CARVE THE SKY

SELECTED AS A *NEW YORK TIMES* NOTABLE BOOK OF THE YEAR

"SMASHING...
Fast, entertaining and well constructed...
this year's most exciting debut."
Los Angeles Daily News

"A FUTURISTIC NOVEL THAT
REAWAKENS OUR PRIMAL PASSION
for the genre... I urge you
to devour it without delay.
The science is right, the writing is astute,
and the sense of wonder
is wonderfully sensual."
James Morrow, author of *Only Begotten Daughter*

"IMAGINATIVE SCI-FI...
An odd mixture of futuristic
and medieval touches,
a world of computers and short swords,
of space satellites and wild boar hunts...
Jablokov sets up a heady premise
that weaves together art, history,
religion and politics."
People

CARVE THE SKY

ALEXANDER JABLOKOV

AVON BOOKS • NEW YORK

AVON BOOKS
A division of
The Hearst Corporation
1350 Avenue of the Americas
New York, New York 10019

Copyright © 1991 by Alexander Jablokow
Cover illustration by Vincent Di Fate
Published by arrangement with William Morrow and Company, Inc.
Library of Congress Catalog Card Number: 90-47772
ISBN: 0-380-71521-X

First AvoNova Printing: April 1992

AVONOVA TRADEMARK REG. U.S. PAT. OFF. AND IN OTHER COUNTRIES, MARCA REGISTRADA, HECHO EN U.S.A.

Printed in the U.S.A.

RA 10 9 8 7 6 5 4 3 2 1

To my parents,
Alla and Victor Jablokow,
who have always helped me on my way

Prolog

Vanessa awoke when Theonave ran his fingertips delicately up her naked back and stroked the nape of her neck. She shivered and arched her back against his touch. Usually braided and controlled, her hair now lay unruly across the cool pillows and the tangled sheets. Theonave knelt and leaned over Vanessa, the weight of his left hand capturing a thick strand of her hair. The sleep after love was always the softest, she thought as she stretched. She was surprised by how rested she was, since she only allowed herself an hour.

She opened her eyes suddenly and sat up with a gasp, pulling her hair painfully from under his hand. The window glowed with the soft color of late twilight. The bright star of Venus was no longer alone in the sky. A breeze from the Bay of Naples stirred the curtains, bringing with it the crockery clatter and the oil and garlic smell of the dinner hour from the city below.

"For God's sake, Theo, what time is it?" she demanded. "What happened to the alarm?" Her clothes hung neatly on the chair near the bed, as if in preparation for a fire drill, and she pulled them on with quick efficiency even as she wished for clean ones from the bureau drawer. And a shower. She had planned on a shower.

Theonave de Borgra, a large man with heavy features

1

and thick, bushy eyebrows, settled down in the hotel room's other chair and pulled his bathrobe around him. "Oh, I don't know," he said with deliberate airiness. He looked out at the gathering darkness that held the glowing windows of the tightly packed buildings of Naples. "I can't tell time by the sun. Remember, I grew up in the corridors of Ganymede and we do things differently there." He yawned and blinked at her. The silver crystals in his irises shone in the half darkness. "I didn't see the naked face of Jupiter until I was ten. An event not without interest, incidentally."

"I'd like to hear the story, but—" Vanessa Karageorge looked at the ornate metal hands of the clock on the writing desk at the other end of the room. They told her that it was four o'clock, about the time she and Theonave had finished making love and she had gone to sleep.

"You looked so lovely lying there, still dewy with sweat. It seemed a pity to disturb you, so I turned the clock off."

"Dewy with sweat." It was just the sort of thing he liked to say. "Dammit, you knew that I have things to do." She pulled on the lemon-colored dress she had worn that morning for their excursion to the vineyards at the base of Mt. Vesuvius. It was completely inappropriate for a cool evening. She was a slender woman with large, dark eyes and wide shoulders. Her brush stuck in her dense, wavy black hair and she swore. It would take more time than she had in order to untangle it.

"Yes," he said, petulant. "But I don't know what those things are. Running around, nocturnal engagements. You never tell me anything important."

"There wouldn't be anything nocturnal about it if you'd have left damn well enough alone!" she shouted, suddenly angry. She was supposed to meet a messenger at a rendezvous point and recover a figurine from him, an important work of art. Her job was supposed to be authentication. Was the figurine, or was it not, an original work of Karl Ozaki? Much depended on her judgment. It was her first really important task for the Academia Sapientiae and it looked as if it would be a disaster, a ludicrous disaster, the side effect of an innocent afternoon of love.

He didn't react, but looked at her, testing. The Ganymedean seemed like an uncomplicated man, as unsubtle as a bull. That was why Vanessa liked him. She now found herself wondering if she had completely misunderstood him.

A long, embroidered night cloak with a hood, suitably mysterious Neapolitan evening wear, hung in the closet. Theonave had bought it for her. She grabbed it and swung into the bathroom with her overnight bag, closing the door behind her.

"Do you need any help, love?" Theonave said, suddenly solicitous. "I'm sorry if I screwed anything up." He rattled the doorknob but she'd managed to lock it.

Water poured out of the dolphin-shaped spout and splashed into the sink, loudly enough that she had to raise her voice to talk, and loudly enough to hide her preparations. "That's all right, Theo. I'm just tense." She pulled out the stiletto she had bought in the flea market the previous day, when Theonave was off on some business of his own, and strapped its leather sheath to her thigh. The stiletto was a weapon rich with associations to Naples and if violence proved necessary she, as a member of the Academia Sapientiae, would prefer it be historically allusive. A length of monofiber line fit into the loose sleeve of the cloak, as well as the bag for the figurine she was supposed to recover. The other sleeve could hold her dress shoes, which she did not intend to wear through the rough night streets of Naples. She began to appreciate Neapolitan nocturnal fashions. There was room for an entire armory in that cloak.

When she came out, cloak on and hood up, concealing her hair, he took her in his arms. As he kissed her Theonave ran his hands up and down, feeling her body through the soft material. His lips were soft and she relaxed against him for an instant before twisting away. His hands had always been wonderfully perceptive, moving across her skin like butterfly's wings. What were they perceiving now?

By the time Vanessa Karageorge arrived at the solemn bulk of the building appointed for the meeting, night had filled the streets. It took her a few moments to find the small and dark front door, the sole gap in the seventeenth-century defenses of the ground floor's heavy, windowless stone. As she entered, two men with an intent grimness inappropriate to the hour brushed past her and ran silently off into the darkness.

She walked through the discreet silence of the lobby, where Ionic pilasters of dark green marble shone like the backs of dragons, pulled open the door to the main hall, releasing a thunder of voices, and stepped through.

The noise inside was deafening, as if to make up for the silence of the dark streets outside. The main hall was large and well lit, with an arched ceiling forty feet high and walls covered with frescoes depicting the magical feats of Virgil Magus. It was packed with a laughing, singing, shouting crowd, mostly male. The larger tables were crowded with red-faced men, fishermen and artisans, while the smaller ones, near the walls, were occupied by discrete groups with interesting business to discuss beneath the clamor of dishes and shouts for more wine. Though most of the musicians who worked the area knew better, a guitar and violin combo was playing at one end. No one could hear them. There was a fair amount of money in the violin case in front of them, the result of the natural human desire to respect artists while not feeling obliged to pay attention to them.

Vanessa stood at the top of the stairs that led down from street level to the main hall and looked for her man amid the busy crowd. Male eyes scanned her appraisingly, though there was little enough to be seen through the cloak she wore. She waited for a pair to linger on her for longer than a casual gawk, but none did. The habitués of this place seemed to have a sense of rough decency.

She found a waitress cleaning off a length of table with several empty places on either side of it. Most of the other seats were filled. She was a strong-armed woman, hair tied back under a kerchief. She picked up a coin and muttered under her breath.

"I was supposed to meet a friend here," Vanessa said, shouting over the din. "I'm late."

The waitress eyed her suspiciously. Neapolitan ladies of quality did not wear their hoods indoors, but Vanessa was not about to lower her status further by revealing her rat's-nest hair. "I can't pay attention to all of these cheapskates," the waitress growled. "Sooner pull one tuna out of a school." She crossed her arms.

Ladies of quality didn't bribe either, but Vanessa was in a hurry. She rang several silver rubles on the table and the waitress added them expressionlessly to the evening's inadequate tips. Vanessa had learned that southern Italians preferred hard coin to bills, notes of account, or digital credit transactions. They retained a sense of the physical, which she appreciated.

"A soft, heavy man, flat face like clay cut with twine," the waitress said. "Not a friend of yours, regardless of what you say. He was waiting for you, but he didn't know what you looked like, because he followed each new person with his eyes. And you *are* late. He'd been here since before six. From the Asteroid Belt, is my guess."

Vanessa was startled. "What makes you say that?"

The waitress shrugged. "Not from Earth, obviously. Trouble with the gravity. Not from the Moon, because he paid with Terran rubles, not Lunar dollars, and you know how Lunies are about our cheap currency." She snorted. "Little enough of it from him anyway. He didn't have the tight-assed look of a Martian or that self-satisfied, arrogant sneer of someone from Ganymede or one of those other moons of the Technic Alliance, and what does that leave? The Belt. Can't get more specific than that, there're dozens of places he could be from. You'd better go after him, though, or your Belter'll be dead when you find him.''

''What?''

''Mocenigo and Rizzoli, the two sitting here,'' she said, pointing at two empty spots. ''They watched him all evening while he waited for you. He's not such a bright guy, you know. He had something that he wore around his neck, like someone who thinks he's found a clever hiding place. He wore his money purse there too, so you could see the thing glitter whenever he paid for another grappa. A figurine of some sort, ivory and gems. Real pretty. You could tell. It had the quality. Mocenigo and Rizzoli know their quality because it brings them money. They watched it like a cat staring at a piece of string in a breeze. They've got claws, lady. They'll jump when it's right.''

Vanessa remembered the two intent men who had passed her as she entered the doorway. She tossed the waitress another coin and ran up the stairs, tripping over her cloak. Several people hooted laughter behind her. The dining-hall door shut and lowered silence over them. She sped through the lobby, almost knocking over several well-dressed couples who were preparing to go up to the finer restaurant upstairs, and leaped out into the street.

The two footpads, she remembered, had gone in the direction of the waterfront. Lacking any better information, she also headed that way. She moved quickly and soundlessly. Her heart beat with excited tension. The Moon had just risen, half full, and rested on wisps of glowing cloud, like a carving freshly uncrated and still in its packing material. Some of its light made it down into the narrow street. Somewhere over her head, behind a shuttered window, a mother sang a lullaby to a fretful child, her own voice sleepy. Alone in the silvery dimness, she moved as if underwater.

After a few kinks in the street she saw the two footpads, Mocenigo and Rizzoli, black on black. They turned a corner and became dark against light. They had the hunched, careful postures of hunters, so had not yet reached their quarry.

Vanessa decided that they had counted on jumping their victim in the passages immediately around the Benvenuto Cellini and making a quick job of it, but had failed. The streets here were too open, too exposed. Vanessa had no idea where her man might be, so was constrained to follow the two robbers as they strolled, reluctantly, across the busy, gaslit Via Chiatomone with its streetcars and roller skaters and down the seaside promenade of the Via Partenope. It was crowded enough that she could walk right up next to them. They were too intent on pursuing to note that they were in turn being pursued. She searched ahead, but could not spot the offworlder with the figurine that had suddenly attracted so much interest.

She stole a glance at Mocenigo and Rizzoli, and almost laughed. They were glum now, as if watching the train they had just missed pulling out of the station while they stood on the platform with their luggage. They scowled at the courting couples on the promenade, who probably thought them sober church elders or fathers seeking erring daughters. Soon their quarry would turn into his hotel, probably one of the smaller ones amid the gardens of the Amadeo district, where she and Theonave de Borgra were themselves staying.

Suddenly their faces lit up, they exchanged a look, and they began to move more quickly. Up ahead a dark figure was just vanishing over the high arched bridge to the island of Castel dell'Ovo. Unready for bed, the unfortunate man had decided to take a stroll in the dense gardens beneath the crenellated bastions of the medieval fortress. Unless Vanessa could do something, it might be the last walk he ever took.

The flagstone paths through the gardens of Castel dell'Ovo were twisted, intended for contemplation rather than directed movement. Mocenigo and Rizzoli had a brief whispered conference and, having agreed upon a tactical plan, split up. Vanessa paused and thought about the touristic impulse. If the victim wanted a view of the city, he would have to go to the seaside terrace beneath the castle. She and de Borgra had taken a walk in these gardens a few days before. Efficiency hadn't been on their minds, so they had wandered at random, but the pattern of paths floated in front of her eyes and she could see that if she went left at the first fork, around the little statue of a frantically running Mercury, and took two rights, she would be at the terrace. She ran, wraithlike, her cloak billowing out behind her. Barely enough moonlight penetrated the trees for her to see. She felt pleased with herself for having mastered the art of running in the cloak without tripping over it.

A shout in the darkness signaled a failure in the footpads' plan. The off-worlder, not familiar with the paths in the garden, had obviously not behaved in a predictable manner, and had run into one of his pursuers. Vanessa tried to place the direction of the cry as she ran, but it was impossible to tell.

The trees vanished on either side and she emerged on the terrace, which was checkered like a chess board. Its edge was marked by a marble balustrade, beyond which were the sea, the city, and the starry vault of the sky. Vanessa stopped at the edge of the growth and breathed slowly through her wide-open mouth, ignoring her body's desperate demands for oxygen. The dark figure of one of the Neapolitan footpads rested casually against the balustrade, silhouetted against the warm lights of the city that curved on the other side of the water.

The Belter emerged onto the terrace, gasping and stumbling in the unaccustomed gravity. The man at the balustrade produced a knife with a slightly back-curved blade that glinted menacingly in the moonlight. It was obviously a weapon he was rather proud of. The man with the figurine stopped, tried to turn, and was confronted by the other footpad, the one he had run into in the darkness. For an instant the three of them stood in tableau, a heavy, slumped man in a rumpled tunic, his face impassive, and two young thugs, their hair slicked back and teeth showing in gleeful success. Vanessa pulled the stiletto out of the sheath on her thigh, then removed her cloak and bundled it tightly around her left arm.

The one behind moved and put his knife against the victim's back. "Mocenigo," he said to the one who had been waiting at the balustrade. "I'll hold him. Reach into his shirt and pull out the figurine. Then we can—"

The Belter turned quickly and jammed his heel viciously against the inside of Rizzoli's knee. Vanessa winced in sympathy. Rizzoli's knife grazed a wound across the stranger's back, but then he shrieked, dropped the knife, and grabbed for his injured leg.

Mocenigo was then borne back by the sudden assault, until he was bent backward over the balustrade. He slashed at his unexpectedly violent victim. "Help me, Rizzoli," he yelled. "Get on your feet, goddammit." He twisted his arm and managed to push his knife into flesh. The stranger did not cry out, but grunted softly, the sound a man makes when he has just remembered something. He stepped back, then drove his knuckles against Mocenigo's throat. Mocenigo choked, but his knife flashed again.

Vanessa ran past Rizzoli, who had just managed to get up onto his good leg, and knocked him back to the ground mercilessly. He screamed in pain. Mocenigo pushed the stranger up onto the balustrade itself, so that he balanced over the rocks, his side now dark with blood.

Mocenigo turned briefly away from his victim to see

what had happened to Rizzoli and found himself confronting a wild-haired woman in a lemon-colored dress. His eyes widened in shock. That was all he had time for. Vanessa felt the stiletto push its way between his ribs with a dreadful smoothness. Blood bubbled on his lips and he fell heavily against the balustrade.

Vanessa stared down at him, shaking. Her hand was suddenly slippery on the grip of the stiletto and she realized that it was wet with a man's blood. She had helped a friend in school once who had cut her forehead by falling down some granite stairs, and she remembered how she had been sickened and terrified by the amount of blood on the stairs, on her hands, on the new dress that she was wearing, all that from one tiny, frightened little girl. She drew in a slow breath.

"You're late," the bloody man on the balustrade said. "I waited for you. We need Nehushtan." He tried to reach into his shirt to pull out the figurine that she could see pushing out against his tunic.

She sensed rather than heard Rizzoli behind her. She stepped back and his one-legged rush carried him past her. He slammed against the balustrade but pushed himself off like a swimmer hitting the end of a lap and swung his knife at her. She caught it in the cloak bundled around her arm. When she pulled, he was yanked off balance and, trying to put weight on his wounded leg, yelped and fell to the ground. Vanessa kicked him behind the ear, and thought that she could feel the delicate bones there shatter. It was her imagination, of course. It had to be. She stood, gasping for breath, the bodies of two men on either side of her.

The balustrade was empty save for a pool of blood. She ran up to it and looked over.

The cliff fell down sheer before her, too steep to climb. At its base the black, shiny swelling of the waves foamed over the rocks broken from its face in ages past. The stranger's body lay sprawled on its back on one of these rocks, its arms and legs moving gently in the ocean. Rizzoli's rush had knocked him over.

A dolphin's head emerged from the water and nuzzled one of the corpse's arms. In the darkness it looked almost as if the stranger patted it on the snout. The dolphin swam fitfully around the rock for a moment, then lowered its head below the water. Even where Vanessa stood, she could hear the deep thrumming of the distress signal, which would be audible to aquatic listeners clear out to Capri.

1

From Household Order of the Week, 13 October 2358, The House at Fresh Pond Verge, Cambridge, Massachusetts. Lord Monboddo and Retinue in Residence. Anton Lindgren, Seneschal:

...I can already hear the curses, but the entire collection of twenty-second-century Turkmen enamel and stained-glass dragonflies and spiders we just finished installing in the East Ambulatory has to be yanked and replaced by a grouping of fourteenth-century Burgundian mourners I had been planning to save until next summer. Miriam Kostal, Justice of Tharsis, is, it turns out, deathly afraid of spiders, an interesting comment on the deep structure of phobia, since there are no spiders on Mars. . . .

... The ceremonial barge *Bucintoro* is ready for Lord Monboddo's planned moonlight tour of Fresh Pond on the 19th. Please recall that guests from Luna, Mars, and Venus are not used to open water, and that stories of sea monsters and giant man-eating anacondas may well be believed. Yes, Param, I do mean you. Andrew Pilbeam of Ishtar Station, Venus, recently wrote me to ask about getting a stuffed pterodactyl, a species

12

Param had given him to understand infest Mount Grey-
lock in the Berkshires. . . .

. . . Two of the wild boar hams should be removed
from the smokehouse for lunch the 17th and 20th. Haul
out some bluefish as well, maybe ten pounds. The
burgundy butter and sugar corn in the southeast field
will be ripe through the week. Pick forty to fifty ears
a day, no more. The kitchen informs me that the ven-
ison in cooler 3 from last month's Vermont hunt is
sufficiently aged to be served at banquet on the 18th.
Cycle it down and raise the temperature to 23 C. . . .

. . . I plan to join Lady Windseth's party late on Sat-
urday night. I will be available for questions and discussions involving Household affairs in the kitchen
garden near the West Wall from 1:00 to 2:30 that
afternoon, where I will be digging parsnips under for
the winter, and will certainly be glad of any assistance.
After that hour, I will be in my study and would appreciate not being disturbed. . . .

The afternoon light had long since faded from the
forested shoulders of Fresh Pond, though the water itself
still gleamed like beaten pewter against the lowering sky.
Anton Lindgren looked up from his work to stare uncomprehendingly at the scene, as if wakened from a nap
on a train, peering out of the window, trying to decide
if he'd missed his stop. He suddenly realized that his
back hurt and that his eyes felt as if they had had sand
poured into the sockets. He put his hands on his lower
back and straightened, unjamming the vertebrae of his
suddenly reacquired body one at a time. He breathed a
long sigh of satisfaction, for he had started to figure a
few things out.

His study was at the top of one of Fresh Pond Verge's
five towers, the one traditionally called Alice's Keep.
Anton turned off the computer and stowed its flat screen

under the desk. The printer spat out the final laboratory report, with its IR absorption and nuclear magnetic resonance graphs, that he had received that morning from Heilbroner Morphognosis, a materials research lab that authenticated art objects and archaeological artifacts for the Monboddo Household under a retainer contract.

He wrapped the object on the desk back up in its velvet cloth without looking at it. Too many thoughts were chasing one another around his mind, and he knew from long, exasperating experience that they had to be allowed to make their peace with one another and settle down before he could make any decisions.

He pushed his chair back and stood up. He was a tall, angular man, with long, nervous fingers and a narrow face, its precision accentuated by his elegant forked beard and moustache. His eyes were wide and blue, and readily expressed his thoughts. His inability to conceal either pleasure or dismay had always annoyed him, for there were times, when acting in a professional capacity as head of Lord Monboddo's private Household, that a stony inscrutable face, with, perhaps, a hint of disdain, was the mask to wear. But he could not control himself. To his horror, when he looked at a photograph of himself at a formal audience with a Gensekretarial Legate or a dinner with an association of local businessmen, he saw that the expression on his face could only be described as a self-satisfied smirk or even a vacuous leer. The fact that none of the other people in the photograph reacted to his expression with any surprise or annoyance only disturbed Anton more.

He strapped on his short sword, scooped the velvet-wrapped package under one arm, and descended the stairs. Behind him the sky had grown completely black, and was brilliant with stars.

A fire burned in the library hearth. Its light caught the gilt on the bindings of the books and vainly tried to penetrate all the complex recesses of the two-story-high room, with its balcony, alcoves, and barrel-vaulted ceiling.

At this hour the library was deserted in favor of the party upstairs. A few days before a corvette from the Technic Alliance had, illegally, stopped and searched the Terran Union vessel *Sulawesi* in the debatable volume of space near Jupiter's Trailing Trojan asteroids. The resulting war talk would undoubtedly lend the party some welcome excitement, and Anton was eager to be on his way. But bright lights and Bordeaux would sterilize the germinating seeds of his thoughts, so he instead folded his long figure into a couch in front of the fire and stared into its shifting shapes. He laid the figurine, still wrapped in velvet, on the table in front of him, but did not look at it.

A fair amount of spilled blood had accompanied the figurine, recovered from the rocks off the Castel dell'Ovo by a rescue-trained dolphin. As far as anyone had been able to determine, the two dead men on the terrace had been ordinary nighttime professionals of Naples. The body on the rocks, however, had belonged to an asteroid dweller of unknown origin. The Asteroid Belt was filled with dozens of independent principalities, but none of their legations had been willing to claim his body. Had he killed the two footpads? If he hadn't, then who had? Why had the Academia Sapientiae, through its contacts near the Gensek himself, put in a claim for the figurine? It was all settling into a puzzle of marvelous complexity.

Anton pulled out the sheaf of papers and looked over them again, examining the graphs of IR signatures, spin state resonances, density profiles, quantum tunneling statistics, and isotope histograms. Some were from labs other than Heilbroner Morphognosis, since it would not have done for one lab to have all of the information. The conclusions were potentially explosive. Anton raised his glass in a toast to himself. "To the ability to draw conclusions," he said. He drained the glass and set it down.

Someone chuckled. Anton stood up and looked

around. There was a glow from one of the alcoves in the otherwise deserted library. He walked toward it. A variety of books lay piled on the shelves of the alcove, many of them open. The broad desk was almost entirely covered by a tangle of papers and more books and was lit by two green glass-shaded brass lamps. The window was open to the dark waters of Fresh Pond, which lapped against the wall of the library. A tiny figure with long white hair was hunched over the desk, scribbling something on a piece of paper.

Anton stood and regarded him for a moment, then cleared his throat.

"Anton," Lord Monboddo said, not looking up from his work. "You've been tromping around the library for the past half an hour, chortling to yourself and drinking toasts to your own cleverness. You need no announcing." He pushed his chair over to one side, and hooked another chair over toward Anton with his right foot. Finally he looked up and smiled. Anton had always thought that Monboddo looked like an animated marionette. He had bright blue eyes, a sharp, down-curved nose, high, flat cheekbones that always showed two spots of color against his pale face. His skin was soft and intricately wrinkled, indicating the passage of a variety of emotions over the years. He wore an old tattered robe, once of good quality, and blue embroidered slippers on his feet, which dangled down from his chair and did not touch the floor.

Monboddo had his own study in another part of the house, but insisted that real work had to be performed somewhere he could be easily interrupted by other people, since significant thoughts survived interruptions while minor ones were better forgotten. Besides, given the people of his Household, such interruptions were often most informative. So he did all of his serious work in the library.

Monboddo pushed the papers into a tall mound at the end of the desk, for the moment dismissing those thoughts. After a few moments of digging, Monboddo managed to reveal several square feet of oak surface, stained dark to bring out the grain. "Put it down here, and tell me what you've found out." Anton set the figurine down on the desk and began to unwrap it. "No. Keep it covered. I want intelligence now, not aesthetics." Monboddo was aware of his own strengths and weaknesses. He knew how easily distracted he was. He sat up straight and opened his blue eyes wide to show that he was being attentive.

Anton settled back and made a temple of his hands. "The figurine was made off Earth."

"A reasonable assumption."

"It's not an assumption," Anton said, mildly testy. "The ivory was grown in low gravity, probably at one of those biological material factories in the Asteroid Belt. The machining on the jewels was done in null-g. Surface impurities indicate that it spent a lot of time in a closed recycled atmosphere, like that on a spaceship or a small asteroid. The magnetic domains—"

"You've made your point, Anton. No need to belabor it with inappropriate details. It isn't from Earth. Go on. Tell me about the ngomite. Those jewels *are* ngomite, of course."

Anton took a breath. "Yes. They are." Since Monboddo was in an interrupting mood, he decided against any more slow, logical development. "From the indications, the jewels on the figurine come from a ngomite strike with a mass no smaller than about eighteen kilograms, probably larger."

He finally got the desired response. Monboddo stared at him for a long moment, speechless. "Eighteen! How do you know that?"

Anton raised his eyebrows. "A reasonable assumption."

"What? Oh, all right. Tell me the story. I'll try not to interrupt."

"Don't make promises you can't keep, my lord."

"I said I would try. I didn't promise success."

"Ngomite has a complex crystal lattice, made up of the quasi-stable elements with atomic numbers 124, 133, and 140, from the Island of Stability in the periodic chart. This lattice seems to have a higher order structure. Some people see this structure as evidence that ngomite is a synthetic substance, left by the Elder Race, the Acherusians, whatever you want to call them, so that humanity could find it and use it in the control cores of fusion engines and thus spread through the Solar System, but not beyond. Maybe. Each gem in the figurine shows a different large-scale structure. Three of them show inadequate particle bombardment, indicating that they are from inside some much larger piece. Mineral impurities vary from gem to gem, which happens only over large crystal distances. If this is true, the gems come from the largest piece of ngomite ever discovered. Eighteen kilograms is the minimal figure. I don't even want to try to think about how much such a piece would be worth on the open market."

"It is not market value that is important here, Anton, particularly as there is no open market in ngomite. No, indeed." Monboddo rested his elbows on the desk, put his chin on his knuckles, and stared into space. "Ah, enough. Let's see it, finally."

Anton unwrapped the figurine and the light shone on the ivory and gems that had so fascinated the two Neapolitan footpads. It was an object that had the property of taking diffuse light and giving it focus, of tying the light's fibers into a tight and complex knot, which made it one of the links that held the human world together.

The figurine, about nine inches long, was carved from polished ivory. It represented the Dead Christ in his winding sheet. He lay outspread on the black velvet. His head sagged to one side and his arms and legs were in positions that would have been impossible to maintain for more than a moment without discomfort. The man was obviously dead. The carving was delicate. Long hair spread out beneath the head, tangled with the crown of thorns. One hand was clenched, the other was loose at the side.

Jewels glinted a mysterious blue-green in the firelight, using the merest excuse of light to display their own energy. There were five of them: one in each palm, one in each foot, and one, larger than the rest, in his side, where the winding sheet failed to cover the abdomen.

Monboddo picked it up and held it in his cupped hands, warming the tiny, cold figure. He looked at it more closely. The ribs poked through the thin flesh, and the upper torso was still twisted with the pain of crucifixion. The ngomite gems stared out at him, for they were inlaid in the form of wide-open eyes, one in each wound. It was an ominous and striking symbol. He allowed himself one more moment of contemplation, then wrapped the figurine back up in its velvet. Monboddo took such concentrated beauty only in small doses, because he was afraid of dulling his senses by excess. To him, beautiful objects had to rest in time the same way the figurine rested on its background of black velvet. Otherwise they would have been lost in a meaningless glitter.

"Is there anything else you can tell me about it?" Monboddo asked. He waited attentively.

"From the style, the artist is Karl Ozaki." Attributing the figurine to the man who had probably been the twenty-fourth century's greatest artist rewarded Anton with a startled look and another long moment of silence. Anton felt some satisfaction. He had never before gotten Monboddo to be silent twice in one conversation.

"Hmm. . . . This is what, I suppose, is called a clue. Anton, what *is* going on here? Ozaki died twenty years ago in that ridiculous accident on the Moon, at Clavius. Blew himself up with some complicated gadget, as I remember. Artists should not be permitted to fool with such things. They have the wrong sense for it. It was Clavius's fault, of course. He should never have permitted it. But then Ozaki went to work for that idiot the Justice of Clavius in the first place, so it was still his decision, after all. Ah. So we have here in front of us a previously unattributed work by Karl Ozaki. Are you telling me that before he died, Ozaki dug an eighteen-kilogram chunk of ngomite out of the wall of the crater Clavius and split five chunks out to make this figurine? How could he keep something like that a secret?''

''I have no idea. No one has ever reported finding ngomite on Luna.''

''Aah.'' Lord Monboddo sprang up from his seat, tied his robe more securely around himself, and paced around the library. With his long nose, and the way he held his head forward, moving it from side to side, he looked like a shore bird dancing in the surf. ''Ngomite. Can you imagine it? Harder than diamonds, and it makes jade look like cheap glass. So what if it's so useful in fusion drive cores? I find that irrelevant.'' He darted back to the desk and snuck another peek at the figurine. ''Ozaki, that old bastard. I met him several times. He was an . . . inelegant man. Picked his nose with his chopsticks during dinner. On purpose, I'm sure, to show his independence from the great and wealthy men and women on whose fickle taste he depended for his livelihood.

''In fact, Anton, if you look into the accounts of the Household before you joined us, you will see that I had contracted with him for a work of art before he died. It was to be a portrait head of Anastasia, to celebrate our twentieth anniversary. I felt betrayed when he died, and he died owing me several thousands of rubles, on account. It was typical of him somehow. He died the way he had lived, crudely and inconsiderately. It seemed like the ultimate irresponsibility. Clavius, of course, would not clear the account.''

Anton was fascinated by his lord's connections throughout the great world of culture during the preceding half a century. When Ozaki died, Anton had been a teenager, a boy whose father had just died. His own involvement with art and the world had still been in the future. But the boy's private mourning for his father had blended with the public reaction to the death of the famous artist, so the figurine's creator was somehow special to him.

He shifted in his seat. It was getting late, and he suddenly realized that he was incredibly hungry.

"Anton, I want that ngomite," Monboddo said with sudden decision. "Do you understand me? We will put all of our resources on it." And that was that. Anton had seen Monboddo debate for two months about whether to buy new carpets for the upstairs hallways, but when it came to the essentials he knew how to act.

"The potential pay off is enormous," Anton said carefully.

This made Monboddo wrinkle his brow. "You know, Anton, I will never cease to be amazed by the manner in which you can make the most interesting things sound about as exciting as trading Venerian mining stocks on the Tycho Exchange. We have beautiful art, mysterious gems, and violent death. What more could you ask for? And yet, all you want to talk about is value returned. You should live on the Moon, Anton, where such things are considered matters of high romance."

Anton often tried to counter his romantic temperament by acting exaggeratedly businesslike, and Monboddo never failed to twit him for it.

"Let's just say that I owe it to the Monboddo Household to make sure it is financially healthy enough to continue to pay my salary," Anton said.

Monboddo snorted and waved his hands in dismissal. "Very well, Seneschal. Enough of that. I will see you at Anastasia's party. She's been secretive all week. Are there to be some particularly interesting guests?"

"I really couldn't say, sir."

Monboddo scowled at him. "Sometimes, Anton, I am not sure if your loyalty is to me or to my wife."

"It depends," Anton said, "on who sounds the most reasonable at any given time."

"All right, all right. Is everything else ready?"

"Yes."

"Good. I will do what is necessary."

Anton stood up. "Certainly, sir." He walked out of the library, leaving Lord Monboddo, figurine in hand, staring out of the window at the dark waters of the pond.

2

From the *Shorter Catalog Raisonné of the Collection of George Harvey Westerkamp, Lord Monboddo, Interrogator of Boston* by Anton Lindgren, Curator:

#0249   Skinning knife in the form of a beaver. Anonymous Tlingit Indian. Chichagoff Island, c. 1885 CE. Handle wood and bone, blade bronze. A good example of the work of these master craftsmen, wiped out by disease and cultural modification by the beginning of the twentieth century.

#0009   Bowl with pedestal, called Blood Bowl, from the specks of red in the surface and its supposed resemblance to a Mithraist sacrificial vessel, by Caroline Apthorpe, 2198 CE. Lazarite, from the Asteroid Belt. Approximately 45 cm. in diameter, massing 2.5 kg. This wide, flat bowl with a curving rim and thin stem is one of the first items made from the new materials Ngomo found in the Belt, and one of the most beautiful items in the collection.

#0108   Statuette, one of the Twelve Acolytes of Honen Shonin, by Klaus Unkei, Hokkaido, 2260 CE. Gilt and polychrome wood. An interesting revival of the Kamakura style of the twelfth century CE for the Temple of Kali Buddha at Sakhalin. Unkei died during a riot between rival monks, and the set was never completed.

#0027   Statuette, *Woman Weeping*, by Barry Wiltern, Oregon Community, c. 2113 CE. Jade and carbonized wood. Typical of the work done just after the end of the wars, when all art was, in one way or another, a funerary monument. This one commemorates the massacre of a farming family by a Brotherly Company. A masterpiece.

The party was, strictly speaking, not a party at all, but instead what Anastasia, Lady Windseth, Lord Monboddo's wife, archaically and perversely insisted on calling a *vyecher*, that is a *soiree*, or *evening*. She felt that the language of the vanished world empire, Russian, gave the proper note of significance to the proceedings. Since an *evening* was of an intimate and somewhat calculated nature, it was held in the cream and light blue rooms of Lady Windseth's own apartments, on the top floor of the West Wing, rather than in the larger Banqueting Hall. Lord Monboddo did not venture into this part of his own house unless invited, and it remained his wife's domain.

"... of course that's true, dear Torstov, but if this sort of thing goes on, the Trailing Trojans will become nothing more than the private estates of the Ganymedean state—Anton, don't try to sneak by me. I'm not a blind old woman, not yet. Where have you been? Come here, come here."

Anton had indeed been trying to sneak by, not because he wanted to avoid talking to Lady Windseth but because he was hungry and wanted to get to the buffet table before there was nothing left at it but celery sticks. He could glimpse its white linen through the crowd that filled the narrow rooms, the brass gleam of the samovar rising overhead. Above the soft mutter of conversation, he could hear the sharp clink of fork against plate. There was a slight smell of garlic, olive oil, and . . . thyme? He sniffed surreptitiously, but realized that that would have to wait. He smiled at her exactly as if he had been looking for no one else, bowed down, and kissed her proffered cheek.

She was a striking woman, with large violet eyes, prominent cheekbones, and a high forehead, her long white hair elaborately braided with ribbons. She had that directness of manner practiced by older women who are adept at captivating men without the use of their bodies. She crossed her legs beneath her long, billowing dress, kicking up one tiny black shoe as she did so, and leaned back in the couch with an arm extended along its back.

Next to her on the couch, sword across his knees, was Torstov Plauger, a lean, almost cadaverous man who in trying to sit at attention on the soft cushions had ended up looking like an abandoned statue half sunk in earth. As quickly as a striking snake, he was on his feet, one hand on the pommel of his short sword. He locked eyes with Anton and bowed, making it a slightly menacing act. Anton returned it more casually and managed an easy smile.

"Good to see you again, Torstov," Anton said.

"Likewise," Plauger responded, ending in a cool hiss. They stared at each other.

"You'd think Torstov, a Martian, would agree with me!" Lady Windseth cried. "Quite the contrary. A Ganymedean warship stops and searches a Terran observation vessel in the Neutral Zone and he counsels moderation!"

"Yes," Plauger said. "I try to stay away from political judgments." He sucked in his breath thoughtfully. "I am sure that the Union of Nations will make a calculated and measured response.''

"We won't at all, Torstov," Lady Windseth said, shaking her head at his astounding ignorance. "The Court is for conciliation. Everybody who matters at the Esopus Palace—Matlin, the Vostoks, husband and wife, even Kang, usually so threatening—all are for ignoring the violation of the *Sulawesi*. The Gensek Varlam hears little other advice. They may expel a few Technics, as a gesture, but nothing more. Believe me, I have my sources at Court.''

"The Court is not everyone," Plauger stated, an opinion not calculated to calm Lady Windseth. He then glowered over Anton's shoulder.

Anton followed the Martian's gaze over to the buffet table. Param Vakante, the Household member in charge of supervising that evening's affair, stood behind it with exaggerated solemnity. His bushy hair, carefully combed when he arrived, was already disheveled. He held a steaming empanada, and as Anton watched, he took a bite out of it. Anton could almost taste the basil and chicken and his hunger became almost insupportable.

He swallowed and bowed to Torstov Plauger and Lady Windseth. "Much as I would like to continue this conversation, I must cut it short. Param and I have Household business to dispose of.''

The Martian silently settled back into the cushions in his Easter Island pose.

Lady Windseth sniffed. "You know the rules, Anton. A *vyecher* is not a place for specifics." She waved her hand dismissively and rings flashed in the candlelight. She was a woman who was convinced that her active intervention was always necessary to a party's success. "But very well. If you get a chance, later in the evening, come and keep an old lady company.''

"I certainly will." Anton knew perfectly well that both of them would be too busy for the rest of the evening to speak again, but proprieties always had to be observed.

He walked to the buffet table. Around him, throughout the crowd, he heard the ominous sibilance of the word *Sulawesi*. It had been a slow season, and all players at politics were grateful to the Technics for having provided such a juicy topic of dispute.

"What did you do to our figure of Martian virtue?" Anton asked as he scoured smoked bluefish, chicken empanadas, and bread from the table. "Tell him there were sea monsters in Fresh Pond?" He poured himself a glass of red wine.

"In contravention of your Order of the Week?" Param said, outraged. "Certainly not. I, ah"—he cleared his throat—"I told him that migrating ducks often drop from the sky and drill their way into the soft banks of rivers and ponds, where they hibernate. My uncle Drogor was killed that way, in fact, while fishing for eels. A mallard through the chest. Boom!" He looked over at Plauger. "I think I've kept the poor man indoors, and the weather's been wonderful."

"How many different ways did Uncle Drogor die? I've heard that he was carried off by pterodactyls, pulled underground by moles...."

"Ah well, Anton, you know how unreliable eyewitness accounts are."

"Apologize to Plauger," Anton said. "Not now. Tomorrow. He *is* the Justice of Tharsis's second in command. I won't have the Martians irritated."

Param slouched down next to him, disconsolate. "He looks annoyed, and I bet he knows how to use that sword. Martians have no sense of humor." Param himself carried a house sword for form's sake, but barely knew which end to hold. He glanced again at Plauger and Lady Windseth, and quickly brightened. "Ah, what have we here? See that woman sitting with Lady Windseth?"

Anton reluctantly looked up from his food. Sitting on a hassock at Lady Windseth's feet, talking animatedly to her, was a slender, dark-eyed woman, her long, thick black hair elaborately braided and pulled back under the lacy headdress lately favored by ladies of fashion. Her bare shoulders were serenely wide and her gestures had an uncommon strength and grace, those of a dancer. Everything about her had a precision of a woman in a portrait, painted by a texture-fixated artist like Vermeer.

"Her name is Vanessa Karageorge," Param said. "She's an Ordinary Fellow of the Academia Sapientiae. She can't be more than twenty-five, so she's young for the office. She must be quite something."

"It does look that way," Anton said. Lady Windseth laughed at something that Karageorge said and even Plauger, miraculously, creased his face in something approaching a smile. Lady Windseth and Lord Monboddo's own children were far scattered, Luka in San Francisco, Frieda at the University of Sydney, a distinct political gesture to the Australians, and Destamin, the eldest, on Venus. Lady Windseth tended to adopt stray young people in compensation. "Do you know anything about her?"

Karageorge suddenly flicked a glance in his direction and caught him staring at her. Her dark eyes were quizzical. She raised her eyebrows as if asking him what, precisely, he was looking at, and he was glad when Param spoke, giving him an excuse to look away. It seemed that her gaze could stay on him forever.

"Oh, this and that." Param was a general repository of gossip. "She was born out in the Great Lakes area, one of those towns that's a small one in the ruins of a big one. Cleland?"

"Cleveland," Anton corrected. "I know it. I put my Long Year in near there, in Detroit, doing ecological restoration work."

"Right. Her parents worked on the fishing fleet and were both drowned in a winter storm. Husbands and wives shouldn't work together that way. First you get arguments. Then you get orphans. Vanessa, about ten at the time, bright girl, ended up at the Northfall Lyceum, near Niagara. A lot of fishermen's orphans get sent there.

I don't know why. I think that huge gush of water would always make me think of drowning."

"Never mind you," Anton said. "Anything else about her?"

"Not much. The Academia Sapientiae snapped her up right out of Northfall. After that, who knows? The Academia plays its cards so close to its chest that they're hidden by ribs. You can check her publications yourself, that's more in your line. She's been in Boston just a few days. She's got a lot of friends, including some from the Technic Alliance. Maybe she's studying them. Maybe they're more fun than they seem at first glance. Young ladies do always insist on having improper affairs. Anything else you'll have to find out for yourself. Is your interest in her professional or personal?"

"I'll let you figure that out for yourself," Anton said, nettled. "Has the kitchen been entirely emptied?"

"What?" Param's eyes flicked over the serving table. "Oh, my God, you're right. That's what I get for letting you distract me. I'll get more food out before the crowd riots." He slid off, suddenly panicked.

Anton walked over to the fireplace, where he could stand, warm his backside, and survey the room. He looked over the glittering crowd the way he would a large collection of gilded belt buckles, enjoying the cumulative effect, but not trying to distinguish individuals, unaware of the pompous appearance he presented, standing there with one arm on the mantelpiece, a glass of wine in the other. He also tried, unobtrusively, to overhear what Karageorge was saying to Lady Windseth in her low quick voice, but the room was too noisy.

A sound cut through the gabble of voices, a sound like the ripping of burlap. It didn't take Anton long to find its source. Lying like a discarded rag doll, almost filling one of the wing chairs facing the fire, was the colorfully dressed figure of Osbert, one of Lord Monboddo's two manservants, dress cap askew over one eye as he snored. He wore fussy little shoes with gold buckles, half trousers and tights that showed off the strength in his calves, and a red tunic, tight across his chest. Even as he slept, he kept one hand on the pommel of his sword. Anton was tempted to reach out and shake him, because his snoring was horrendously loud, but he didn't. That sort of thing could be dangerous and besides, where one slept the other was surely watchful.

He looked around and, as expected, found Osbert's companion Fell, a burly six-footer as blond as Osbert was dark, who stood in partial shadow in an alcove, watching the party with the air of a line judge at a particularly dull tennis match. He raised a finger to his temple, but did not otherwise acknowledge Anton's greeting. It took just a slight throat clearing, however, for him to understand Anton's desire. Not taking his eyes from the crowd, he nudged Osbert with a foot. Osbert woke up with a start in the middle of a snore and immediately began coughing. He looked around, disoriented. When he saw his comrade standing guard he knew all was well and turned over on his side and went back to sleep. In this new position, at least, he did not snore.

"Did they come as a set?" a low, hissing female voice asked.

"Miriam," Anton said. "I thought I'd find you eventually." Anton took a step to the other wing chair, where she had been sitting concealed. He bowed. "Lord Monboddo picked them up separately, though now they are inseparable. He simply has a talent for collecting. How are you? I want to apologize about the spider sculptures in the Ambulatory. I didn't realize your phobia."

"No reason why you should have." She moved her feet far enough over on the footstool for him to sit, but did not remove them completely. She smiled and raised her wine glass to him. Typically, it was half full, and would probably remain so at the end of the evening. Miriam Kostal, Justice of Tharsis, was a tall, beautifully figured woman in her mid-forties, with clearly defined muscles and dusky skin. Her low-cut dress showed the intricate structure of her neck like sculpture.

Her wavy brown hair, now filled with gray, was held back by a silver comb in the shape of a stylized, elongated springing panther. He stared at it for a moment, mesmerized. He had forgotten that what she had worn in her hair since before he had met her was an original Karl Ozaki. It was a rare woman who could wear a work of art like that and not be diminished by comparison.

"It has been such a long time since you have visited us, Anton," she said. Her voice was a throaty whisper. The air of Mars was thin and dry, even in the covered spaces of the Valles Marineris and the four volcanoes on Tharsis Ridge where most Martians lived. "The last time you were with us, it was wonderful. Years ago, much too long. But now . . . those *bastards*." She turned the intensity of her gaze on him. "We must act, Anton. You of Earth have relaxed. You don't understand, the way we of Mars do. We feel the hot breath of those machines on our necks, and know that soon we shall feel their teeth at our throats. The entire Union of Nations must act."

She had leaned forward and taken his hand while making her point. He could feel the sharp nails resting against the skin of his palm. Sitting next to her, hearing her throaty voice again, made his blood run faster, despite himself. She smiled slightly at him, just enough for her prominent canines to show between her lips.

"Torstov thinks we will make a calculated and measured response," Anton muttered. "I think that's how he put it."

"I don't doubt that's how he put it. Unlike most men, Torstov knows when not to speak his mind."

Anton found this praise obscurely irritating. He remembered the first time that he had spent a month at Pavonis Mons. That time had changed him. Left at loose ends after the completion of his studies at the University of St. Petersburg, unsure of what to do next, he had made a decision long traditional in the Lindgren family and traveled off-planet to complete his education. He became a guest in the rambling house of the Justice of Tharsis. The families of Kostal and Lindgren had some ancient connection, the source of which no one could quite remember, though everyone valued it. The house was furnished in the Martian style, austerity struggling with luxury. Much of the best Martian art came in the form of decorated but extremely functional weaponry.

She looked at him, sensing his discomfort. She stroked the palm of his hand. "You should come back to us, Anton. Coprates is still that irritating maze of crooked streets that you would always get lost in. And Pyramid Square is still a hundred meters high and full of light. I remember when you got back to Pavonis from there, jumping around like a sun lizard. Your first duel! With that ridiculous businessman from Hebes who insisted on claiming that Terrans could fight only with clever magazine articles. You used the sword I lent you, no blood was spilled, and Earth's honor was satisfied. Do you still have that little head you bought to celebrate?"

"My bust of the Gensek Timofey? Yes. He still sits in my bedroom, frowning at me." Buying the finely detailed marble bust of that gloomy twenty-third-century monarch had taken almost all of the money he had at the time.

He'd arrived at Pavonis so excited he could barely breathe and run up the crazily twisted stairs that hung out over the cliff, almost pitching himself into the volcano's fumarole, because Martian stairs had no handrails. The house had celebrated, in cool Martian fashion, since it was not polite to regard surviving a duel as something worthy of discussion. And the Justice herself, who had taken into her hands a number of aspects of his education, saw fit, that night, to continue it.

"That was a delightful time," Miriam said. "I'll always remember it. And it's led here, hasn't it? Anton Lindgren, Seneschal to Lord Monboddo, Interrogator of

Boston. It will lead further yet." She rubbed her hands together delightedly. "This is going to be important. I can sense it, even though you are not allowed to tell me anything about it yet. Mysterious figurines and romantic murders. . . ."

"We can discuss it in three days time," Anton said hastily. This was no place for such matters. "You will have helped to make the decision by then."

She leaned forward. She wore a scent at the hollow of her neck, a dark, spicy aroma. "I'm sure, since you recommend it, that it will be approved." She took a sip of her wine and smiled at him. He pushed the footstool back slightly, away from her, and slowed his breathing. What had happened between them was long over, and he knew that sequels are seldom as interesting as the original works. Still, there was something about her that he had never gotten over.

She was now his superior in the Division of External Security, an organization she herself had recruited him into, another old family tradition, as he only discovered much later. They lay together in her bed that next morning, looking through her window at the plunging depths at the center of the volcano of Pavonis Mons, and talked. The room was cold, as all Martian rooms were. Miriam didn't notice and stretched out, gloriously nude, on the pale blue silk, while Anton burrowed in the sheets for warmth. They had talked about responsibility and duty. And about reason and passion.

Those were subjects that still interested her. She sat back in her wingback chair. What part of their time together at Pavonis was she remembering? "That's good, Anton," she said, eyes gleaming. "It never does to be too controlled. Reason must be the handmaiden of passion. If she is allowed to rule the house it becomes nothing but an overdecorated tomb."

He grabbed the legs of the footstool and dug his fingers painfully into them. "Reason tells me you are correct," he said. "It doesn't tell me much else." It had been too long since he'd felt anything like the surge of . . . lust that he had just had. And she had noticed, and approved in the abstract, with one of her aphorisms. He looked away, suddenly angry with her and himself.

The party's talk had focused from general hubbub into tight, intent groups. Vanessa Karageorge and Torstov Plauger now stood some distance from Lady Windseth, concluding a conversation. He took her hand, bowed farewell, and walked toward Anton and Miriam. Vanessa's eyes followed him, then scanned across Anton, barely flickering, as if he were an andiron or a decorative vase. Anton stood up convulsively.

"Ah, Torstov," Miriam said softly. "It is time to go. We have business in the morning." She put up her hand and he helped her out of her chair. She leaned against him slightly. "Good evening, Anton. I leave in the morning, but I'll be back in three days. We can talk then."

He kissed her formally, on the cheek, and watched her sway out of the room on Plauger's arm.

The *vyecher* at Lord Monboddo's famous house at Fresh Pond Verge was Vanessa's first chance to relax since Naples, even though she was still officially on duty. Any duty that did not involve night knife duels or, almost worse, the intense Academia Sapientiae debriefing that followed seemed easy by comparison. She tried to wash the gall taste of defeat from her mouth with a dry, straw-colored wine and idle talk. It almost worked.

Soon after Torstov Plauger left her, the room began to seem too hot and too crowded for her. She slipped out, to wander those parts of the house that were open to a casual visitor. She finally emerged on the East Ambulatory where carved mourners from the fourteenth century were on display. The Ambulatory would be enclosed in the winter, and the glass panels for that purpose were already leaning against the wall near the door, but for now the archways were still open to the evening breezes. The cool air off the pond was pleasant, and she strolled back and forth, admiring both the night and the Burgundian mourners, who stood in their niches in the wall, now lamenting their own exile in time and space rather than the death of their long-vanished lord.

She sensed a flicker of movement and swung quickly to face it, stepping back to balance on the balls of both feet. Facing her was a slightly startled Anton Lindgren. He recovered quickly, though he looked irritated at being pulled from whatever reverie had kept him from seeing her in the shadows.

"Ms. Karageorge," he said, inclining his head. "I am Anton Lindgren, Seneschal of this House."

She bowed in response and shook his hand, which was warm and oddly rough, with astoundingly long fingers. "Pleased to meet you." Household etiquette did not allow the carrying of concealed weapons, thank God. Otherwise, still nervous after Naples, she might have pulled a knife on him.

He seemed tense, distracted, and unwilling to start a conversation, which Vanessa, trying not to flatter herself unduly, found unexpectedly annoying. He'd spent all that time talking to Miriam Kostal, and then she'd left with Plauger. What interested him? Was he as dry as he appeared? Where did he really live? Vanessa turned half away from him and patted the fat, gloomy monk in the niche, whose hands automatically counted a rosary as he stared off into space. "This one, and the Abbess at the other end. They're by Claus Sluter, aren't they?"

Anton smiled in honest appreciation. "Yes. Brilliant, though Sluter is almost unknown these days. It's a delight to find someone else familiar with his work."

She ignored his compliment. "One of the others is by his student, Claus de Werve. Not as good as his master."

"But good enough. Good enough indeed. He's even more obscure. I hadn't even heard of him when I found that figure. I didn't know that you were an expert in fourteenth-century Flemish sculpture. I could have used you."

"I'm not an expert in it. You don't have to be an expert to see what's obvious." She walked to the other end of the Ambulatory, and he fell in step beside her, no longer in a hurry to get to wherever he had been heading. She allowed herself a little satisfaction. "But these other three," she said, pointing at the nearest, a balding man in the elaborate court garments of the Gensekretarial Court, carved in the style of Claus Sluter. "Do we continue to mourn the Duke of Burgundy in the twenty-fourth century?"

Anton laughed. "It's a whimsy of Lord Monboddo's. He commissioned them from an artist out in the wilds of California. It was quite an adventure hauling them back. He says they can stay here with their comrades until such time as they support his own catafalque. I don't know if he's joking or not."

"Sluter and de Werve have been dead for a thousand years. Why go through so much trouble to make imitations of their work? It's absurd."

"I don't think so. The six mourners, besides being beautiful, show something about what fourteenth-century Burgundy and twenty-fourth-century Terra have in common: a court with an elaborate ceremonial, and a fear of death. The two eras in this Ambulatory look across the centuries at each other with surprised recognition."

"Hmm. Does everything in the Monboddo collection teach a useful and wholesome lesson?"

Instead of being offended, which she had half expected, Anton laughed again. "Am I hearing a Fellow of the Academia Sapientiae?" He examined her carefully, unembarrassed to be seen doing it, like a connoisseur finding something in a dark corner of a gallery. Is it a fine early effort? The idle daub of an amateur? A superb, but minor work? "School of" or "influenced by"? She felt, for a moment, vulnerable, as if whatever decision he was making affected her deeply. At the next instant he might take his leave and stride off out of the Ambulatory, to disappear. In that case she knew she would never see him again. That seemed, suddenly, a pity.

"I have some time before I have to get back"—he gestured to the lit windows of the West Wing—"to my social responsibilities. Would you care to see part of the collection?"

She let out a breath she hadn't even known she was holding. "That would be wonderful," she said with open gratitude. She had heard a lot about the Monboddo collection. In addition, she knew that it now included a new object: a carved ivory figurine, which, the last time she had seen it, had been hanging around the neck of a dead man in the Bay of Naples.

Only part of the collection was on display at any one time in the house, but key parts of it stayed permanently in Martin's Tower, called after the birds that had once supposedly nested under its eaves. It stood at the high end of the house, toward the town of Cambridge, whose high-pitched roofs could be seen above the surrounding pines and hemlocks. The octagonal tower was roofed with cedar shingles.

The base of Martin's Tower intersected the library, and held reading and study rooms and two artists' studios as well as the art collection, so books, papers, and occasional children's drawings lay scattered among the artworks.

Vanessa stepped through the works in quiet awe. The collection was small by museum standards, but there was nothing in it that was not significant. Wiltern's *Woman Weeping*, kneeling in an alcove by herself, still had the power to move, two and a half centuries after its creation. A case of silver portrait coins from the Greek kingdom of Bactria, dating from the second century BCE, showed how high the art of coinage could go. Anton took several of his favorites out so that she could look at them more closely.

She stopped dead next to something that should have been simple. It was a bowl carved out of a green-blue stone flecked with bright red, with a slender pedestal. The bowl seemed almost liquid, like a stop-motion photograph of a droplet falling into some impossible liqueur. With a glance at Anton for his permission, she reached out and stroked it. It moved beneath her touch as if alive.

"It's called the Blood Bowl," Anton said. "It's carved out of lazarite, a close relative of ngomite. It's just as strange a substance, though in a different way. When she was very young, the artist, Caroline Apthorpe, met Aya Ngomo, just before Ngomo disappeared from this earth. She waited another half a century before carving this bowl from one of the substances Ngomo found in the Belt. We have no evidence that she ever carved anything else."

"She must have," Vanessa gasped. "Something like this doesn't just come out of nowhere. Lazarite is almost impossible to work with."

She looked up at Anton, who shrugged. "Perhaps all of her other works have vanished. Perhaps she destroyed them herself, so that no one could ever attribute to her anything less than perfection. Perhaps the bowl doesn't actually exist. Perhaps it's the only thing that does."

3

The sky was lightening to the east. Anton crunched through the dry leaves that covered the path along the shore of Fresh Pond, watching the water catch the light and come alive. Maples glowed orange among the solemn green pines. The five towers of the house at Fresh Pond Verge stood reflected in the still pond, the growing day behind them.

He left the path to sit on a bench facing the pond and think. A square of thick grass, silvery with dew, led out to the water. He stopped. Facing away from the pond sat a shaven-headed woman in a white wool robe, cross-legged on an embroidered carpet. The dew was undisturbed all around her, so she had been there a long time.

Anton sat down on the bench. She stared at him levelly for a long moment, brown eyes under a high, eyebrowless forehead creased by a column of wrinkles as precise as if marked with a straightedge. Her skin was mahogany dark. "Good morning, Anton," she said in a voice as soft as shifting sand.

"Good morning, Rabiah."

"It is fat here. Too much water. The grass is as soft and thick as the flesh of men. Reality itself is swollen like a dry reed sunk in the Nile, wet and ready to fall apart. How can you think here?" She ran her hand across the dew-laden grass and let the water drip from her fingers. She shivered.

"I'd have trouble thinking in your desert," Anton said. "I would always be worried about where my next drink of water was coming from."

She looked scornful. "God has ever walked only in the dry places. All of His prophets—Abraham, Moses, Jesus, Muhammad—have been desert dwellers."

Rabiah umm-Kulthum was a Sufi mystic who had lived most of her life in the dry hills of the Eastern Desert, between the Nile and the Red Sea. She was one of the most respected Muslim legal scholars of her generation. She was also, paradoxically, a member of the Joint Working Group for Collateral Diplomacy, which was why she was sitting on the lawn at Fresh Pond, getting her knees wet, rather than seeking Allah in the desert. Anton had first met her before leaving on his first independent mission, to ferret out the Martian connection with the Australian Nullifiers. Even with Kostal's assistance it had proved a vicious introduction to intelligence work.

"Some of us have other roles," Anton said slowly, "and serve God in other ways."

"True." She breathed for a moment. "It is a striking object, your figurine. The dead prophet in his winding sheet. I would be careful of it, and the conclusions you draw. Think of it: a mysterious stranger, dead on a rock in the ocean, a magnificent figurine around his neck. A real event? Or a bizarre shadow play? Truth often cloaks itself in so many garments that its flesh is invisible. I rather think you may have gotten a hold of one of its more brightly colored scarves."

Anton finally couldn't take it anymore. "But did you approve? Can we go ahead?"

A lark sang in a tree overhead. A breeze rustled the leaves of the maples and red leaves drifted down to settle on the grass. Ripples chased one another across the water. Rabiah umm-Kulthum glared at Anton. "I would teach you patience, but that cannot be done in a morning. I come here to this hole filled with water because I was the dissenter.''

Her voice took on a formal tone, as if she were reciting the Koran. ''The Joint Working Group for Collateral Diplomacy, an executive organ of the Division of External Security, acting under authority granted it by the government of the Union of States and Nationalities under the Treaty of Jakarta, has approved your project. Consider this your formal notification. The plan was presented, and Miriam Kostal, along with the other five members of the group, agreed, after some debate, to grant your request. You have full support to mount an expedition to recover the eighteen kilograms of ngomite you believe exist, whatever its location.''

Anton felt a deep joy. He hadn't realized how much he wanted it, but he now found that he wanted it desperately, as if the ngomite were something beloved that he had lost in childhood and been seeking ever since.

''But you didn't agree,'' he said.

''I did not.'' The sun rose high enough to shine directly on them. Anton enjoyed its warmth on the side of his face. It illuminated the bony details of umm-Kulthum's skull. ''I think you have misunderstood almost everything. Colonel Westerkamp and Miriam Kostal will be here this afternoon. They can give you their version of events, although I suspect that Kostal has her own program. I am here to give you my opinion, if you want it.''

Since their contact was purely a matter of serving together on the Working Group, umm-Kulthum did not call Monboddo by either his noble title, granted by the Gensek, or his legal title, Interrogator. Instead she referred to him by his rank in the Division of External Security, and his birth name, George Harvey Westerkamp. Terrans were so fascinated by hierarchy that they used several contradictory sets of ranks simultaneously. In the world of intelligence, at least, Monboddo outranked Kostal, umm-Kulthum, and certainly Anton Lindgren, a lowly Lieutenant, particularly as Monboddo was his immediate superior.

"I wouldn't proceed without it," Anton said simply. He had met umm-Kulthum only a handful of times after that initial meeting during the frantic days at the start of the Australian Expedition, but found that he valued her opinions highly, though they came from a way of thinking very different from his own. Her thoughts were like basalt monuments standing on a desert plateau, their purpose and means of construction mysterious, their presence and solidity unarguable.

"Certainly. Excuse me a moment, Anton. It is time for prayer." Anton stood up and walked a few steps away to give her privacy, even as he realized that this did not make sense. For a Muslim, prayer was a public act. Umm-Kulthum turned her rug into the rising sun, since from Boston Mecca lay to the southeast, and knelt with her forehead down. Anton could almost imagine a muezzin calling from the bell tower, the highest tower of Fresh Pond Verge. The wet grass around her steamed slightly in the sunlight.

Across the pond the backlit house looked as flat as the painted backdrop to a play. A stiff breeze could have blown it over into the water. And Vanessa had stood in the darkness of the Ambulatory, her lacy headdress and erect carriage making her look half like one of the carved Flemish mourners herself, a live woman among the ancient stone figures. He thought about the way her slender fingers had slid along the mysterious surface of the Blood Bowl. It seemed to him that she had come to the gallery with a purpose, a purpose that was largely forgotten in the face of the objects she found there. What had she been after?

"Your Dead Christ," umm-Kulthum said, breaking into his thoughts. She sat, facing him again. "A figurine, which you interpret as a sign, a symbol of another reality, a reality that you believe is eighteen kilograms of a rare crystalline substance. It is commonly believed that this substance, ngomite, was created by an Elder Race a million years ago, a race that may itself symbolize humanity's desire for an orderly universe. I don't argue with your physical evidence, which Colonel Westerkamp presented to us in somewhat excessive detail.''

Anton smiled. ''He complained when I did it to him, of course.''

''The Dead Christ is a symbol. You are blinded by its beauty, by its ivory and gems, by the genius of the man who carved it. If it were a crude figure, molded out of clay by untrained fingers, its essence would not be changed. It would still be the corpse of a man who died on a cross, with iron nails through his feet and wrists, and the wound of a spear thrust in his side, in thirst and agony, abandoned by all who claimed to love him.''

''But why should that cause you to oppose our search?'' Anton said. ''If you accept our conclusions.'' Umm-Kulthum's opposition could be dangerous. From her dry cave in the Egyptian desert she exerted an enormous influence over the operations of ExSec.

''I do not oppose. I question. A symbol ties together more than one reality. This is the strength of symbols. What are the realities here? You must know they are there. You are being fascinated by the brightness of the scarlet cape, and are ignoring the flash of steel in the hand of the matador, the necessary consequence of the cape's meaning. The figurine is much more than a treasure map.''

''I realize that.'' The Dead Christ floated in Anton's imagination. The eyes in the wounds stared at him with an impassive attention similar to umm-Kulthum's. ''But I have no choice. If I'm to find the matador, where else should I look but behind the red cape?''

''You talk sensibly, but I'm not sure you are thinking sensibly,'' umm-Kulthum said, frowning at his attempt at cleverness. ''You have fallen into a treasure cave, and rejoice that you have found a gold hinge with which to fix your kitchen door. What other wonders lie around you? And what djinni guards this hoard? What mysterious door was that hinge intended to hold? And, on a more mundane level, what does your friend Kostal want?''

''What we all want. A favorable balance of power against the Technics.''

''Does she?'' Umm-Kulthum was sardonic. ''She is a Martian. The Martians are angry. Many want war. Does she? Do they intend some independent act? The Technics themselves maintain that their search of the *Sulawesi* was in response to a Union attack on Europa.''

Anton was startled. ''How did you learn that?''

Umm-Kulthum smiled a secret smile. ''I should point out that Technic diplomatic personnel are sometimes in need of spiritual guidance, just as anyone.''

''I find that a little dubious.''

''Find it however you like, Anton. But consider the fact that if the Union itself did not authorize an attack on a Technic military base, Mars might have.''

She stood and rolled up her rug. It was dark red, of intricate pattern. A gift from someone who had once sought her advice, it was the one object of beauty that she permitted herself.

''I dissented from the rest of the Working Group, not because I felt that you would fail in your quest, but because I fear you have no idea of what success will entail.'' Standing, she was a strong woman of middle height. ''If I were to give you any specific advice it would be to come to the wilderness of rocks and wadis east of the great Aswan Swamp. I am returning there this morning, and you could travel with me as far as the base of Wadi al-Kharit. The Earth's ribs show there, the air is clear and dry, and the sun is merciless. The mountains roar. There you will see where reality lies, between the thumb and forefinger of God.''

''We have to move quickly, Rabiah,'' Anton said, facing her. ''You know that. We will.''

''I know it,'' she said serenely. ''You don't have time

to think. But when you awake at the end of it, and the whole world is different, I hope you will finally have a chance to understand why.'' She walked past him and disappeared into the trees.

The room had one of the best views at the New Montevideo Hotel, looking out over the curve of the Charles River to the long steep roofs of Cambridge on the other side. Typically, both of the Technics sat facing away from the window, which in any event was tightly irised shut as if to ward off the effects of a nuclear blast. They looked, instead, toward the light screen on the opposite wall that flickered with the images of a reality put through a blender: an endless corridor cut through stone, a screaming rally in an underground space, three people screwing in free-fall, beautiful children playing on a green lawn, a prospecting ship hurtling past the rings of Saturn, twenty-first-century Chinese troops attacking a Russian tank across a frozen land covered with bodies, an abstract pattern of vibrant colors. None of the scenes lasted longer than a few seconds.

There were two other screens in the room, both spilling images. One showed Terran data: energy use patterns for the province of Massachusetts, inwarding orbits of nickel-iron asteroids bound for the circum-Terran orbital smelters, known troop movements of Union Army units, comm surveillance of optical trunklines in eastern North America, concentrations of volatile organics in the outflow currents of significant biofactories. It was a cornucopia of excessive public intelligence data.

The second screen was a permanent news channel from the Technic Alliance, showing segments on current fashions, popular figures, sports contests, and local politics.

The walls themselves glowed and flickered, roaring like waterfalls and tinkling like wind chimes. The two people sat on the couch, their faces smeared with colored paints that swirled like the surface of a gas giant. They looked like effigies in the cool blue-green light of the walls. It was here that they could relax in the manner of their own society, away from the social insistence of Earth. A tea set, a Terran intrusion, sat on the table between them.

Theonave de Borgra let the sound and light wash over him. For the first time in weeks his thoughts were not distracted by silence and the regular glow of sunlight. What would Vanessa feel to see him now? She thought he was an official at the Ganymedean Commerce Agency, drumming up business on Earth. It irritated him sometimes that she had been so easily convinced that he was nothing but a dull businessman.

That morning, in her bedroom at Harvard, she had been tense and irritable, a part of her personality that had been more prominent since their time in Naples, a little over a week before. He had distracted her with an idle, and false, story about his childhood, which in reality he barely remembered. What had she thought when he had followed her to Boston? That he was devoted, and a little foolish, he hoped. Coming to Boston had proved convenient in several ways. For one thing, it let him meet with the local officer of Titanean Intelligence, one of his subordinates.

"What happened at Europa?" he said.

Tamara Sellering tensed the long spring of her body next to him and extended her nails a few millimeters. In idle moments de Borgra sometimes wondered why he never found her sexually attractive. Maybe it was the fact that she could kill him with her bare hands inside of five seconds. He preferred to think it was because he didn't like bony women, particularly not ones that resembled some sort of hunting creature.

"Europa," she whispered, and the Jovian satellite, a greenish-white sphere of ice crisscrossed by a network of dark lines, suddenly filled the room and turned in front of them as if on display for purchase in a video catalog.

The room's computer contacted their brains directly, through a link in each of their cerebral cortexes. The maker of the computer, Interval, of Callisto, identified itself in their minds with the mental image of a pair of hands with a lightning bolt between them, with the emotional content of a long-ago memory.

Their point of view swooped down toward Europa and entered one of the dark lines, a deep canyon cracking the ice.

"The Union hit Feld's Terminus with a single assault ship," Sellering said. "No one at Feld was on the lookout for an attack. The ship came in low, at high speed, down through the ice canyon of Asterius Linea, just below the level of the surface."

The ice walls sped past at incomprehensible speed. The computer dumped the velocity and the g-forces associated with the turns, to four significant digits, into de Borgra's brain, but he still did not comprehend it. "Good God! One ice column in their path and they would have gone up in flames." He thought about it and shivered. "The ice changes every day. They must have been crazy."

The image of Feld's Terminus appeared, a cluster of silver bubbles at the canyon bottom, like the heads of giant screws driven into the surface of the planet. The scene cut to a fuzzy shot of a spaceship, almost invisible except for the blue-white glare of its fusion flame. "Which Union ship it was is entirely unknown," Sellering said. "They made it, landed at Feld, blew the hatches, and charged in, achieving total surprise."

Ten men ran lightly through the hotel room and into the interior of Feld's Terminus. They wore dark uniforms covered with lightweight body armor and helmets with reflective face plates. They carried short shields and swords, like riot troops. Personnel in the enclosed environment of Feld's Terminus did not carry personal weapons, so the Technics were quickly overwhelmed. Two of them died. De Borgra felt fear, hatred, elation, all a result of endocrine stimulation through his computer link.

"The attackers weren't trying to take the base," Sellering said. "They were only fighting off resistance. No projectile weapons were used, and they weren't wearing vacuum suits, a tacit reassurance that atmospheric containment would not be breached. That makes me think they were Lunar troops, or perhaps Martians. Terrans don't understand vacuum. And see? They have no problem with the low gravity."

The invaders stormed through three levels of the base. They had hit the illusion generators as well, and the background was nothing but bare wall, with none of the usual magical forests or flowing waves. Suddenly made visible, the walls were patched and ugly.

Four of them set up a barricade with some furniture, and defended themselves against the attacks of base personnel, while the rest vanished from the range of the cameras.

"They weren't after anything in the base itself," Sellering said. "It looks like they were after something down in the deep tunnels, which extend down below the ice into the silicate layer."

"The deep tunnels?" De Borgra frowned, bringing his thick eyebrows together. "Why did they dig tunnels there? I thought Feld's Terminus was a military research base. Hell, there's nothing to mine on Europa. It's just a big lump of sand and ice."

A composite holographic map of Feld's Terminus appeared. The base itself was based on five centers, and spread a considerable way down into the depths. But all around, dwarfing the base itself, was a vast maze of tunnels, many of them penetrating dozens of kilometers down into the crust. Many of the tunnels were marked with jagged lines, indicating that they were impassable. Those tunnels that were pressurized and used by the base were marked in yellow. De Borgra felt the thrill of direct geometric perception, a thrill that was as illusory as the perception itself, for it all entered his mind directly from the computer.

"True enough," Sellering said. "The tunnels were there when they built the base. They were convenient for storage. They might be the result of outgassing during the early period of Europa's formation." She paused. "Or they may just be Acherusian."

"Bah," de Borgra said, who made it a point to disbelieve in the existence of the so-called Elder Race, based more on a principle of man's uniqueness than because of any judgment on the archaeological evidence. It pleased him to have prejudices, because he felt they were more individual and personal than considered opinions.

"Be that as it may, the tunnels exist, and the Union assault squad went down into them. Those four held the passage for about half an hour. It was incredibly risky. A brigade of Callistan marines is stationed at Norgol, near Tyre Macula, halfway around Europa. As soon as they got the alarm they took off from their base to reinforce. There is no way that the Union troops could have done anything against them." The screen showed a Callistan corvette, heavily armored, blasting dramatically out of a shielded launch tube. Flakes of frozen ammonia fell from its sides. A notice at the bottom said, "Stock Footage: S.S. *Beck*."

"But they emerged before the marines could get there." The invaders rushed back out of the tunnel, this time carrying a man-sized object wrapped in a cloth. "They met no resistance on their way out."

"What *is* that thing they're carrying?" de Borgra asked.

"You'd think with the film and the eyewitness reports we would know. But we don't. No one got a good look at what was under the cloth. Someone who had seen a Terran video show said it looked like a . . . bassoon." She paused, and looked irritated. "Even the *word* is ridiculous. They got out fast. They left one thing behind them. A garland of roses." De Borgra looked at it, water glistening on the delicate petals. "They're getting crazier all the time. By the time the marines got there, they were gone.''

De Borgra felt a sudden sense of limitation. Since the computer had no idea of what was underneath the blanket, he didn't either, and he had largely lost the ability to draw such conclusions on his own. The unexpected blind spot was frightening.

"With the bassoon," he said. "But that Terran assault boat wasn't the *Sulawesi*."

"No, it wasn't," Sellering said. "The *Sulawesi* seems to have been exactly what the Union has been claiming, an entirely innocent passerby. The assault boat vanished completely. There was a good chance, or at least it must have seemed that way at the time, that the *Sulawesi* had something to do with the attack. At least it was all the marines could get their hands on." The screen showed the flare of a fusion flame, taken with the forward cameras on the *Beck*. The Callistan vessel closed in on it.

The *Sulawesi* could not possibly fight the *Beck*. "Target Submits," the screen said in disappointment. The Union vessel loomed in the screen and the image dissolved back into random flickering.

"The Union's hysterical now, but they'll get over it," de Borgra said. "It provides good material for party conversation, but not much more else. The Union certainly isn't going to go to war over it, much as the Martians may fume. What we have to do is find out why they hit Feld's. Why did they take so much risk for a bassoon?"

"He just said it *looked* like a bassoon," Sellering said with some asperity. De Borgra could see that the word, with its mocking *oon* sound, annoyed her. He resolved to use it more often. "It might have been anything. Until we find out what it was, we have to maintain our position that the *Sulawesi* was violating our claims to the Trojans. It gives us cause to move a military force there. We can turn this situation to our advantage yet."

"The Trojans. Bah. Who needs the damn things?

Chunks of ice named after heroes from some stupid Terran book. I want Earth, and nothing less.'' And he did, with an almost physical passion, as if the Terran women he had affairs with were merely a temporary, unsatisfactory substitute for the entire globe. It was ridiculous. The wealthiest planet in the Solar System, it deliberately kept itself poor, through some sense of guilt, an emotion de Borgra did not understand. "We need to run it. It will be ours. Why mess with asteroids?''

He poured himself another cup of tea. The tea service was of Terran design, but based on Technic motifs. The delicately fluted porcelain cups had their origin in the sort of cup popular on Titan, which looked like a flower and was extravagantly decorated. A bow to their place of inspiration came in the form of a double silver line, a stylized Rings of Saturn in an angled ellipse around the cup. It pleased Terran artisans to demonstrate what they could do with the unexploited potentials of Technic civilization, but the Technics who used their creations did not care.

De Borgra pulled at the long, curling lapels of his shiny red jacket, that month's fashion on Ganymede. Everyone he met in the hallways of the New Montevideo, the central gathering place of all Technics in Boston, wore the correct, fashionable clothes. He had forgotten how much that relaxed him.

The computer began to dump a précis of other intelligence data into his mind. It was mostly a variety of small tasks whose importance was only cumulative. One item was flagged.

"There was a meeting of the Joint Working Group on Collateral Diplomacy three days ago,'' Sellering said. She fully extended her nails and examined them. De Borgra had watched her shred paper with them. He knew that at least four of her nails could also inject poison and drugs but had never been able to figure out which ones.

De Borgra thought, and the computer supplied him with images of the known members of the Working

Group: Lord Monboddo, Miriam Kostal, and Rabiah umm-Kulthum. The other four were vague, hazy figures in his mind, like long-forgotten relatives. That was frustrating. To satisfy his mental itch for more data, the computer gave him vital statistics, educational records, and behavior patterns on the three known members until he lost track of what it was he was trying to understand about them.

"Anything to do with the raid on Europa, do you suppose?" he asked.

"Possible." She ran her fingers through her dark, close-cropped hair. De Borgra watched with interest. Wasn't she ever worried about injecting herself with some deadly alkaloid? "But there's no way to confirm. Their security's too tight. I traced back the activities of the known members. Umm-Kulthum, nothing. Kostal attended a party at Monboddo's the day before the meeting. Among the other guests was your girlfriend, Vanessa Karageorge."

"Eh?" de Borgra said, startled. "Are you implying a connection?"

"No. A correlation. Monboddo is a well-known host, and a variety of people were there, so her simple presence means nothing. However, two days before, a special Gensekretarial courier arrived at the house at Fresh Pond Verge direct from the Esopus Palace with a package. An important object."

"Our bassoon?"

"Too small. A part of it, perhaps. They went through a great deal of trouble to keep security high while making it look casual. It's a key though, I know that much."

"How do you know that?" de Borgra said. His colleague's thought processes always interested him. "The Gensekretarial Court doesn't usually get involved in intelligence. What does the computer say?"

"I don't give a damn what the computer says!" Sellering exclaimed, suddenly irritated. Through a mental resonance, the screen began to show quicker, more violent scenes. A man cut a woman's throat. A volcano on Io exploded, sending streams of flaming sulfur high into the black sky. Figures in clumsy spacesuits grappled in silent vacuum. "It's a hunch. Their security isn't perfect, particularly since Internal Security is involved. I got one word out of it: ngomite."

"Ah," de Borgra said. "Now that's one hell of a word."

Vanessa managed to get her fingers to relax on the girder and just rest casually on it as if it were a column in a reception hall rather than the only thing other than fifty meters of empty space between her and the pavement below. She looked up through the spidery network of old rusted metal at the sky. The elegant yet bumbling cylinder of a dirigible drifted by like a mysterious undersea creature, its outer layer transparently iridescent and its inner layer dark, since it used the heat of the sun to help it generate lift. She couldn't hear its buzzing above the rush of the wind through the girders around her.

Nahum Torkot squatted on a girder above her like an owl on a tree stump. He looked past her at the city around them. "Just think," he said. "People used to live and work at this altitude. This is what's left of the John Hancock Building, an insurance office. Their environment was carefully isolated so that they wouldn't know how high they were. And there was no way they could fall." With a sudden graceless but effective leap he swung his heavy, blocky body out over the open air and dropped down onto a resting place on the other side of Vanessa.

"Maybe that was so that they could get their work done," she said.

"We're getting *our* work done, aren't we?" He closed his eyes and raised his face to the sun. His skin was dark and seamed like old leather. "So the Justice of Tharsis wears an Ozaki in her hair. What sort of person would wear the work of a genius as a personal ornament?''

Vanessa looked out over the city. The skeleton of the John Hancock Building stood over the herringboned brick of Copley Square, opposite the ornate Russian Second Empire bulk of the Boston Public Library, with its bright red and green wooden-shingled roof. Toward the river was the New Montevideo Hotel, the flowing golden stucco of the twenty-third-century Pampas Style more suited to the open stretches of Patagonia or Kansas than the narrow streets of Boston. Theonave was in that building now, doing God knew what odd Technic things. Her eyes followed the Charles River, crowded with sailboats, upstream. On the opposite side, amid the orange and yellow woods that marked the edge of Cambridge, was the glint of Fresh Pond. Were those the towers of the house at Fresh Pond Verge? She wasn't sure.

"A powerful one," she said, remembering the stalking panther that suited Kostal so well. "But she doesn't seem to have anything to do with the figurine. She's a personal friend of Anton Lindgren's."

Torkot twisted his full lips in a frown. "You're the one who insisted on going to that party. For information. There's a lot of information to be had, and the Justice of Tharsis's habits are part of it. The figurine itself, I fear, is lost."

Vanessa turned away from him. She served Preterite Torkot as his personal assistant. He had never rebuked her for having fumbled the recovery of the figurine in Naples, leaving her to do the job of rage herself. A sea gull flew by and shrieked at her. She felt like wringing its neck.

"I don't think it has to be," she said.

"Lindgren and Monboddo. A couple of magpies who pick up shiny things to decorate their nest. They picked up my figurine. Why that of all things? Damn them."

"They enjoy beautiful objects," she said. She remembered the artworks in the gallery at Fresh Pond, and the way Anton had looked at them as he took her through, as if wonderingly seeing them for the first time himself.

She relaxed and sat down on a girder. Only a third of the original framework was left, rusted a mellow orange-brown. It was protected by a nonreactive coating, kept in a state of arrested decay. Four massive bronze bells hung below, looming over Trinity Church's squat nine-teenth-century tower. The framework had served as the bell tower of Boston's Russian Orthodox Cathedral in the twenty-second century. The ruins of the Cathedral itself, burned during the Tumults that marked the end of the Orthodox Empire, still lay below. Torkot, after sev-eral minutes of dedicated effort, managed to pull a bolt out of the girder. He tossed it down, and it struck the largest bell with a muted golden sound.

"How did they manage to get the figurine in the first place?" Vanessa asked.

"It's odd. The figurine was recovered by a trained dolphin. Dolphins are legally wards of the Gensek. It went to the Esopus Palace." He scowled. "It should have come to the Academia. I talked to Varlam himself. I put in a formal request. He said it was impossible. Impossible!"

In his younger years Torkot had been head tutor to the Household of the Genseka Akulina, Varlam's great-aunt. He had thus been in charge of Varlam's moral and in-tellectual education. The Academia Sapientiae had been educating Genseks for almost a century, one source of its cultural influence. To have his former pupil—now monarch of the Earth, Moon, Venus, and Mars, and the spaces between—refuse such a simple request had thrown Torkot into depression.

"Did you at least get a look at it?" he sighed. "At last?"

"It's hidden somewhere," Vanessa said, frowning. "Which is odd in itself. It's an art object, a brilliant new acquisition. Why haven't they put it on display? Senes-chal Lindgren didn't even mention it, and I didn't see any case being gotten ready for it." She looked thoughtful. "Lady Windseth, Monboddo's wife, has influence at Court. Still, I don't see why it went to Fresh Pond. The Gensek should have kept it for the Palace collection."

"Maybe Varlam won't let them keep it," Torkot said hopefully.

"Preterite!" Vanessa said, suddenly exasperated. "Losing the figurine was my fault. I concede that. But we can't proceed on hopes and prayers." She stood up quickly, as she did when she was passionately interested in making a point, and almost toppled down into Copley Square. She grabbed for support, fighting vertigo. At this altitude, the smallest act could have serious consequences. Torkot was a specialist in symbolic dialogue.

She took a breath and let her thudding heart slow. "There's something we're not seeing here. Someone must see a significance in the figurine beyond its being an original Ozaki in an antique style. How important is the figurine?"

Torkot had really told her little about the figurine's origins and significance, but she was used to that. Many of the Academia's operations were secret even within itself. She would have felt more comfortable, however, if she had the feeling that Torkot knew what he was doing. He tended to rely too much on personal influence in the Esopus Palace and among his fellow leaders in the Academia, and not enough on hard procedure.

"Lindgren," Torkot said thoughtfully. He smiled at her look of surprise. "He's the curator of the Monboddo collection. What did he see in that figurine, do you suppose? What is he like?"

"Ah, intelligent. Distant. Oddly unsure, given his position and his skills. And as for the figurine . . . I don't know. He has a good eye and a clear mind. And he's seen it. I haven't." Except dangling around the neck of a dead man twenty meters away. Except in failure.

"What should our next move be, then?" Torkot said.

He watched her carefully, sharp eyes under disconcertingly long, ladylike lashes.

"We should watch Lindgren," she said, somewhat reluctantly. She thought of Anton's lean figure, his dreamy expression. He was a man of parts, but somehow disconnected from the world around him, an attitude she didn't like. Quite unlike Theonave, who held on to the world with both hands, though she was never quite sure what he wanted to do with it. "He's the key, the figurine's visible part. He's our only option."

Torkot nodded. "Good idea, Vanessa. Watch him, follow him." Torkot was a genius at surfing on the breaking waves of others' thoughts. "He will be a lamp unto our feet, a role I think he would enjoy, if only he knew about it."

4

From *A Brief Life of Aya Ngomo*, by Mary Bartholdi, Educational Press, Buenos Aires, 2332:

By this time, distinguishing Ngomo from her ship was almost impossible. Her eyes were the scanners, her lungs were the ventilation system, her skull was grotesque and deformed, the bone soft. Identity with the machine is a common feature of space dwelling, and Ngomo, of course, had lost the use of her legs long before leaving Earth. She was a cyborg, plain and simple. Nowadays, the Union does not use cyborgs. They were banned after the Seven Planets War, in 2255, and many of them were banished to Mars or the Asteroid Belt, their service in the war forgotten. But under the Orthodox Empire, in the twenty-second century, it was allowed. You often see pictures of Ngomo as a pretty woman in a wheelchair. Remember what she really was. She was as human as you or I, though she was a steel cylinder hurtling through the Asteroid Belt, with a soft inside of human flesh. . . .

. . . Finding ngomite was no accident. It was the "jewel" of her childhood, which she thought was a part of each person's brain. Her jewel had been lost, and she was looking for it. Until she found it, she could not be complete. How she had sensed it, across millions of miles of space and millions of years, is still a mystery. Did the Elder Race, which seems to have created ngomite and its relative, lazarite, leave the young girl a message? She never told anyone....

... It was supposed to be just an experiment, of course. The new fusion engine that ngomite made possible was, in honor, going to be tested by Ngomo herself. Her flight was blessed by the Patriarch of Moscow. "I'm sorry," she said. "I have to go home." And, on 13 April 2146, she blasted at an acceleration of three g's, straight out of the Solar System, perpendicular to the ecliptic, toward the constellation Draco. The new engine was certainly a success. Ngomo is still traveling, ever closer to the speed of light. She may even still be alive, due to time dilation effects of travel at relativistic velocities. Someday, perhaps, we will be able to follow her.

Vanessa stood at the edge of the sunken bowl of the Summer Theater and looked down over its curved benches and autumnal brown grass toward Theonave de Borgra, who leaned back carelessly in the second row of seats from the now boarded-up stage. Beyond the stage, where the Boston Symphony Orchestra played its summer concerts, was the organized wilderness of the Fens, its almost-bare trees austere in the steely light of the overcast sky. This was the edge of densely inhabited Boston.

To the left, through the trees, Vanessa could see the granite portico of Symphony Hall, with its ponderous metal tracery and statue of Henri Lastesse as a young man, when he wrote *Final Songs*, anticipating his death by some five decades.

Yesterday, she had looked down over this area from the skeleton of the Hancock tower. If that sunny, warm day had been a late memory of summer, today was a presentiment of winter. It had rained heavily the night before, and the wind had grown teeth. Usually she looked forward to the approach of cold weather, but this rawness struck into her bones.

Theonave wore a long coat and a felt hat. Under it, she knew, was his gray jacket with the lace at the collar and cuffs. He always wore it in public. It amused him to no end that he could keep wearing it month after month and still have it be in fashion. She hadn't told him how dowdy it had looked in Naples, where brighter colors were the norm.

He stood up and bowed, awkwardly, a Technic mimicking a Terran social gesture without quite understanding its purpose, then stepped forward and took her into his arms. His eyes gleamed with the silver microcrystals sprouting through his irises. His face was soft, save for the dimpled chin and the dark eyebrows. He had the dissipated elegance of a late Roman senator, granted an automatic superiority by his birth. She kissed him.

A wide V of Canada geese flew overhead, honking at each other. Theonave looked up. "Ah, another *vyecher*. Terrans do like to socialize." Though heavily dressed, so much so that she could barely tell there was an actual person under his coat, he shivered. "I hate weather. It's a nice idea, but I think you've gone overboard by putting it all over the place like this."

"Today, I think I agree with you," Vanessa said. "Let's walk."

A path of crushed stone led from behind the stage through the Fens and around to the quiet houses and cafés of the Avellaneda District, the area that had been favored by the Argentinean and Uruguayan businessmen who had helped rebuild Boston in the middle of the previous century. The small hotels there, with their shuttered windows and enclosed rose gardens, promised a concealed intimacy popular with lovers of all sorts. But now, in the cold late October light, the colored stucco walls seemed falsely cheery, and the cafés with their empty outdoor patios, tables and chairs stacked against back walls under tarpaulins, puddles on the stone paving reflecting the metal sky, were like weary entertainers conceding that their audiences could not be moved.

The Brasilienne, a restaurant that she had chosen, was warm and steamy inside, the air sharp with spice. The clatter of dishes was pleasant in contrast to the wet silence of the streets.

"But where are you going?" he asked. "And so soon. Tomorrow morning, you said?"

"That's what I said. It's a surprise to me too, believe me."

"But where—"

"I'm not allowed to say. Academia business, is all." She wondered at her own exasperated mood. Maybe it was the weather. In literature, the pathetic fallacy is often invoked to match the weather to the moods of the characters, an unnecessary ploy, since people's moods often fall into place with the weather, which is the mood of the sky. The sky's mood was foul, and so was hers.

"Vanessa?" Theonave said. "I saw something odd today. Can you explain it to me?"

Vanessa acted as Theonave's interpreter of Terran culture, a role she usually enjoyed. She peeked around the edge of her menu, though she was not feeling at all flirtatious. "What was it?"

"It was a path through the woods. It crossed a stream on a bridge, which kinked back and forth." He drew a lightning bolt on the table with his finger. "Why did it do that? Did someone fold the plans by accident?"

She smiled. "No. In Japanese legend, demons can't cross running water. They need bridges to do it, but they have to travel in straight lines. They can't use a bridge like that."

"What? But this isn't Japan, it's Massachusetts." He showed outrage at Earth's confused mass of folklore, an outrage that always delighted her.

"You can't be too careful."

He snorted in contempt and leaned back in his chair,
like a billiards player who had just sunk a difficult ball.
She set her menu down. The waiter brought their black
bean soup, which served to chase away the last chill of
the fall day outside.

Vanessa thought idly about his story. Since when did
Theonave take walks in the woods? That was an easy
one. He didn't. Had he made the whole story up, then?
That wasn't likely either. Bridges of that sort were rare.
He'd probably been looking at a map. For some reason,
the thought would not leave her alone, though it was
ridiculous. What difference did it make? But a map of
where? There was only one place around Boston where
such a bridge stood. It spanned Alewife Brook, which
marked the western edge of the Monboddo estate. So
what? He'd probably been looking idly at a map. But
that didn't match up with her understanding of Theonave,
a man whose every act had a goal.

"What are you staring at?" he demanded. "I don't
think you're listening to me."

She leaned over and put her fingers through his curly
hair. "Of course I was listening," she said. What had
he been talking about? Ah yes, he was complaining
again.

"It makes no sense at all. It took me three days last
month just to get to New York from San Francisco.
Trains! Steam engines. I don't care what they say about
the availability of coal, they're a stupid idea. Sleeper
cars and dining cars with big brass samovars and nothing
to do but read and look at the scenery. And the woman
serving the tea was unbelievably ugly. It used to take
three hours for the same trip. *Hours*, not days. And the
women were better looking. They had to have been."

"Theo, I've lost track. Are you complaining about the
ugliness of the women or the speed of the transportation?"

"Both, by God. It's a ridiculous game you Terrans
play, pretending that it takes a long time to get anywhere,

when I could take a spaceship to L5 maintenance dock and take another one down and be in, in . . . *Brisbane* in half a day. Or what's left of it.''

Vanessa winced. He'd picked that city deliberately to be annoying. She saw heads turn at other tables.

"You'd need a special Gensekretarial order to do it,'' she said. "The less time it takes to go from place to place, the less difference there is between them. Is there a difference between one side of Ganymede and the other?''

He looked surprised. "No. Why should there be? We all know what we want, so we have it. We don't have an Academia Sapientiae to tell us different.''

"But don't differences matter to you? Don't you remember Manaus?''

He smiled and put his hand over hers. "Of course I remember. But we could have met anywhere and it would have been beautiful. Manaus itself was irrelevant.''

"But it was there, there above the jungle. That's important. The terraces, the dark Rio Negro, the way the city was split up by the deep channels of the river. All that's important, just like that iridescent silk jacket you were wearing. Remember? With the high collar.''

Theonave looked uncomfortable. "Come on, Vanessa. That's been out of style for months. I don't even know what happened to it.''

"That doesn't matter. I remember it.'' He had worn the jacket with the serene confidence of a man who knows he is in fashion, even if no one around him is.

She also remembered the wet jungle that finally grew again on the side rivers of the Amazon. Much of the basin was still scrub wasteland, utterly destroyed, but Manaus again stood above an aromatic, flowered, dangerous jungle. Which was a silly thing to remember because Theonave had never strayed out of the city, had never felt the water drip on his head from leaves thirty meters above, smelled an orchid as it hung from its tree, or stared into the eyes of a jaguar. Still, when she remembered those things, she remembered him.

"But tell me, dear," he said. "What are you going to be doing?"

Vanessa found herself, suddenly, suspicious. His interest in her work for the Academia Sapientiae had always seemed paradoxically strong for a blandly businesslike trade official. When they met in Manaus, he had been in the process of selling the Terrans heavy topomorphic equipment developed for use on Io, now to be used to reconstruct the Amazon jungle.

"I told you, Theo. Academia business. I can't tell you any more. Please don't ask."

"Not more Academia business. Haven't you had enough? You should quit while you're ahead. You've set this whole planet up as a museum, with yourselves as the guards. It's dead."

"It's as alive as life itself," she said sharply. "You don't understand, because you do all your living on the outside, where it can be seen. Is a Technic alive when no one is watching?" It had always been an exasperating part of Theonave's personality that he hated to do things alone. He needed company for even the most mundane errands.

She thought she understood why. All Earth children imagined that their stuffed animals talked, but his really had: the clever snake with the jeweled scales, the bear that giggled when he squeezed it, and the mouse that tickled his toes when he took a nap. He had never in his life been alone. How could he know who he was, then?

"But you never *do* anything," he said. "You just study, store, collate. You pile up the facts. How can you live this way? Not everyone agrees with what you've done to this planet. Obviously not. Five years ago an entire continent tried to throw off the shackles."

A number of topics were taboo in polite public discourse, but none more so than the dismal rancor of the Australian Expedition, the counterinsurgency operation that had kept Australia within the Union of States and

Nationalities at the cost of half a million lives. Like an excised tumor that might well have been malignant, it had resulted in a planetary political hypochondria. To have the subject brought up by a Technic was beyond the pale.

There was silence at the tables immediately around them. Vanessa practically pulled Theonave bodily out of the restaurant. She was less angry than simply irritated. He usually had a sense of how to behave in public places. Something about her refusal to tell him where she was going galled him, more than she would have thought possible. She wondered, again, why he was so desperate to know.

They stood silently together, their breath steaming, until the streetcar arrived, quiet on its rubber wheels.

The streetcar passed the New Montevideo on its way up Massachusetts Avenue, stopping opposite the twisted columns of the hotel entrance, but Theonave didn't invite her in. Nor did he get off himself.

"You can't stay with me," she hissed as the car started again. "It's not allowed."

He chuckled. "Morality enforcement. Are you scholars all pure?"

"We're not pure. We're polite."

The streetcar rolled its way up the street from the river to Harvard. A main avenue for hundreds of years, Massachusetts was lined by a double rank of graceful elms. The drizzle had started again. Water droplets on the windows refracted the lacework of tree branches and the yellow streetlights. Just visible between the tree trunks were the deep doorways of Cambridge, their flanking windows shining warmly. Vanessa leaned her forehead on the glass and wondered what private lives went on within those dignified and slightly dowdy houses.

Theonave walked her to her dormitory, a squat brick building resembling an armory or a fort, built during the declining days of the late twenty-second century. He kissed her in the doorway, and she did feel the sudden

urge to smuggle him in somehow. She pulled herself
back a little and looked at him. He gazed back at her,
but his mind was somewhere else entirely. She had never
seen him when he was other than intent on her, and only
her. He kissed her once more, then walked off into the
darkness. She looked after him. His calm, measured walk
did not look like that of a man eager to get home on a
rainy night. But this was really too much. She was ana-
lyzing everything. She hurried inside.

The main room, which served as library and meeting
hall, was crowded, dominated by an immense samovar
at one end and an open fireplace at the other. It was filled
with the quiet intentness of argument, young men and
women displaying ideas to each other, ideas blazing with
newness and truth, not yet covered by dim layers of
equivocation.

She felt shut off from it. It did not reject her, but she
suddenly felt that it accepted her falsely, not understanding what she was. But what was she? A scholar? A
murderer? A spy?

She crossed the room to one of the narrow windows.
The streetcar platform outside was calm, an oasis of light
amid the trees. Theonave's bulky shape stood on the near
side and, as she watched, climbed into the haven of a
streetcar bound for home. She turned away, oddly com-
forted, and froze. The two of them had gotten off the
streetcar on that side. If he had gotten back on in the
same place, he wasn't going back toward Boston but was
heading west, away from the city. What lay in that direction? Arlington, the hamlet of North Cambridge, and
Fresh Pond.

She whirled, suddenly decisive. She soon found the
person she wanted, a blond woman with fine features,
sitting carelessly in a pile of pillows near the fire. Four
or five men sat around, intent on her.

"Ah, don't talk to me about Martians," she said,
raising her hands in dismayed surrender. "Everything's
calculated to them. Even sexual violence follows aes-

thetic rules. I wouldn't be surprised to find out that they had some precise canon of proportion for bruises and whip scars. It can be a bore."

Vanessa finally managed to catch her eye. "Lauren," she said. "I need to borrow your bicycle."

"Come on, Vanessa," Lauren said lazily. "It's the middle of the night, and pouring rain besides. Why aren't you in bed with that Technic businessman of yours?"

Vanessa was surprised to find that she could still be embarrassed, but Lauren did have such a penetrating voice. "Dammit, I want the bicycle. Will you lend it to me? Now!"

Lauren shrugged in surrender. "If you tell me the story later. The key's in my room, in the left drawer of my desk. Don't run it into any trees!" These last words were shouted after Vanessa as she ran from the room.

A few minutes later, wearing a dark, waterproof jumpsuit, she was pulling the bicycle out onto the cold, windswept street. At least she wasn't wearing a lemon-yellow dress this time. Lauren's bicycle was a high recumbent with a smaller front wheel. The fairing was folded back on either side in two spindles. She twisted a lever and it opened out like butterfly's wings, enclosing the bicycle in an aerodynamic shell.

The forest beyond the north wall of Harvard was largely uninhabited until North Cambridge. The streetcar track left the road and made its way through the woods, unaccompanied save for a wide bicycle path. Vanessa hissed along through the darkness. Rain pattered steadily on the fairing.

It did not take more than a few minutes for the rhythm of the bicycle to warm her up. The two pairs of tracks gleamed parallel in her headlights, and the trees whipped past, dark shadows at the periphery of her vision. An occasional fellow bicyclist passed her, heading in toward town. In past eras, this area had been densely inhabited, and an occasional tumulus loomed from the woods, marking the piled remains of smashed buildings. These were usually surmounted by a monument, a pillar, a statue, a burning blue flame surrounded by glittering shapes like shards of broken glass. At the beginning of the twenty-first century the population of the Boston area had been over five million. Now, after centuries of war and plague, it was roughly a tenth that number. For years, funerary monuments had been a mainstay of the arts.

She finally spotted the lights of the streetcar as it scuttled its way through the woods like a gleeful insect. She slowed and peered at it. Was that Theonave's large head? It was hard to tell. The streetcar windows were a mass of heads, diligently reading papers or peering out into the darkness at the barely visible trees. She flicked off her headlights. The streetcar stopped at some anonymous crossing in the forest. Dark-cloaked figures stepped out, gossamer umbrellas blossomed, and they marched off into the night, shouting farewells at each other.

She chased the streetcar again, not pulling near it. She would have been by far the most interesting thing to look at, and Theonave would have noticed her immediately.

Now that she found herself suspicious of him, she realized that she had never quite trusted him. The son of a bitch was clearly hiding something, and he had absolutely no urge to confession, a useful weakness in a man. So she had to shadow him in the rain to find out what it was. Another lover? The thought almost made her brake to a halt. What a ludicrous thing that would be, to chase Theonave around dramatically, only to watch him in some romantic rendezvous, and then bicycle sadly home. What else, indeed, did she expect? What other secrets was a man like him capable of having?

The streetcar tracks finally crossed Alewife Brook on a high trestle, and it was there, not far from Fresh Pond, that Theonave alighted. Vanessa skidded to a halt before she came to the trestle, her decision made. Turning back now would be silly. She folded the fairing and hauled the bike into the shrubs at the edge of the path, praying she would be able to find it again.

By this time Theonave had left the tracks, but she could hear him thrashing and muttering in the wet, dark woods. It certainly didn't sound as if he were on his way to an amorous rendezvous.

The trail's surface of crushed stone wound its way through the trees in a manner that, under more favorable circumstances, would have been picturesque. It crossed over the zigzag Japanese bridge, whose bizarre configuration almost dumped Theonave into the rush of Alewife Brook. That was where Vanessa stopped. She had examined the security system of the house at Fresh Pond Verge during her visit there for the *vyecher*. It was incredibly sophisticated. Her crossing the bridge would be immediately detected. She stood and watched him disappear into the wet darkness.

Theonave was no fool. If he crossed into Monboddo's territory with such insouciance, it was because he knew a way to do it without detection. What sort of man could violate Fresh Pond Verge's security system with impunity? She longed to follow him, but her being apprehended on the grounds would create more trouble than it could conceivably be worth. She wondered, for an instant, what Anton Lindgren would think to catch her and the Ganymedean Theonave de Borgra wandering the woods at night. Perhaps he and Lord Monboddo could then figure out what she had been unable to. She rejected the idea with a chilled shudder. She would have to solve the problem of her wayward lover on her own. Wet and irritated, she turned back to her bicycle.

The dead man lay in the wet grass like something dumped and forgotten. His throat had been cut, and his tongue sliced out of his head and flopped in the grass like some grotesque slug. The rain had washed the blood away, leaving the corpse with the pale slickness of a refrigerated chicken. Anton looked down at the face, its eyes rolled up under half-closed blue eyelids, then glanced at Fell, who shrugged.

"He's not our fault," Osbert said viciously. "Ask *him* what happened." He jabbed a thumb at a slope-shouldered man with a prominent Adam's apple who stood on the hillock above, dictating a report to one of his colleagues.

"I'm not interested in his opinion," Anton said, loudly enough to be heard above. The man stopped dictating for a moment, then resumed. "I want your account."

"Right." Osbert turned away and looked off across the lawn at the pond, its surface dull from the muddy runoff of the storm. "It's a complete fuckup is the account."

Fell curled a lock of his blond hair around a finger. "We caught this guy in the Collection at about two this morning. He was near that thing you call the Blood Bowl. He got through the security systems all the way, but we heard the floorboards creak. Low technology pays off again. We called you."

"And you called them," Osbert said.

"Yes, Osbert, I did," Anton said, his voice suddenly low. "Are you stating an objection?"

"No," Osbert said, startled. "No, of course not. Why should I?"

"That's what I was wondering."

Martin's Tower had been brightly lit when Anton got there, still rubbing the sleep from his eyes. Osbert and Fell had immobilized and searched the man they had captured in the Collection. External Security had no authority within Union territory to hold or interrogate captured agents and any attempt to do so would have resulted in serious punishment. So Anton had put in a call to the local office of the Division of Internal Security.

Osbert turned away, rubbing the back of his neck. "We caught him, alive. You saw all that. As soon as you got down you ordered a full search of the grounds. While you were taking care of that, we turned him over to bozo over there, yeah *you*, you know who I mean, and—"

"Osbert!" Anton said. "Either tell me what happened straight or shut the hell up. I'm not interested in anyone's *opinion*. Got that?" He'd been woken up twice in one night and had barely gotten his eyelids unstuck the second time, when he'd been dragged from bed at dawn to examine a mutilated corpse.

"He's a citizen of Callisto," Fell continued. "Paul Malan. A metals trader, works with asteroid smelting. No file. Until last night, we thought he was clean."

"You mean the *insects* thought he was clean," Osbert contributed.

"Internal Security has nearly a hundred thousand resident Technic citizens to keep track of," Anton said with reluctant reasonableness. As an ExSec officer he held no brief for the Division of Internal Security, but there was no reason to start interdepartmental brawling now. "Most of them are not spies."

Anton turned to the man on the patio. "Then what happened, Snodgress? Aside from your refusing to help in an immediate search of the area."

Snodgress walked down, reluctantly, darting a glance at Osbert, who ignored him. His Adam's apple bobbed up and down. "My men have better things to do than crawl around in the wet woods in the middle of the night. The security system of your house—"

"Is inadequate. Obviously." Anton controlled himself, keeping his voice modulated, professional, though he suspected that his face showed his irritation.

"He was a Technic spy," Snodgress said.

Anton waited.

"We took him off for a full interrogation. En route, we were attacked, here in the woods, by some substantial body of men—"

"Our security system isn't that bad, for God's sake. We don't have armies wandering around in our flower beds. There couldn't have been more than one or two others. They decoyed you away, and murdered him. How did they do it?"

"Mr. Lindgren. You asked for a report, and I am giving it to you. I am not, as you know, legally obliged to do so."

"Legally—!" Anton took a deep breath. "So the Ganymedean army, which had concealed itself under the compost heap—"

Snodgress glared venomously at him. "Read the formal report later. Meanwhile, you had best check your security systems. They seem inadequate." He signaled his men, who picked the body up and carried it off. Anton looked after them.

"They sure screwed that one up," Osbert said.

"Not any worse than we did," Anton answered.

The government of the Union of States and Nationalities felt that the political threat of a competent and powerful intelligence organization far outweighed any advantages to be derived from using it on Earth. The principle was that there is no better guardian of the people's freedom than a corrupt and incompetent secret police. Occasionally ExSec officers sought to alter this policy. Executions rarely proved necessary to curb their ambition.

"There were others in the woods, obviously," Miriam Kostal said, twisting past the wet drooping branches of a willow.

"Obviously," Anton said. "Not many of them. The rain has washed away any signs."

"Then why are we here? There's too much life. It oppresses me." Miriam wore a light shirt, despite the cold. Anton had once seen her on Boston Common, walking through a winter snowstorm in a similar outfit, the snow glistening on her skin. Her rib cage was high and wide, a Martian characteristic.

"You're starting to sound like Rabiah. We're here because you wanted to talk. Isn't that what you said?"

"I only like your woods in the winter. Everything is so clear then. Structure is visible."

"Snow does show blood well," Anton said.

She looked at him levelly, her eyes the green-brown of polished agate. Used to the dry air of Mars, she blinked disconcertingly seldom. She reached up and plucked one of the last red leaves from a maple. "I can talk to you if you're irritable. I won't if you're irritating."

Anton turned away with a sigh of exasperation. The trees around were almost bare, their trunks wet and black. The sky was gray, though less heavy than the day before. "I'll try not to be," he said.

She came closer. He could feel the warmth that came from her. As he looked down at her he remembered the texture of her skin, like rose petals.

"What would Torstov think if he knew who you were with?" he said, even as he wondered at himself. Was he really so jealous of that walking statue?

She tossed her head and turned away. "Don't be a fool. Torstov acts, he doesn't think. That's his great strength. It will also be his final weakness. You don't have anything to fear from him. He rather likes you, in fact."

"He *likes* me? I didn't think he liked anyone."

"Stop it! He respects you because you're clever. Do you respect him because he's strong? No, of course not. Like a rabbit, you only respect animals with long legs who hop. All other accomplishments are worthless."

"Don't be ridiculous," he said, though it was absolutely true.

"You understand more about . . . Burgundian sculpture than you do about yourself," she said. "What's happened to you, Anton? You've become a petty administrator, a man who endlessly reshuffles the same hand of cards, terrified to draw. Not the man I remember from even a few years ago, who saved me from being dropped into a fumarole on Ascraeus Mons and then demonstrated the Academia's complicity. Who are you now? You have a comfortable bed, the Lord Monboddo feeds you well. God knows that was always important to you. Is that it, then? The heat death of the universe, here in a country estate?''

''It *is* banal, isn't it?''

''Don't try to be the world-weary hero. You haven't lived enough for that to be convincing. It's not the situation that's banal, it's your response to it. Lord Monboddo lives here too, remember. He hasn't let the vines crawl over him, as if he were some sort of statue.''

Being himself compared to a statue was annoying, as if Plauger were getting back at him through Miriam.

''I don't know what happened,'' Anton said quietly. Martians drank boiling hot tea with bitter herbs, accompanied by honey cakes spiced with pepper and cardamom. Ever since his days on Mars, if the house was cold and silent and he smelled the sharp aroma of Martian tea, he still felt a surge down his spine and into his groin that was almost unbearable. Nothing since had ever matched the feeling she had given him. ''I feel like it's not entirely my fault. I could never live up to what we had on Mars. There has to be a time when life is sweetest. If that time comes too early in our lives, the rest is a dull coda, an explanatory appendix. All the landmarks I can see are behind me.''

''They're the only landmarks you can see because you walk backward. It's not like you to set up metaphors so that you can take a pratfall. That shows the weakness of your position. Don't blame me, or Mars, or your youth. Blame yourself.''

They came to the angular Japanese bridge. Alewife Brook rushed beneath it. During the spring the water filled with the squirming silver bodies of mating alewives, so dense that it seemed one might walk across on their frenzied backs and not get wet feet. Now the brook ran dark with the tannic stain of decaying leaves, and seemed slumberous, as if already preparing for its icy winter's sleep.

She put her hand on his chest, above his heart. She smiled. ''But what are we talking about? The past?

You're lucky, Anton. Most of us, when we fall asleep, sleep until we die. It's a rare person who stays awake through an entire life. But sometimes we are granted a reprieve, and something wakes us up. It can be love. It can be hate. It's not usually something so dramatic as a dead body with a masterpiece around its neck.'' She stared at him fiercely and struck his chest. "Come now, Lazarus. If you don't listen to this call, you will be damned. Of that I am sure.''

"So we learned nothing,'' Tamara Sellering growled. "Less than nothing. We gave away information.'' The room swirled with the colors of Jupiter, as if they were settling into its heavy atmosphere. Lightning bolts crackled in time to her voice. Her fingernails extended, then pulled back in. "We let them know we can break through their security systems. We let them know that we have a spin-state induction detector for Island of Stability elements—''

"We don't know that they figured that one out,'' de Borgra protested.

She slammed a table with her fist. De Borgra's teacup jumped, dumping hot liquid in his lap. He knew better than to yelp. "If they haven't yet, they will. Didn't it occur to you that there would be more than one piece of ngomite in that house? They're art collectors, for God's sake.''

"It was a calculated risk. We didn't give anything up.''

She coiled her body up, a snake ready to strike. Her extended fingernails clicked on the table. "I had to kill Malan, Theonave. Right there in the middle of the goddam Monboddo estate. He could have blown our whole network. Is this supposed to be our way of relaxing them and keeping them quiet?''

"And I decoyed them into the woods. We both did what was necessary. Our network is safe. His dead body will tell them nothing.'' De Borgra was angry with himself. The idea that Vanessa had a mystery he couldn't immediately unravel had annoyed him and led him to act out of character at dinner, directly attacking Terran mores. He tried never to show his hostility directly. Then, the Monboddo operation had been a botch, and he had gotten soaked and cold in the rain. Fortunately, the Union Division of Internal Security had matched the Technics' incompetence, and the result had been a draw.

Sellering straightened, and the room suddenly opened out, walls, floor, and ceiling all seemingly receding into space. "Those bastards don't put anything on a data network," she muttered bitterly. "How do they ever get anything done?"

"They get it done," de Borgra explained. "They just do it more slowly." Were Vanessa's arguments starting to convince him? He laughed to himself. When Technics ran this planet he could decide what features to keep, and which to get rid of.

"We'd have to kidnap Monboddo and brainstrip him." Sellering's voice was distant, dreamy.

"And start the Second Solar War?" de Borgra said, startled. "That might just do it."

A wind thundered past. He could see other figures in the distance, all dressed in clothes of the proper cut and color. Thurman, Okono, Vangwill, Amberden, all other members of the Technic intelligence services. An empty space for Paul Malan. Was he actually seeing them, or were they a generated illusion?

"We're starting it anyway. They hit Europa. We hit the *Sulawesi*. The Martians are ready to jump. If they do, the rest of the Union will follow."

"War." The future was a blank to de Borgra. Had the Solar System gone so quickly from peaceful balance to the edge of war? How?

"I don't know how." Either he had spoken, or the computer had transferred his question to Sellering. Or he had imagined her reply. He looked down at his fellows and felt a sense of loyalty, of trust. He thought that was his own. He could trust by himself, couldn't he? Did he trust Vanessa? No. Men and women never trusted each other. What for? Might as well play tennis with both players on the same side of the net.

The Technic Alliance whirled by. Io, Europa, Ganymede, Callisto. Titan. Triton. At home around the gasbags.

"They can fiddle around however they like in peacetime," de Borgra said. "But if they fight, they'll have to do it on our terms. Technology will determine the victor."

Suddenly, each of the Technic worlds flared up and vanished.

"Yes," Sellering murmured. She lay utterly relaxed in her seat. She was like a null-g cat that could relax and yawn in the middle of a silent spring on its prey. "On our terms. We can clean the Solar System up." Shiny pieces of the destroyed worlds tumbled through space.

De Borgra felt a chill. "Let's stick to intelligence work, shall we, Tamara? I don't need editorializing."

The room receded into darkness.

When he got back to the house, Anton headed up to Monboddo's study past a crowd of pushing and shouting children having a party in the front room. It was Tomas Vakante's tenth birthday. He was Param's second son, as studious as his father was whimsical, and was a particular favorite of Anton's, so he stopped by to give Tomas his present, a book about eagles and hawks, with pictures. He sociably shared a drink of grape punch with Tomas and his friends, and then proceeded upstairs, pleading urgent business.

Monboddo was lying on his chaise lounge. He wore a green quilted robe and a little embroidered cap from central Asia. He drank Turkish coffee from a demitasse. Loose papers lay scattered around him, and a cat sat washing itself on the windowsill. Monboddo had obviously been up all night, as he often did, in defiance of all medical and personal advice. He said he thought better then, when life pressed less heavily on him. He looked old, old and tired, with sunken cheeks, but his eyes were as bright as those of a child watching a circus for the first time.

"Ah, Anton!" he cried. "Everyone's been giving you advice, I trust?"

"Inordinate amounts of it," Anton grumbled. "Most of it, unfortunately, perfectly valid."

Anton slumped down in the only other chair in the room, an uncomfortable thing with huge arms and a lumpy, overly soft cushion. After a few moments of rearranging himself in it, he threw his long legs over one arm and leaned back against the other one, the position he was usually forced to assume.

Monboddo poured him a cup of Turkish coffee. "It seems that the Technics are on to us," he said. "We know who Paul Malan, citizen of Callisto, was, now that it's too late to be of any use. Who killed him? And what, precisely, were they after? One would like to believe that since the Technics have no taste, they have no brains either, but this is not the case."

"We have to assume they were after the figurine," Anton said. "So how did they think they could find it in Fresh Pond Verge? I'm sure they didn't think they could spend the whole night pulling open drawers."

"I fear you are right, Anton. We know that it is physically possible to detect Island of Stability elements, at least at a distance of some meters. That must have been what they were doing, which is why Malan ended up staring at Apthorpe's Blood Bowl. Unless he was simply a thief with excellent taste, and we're chasing after false theories."

"Thieves don't kill each other like that. Not unless there's a lot more to be revealed."

"True," Monboddo sighed. "But this is unnecessarily complicated. At the moment, the figurine itself eludes us."

"Rabiah talked of signs and symbols," Anton said. "A symbol is like the handle of this cup, the thing that lets us pick up meaning without burning our fingers. She suggested that I was paying more attention to the shape of the handle than the contents of the cup."

"Did she really say that?"

"Or whatever. Talk to a Sufi and you find yourself mired in metaphors. Why are hers any better than mine?"

"Don't get competitive over trifles, Anton."

The figurine lay on the table. Anton unwrapped it and looked at it. "My father died when I was fourteen. Karl Ozaki died in the same month. I still have their obituaries, together. After that I collected every bit of information about Ozaki that I could, though I hadn't given him much thought before. Rabiah's right. The strength of a symbol is that it ties together more than one reality."

Monboddo nodded slowly. "And we have to be careful that we understand what it is we're searching for. Are you ready? I've read your notes, and concur. You have quite a journey ahead of you. All the way to the Hypostasium. I'm sure Torkot will be delighted to see you in the heart of his own headquarters."

"Of course," Anton said. "The Academia Sapientiae has its own interests, whatever those are."

"Most past antiquarian organizations have consisted of crabbed and constipated men poring over dusty manuscripts in obsolete alphabets and dreaming of times when antiquarians were respected. The Academia is a different matter altogether. They affect to study the human race, but actually feel responsible for its destiny. They have more at stake than you might think."

"I've never been to the Hypostasium." Anton found himself with a terrible desire to be on his way, to leave the house in which he had spent some of the most pleasant years of his life. He'd been shaken awake. The only way to keep from falling back asleep was to get out of bed.

Monboddo grimaced. "Do they call their headquarters something reasonable like Center, or even Headquarters?

They do not. They get all fancy and portentous and call it the Hypostasium. 'Hypostasis' can mean a basic truth, it can mean one of the Persons of the Trinity, it can mean rational nature. I looked it up. Which of these meanings stimulated them to choose that ridiculous name? They are all more or less misleading.'' He picked up a piece of lemon peel and nibbled on it. "Do you foresee any problems on the way?"

"Nothing in Paris. But Constantinople. . . . I don't know what compelled Ozaki to leave his private papers to the library of the Monastery of St. Gregory of Nazianzus—''

"A perverse desire to cause trouble, I should think,'' Monboddo said primly. "He never in his life showed any trace of religious vocation.'' Monboddo himself would have been pleased to end his days in one of the scholarly Orders, though not on Mt. Athos, which permitted only men. He liked women too much for that to please him. But the concept of a "religious vocation'' was something that actually meant something. "I will give you a personal letter of introduction to the Abbot Phalaris that will give you access to their private collections.''

"He's a friend of yours?'' Anton was interested by the fact that most of the important actors in the Union, for all of its nearly a billion citizens, seemed, in one way or another, to know one another, or at least of one another, in a personal way.

"We were at Chicago together. At that time, in our youth, we were both studying engineering, the queen of the arts. We both descended from that point, he to theology, I to law. I haven't spoken with him in many years.''

Anton hid the Dead Christ back in its velvet. "I'm sure I'll just collect a few more questions, just like this Technic body in the garden and the figurine itself.''

"Ah, show more optimism, Anton. You are putting a puzzle together. Don't be upset that you have found a piece of blue sky when you want the hindquarters of the cow. It will come."

"I think that Rabiah umm-Kulthum suspects you, Lord Monboddo, of not taking intelligence work seriously."

"Rabiah has a suspicious nature."

5

From "A Preliminary Report on the Artifacts of Aspiration Cliff in the Tantalus Fossae, Province of Tharsis, Mars," by Prof. G. Subramanyan, University of Addis Ababa, *Papers of the Society of Pre-Human Archaeology*, December 2347:

The fused channels of the crystals of variant morphology follow distinct helical paths to a distance of some five to six meters (Fig. 8). They emerge in the undercut section of the cliff, their one-time path of egress, if any, buried under talus. Their purpose, like that of the elliptical tunnel and the absorption layer under the cliff itself, is completely unknown.

No natural mechanism can account for the complexity of the substratal variations in this area, yet no unambiguous markers of intelligent origin exist. The major contribution of our work at Aspiration Cliff is to provide a causal explanation for the ambiguity.

The Aspiration Cliff remains are obviously cognate to those of Mallow Cave on Phobos, Harry's Cut in the Cleopatra Patera on Venus, the crater Clavius, and, of course, Cap Acherusia on Luna (18–23), leading to the necessary intellectually parsimonious conclusion of intelligent, or at least volitionally creative origin, with its time of action somewhere between one and three million years before the present time, though whether this origin is called the Elder Race, the Acherusians, or some other term is a matter of debate.

As shown above (Figs. 3–5), our excavations indicate the presence of relatively recent (100–200 years bpt) intrusions in ancient strata. The first recorded excavations of the Aspiration Cliff remains was in the 2270's, under Sansavino and Zeldin (24, 25). It is now clear that they were not the first to explore these deposits. During the time of the Orthodox empire or during its death throes in the Tumults someone dug through the richest lodes, both on Mars and Luna. According to Hann (26), Acherusian artifacts could be found on the art market as early as 2190, the extreme late Empire, though they were not labeled as such. Aya Ngomo, of course, discovered the synthetic minerals ngomite and lazarite in the Asteroid Belt in the 2130's, though no one at the time suspected them of being anything other than natural.

Aspiration Cliff, as well as Clavius, Cap Acherusia, and perhaps other sites, are thus at an intersection point between pre-human and late-human archaeology. The first question remains: who were the Acherusians? A second has now been added: who discovered them first and what use did the discoverers make of their findings?

It was late afternoon. Anton, still dressed in striped silk pajamas, sat cross-legged in the middle of his large bed, completely surrounded by piles of paper. A small tray with a pot of coffee and the remains of breakfast sat next to him. Sunlight streamed in through the high windows. His rooms at the Hotel Gonfalon were ornate in the style of about fifty years before, during the long reign of the Genseka Akulina. The bed was heavy and canopied, and the chairs and desk had a curving solidity, as if intended to resist high winds. The view through the casement windows included a generous number of rooftops, which had always been one of Paris's greatest charms.

The trip over on the dirigible *Star of Copenhagen* had been uneventful, for which Anton was grateful. The laser satellites, lofted in the late twenty-first century by the shaky world Russian government, shot down any small, fast-moving, air-breathing atmospheric vehicles, as well as non-slaved spacecraft entering or leaving the atmosphere, but somehow, through the rigidity of their programming, ignored large lighter-than-air craft. The Union maintained the satellites, since the lack of aircraft kept local wars from becoming more than locally destructive. It had taken the *Star of Copenhagen*, with a hundred passengers, thirty-six hours to cross the Atlantic from Boston to Paris. Anton had spent most of the trip in the aft lounge at a table with a view of the sea, feeding himself on hors d'oeuvres and doing documentary research.

Anton sighed and leaned back on his pillows. His brain felt numb. He'd gone through dozens of documents concerning Karl Ozaki's life and works and the subsequent ownership histories of his creations, including Monboddo's contract with Ozaki for the portrait of Lady Windseth. Anton had studied the art trade to and from the Asteroid Belt. That tangle met in favorable conjunction with Monboddo's current art-collecting interests at a gallery in St. Germain. This coincidence enabled him to combine business as Monboddo's Seneschal with his role as an officer in ExSec.

He reached carefully across a pile of documents and picked up the phone on the little night table with the spiral legs. His bust of the Gensek Timofey stood grimly next to it. He searched through another pile and found a scrap of paper with a number on it. He punched it.

"Galerie Huygh," a woman's voice answered, with the lazily sophisticated arrogance that successful gallery owners all possess. Particularly French ones. "How may I help you?"

"My name is Anton Lindgren. I am the Seneschal of George Harvey Westerkamp, Lord Monboddo, Interrogator of Boston." His role as curator to an eccentric art collector allowed him to chase after almost anything without appearing out of character. "I am interested in acquiring some new . . . object for Lord Monboddo's personal collection, and was informed that your gallery might be of assistance. Could I speak to someone in authority, please?"

"You are, my dear Mr. Lindgren. My name is Helena Huygh, and this is my gallery."

"Excellent," Anton drawled in his best aristocratic flunky voice. "I should like to make an appointment for tomorrow afternoon."

"Would three be convenient?"

"That would be excellent."

"Good. I have a number of things to show you that I think you would be interested in. We have several Farenas, a small Maillol, and even an Ozaki."

"Ah, Ozaki," Anton said. "Much overrated, in my opinion, but, of course, I am always willing to look. At three, then."

"I shall be expecting you," Mme. Huygh said, slightly nettled.

It was dinnertime, according to the bronze clock supported by the triton and mermaid on the other side of the room. Until he had disabled it with a screwdriver, it had bonged out the hours with the sounds of a ship's bell, from one to eight every half hour. The little dial just below twelve o'clock still told him that it was an hour after high tide.

He climbed carefully out of his bed over his ramparts of paper. Despite having worked hard the entire day, he had the suddenly worthless and decayed feeling that comes from having spent the day in one's pajamas. He took an intensely hot shower, waxed his beard, and combed his hair. Once again he noticed, as he did whenever it was wet, that he had very little hair left.

It would have been pleasant to fall down on the bed and lie on its softness for a moment, but, unfortunately, it was entirely covered with his work. He rummaged through the desk drawer, pulling out a patella reflex hammer, a marzipan skull, several rock crystals, some peacock feathers, and a sachet of lavender, which sent up a strong scent, either vestiges of former residents or an attempt by the hotel to be amusing, before he finally found a pad of paper marked "Hotel Gonfalon," with the colored banner hanging from a crosspiece from which the hotel took its name. Ripping off a sheet, he wrote "Please Do Not Make The Bed," and attached it to the canopy. After a moment's thought he put another on the pillow. He took the tray with the plates and cold coffee and put it outside the door.

The dining room was high and narrow, with a balcony running around three sides. It looked as if it had once been a theater of some kind, but there was no trace of the stage, and the maître d'hôtel indicated that anything before his time was prehistory. At Anton's request, he was seated up on the balcony, partially screened by a pillar. There were few other people up in the balcony, since it was slightly uncomfortable and the tables were small. Anton could tell by the maître d's slightly raised eyebrow that he had been pegged as some sort of minor celebrity, unwilling to be seen by his fans, or perhaps a man escaping creditors.

Anton decided to make the man's evening more interesting. "If you see a woman," he said in a conspiratorial whisper, "a black woman with a tall coiffure, covered with jewels, wearing a sea-green gown, let me know. She will ask for me, speaking in the accent of a Sinhalese aristocrat. Reveal nothing! She will offer you a reward. Tell me what it is, and I will match it. Understand?"

"Perfectly, sir," the maître d' said, and walked away

with a secret smile. Restaurant work could get dull, Anton knew. He pulled out an old, battered copy of Boswell's *Life of Johnson*. Like any traveler, he drew solace from the well-considered acid words of the great curmudgeon stay-at-home. He sipped his bitter aperitif.

"Do you really prefer eating up here, like a bird?" a woman's voice asked.

Vanessa leaned over him, one hand on the pillar that had supposedly screened him from observation. Even as he stood up, Anton ran through the possibilities. Coincidences happened constantly, and most of life's perceived structure was entirely accidental. All bets were off, however, where the Academia Sapientiae was concerned. How had she found him?

"Would you like to join me in my aviary?" he said.

She looked dubious. "Is there room? Down on the main floor—"

"And join the groundlings? Nonsense. The show's much better from up here. Let me move Dr. Johnson, and we won't have any trouble." Below, Anton could see the maître d' peering up at him with a raised eyebrow, so much as to say "she doesn't *look* Sinhalese." Anton shrugged down at him.

"Is Paris your home?" Anton asked, working from the most obvious hypothesis down.

"No. I can't be said to have a home, really. Not the same way that Fresh Pond Verge, Boston, is your home." Her black hair was pulled straight back off her forehead, held by a fillet. Her gaze was solemn, but her eyes danced. If she had been medieval in the Ambulatory at Fresh Pond, here she was classical. Anton imagined that Nausicaa, the young princess who found Odysseus on the beach and aided him, had looked much like her. "I'm on my way to the Hypostasium, in the Pamirs. That's definitely not home, by the way. It's the headquarters of the Academia, but that's all. Preterite Torkot wants to get back there."

Anton flicked his eyes across the restaurant, searching

for the mercurial and difficult philosopher amid the local bankers and shopkeepers who seemed to make up most of the clientele.

"Oh, you won't find him here. He's off wandering the streets somewhere, dressed as a bricklayer, or something."

"In disguise, like Haroun al-Raschid in the streets of Baghdad."

She laughed. "I'm sure that's exactly how he feels, a Caliph concealed. Checking on the people influenced by his decisions, and deciding what new obstacles might best be put in their way so that their lives may be enriched."

"Hmm. A remarkable admission from someone in the Academia Sapientiae."

"Come on, Anton. You don't think we're all grim fanatics determined to throw the human race back into the Paleolithic, do you?"

"Of course not," he said. "I doubt you have any interest in going back past the Neolithic. Nahum's just one of the grand eccentrics who we have chosen to characterize our century. How did you end up as his assistant?"

"Chance. How else does anything happen?"

"I've always had a soft spot in my heart for will, myself."

"So do other people I know," she said.

This, for some reason, seemed a significant thing to her, so Anton momentarily turned his attention to his food and allowed her to sort out her thoughts.

"My parents died when I was young," she said, "and I went to a school called the Northfall Lyceum at Niagara. After four years there, with the falls next to my ear, I found everywhere else to be almost silent. Particularly since the next place was Venice."

Anton was startled. "The Academy of Ancient Arts?"

"Yes. Do you know it?"

"I was there too, though I probably left before you came. Wang Zhen was my tutor."

She clapped her hands in delight. "I was so frightened of him when I was first there! He looks like a court executioner, huge, built like a rock, with that horrible beard. It was amazing to watch him paint those landscapes with a camel's-hair brush with about three hairs in it. Such delicate hands."

"He was just as cruel as he looked," Anton said sourly. "We had an argument about the nature of artistic representation once, and he picked me up with those delicate hands of his and pitched me into the Grand Canal. I smelled for days."

She threw her head back and laughed so loudly that the diners below looked up. "Did that end the argument?"

"Certainly not. It went on for another year, at least. Don't ask me what exactly it was about. The process of argument was what was essential, not its subject."

They described their lives in Venice to each other, tying different incidents to the same locations. Anton remembered his eternally damp-smelling room with its windows only a couple of feet above the surface of a dark and silent canal. She recalled the narrow campanile she could see from her window on the third floor of a seventeenth-century terrace block. The white kitten that had always sat at the front hoof of Colleoni's horse watching passersby had, by Vanessa's time, grown into an obese, dignified cat.

Anton remembered that he had been full of romantic fancies and dreams in that time. The dreams had not changed so much as they had grown darker and harder to see, like ancient paintings with darkened varnish, covered with dust and cobwebs, awaiting only the hand of a patient and talented restorer for them to shine forth again.

Vanessa checked the time on her fingernail and jumped

up. "I'm late. I promised to meet the Caliph in the Luxembourg Gardens."

"Salaam to him for me," Anton said. "I'm sure I'll see you again, somewhere."

"It's a date."

He sat thoughtfully, sipping his coffee.

"Was that her?" asked the maître d', who had crept up behind him.

"What?" Anton said, startled. "Oh, no. That was someone else."

The maître d' looked impressed. "Indeed."

"Yes." Anton reached into his pocket and pulled out a new, crisp fifty-ruble bill. He snapped it to show how fresh it was. In Paris, particularly, you did not bribe with old, tattered, and stained money. Not if you wanted to be taken seriously. "Could you find out when Vanessa Karageorge and Nahum Torkot arrived here, and when they made their reservations?"

The maître d' made the bill vanish silently. "Certainly, sir."

A few minutes later, he was back. "They are in rooms 232 and 234. They arrived just this afternoon, and they made their reservations four days ago, October thirtieth." That was the day before Anton had left on the *Star of Copenhagen*, his plans unknown to anyone save Lord Monboddo. It implied that their presence was sheer coincidence. Anton did not believe it for an instant.

The Musée de Cluny was an ancient institution. Built in the ruins of a twelfth-century abbey, it included a great deal of that art called "medieval," a term that had ceased to have much meaning, the modern era having ended three hundred years before. It stood in an open park full of now-bare horse chestnuts. The newer part of the museum was an impressive granite construction whose ribs sprang from thick porphyry pillars.

Anton did not walk straight to the gallery that contained the Ozaki exhibit. The museum was too distract-ingly designed for that, full of interesting culs-de-sac and rooms of colored tapestries dramatically lit. Anton had a weakness for museums. They reminded him of the contents of his own mind, a clutter of interesting objects with little apparent connection between them.

The Ozaki exhibit was in the center of a high, domed room, eggshell-colored, with a slightly rougher texture than an eggshell that size might have had. Light came through shifting, translucent sections of the dome, resulting in a subtly changing light, altering the facial expressions of statues and revealing color variations in what had seemed solid blocks of paint. Supplemental light came from fixtures concealed at the dome's lower edge.

There were four Ozakis, two from the University of Shanghai, one from the collection of Ernest Tallgrass of Lakshmi Station, Venus, and one from the collection of the Justice of Clavius, Luna.

As he had half expected, Vanessa was already there, leaning intently over the Shanghai case. She wore a dark blue dress with long sleeves. Did she really become more beautiful every time he saw her, or was that an illusion?

Her presence was starting to make sense. She didn't have to follow him. If she knew he was interested in Ozaki, and knew that his final destination was the Hypostasium, in the Pamir Mountains, it didn't take much thought to predict his route. But how had she guessed Paris? These four small objects were delaying him by more than a day, which didn't make reasonable sense. To Anton, every work of Ozaki's was important, a word in the interrupted sentence of the artist's life. It was interesting that she understood that.

She looked up at him and smiled, not feigning surprise. The Shanghai case contained two heavy brooches.

"He was something," she said. "It's too bad he died so young."

"Sixty isn't young. Not for an artist."

She looked at him, as if, he thought suspiciously, wondering exactly how old *he* was.

"True, I guess. But he wasn't finished. Not near finished."

The two brooches were sea creatures, one a dolphin, the other a killer whale, both highly stylized, owing something to the style of old Pacific Northwest Indians. They were copper, inlaid with enamel and titanium. The date was 2308, which put them early in Ozaki's career, when he was thirty-one years old.

"He didn't do much jewelry," Anton said.

"Your friend the Justice of Tharsis had an Ozaki panther in her hair," Vanessa said with a sideward glance. "I saw it at Lady Windseth's *vyecher*. It suits her."

"The panther looks as if it were made for her, and no one else, but Miriam inherited it from an aunt when she was seven."

"Maybe she has spent the rest of her life making herself someone who is worthy of wearing it." She gestured at the killer whale and dolphin in the case. "These are different. I wouldn't even call this stuff jewelry. I mean, you couldn't really wear it."

"Why not?"

"Are you kidding? Each of those pieces weighs over one hundred fifty grams, at least. In order for a woman to wear a brooch that weighs six ounces and is shaped like a leaping killer whale, and carry it off, she would have to be an Amazon."

"Perhaps he designed them for an Amazon."

"That's what I'm saying. I don't think he designed them for anyone. He didn't really do things *for* people, even when they were commissioned works. The work was certainly more important than the patron. Besides, Amazon or not, whose jewelry box would they fit into?"

"A significant point, I suppose," Anton conceded. "So you think these pieces are still waiting for someone to influence?"

She shook her head violently. "No. Tharsis wears her

panther in her hair, and probably keeps it by her bed when she sleeps.'' She looked at Anton as if waiting for him to confirm or deny the last statement. He looked up at the shifting light of the dome. ''This whale and this dolphin are in the public collection of a university. No one will ever wear them, Amazon or not. All we can do is look at them. They are made that much less alive by that.''

Anton thought about the cases at Fresh Pond Verge, full of coins that no longer circulated, cups and bowls that no longer held food, and a Blood Bowl that no longer . . . well, no one ever had figured out what Apthorpe intended it for. He had shown Vanessa the beauty Monboddo possessed. Did she believe that any art gallery was a mortuary for dead art?

Ozaki's next work was a pattern of cast silver that looked like water spilling down over rocks, though it hung in space unsupported. A second look revealed that the pouring water was also a water sprite, leaning back in an exquisite stretch, with long flowing hair. The revelation of the nude figure in the water was quite erotic.

''Notice the modeling on the thighs,'' Anton said, just to be difficult. ''It's hard to do good thighs.''

Vanessa wrinkled her nose. ''Her toes and fingers are too long. Isn't that odd?''

Anton felt this to be a typically irrelevant female observation, even if true. ''You're right,'' he said. ''They are.''

''It's dated 2325. Who was his mistress then?''

''You think she was the model? I have no idea. He had too many for anyone to remember.''

''I think it was Sena Ameling,'' Vanessa said. ''She came to Northfall once to talk about her life with Ozaki.''

''Is that what the famous Northfall Lyceum considers to be an artistic education? The bedroom habits of famous artists?''

''That's *not* what she talked about,'' Vanessa snapped. ''It was actually more interesting than that.''

"Oh? Did she discuss how Ozaki got patinas on his bronzes?"

"She talked about life with a genius," Vanessa said carefully. "She said that he would be in incredible states of depression for weeks, sometimes months at a time. He would pick fights with his closest friends, and lie facedown on the stone floors of churches. Any churches, he didn't care what religion they were. That, she said, was when his mood would break. He'd come back, muttering about the abortions most people thought were religious art, which made reality look good by comparison, and he would dive into his studio. Commissions and contracts that had been waiting would wait longer, while he did some little work to distract himself, things like this statuette. It was in one of those moods that he drove Sena out of the house. He only broke with his lovers when he was out of his depression and didn't need them anymore."

"Why should he need them?" Anton said. "He had replaced them with silver."

"She was old when I saw her. Those long fingers look much better on an older person."

Anton looked at the taut young muscles on the water sprite and thought about an old woman lecturing students on her life with Karl Ozaki. "Are you really so jealous of her?"

"What? That's absolutely ridiculous. I don't think she was ever more than a tool to him, like a drill or a grinding wheel."

"Of course it's ridiculous," Anton said soothingly. "But don't blame her for having been beautiful, and for having inspired the greatest genius of the last two hundred years. I'm sure she couldn't help it. Any more than she could help growing old."

Exasperated, Vanessa turned away from him and moved to the last case. Anton admired the erect grace of her walk, and the way her hair swirled over her wide shoulders. He looked back at the silver water sprite.

Vanessa really didn't have anything to be jealous of.

The last statue, from the Justice of Clavius's collection, was a large warrior's head wearing a high, pointed helmet, with long flowing hair and beard. The materials were silver and null-g vat-grown ivory. It was dated 2320.

"He did a lot of mythical and legendary figures in the twenties," Vanessa lectured. "They were popular, and Ozaki liked being popular. This one is a figure from the poem *Ruslan and Ludmila*, by Pushkin. Ozaki was living in Rome then. He'd just learned silver working at the time, and a lot of his works show it. He didn't really get the hang of silver work before the 2330's. The solder's often sloppy in the older stuff." Having demonstrated that she knew a lot about the subject, she knelt down and looked up under the rim of the helmet. "For example, here . . . huh, that's odd. The solder here is perfect. But it's vacuum solder, the kind they use . . . but why would he be soldering in a vacuum in Rome?"

Anton knelt and looked with her. The solder did indeed have that sheen associated with vacuum work. But he noticed something else. There were two odd drops of solder, perfectly spherical, just by the helmet's nosepiece. It looked as if they had not been dripped, which would have deformed them, but as if they had floated there in a weightless environment. A rather cranky conservative, the sculptor hadn't gotten off Earth until 2332, more than ten years after this figure was supposedly made.

She turned, forgetting her irritation with him in a rush of thought. Anton was relieved. He'd been wondering if he'd pushed her too far. "Are you familiar with a twentieth-century artist called Giorgio de Chirico?"

He knew better than to fake it. "I've heard the name. I don't remember him."

"An original, if minor artist. He specialized in strange, dreamlike architectural scenes, *Nostalgia of the Infinite*, *Melancholy and Mystery of a Street*, a variety of others.

Then, suddenly, he stopped being original, and his work became banal. Realizing that if he couldn't move forward he could move backward, he began to forge his own early work, backdating the paintings to his most creative period. He's been a desperate headache for collectors ever since.''

''The hardest forgery to distinguish is one done by the artist himself,'' Anton said. He gestured toward the warrior's head. ''Do you think that that's what Ozaki's done here?''

''Yes, definitely. Isn't it obvious?''

''I don't know that it is. Ozaki never became banal.''

''Well, it would be hard to *prove*. It's all stylistic. Look here. See the way he's formed the beard? It's all simple lines. In the twenties, he would have worked at it a lot harder, and put in more detail than this. And the helmet. It has a slight reverse curve near the crest. That's characteristic of Arabic armor of the premodern era. Ozaki never used anything like that until he saw an exhibit on Islamic art in 2335, just before he left to work on the Moon. He was quite taken with the style, and used various aspects of it quite a bit in his work for Clavius.''

''So you think he made this figure after 2335—''

''And before he died in 2338, on the Moon. His final period. I think it's pretty obvious. Ozaki probably did it as a joke. He liked jokes like that. The Justice of Clavius must have kept it in his personal collection until now.''

''Hmm. Interesting.'' They walked on.

Ozaki had never had access to a weightless studio in the years he worked for Clavius, the only time, Vanessa had convinced him, that he could have done the warrior's head.

Unexpectedly, Anton had an urge to ask help from his father, Josiah, dead with Ozaki twenty years before. Anton had only found out years later, from Miriam Kostal, that his father had been an officer in ExSec. Josiah had died preventing the assassination of a Union official in

Borneo. His father had always entertained Anton's most absurd questions and theories with a solemnity that had led the young boy to try to think in a way that deserved such attention. Josiah's death had taken him away before Anton ever really had a chance to talk with him, and now it was far too late to ask him to explain why Ozaki was taunting everyone from beyond the grave.

He and Vanessa walked a little farther. Standing in a clear beam of sunlight from somewhere high on the dome was an assemblage of crystalline metal tubes. Each tube had a simple curve, some catenary, some hyperboloidal, some circular, intersecting each other at odd points. It seemed like a part of something larger, as if each of the curves should have continued into some other joining. The sheen of the metal made it look even more complicated than it was.

"It's amazing," Vanessa said. "Even as clear an Acherusian artifact as this still looks like it might be something else. Do you suppose they left this stuff for us to find?"

"Us? This thing is at least a million years old. At that time the human race was just a gleam in some hominid's eye. I think we're just digging through their garbage dumps. This thing was probably a drink container, or something."

"And ngomite?"

He paused and looked at her. "Ngomite is a pretty bauble. We value it because it looks like something someone else has lost. And what are you doing with your afternoon?"

The Galerie Huygh's doors were massive bronze, with a rich green patina, curving outward as if under intense pressure. Sections of the surface had peeled back, like dry paint, and the layers glimpsed underneath were shining clean new metal. The doorway was deep, keeping the doors always in shadow, so that they seemed like the entrance to some troll's abode.

Pushing the doorbell resulted in a low sound, like a
large gong being struck. It was an impressive and ponderous enough sound that even the most impatient doorbell ringer would hesitate for a moment before trying it
again. Ten or fifteen seconds later, the two doors swung
inward, to reveal a set of marble stairs with twisted metal
balustrades. Light came from a skylight high overhead.
The stairs split at a landing, to climb up either wall of
the foyer. As Anton and Vanessa turned on the landing,
they saw a heavy woman of middle years, who stood on
a balcony just over the door, where it could not be seen
by someone entering. She was wearing a white dress,
off one shoulder, and was watching their progress super-
ciliously. She had arching dark eyebrows, which made
that expression easy for her.

"Mr. Lindgren," she said. "I had not expected a
guest, but"—she made a gesture indicating that she was
worldly, and that nothing, no matter how scandalous or
ridiculous, shocked her—"Paris is a city where one
makes . . . friends easily."

Vanessa stopped and glowered. Anton laughed.
"Mme. Huygh," he said. "I am afraid that no matter
how you may do these things in Paris, that is not the
way I transact *my* personal business. Ms. Karageorge is
a colleague of mine from the Academia Sapientiae."

Mme. Huygh raised an eyebrow. "Ah, the Academia
Sapientiae. What an honor for my humble establishment.
Please come up."

The main chambers of the Galerie Huygh were high
rooms, with floor-to-ceiling windows and skylights overhead. Its collection was small but impressive, tending to
works from the Moon and the Asteroid Belt. Anton admired a painting of two bow-and-arrow-armed cat hunters
in the null-g trees of the asteroid Boscobel, their bodies
lapidary gleams of sweating muscles.

Most of the other works in the gallery tended toward
classical themes, as if out there, in the harsh environments of the tumbling rocks between Mars and Jupiter,

the artists harkened back to the ideas that had first evolved among the bare rocks of ancient Greece. Aside from a terra-cotta Diana by the twentieth-century artist Maillol, there was a cruel bronze of the satyr Marsyas, having lost a musical contest with Apollo, being flayed alive, his pipes crushed at his feet, from the asteroid Hellebore, and a severe bust of Abraham Lincoln, done as a Greek herm. There was also the Ozaki Mme. Huygh had mentioned, a minor work, a baroque pearl that he had carved into a grotesque eyeball as a house gift for a hostess he was visiting, which had been hidden away in a closet of a family with no idea of its real value for the last thirty years.

One sculpture was particularly striking. It was a brilliantly rendered hand carving itself out of a block of finely veined Pentelic marble. It was titled *The Hand of Phidias*. The hand had obviously labored, for it was callused and scarred and one of the fingers had been broken, perhaps more than once. The hand looked as soft as a human hand, while the rock it was carving, exactly the same material as the hand, looked hard, harder even than marble normally looked. The artist, Anton was interested to note, was Clavius's current court artist, John Addison, who had filled the office left vacant by Ozaki's death.

Mme. Huygh had retreated to a desk with curved golden lion's legs at one corner of the room, where she was busily talking on an archaic phone while staring right at them. She held a lit cigarette in one hand, but did not smoke it much, content, rather, for its smoke to spiral lazily up into the still air of the gallery, making interesting patterns.

"What do you think?" Anton said, pointing out the Addison.

"Excellent," she breathed. "You can tell who the major influence in his career was."

"Hmm?"

"Ozaki, of course. But I don't know if Addison ever

actually studied with him. Ozaki did like to take young artists under his wing and influence them. It was a way of trying to extend his influence into the future. You can see it in this work, particularly in what you might call the 'literary' quality of the thing. It's not usual. Ozaki is one of those artists everyone admires but no one can imitate.''

Now that she mentioned it, Anton thought he could see what she meant. It was a young man's work, but it did show something of homage to the old master, particularly in its somewhat arrogant assertion that an artist creates himself. He looked at it and made a decision. He signaled to Mme. Huygh. She quickly finished her conversation and came over.

"How much are you asking for this one?''

"The Addison? Quite an interesting work, wouldn't you say? It was gracious of the Justice of Clavius to release it.''

"Clavius is always gracious,'' Anton said dryly.

"The Justice of Clavius is one of the great patrons of our time,'' said Mme. Huygh, as proud as if she were his mother. "Tennerman, Ozaki, and now Addison. It is quite remarkable, and the Galerie Huygh has always handled the work of his artists, under contract.''

"Tennerman, as I recall, took cyanide and flash-froze himself solid in a cryogenic chamber, with instructions that he be placed into his sculptural figure group *The Nuremberg Trial*, as Hermann Göring,'' Anton said.

"That's right,'' Vanessa said. "The whole thing has to be kept at -10 C, so that he won't melt. It's easier to do on the Moon than on Earth, I suppose, though it's still not a popular tourist sight.''

Mme. Huygh looked a trifle nettled. "If an artist chooses to include himself in his own last, greatest work, I think that it is his own business.''

"And Ozaki . . . blew himself up in his studio, trying to incorporate what he thought was an Acherusian artifact into some work of his.''

"Karl Ozaki was a great artist," Mme. Huygh said, eyes flashing, "but a poor engineer. He proceeded against Clavius's express wishes."

"And now Addison," Anton said, looking down at *The Hand of Phidias*. "Who has managed to survive so far. Clavius does have taste."

"I'm glad you agree," Mme. Huygh said briskly. "Now, are you interested in purchasing this piece?"

"I am. While they share almost nothing else, Lord Monboddo and the Justice of Clavius do share a taste in art." There could be no price negotiation on a work of a living artist whose agent the gallery was. The price, while high, was not unreasonable, so the arrangements were quickly concluded. Mme. Huygh, though clearly cherishing no great love for her customer, insisted that they toast the deal with some superb Calvados, which she kept in a cabinet in the office off the exhibit rooms for just such occasions. Anton took a sip and felt friendlier toward her immediately.

Mme. Huygh suddenly turned to Vanessa, flashing a bright and patently insincere smile. "Ah, my dear, now I recognize you. Do you not remember? It was at the Delachazes's garden party, two or three months ago, yes? You and Nahum Torkot. He was pressing me extremely, I remember."

"What about?" Anton asked, because it was expected.

"Why, Karl Ozaki. An odd thing, for the Academia Sapientiae, no? He has not been dead for nearly long enough."

"He has a personal interest," Vanessa said quickly. "Many people do."

Anton took a gulp of his Calvados. Of all human beings, Nahum Torkot had no private capacity. He was always Preterite of the Academia Sapientiae. Why had he been interested in Karl Ozaki two months before the figurine surfaced in Naples? Hunting the truth was like old-time whaling from wooden ships. It kept rising to the surface, spouting, and diving ever deeper, hauling lines and harpoons with it. One could only hold on and hope for the best.

"Ah, yes, of course," Mme. Huygh said. "As does Mr. Lindgren himself, though he wishes me not to know it." She shook her head. "Why all of this concern for a man who, after all, died twenty years ago?"

Understanding finally came, and Anton found his heart beating with wild surmise. He arranged for the shipping of the *The Hand of Phidias*, bid Mme. Huygh farewell, and accompanied Vanessa back to the Hotel Gonfalon, all in a complete daze. Sometime after 2335, when he went to work for the Justice of Clavius, Karl Ozaki had made a clever forgery of his earlier work, but did it in null-g. Between 2335 and 2338, when he destroyed himself in an explosion, he had never been off the surface of the Moon. And Lord Monboddo had, resting in his cabinet, the Dead Christ, created in null-g, incorporating a material found only in the Asteroid Belt, and stylistically unattributable to any period in Ozaki's known career.

Anton Lindgren knew that somehow, somewhere, twenty years after he had supposedly died, Karl Ozaki was still alive.

6

From "Traveler's Advisory: Cappadocia and Lyconia, the Anatolian Plateau," Terran Union Travel and Tourist Office, May 2358:

The patchwork of cultures and religions in this area is almost incomprehensible to the outsider. Be cautioned that missionary foundations of the Patriarchy of Constantinople, despite the long tradition of Orthodoxy in the area, have resulted in some tension. Bektashi Dervishes are not welcome in Kayseri. Do not point at a dog in Yarma, it is bad luck. A Turkish army hides in the Taurus Mountains, and occasionally raids the lowlands, with the avowed goal of reconquering all of Asia Minor, which ethnic Turks ruled from the thirteenth through the twenty-first centuries, though mostly they just steal sheep and guns. Avoid contact with them if possible; surrender if challenged; armed resistance is not advised in numbers of less than twenty. Passengers on the Constantinople–Erzurum leg of the *Bay of Bengal* Direct Express may note flaming pyres in the vicinity of Sivas. These are an Isma'ili ritual, for which they occasionally kidnap strangers. Most of their involuntary guests do survive the experience; nevertheless the train, until further no-

103

tice, does not let through passengers off at Sivas. The flames are best appreciated from the observation car, where, at dusk, they can be quite striking. . . .

The train shed at the Gare d'Inde covered more than sixty tracks and was full of the bustle of all the trains leaving for points east: quick, sleek interurbans leaving at regular and precise times like seven minutes after the hour and half hour for destinations like Munich, Milan, and Mannheim, the busy, grunting engines and narrow high-slung cars of local commuter trains with their rows of silhouettes reading newspapers, the sly elegance of the violin-brown cars of the Moscow Express, their fan-shaped windows partially frosted, as if by snow. Baggage cars stopped and dumped their loads of luggage into the chutes that automatically routed the tagged suitcases and valises to the claim areas within the station. Crowds of passengers bound for destinations as distant as Peking or as near as Montreuil ran frantically about, trying to hear train announcements above the din. A lone yellow balloon, lost by some unfortunate child, bumped up at the top of the shed's high vault.

But, at least in Anton's mind, the *Bay of Bengal* dominated everything. It pulled in with a quiet hiss, three minutes late from London, for its ten-minute stop in Paris. It had thirty cars, each the famous dark red with the gold details. Their windows alternated narrow and wide, for there were no regular cars on the train, only sleepers. The train was pulled by three low and powerful engines, like jungle cats crouched to spring. They burned a liquefied coal slurry, and even purred.

A sourceless voice spoke. "*Bay of Bengal* Direct London–Calcutta Express, departing in five minutes, Track 18. Strasbourg, Munich, Vienna, Budapest, Belgrade, Sofia, Constantinople, Erzurum, Tabriz, Tehran, Multan, Lahore, Delhi, Kanpur, Benares, Calcutta. All aboard, please."

A few cars down the platform Anton could see Vanessa

and Nahum Torkot. Torkot, as usual, was dressed anonymously, like a commercial traveler of some sort. So they would be with Anton until Constantinople, at least.

The conductor saluted and waved him aboard. He could hear the low thrum of luggage being loaded into the baggage car from below. Then, almost before he could find his seat, there was a whistle, and the train accelerated smoothly out of the station. Within five minutes it had reached a speed of one hundred sixty kilometers an hour. Ten minutes after that, having left the metropolitan area of Paris well behind, it reached its cruising speed of nearly three hundred kilometers an hour, which it would maintain until it reached Strasbourg.

As was considered good form on a railway journey, Anton acquainted himself with the other travelers in his compartment before plunging back into his work. Two were a comfortable middle-aged couple named Kramer, from York, and the third was a gloomy Spanish Hindu named Garces who was on a pilgrimage to Benares. The Kramers showed each other things out of the window, while Garces read a brightly colored book called *Christ the Avatar* and ate chocolates out of a large gift box.

The conductor came by and Anton signed up for the third seating at dinner. Then he seized half of the compartment's double writing desk as his territory and settled down, once more, to his paperwork and his thoughts.

They were starting to circle more and more around the Asteroid Belt, mysterious territory. An anonymous man from the Belt had brought the Dead Christ to Earth. Was Ozaki there as well?

By the Treaty of Juno, which had ended the Seven Planets War in 2255, the space between the orbits of Mars and Jupiter was declared a Neutral Zone, forbidden to the military forces of both the Union of States and Nationalities and the Technic Alliance. As a result, those thousands of tumbling rocks, filling a volume larger than that within the orbit of Mars, became a *place*, mentally, which they physically were not. The place was one of exile, one of experiment. No one could keep track of what went on there. The Academia Sapientiae regarded it as a cultural lab bench. Martians saw it as a dangerous threat on their doorstep, where fleeing criminals could easily hide, and where most of the next war would be fought. Cunning passengers brought art from there to Earth. Anton strove to untangle the skein of contrivances and see the underlying pattern.

While he studied, the train stopped in Strasbourg, where the Kramers ran out and bought buns from the sellers on the platform, and Munich, where they bought sausages and leberkasse. At each place they also bought fruit and offered it around. Garces diffidently accepted a pear at Strasbourg and devoured it, stem, seeds, and all. The crumbs of the sausage rolls they had come on the train with in London and the croissants they had bought in Paris had already worked their way underneath the cushions of their seats, whence they would have to be vacuumed by the cleaning crew during dinner. A woman had come by with a cart carrying a huge enameled tureen of steaming bean soup, a bowl of which had served Anton as lunch, but the Kramers seemed to need, Antaeus-like, to reaffirm contact with the soil over which they traveled, which they did by eating its produce.

After Munich the land grew dark, and before the train got to Vienna, it was night. Anton had been looking up increasingly often from his work to watch the passing landscape proceeding with frenzied speed nearby and at a more leisurely pace near the horizon. At the speed of the *Bay of Bengal*, the human landscape changed slowly but perceptibly, the pitch of the roofs rising and the windows shrinking as they proceeded from Paris to Munich. The crossing gates in the Free State of Bavaria were more colorful than they had been in the Paris Jurisdiction. Now that it was dark, the floating lights of the villages and houses made it seem as if he were traveling through interstellar space. Anton packed away the papers concerning Ozaki's own critical writings as the third bell rang in the compartment, telling him that it was finally time for dinner.

The dining car was dark wood and white linen, the way dining cars always were. The Kramers had been cheery and bland, while Garces had manifested the melancholy of a man who had spent years practicing a religion with difficult precepts and ritual requirements whose essential truth he doubted. Their company had not satisfied him, and now, though there were several empty tables, he looked around to see if there was anyone interesting to sit with. He found Nahum Torkot and Vanessa.

His action of inviting himself to join them, which would have been rude in a restaurant that was not moving at three hundred kilometers an hour, was quite acceptable on a train, which mimicked the entirely random joinings of life but revealed their true nature by making them last only hours or days, rather than years and decades. People on a train form an alliance, as if the world that surrounded the parallel rails were hostile and they refugees from it. The dining car, humming and rocking gently in the night, annihilated past and future and made all associations outside of itself seem vaguely unreal. So they welcomed him at their table, for he was one of them, a traveler, and not one of those wraiths through whose night-lit cities they passed.

Vanessa poured him a glass of wine, then sat calm and demure, her manner here more opaque than he had yet seen it. Anton looked at her, and again wondered at the precision of her words and actions. Style is typically something one either develops with age or has assigned by someone else. Her style—the braided hair, the clear aesthetics, the slightly angular clothes—all seemed parts of a self-developed whole. Anton had never felt as if anything about him was part of a whole. He was a collection of oddments, like things forgotten at a railway station. She was complete, like an apartment furnished by someone who knew exactly what she wanted.

Torkot was something else. His dark, worn-leather face showed little expression. His hair was close-cropped. The power the Academia Sapientiae exercised over Terran civilization was ambiguous, but undeniable. As Preterite, Torkot directed that power. To what end? No one was ever sure.

Torkot blinked his long eyelashes at Anton, the only movement on his face. "Mr. Lindgren. It must be difficult for you to be away from the Monboddo Household. Vanessa tells me it's a pleasant spot. A place of contemplation. A place one could stay forever."

"It is," Anton answered, not sure how to respond to a pleasantry that seemed to conceal a challenge. "More pleasant than the Hypostasium, by all accounts."

"Doubtless." Torkot pulled his lips back. A smile? "But peace isn't the language the Hypostasium speaks. The proper mood of the place is disquiet."

"Is that the mood of the Academia Sapientiae as well?"

"Utopia is not a place. It is a process. All processes involve disquiet."

Anton gulped his wine. He hated sitting and listening to gnomic utterances, and Torkot seemed prepared to produce them all evening.

"In order to read the hieroglyph of human history—"

"Stop talking like some sort of Sibyl, Nahum," Vanessa said. "You're making Anton squinch his face up as if the wine tastes bad." She took a sip of her own. "It doesn't, does it?" she asked, with the air of someone nervous about the arcana of wine-tasting.

Anton was grateful, but felt dismay that she had read his expression so easily and interpreted it so accurately. "The wine is excellent. The Atlas Mountains produce these flinty whites. A Tighennif, isn't it?" Wine identification was one of those useful tricks that gave a misleading impression of understanding. Vanessa took another sip and watched him.

"You deserve your reputation for discrimination," Torkot said sourly. "You should use it to better purpose."

"To assist the Academia in its modification of civilization?" Anton said. "I would prefer to let civilization take its natural course."

"Natural, Anton?" Vanessa said softly. She licked her upper lip thoughtfully. "You're the Seneschal of a Household. How natural do you think that is?"

Anton thought of the great five-towered house at Fresh Pond Verge and the Household that lived within it. It seemed like an eternal entity, the basis of civilization. "All social structures are, to that extent, arbitrary. It suits me. That's all I can say."

"The essence of dominance," Torkot said. "'It suits me.' And you criticize the Academia for its arrogance?"

"I said it suited me. I don't try to make it suit everyone else."

"You are evading the issue. For that type of life to suit you, it must exist." Torkot leaned forward, suddenly intent. "Do you think our civilization exists by accident? Your house at Fresh Pond, for example, with its Household, art collection, hunting forests. It exists because something else doesn't. Fresh Pond could be covered with pavement, and you could live in a mile-high tower. You could fight on its shore in blasted ruins for ancient cans of preserved beef. You could be the manager of a factory that uses the pond for cooling and dumping its waste. These are all choices. Each benefits someone. Each displeases or oppresses someone else."

Anton didn't try to argue the point that a world of blasted ruins benefited someone. He'd met people who would have been perfectly suited for such a world. "And who benefits from our form of civilization?" Anton asked.

Torkot leaned back. "The three of us do. As you've pointed out, it suits us."

One hundred fifty years before, in the midst of the Tumults, the Academia Sapientiae had appeared, sprung full-formed like Athena from Zeus' brow, and immediately commenced to bend human society to some specific but unknowable end. They had, from the first, used any means available.

"You began as assassins, didn't you?" Anton said.

"Eh?" Torkot looked up from his dissection of his fish, bare of sauce or spice. "Is this your version of polite dinner conversation?"

Vanessa laughed. "Your trout offends him. He wants to add some savor to it by arguing with you." Her eyes flashed at Anton with a slightly malicious glint.

"Is this man's intellect entirely determined by his palate?"

To his horror, Anton found himself blushing. How the hell did she peg him so quickly? He sawed industriously at his beef Wellington. "I'm discussing ancient history," he said. "Purely theoretically."

"You of all people should know that history is not theory," Torkot said. "Any more than your childhood and education are theory. They make you what you are. The Australian Expedition is not theory. Neither is the Massacre of Syrtis Major." He poked with his fork and lifted the fish's skeleton out whole. "The Academia started as a cabal of assassins. Yes. We killed Zhao Wang-Mang, Chairman of Sinkiang. We killed Eugene Fabrieux, Controller of the Technocracy of Paris. We killed Kirstin Gunderson, President of Sweden. They wanted to lead in a direction in which we did not wish to go." Torkot spoke with a clean relish, as if he himself had pointed the rifles, slid home the knives.

Anton looked at Vanessa. She smiled serenely. While his plate was surrounded by crumbs and sauce stains from his beef Wellington, her place was clean, and she had even refolded her napkin into the elaborate form it had

had when they sat down. "Well, Anton, you asked him. You should be happy that he gave you an honest reply instead of some homily."

"Ah, yes," Anton said, slightly disconcerted. "That was a century and a half ago. What are you after now?"

"The same thing you're after," Vanessa said. "A life worth living." Her gaze was direct. Her eyes were the darkest Anton had ever seen, like ripe olives. "That *is* what you're after, isn't it, Anton?"

"Yes," he said. "I suppose it is."

"Long ago, this was a cistern," Hieromonk Stephen said. "It was built in the late twenty-first century, after the wars, but the bricks are from a sixteenth-century mosque. You can see maker's marks on some of them." The room was a cylinder, about three meters across and six meters deep, lined with irregular gray bricks. Light came from a dome overhead. The floor was poured metallic glass, pearly gray and almost impossible to scratch. One narrow door led out into the hallway.

Anton looked up at the rough walls, and thought about the people who had once owed their lives to the water filling this cistern. In was in that time, when people had dug themselves out from under the rubble and contemplated the poisoned seas and ruined lands around them, having worked hard enough to have a few minutes to wonder where they had gone wrong, that the roots of the modern civilization of Earth could be found.

"There are twelve of these cisterns," Stephen said. "One of them cracked in an earthquake and ever after leaked its contents, no matter how often it was repaired. Each of them has the name of one of the apostles. This one is St. Jude. The leaky one, of course, is Judas Iscariot."

Hieromonk Stephen, his title indicating that he was an ordained priest as well as a monk, had been assigned as Anton's guide to the Monastery of St. Gregory of Nazianzus, which sprawled across a hillside several miles from the walls of Constantinople. He was a quick man with a scanty beard, in his mid-forties. Anton barely listened as Stephen prattled on about the history of the monastery. He was, instead, distracted by thoughts of Vanessa. He had left her and Torkot aboard the *Bay of Bengal* to continue their journey. What was she after? He thought of her, dark and controlled, with the mysterious Torkot. He thought of the way she moved, and the curve of her breast. Inappropriate thoughts for a monastery. He turned his attention to the Hieromonk.

"We, as an Order, have always had an interest in the art of the sacred," Stephen said. "Sacred images can focus the spirit, but they can also delude it. The danger is always there, but we flirt with it." He grinned. Theologically obsessed Byzantines had shed a lot of blood over the issue of iconoclasm in past centuries, and it seemed that the issue was not yet dead.

The cisterns had been turned into large display cases. St. Andrew held a stunning twenty-third-century crucifix, and this one, St. Jude, held an Ozaki, dated 2330. It was a statue of St. Ambrose, the fourth-century Father of the Church, sitting in his episcopal throne. He was leaning forward slightly on one elbow as if speaking to the onlooker. In the other hand he held a scourge with three knots, symbolizing the Trinity. His face was worldly and a bit tired. The skin was tight over the bones of his face. He had worked hard at founding a Church that would survive, and had lived to see that it would, though darkness was closing in on all sides.

"Abbot Phalaris comes in here sometimes and just sits with him," Stephen confided. "He says that it helps a piece of scrollwork in one of the church's upper galleries to come down and talk to one of the pillars, even if the pillar is working too hard to talk back."

"Hmm," Anton said. He was mesmerized by that strong, weary face. He examined it closely, trying to understand why it struck him so. Ozaki had not himself been a practicing Christian, but he had had the skill of creating art that inspired emotions that he himself did not feel. Anton found himself looking, not at a statue carved by Karl Ozaki, but at the face of Ambrose. What would that man have seen in the figure of the Dead Christ in his winding sheet? How would he have acted? Suddenly, Anton had it. As they walked, Stephen continued his commentary, but Anton didn't hear a word of it. He was still marveling over how much the face of the tired St. Ambrose reminded him of how Lord Monboddo's face had looked on the last morning he had seen him.

The library, a set of large, well-lit rooms high up on the hill, just below the main chapel, contained all of the monastery records since its foundation in the twenty-second century under the Orthodox Empire, and a huge variety of interesting documents. Among them were the private papers of Karl Ozaki.

The Chief Librarian, a gray-haired monk named Theophanos, glowered at Anton over a pair of spectacles. The glasses were totally archaic, since vision was readily correctable by simple ocular remolding, so he must have worn them simply for effect. He closely examined the research permission with Abbot Phalaris's own signature on it as if wishing to declare it a forgery. "Are you a researcher in heresy?" he asked in a hissing voice.

Anton looked surprised. "No, of course not. Art. What does heresy have to do with it?"

Theophanos laughed, with dry, unpleasant sarcasm. "What does heresy have to do with it, he says. Some researcher. The twenty-fourth century has managed to forget much, but I had not realized how much." He folded the permission in half, though it had not been folded when Anton gave it to him, and handed it back, his face scrunched with disgust. "Very well. I hear and obey." He shuffled back tiredly into the sealed stacks, hunched over, muttering, "I hear and obey, I hear and obey."

After about five minutes Theophanos came back pushing a creaky cart loaded with volumes. The cart had one bad wheel and kept pulling to the right. Every time it ran into one of the shelves, Theophanos would stare at it with a look of betrayal, mutter a prayer to the Blessed Maria Theotokos, Mother of God, pull the front of the cart straight, then proceed, to run afoul of the bad wheel once again.

Despite himself, Anton felt dismay at the mass of volumes and bundles of paper that filled the cart. Theopanos handed him a receipt to sign. Just to be annoying, Anton did not sign it immediately, but instead checked through the documents on the cart. Receipts, contracts, preliminary sketches, and fifteen black leather-bound volumes.

Anton flogged his weary mind. Hadn't one of the papers he'd read on the train referred to sixteen volumes of notes? He knelt. The embossed gold numbers on the spines ran from I to XV without a break. He glanced up at Theophanos. The librarian's face was tense, almost terrified. Anton glanced in Volume XV. It definitely seemed to be the final volume in the series, only three-quarters full, the last entries dated mid–2338, just before Ozaki vanished. Anton signed the receipt, and Theophanos's relief was palpable.

"What's his problem?" Anton asked as he wheeled the cart toward his assigned study carrel. The bad wheel kept bumping the cart against the right-hand wall.

"You must forgive him," Stephen said. "He is a man of religious passion. The shame he feels is our glory here at St. Gregory's. Why is he ashamed of things that would make other men feel pride, such pride, in fact, that confession would be required? I don't know. You must forgive his rudeness."

"Of course," Anton said, not knowing what Stephen was talking about. "How much longer is he on duty at the library?"

"Until after dinner. Enjoy yourself."

The carrel was a plain white cell with an Orthodox cross on the wall and a simple desk of light-colored wood.

A window opened out into a courtyard full of flowers, where some monks dug in the soil while others animatedly discussed important matters in the shade of a colonnade.

Anton sat down and checked through the fifteen black-bound volumes in detail. They contained many working drawings, some for works now famous, others for things never made. He looked over them in wonder. What a strange and closed place the modern world seemed sometimes, so full of wonders that no one had time to examine them all. These pages were priceless, and were sitting here concealed in a monastery, examined by him solely because he was interested in finding the whereabouts of a ngomite strike.

The window of the carrel received not direct sunlight, but the glowing north light of a good artist's studio. Ozaki was known mainly as a sculptor, but his anatomical and perspective drawings were superb, drawn with a fine black ink pen on thick paper. Volume IV contained drawings of his mythical and legendary figures of the years around 2320. There was a griffin, a Cupid, the elaborately armored figure of Parsifal, a fox fairy changing into a beautiful woman, a gnome digging. Nowhere did he find the bearded head of a warrior with an Arabic helmet.

The drawings were so beautiful that they kept distracting him, but he had a definite purpose in mind. The more he thought about it, the more he became certain that Ozaki had donated sixteen volumes of notes to the Monastery of St. Gregory of Nazianzus, not fifteen. He flipped past exploded drawings of metalwork, sketches of monumental heads labeled "Mt. Rushmore," and a wealth of others, seeking a pattern.

He would have missed the gap if he hadn't been looking for it. Some pages from the end of Volume XI had been shifted to the beginning of Volume XII, which concealed the fact that everything relating to 2335, Ozaki's first year on the Moon in Clavius's service, was missing.

Anton sucked in a long breath. Missing, or destroyed? The courtyard outside the window was now the violet of evening. The bells had sounded for dinner. If not destroyed, he had a good guess as to who knew where they were.

He headed quickly down to the library. Theophanos was not on duty, and none of the other monks there were certain of his whereabouts. After several wrong turns in the complex hallways, Anton came to Theophanos's cell. All the other cells were places of precise order, but this one was a mess. The cot had been overturned and the fabric on the bottom of it ripped apart.

Certain now of what he sought, Anton pounded down the hallway, stopping every monk he came to. Theophanos? I saw him earlier, heading toward the dining hall. Theophanos? Not today. Theophanos? Well, I saw him this morning, but I was in a hurry and didn't have a chance to talk with him, not that I was ever much for— Theophanos? He looked like death. He was on the stairs leading to the back-kitchen courtyard.

The courtyard behind the kitchen was a maze of piled cords of wood, stacks of coal, pallets of food, and piles of kitchen rubbish being turned over for compost. Anton dodged through it. It was nearly dark. Ahead of him he saw the red-orange glow of a fire. He ran toward it desperately. A dark figure knelt in front of a glowing orange rectangle, the access hatch to the fluidized bed furnace that provided heat to the kitchen and the rear of the monastery. Anton launched himself forward and hit the other with his shoulder. He felt like he had hit a scarecrow, all dry bones.

The pages of the book Theophanos had been feeding into the fire went flying around the courtyard. Anton scrambled to pick them up as Theophanos, painfully, found his glasses and pulled himself off the ground. He held his abdomen and gasped for breath.

Anton grabbed him by the collar. "What the hell are you doing, you son of a bitch?" he shouted.

"What I should have done twenty years ago," Theophanos said, not trying to pull away.

Anton looked down at the sheets he held. The bright firelight revealed drawings and notes in Ozaki's hand. Theophanos slumped back down to his knees and stared into the roiled glow of the furnace. Anton shivered. The warmth of day had fled with the sun, and he wore indoor clothes.

"Are you insane?" he said.

"Most likely," Theophanos groaned. "Haven't I thought that often enough?" He turned a ravaged face up to Anton. "Haven't I thought that every day of these twenty years?"

"What was Karl Ozaki to you?" Anton whispered.

"He was the Tempter," Theophanos answered, his voice suddenly savage. "He showed me the wrong path, and I almost took it. Because he told me I was brilliant." He choked out a laugh. "Heady words for a novice, coming from the artistic genius of the age. Words of temptation. Have you wondered why he left his papers and books here, at St. Gregory's?"

"Yes," Anton said. "But he was an unpredictable man."

Theophanos snorted. "Nothing is more predictable than sin. He left those things and *that*"—he pointed at the papers Anton held—"for the purpose of converting me to his heresies. When I was young, I was a sculptor. Can you believe it? I carved a statuette, a little thing, a statuette of the Repentant Magdalene. Everyone said how beautiful it was, what a brilliant work it was. Ozaki himself admired it. This was just before he left for the Moon. When he died, he left me his papers, to show me the true meaning of images for a Christian."

"Where is the statuette now?" Anton asked. "I didn't see it in the cisterns."

"I destroyed it," Theophanos said. "I burned it in

this very furnace. A sacrifice to my vanity.''

"Why?" Anton asked in horror. "How could you destroy a work of art?"

"To make way for the work of God! Can an image stand in the way of the truth? Images mislead us, change us into what we are not. They are false guideposts, each pointing in a different wrong direction, and their beauty tempts us to follow. How can you love a work of art above the meaning it seeks to express?"

"Beauty is its meaning."

Theophanos shook his head. "I knew you wouldn't understand. I sought to mimic God by becoming a sculptor. Look in the book you hold. See what evil the Dispossessed Brethren of Christ create, in the urge to remake the universe. See what sins Ozaki fell into, before he died, perhaps by his own hand, on the Moon. It's all there. Look."

"So images may show more truth than you think," Anton said. Theophanos turned away. "Why did you keep the book all these years? And when it came time to destroy it, when you knew I was looking and would see where it had been, why did you burn it one page at a time rather than throwing it whole into the fire?"

When Theophanos turned his face to him again, tears were streaming down his face. "I don't even keep icons in my room, for fear of images. Only a cross. When I pray in church I avert my eyes from the iconostasis, though I feel the glowing color of the images, like soft caresses on my eyelids. Our sins are those things we desire, not those things we loathe. I kept that book because I loved the images in it. Before I burned them, I took each page up and looked in the light of the fire, to see for the last time the lines of beauty. Such things the man created!" He sobbed. "They changed me and I could do nothing. By themselves they almost made me a heretic, like the Dispossessed Brethren of Christ. To escape I have almost become the opposite sort of heretic, fearing images so much that Abbot Phalaris is concerned.

Burn the book. Free me and free yourself!'' He wrapped his arms around Anton's knees.

"I can't," Anton said, near tears himself. To have such a longing for beauty and such a fear of it! How could the man live? "I can't destroy beauty."

"And you need it," Theophanos whispered. "I don't know why, but you need it. That's why you can't destroy it. Beauty has nothing to do with it."

"You're right," Anton said, pulling out of the other's grasp. "I need it."

Anton continued looking through the mass of Ozaki documentation in his study carrel during the day, but his real work was done at night, in the small room that had been assigned him. There he lay under his sheet with a light, like a schoolchild reading adventure stories instead of sleeping, and examined the hidden volume.

He didn't know how many of the pages Theophanos had managed to burn. The volume started in the midst of a set of drawings that were studies for four caryatids Clavius had apparently commissioned for a domed hall in his palace. Interesting, certainly, but nothing to frighten an Orthodox monk, even if they were bare-breasted women. The next series of drawings showed some sort of ruins with cracked lintels and large, empty halls. They radiated a feeling of abandonment and were labeled "Remains. Clavius." Anton turned the page, and stopped.

The sculpture was an arm, muscles standing out taut. The fingers were curled up in agony and, in the center of the palm, a calm eye stared out at the viewer. The arm seemed to be hanging on a wall, in those same ruins Ozaki had been drawing for the past several pages. In the corner, in sharply angled letters, Ozaki had written: "Tip of index finger to end of arm: 145 cm. Material: granite."

The next few pages showed tombs, each with a dead body carved on the sarcophagus. The first page was titled

"The Brethren Are Dispossessed of Their Lives." The carvings were extremely realistic, and each depicted the body in an advanced state of decomposition. Each sarcophagus had a brief notation next to it, with its length, the stone of which it was made, and any special information. One of them, next to a body that was almost a skeleton, said: "Biblical literalism: statue has one too few ribs on the right side."

The next ten pages showed a series of deep cuts in rock, like those of a mine. Wraithlike figures in monastic robes wielded hammers and chisels. The scenes were strange, dreamlike, and resembled a Piranesi. The pages were labeled "Excavations: hypothetical."

After that there were a few more pages of carved walls and arches, then some drawings of curving lines and odd shapes that reminded Anton of the Acherusian artifact he had seen in the Musée de Cluny. Ozaki had supposedly died while experimenting with an Acherusian artifact, so Anton examined them carefully, but they might as well have been abstract drawings as far as he was concerned, for they contained no meaning.

One of them had more structure, a set of interlocking tubes, and rested in some sort of rock niche. Its title was Boaz. There was a scribbled notation on one corner of the sheet. It said: "If Abakumov had been an artist rather than a physicist, he would have been considered a genius. Someday, perhaps, his work will be completed." Next to it were doodled some roses. They seemed out of place.

Anton returned to these pages night after night in frustration, for though the emotion of the pages was strong, the meaning he could gain from them was small. Somewhere in the crater Clavius were the remains of a religious brotherhood, Theophanos's Dispossessed Brethren of Christ. The Brethren had an odd iconography, involving eyes in wounds. The image had struck Ozaki strongly, and he had incorporated it into at least one work, the Dead Christ now in Monboddo's possession. What had

Ozaki learned from the ruins of these vanished monks that had so terrified Brother Theophanos?

On his fifth day in the carrel, Anton rang the bell, indicating that he was finished with his research. Then he stacked the volumes carefully back on the cart, all fifteen of them in order. The pages he had obtained from Theophanos now rested in one of the hidden spaces of his suitcase where he kept the instruments necessary to the work of an officer of ExSec.

After a moment the door was opened by a very old man with long ivory-colored hair and bright blue eyes that glinted within those folds of skin that can give elderly Caucasians the look of Asians. He wore a blue skullcap and a black robe, with no decoration but a gold Orthodox cross on his breast. He had obviously always been a large man, and even in age had broad shoulders and big, muscular hands. On one finger he wore a ring.

"Finished?" he said. "Any important discoveries?"

Anton cocked an eyebrow at him. "What happened to the days when monks obeyed a rule of silence?"

The monk laughed. His teeth were strong and white. "George warned me that you would be difficult."

"George?"

"Oh, I suppose he hasn't used his name in years. George Harvey Westerkamp. He never liked any of those names, and so, when he had a chance, he got that strange one he has now, Monboddo. Some eighteenth-century English lunatic who thought that children were born with tails. George, for some reason, had always liked the name. I remember that. It suits him, somehow."

Anton quickly bowed to kiss his hand. "Abbot Phalaris. Forgive my insolence."

The Abbot blessed him. "Come. George spoke very highly of you and I'm interested in hearing about what he's been doing."

They walked out into a large garden filled with flowers, that same garden Anton had been seeing from his carrel window. After five days in a whitewashed room, it seemed like paradise. Butterflies moved from flower to flower, and lemon trees peeped at him from over a wall.

They talked about Monboddo, about his days at the University of Chicago. Anton told about the life at Fresh Pond Verge, of Lady Windseth, and about the growing of parsnips.

Abbot Phalaris shook his head with a smile. "Ah, Lord Monboddo, a minor functionary now playing the good country squire, in quiet retirement, growing prize roses and, perhaps, writing his memoirs? Ha. We are not so far from life here in this monastery as you may think, Mr. Lindgren. After all, I know perfectly well that George spent the better part of 2355, right after the Australian Expedition, interrogating Murad Luo and George Macklevore in Jakarta before their executions. Two men who almost tore the Union apart, and then there's the rumor that nuclear weapons were found after the Fall of Brisbane. The Gensek has denied it, officially, but still. . . . We'll never know what George found out, since the documents are under a seal of . . . thirty years?"

"Fifty," Anton said shortly. He'd always wondered what Monboddo had discovered, but Monboddo would not tell him, and never would, though Anton could figure some of it out for himself, from what he'd learned on Mars before the war began. He sometimes wondered if the Union established by the Treaty of Jakarta, in 2225, ending the Tumults, was now itself breaking up. The Massacre of Syrtis Major was twenty-five years ago, the Australian Expedition four. Would future historians see those brutal events as the first signs of the end of the Union? How would they view this ridiculous chase after a perhaps nonexistent chunk of ngomite?

"Fifty. You might see them eventually, but I won't. At any rate, provincial Interrogators are just not handed that sort of responsibility. So now George is after something else." Phalaris raised a hand, seeing that Anton was about to protest. "Oh, don't worry, Mr. Lindgren. I won't pry, like a nosy old man, and embarrass you.

I've learned something from years of ecclesiastical dignity, after all.'' His eyes twinkled, and Anton wondered at the resilience of these two old friends, influencing society for over half a century, and still going strong. He could see that Abbot Phalaris, though full of respect for his friend, still thought of the Interrogator of Boston as an unpredictable young student, who had somehow acquired wrinkles and high office on a lark, and would set them aside when he grew tired of the joke.

Abbot Phalaris stopped at a bench under a densely gnarled fig tree and sat down, trying unsuccessfully to conceal the fact that the short walk around the garden had tired him.

"Three nights ago," he said, "Brother Theophanos attempted suicide." He raised a hand before Anton could say anything. "Your arrival set him off, but it is in no way your fault."

Anton sat silently in the shade of the fig tree, thinking of the weeping man holding on to his knees with a death grip, and of the forbidden volume that he was even now preparing to steal from the Monastery of St. Gregory of Nazianzus. In a sense, perhaps, it still was not his fault. That did not relieve him.

"He—" Abbot Phalaris stopped and gazed into space. "He tried to carve himself, with a tool used to repair windows. The wounds are painful but not fatal. I've sent him off to our vineyards in the Thracian hills. We need help with the harvest, and the physical labor in the sun should help him in turn. He'll be taken care of."

He turned his bright blue eyes on Anton. Did the Abbot see the truth? And what was the truth? Anton bit his lips at the old question, asked by those who knew only falsehood.

"The late twenty-second century was a difficult time for the Church, both in the East and in the West," the Abbot said. "Cracks were forming in that empire the Russians had founded over Earth, and their Orthodoxy was failing everywhere. Hundreds of sects sprang up in that time. Some are still around: Kali-Buddha, the worship of the bloodthirsty Bodhisattva, for example. Most are gone, just like Waldensians, Christian Scientists, and Episcopalians.

"The Dispossessed Brethren of Christ were one of those groups, and no one knows where they came from. A lot of things were lost in the Time of Tumults. At any rate, they left Earth as soon as they could, which was wise considering the times, and settled in the crater Clavius on the Moon. They dug into the walls of the crater and built their monastery.

"These men and women were heretics, Gnostics, with the usual Gnostic suspicion of the physical world." He gestured around himself, taking in the sparsely decorated buildings of the monastery, the chapel with its gold dome, the blue sky with its doves, and the entire world around. "It seems impossible that someone might hate this world that God created, but hatred of the physical has always been a besetting intellectual sin of Christianity."

"It generates a lot of passion for an intellectual sin."

"It does. Do you not understand it?" Again, the blue eyes regarded him.

Anton thought of the desperate Theophanos, so in love with beauty that he thought himself damned. He shook his head. "No, I understand."

"The Brethren believed that God did indeed make this universe, but that, in the process of creation, He became trapped in it, like a fly in amber. Everything around us partakes both of the mundane and of the Godhead, because He is imprisoned in everything around us. They believed it to be Man's job to free God from the universe, the same way a sculptor frees a form from a rough block of stone. That this metaphor means they are creating God rather than simply freeing Him seems to have escaped them. That's the main thing that makes heretics, after all. They just don't think things through.

"The Dispossessed Brethren of Christ made the metaphor real. They became sculptors. Not many of their works survive, at least on Earth, but general account makes their work brilliant. Their favorite symbol was the wounds of Christ with eyes in them, because the nails of the Crucifixion and the spear point that wounded His side were the tools of a sculptor, starting to reveal the form of the awakening God beneath the flesh of the man.''

The ngomite eyes peered out at Anton from the ivory figurine of the Dead Christ, gleaming in the light of the fire in the library at Fresh Pond. What would Theophanos have made of that? The Brethren seemed to have thought that only images existed. The universe was an image that concealed God, and God himself was an image to be abstracted from the universe. And Theophanos had been tempted.

''The most important part of their Mass,'' Abbot Phalaris said, ''was called the Dispersal of the Instruments. The hammer, the nails, and the spearhead were handed out to the congregation for use in the liturgy. Though there is some question in my mind about that. . . .''

''What do you mean?'' Anton asked.

''I am not an expert on the history and theology of the Dispossessed Brethren of Christ, but even I can detect gaps in the record and deliberate lack of clarity. The term 'Dispersal of the Instruments' seems also to refer to an actual historical event, and not just a ritual. Various Grand Masters of the Brethren are mentioned, along with someone named Abakumov, one of their great holy men. Perhaps Abakumov was a soldier, for they were also warriors, fighters, like ancient Israelites. Hammers, nails, and spears are also weapons. Life is a constant carving out of the universe.''

''And Ozaki?''

''Ozaki, it seems, excavated part of their colony on the Moon. They had burrowed deep, and there are many areas still unexcavated. They are gone from there, however, for sometime in the early twenty-third century, all of the Brethren left the Earth, the Moon, and Mars and traveled to the Asteroid Belt, there to begin the construction of their great temple, to be called Jerusalem the Lost. What happened to them then? No one knows. A civil war, started by a Grand Master whose name has been blotted out. After which they vanished. They said they were going to the stars and perhaps they did, though I suspect they simply ceased to exist as an organized group. It is this civil conflict that seems to be associated with the Dispersal of the Instruments.''

He winced, whether at a thought or at some internal pain, Anton didn't know. "And if there is a time for dispersing Instruments—''

"There must be a time for gathering them together,'' Anton completed. "Do you really believe that?''

"I'm sure they believed it. When the Instruments are reassembled, who knows how the universe may be transformed? Their belief was apparently that they could travel to the stars. I'm sure many Brethren died in brutal combat believing that they were giving their lives for that eventual reassembly of the Instruments.''

"Did they manage to build their temple?'' Anton asked.

Abbot Phalaris smiled. "They did. Jerusalem the Lost. They lost it again, because it is now the entertainment complex called the Dead End, though its rulers are still called by their old religious name, the Syndics of Jerusalem the Lost. You've heard of it?''

Anton snorted. "How could I not have heard of it? So Jerusalem the Lost became the Solar System's largest disneyland?''

"God was obviously trapped more securely than they had thought,'' Abbot Phalaris said, with the satisfaction the orthodox feel for the confusions of the heterodox.

"But how does Ozaki fit in with all this?'' Anton said. "He never struck anyone as a religious man.''

"Many of Christianity's greatest saints did not strike

anyone as particularly religious, before God called them.''

''Are you trying to say—''

''Of course not,'' Abbot Phalaris said, obviously irritated with himself for having, even for the purposes of illustration, compared Karl Ozaki to a saint. ''But Ozaki seems to have had some sympathy with the strange dogmas of the Dispossessed Brethren of Christ. Could he have become a convert, there in those abandoned tunnels, simply by looking at their works and feeling their strength?''

''Perhaps,'' Anton said. ''Art does have that power. As Brother Theophanos discovered. Though he resisted.''

The Abbot nodded. ''He is an extremely brave man. He feels the power of beauty so strongly that it terrifies him. He will never be at peace.''

''Is that a curse,'' Anton said, ''or a blessing?''

7

The Academia Sapientiae had chosen to build the Hypostasium in the windswept heights of the Pamirs, far from where any historical civilization had ever thrived. There were no ruins there, no archaeological remains, save for the frozen skeletons and corroded equipment of generations of mountain climbers. The peaks in that area were notoriously treacherous because of the unpredictable weather, which could change from bright sunlit day to vicious blizzard in a matter of moments.

To get to the Hypostasium took time, effort, and determination. No rail line led there, and the winds were too unpredictable for airships. The roads were notoriously bad, the hills were infested with bandits, some, according to rumor, in the pay of the Academia itself, and the welcome at the Hypostasium itself tended to be cold and grudging. Though the Gensekretarial Charter for the Academia Sapientiae obliged the Hypostasium to provide free and equal access to all citizens of Earth, the Preterites, Fellows, and Aspirants of the Academia had managed to insure that this access was equally difficult for all. Thus, scholars, wary of being attacked by highwaymen and dropped off a cliff to be eaten by snow leopards, often contented themselves with the research collections in the cities, which were, after all, more than adequate for most needs.

From Lahore, where Anton had left the *Bay of Bengal*, a train of the Hindu Kush Mountain Railway proceeded northwest, via Rawalpindi and Kabul and then through the tunnel to Dushanbe. Dispensing with a locomotive, each short, stubby car on the train had its own engine, for better traction. The rail line curved dramatically and went up extraordinarily steep inclines, since the cars had cogwheels underneath, and climbed the hills by means of a cograil. Anton thought of a high-velocity spider pulling itself across a rough landscape by means of its own silk.

When Anton arrived at Dushanbe's elaborate wedding cake-decorated railway station, the waiting area was almost totally empty. A sullen baggage handler was only reluctantly persuaded to leave his card game with three other underemployed railway workers to find Anton's luggage.

The baggage handler wiped his nose with his sleeve and stared at him. "Where you going?" he said.

"To the Academia Sapientiae. The Hypostasium."

"Hah. Good luck. I think they're closed." Then he shuffled back to his card game.

"What do you mean, they're closed?" Anton called after him. The other three card players looked at him blankly, as if he were an advertisement for some product none of them used.

He went outside to look for the car that was supposed to be picking him up to take him to the Hypostasium, but there was nothing in front of the station but a local bus, an ancient model gaily decorated with bunting for some festival. Its engine had failed, and a group of locals wearing embroidered shirts and black caps was gathered around the mechanic where he sat on a carpet, surrounded by the parts of the dismembered engine, offering him advice. Two Bactrian camels foraging in the field across from the station looked up and stared at Anton in bemusement, as if to say "I wonder what he's doing *here*." Beyond them rose the snow-covered peaks that were the foothills of the Pamirs. He was about to go back inside to call the Hypostasium when he was stopped by a villainous-looking Pathan with a hooked nose and scars on his face, who wore a long coat with huge flowing sleeves, like that of a grand vizier.

The Pathan's eyes widened in pleased recognition. "Lieutenant Lindgren!" he cried. "I have found you at last. Thank goodness. I was warned of your coming, but was unsure of your schedule. Never fear, I have booked you a room, and everything is taken care of. And you have an important call."

"A room? Where? Why? Who are you? What call? And don't call me Lieutenant."

The Pathan thought a moment, sorting out the questions and deciding what order to answer them in. "I am sorry, Mr. Lindgren. There has been a difficulty with the transportation, and the Hypostasium will not be receiving visitors until tomorrow, so I have found you a room in one of our fine hotels for the night. My name is Azal, and I am an agent of Internal Security here in Dushanbe, where I grew up and still remain. Your call is top security and comes from the Lord Monboddo." He looked thoughtful, and ticked off Anton's questions and his answers to them on his fingers, counting silently. Concluding that there was a one-to-one correspondence between questions and answers, he smiled at Anton.

Anton looked up at the mountains that hemmed Dushanbe in from all sides. This was no accident. The Academia had some reason for not wanting him at the Hypostasium that night.

He turned to Azal. "It is imperative that I get there tonight, not tomorrow. Do you know of any way?"

Azal looked gloomy, something his long face, hooked nose, and down-curved mouth seemed designed for. "No, there is no way. No buses, no train. It is so seldom that I am called upon to make decisions of this sort, I am afraid. A camel would take far too long. . . ." He began to pace back and forth in a frenzy, Anton himself apparently forgotten, hands behind his back, swinging his long coat from side to side. He muttered to himself. "Wait!" He stopped and thrust a finger at Anton. "What for are relatives?"

"To be useful," Anton answered promptly.

"Exactly! Exactly! My sister's husband's cousin is Najil. Najil!"

"That is excellent."

"No, no!" Azal danced around, swooping his long sleeves. "You do not understand. Najil has a car, a vehicle of his own, and knows the roads. Once upon a time he drove for the Hypostasium itself. Regrettably, he was fired. He drove badly, they said. He says this is a lie. He is in need of money now, and drinks far too much, poor fellow. Drink too much kumiss, which is fermented mare's milk and quite disgusting, even to maintain national traditions, and you become quite ill. He has become impossible to deal with. It is a pity about Najil!"

"Sounds like just the man. Is he available?"

"I will make him available. I am an officer in Internal Security." He pulled a short, curved knife from a scabbard at his belt and brandished it. "I am a man of authority. Yah! But now we must go and connect you to Lord Monboddo." He set off down the street at a brisk pace. After dithering for a moment, Anton shouldered his travel trunk, grabbed his other bag, and tottered after him. Passersby stopped and watched this odd procession through the wide, rectilinear streets of Dushanbe.

"This is an important message," Azal said over his shoulder, not offering to help. "We rarely get such messages here. I am qualified to handle them, of course, though I deal normally with the pettiest of petty criminals and their ilk. Men who would sell their aged mothers to the Technics, only Technics do not come here to Dushanbe, you understand, or even to Tashkent, because they are afraid of the out-of-doors when it is vertical, I am told. And they are banned from the Hypostasium, and why else would anyone come here? I am trained in counterintelligence. I received top marks. Where then is the intelligence to counter, you see. I am thinking of transferring, but where? Where? And how?'' He glanced over at Anton, who was having trouble getting enough oxygen at Dushanbe's altitude and could not muster the breath for a reply.

The local office of Internal Security, fortunately, was not far, on the bottom floor of a four-story hotel with many balconies and few guests.

Azal led him inside, into darkness. ''Here we are!'' he announced. ''Now, the call . . . and Najil . . . what to do . . . you have many contacts, I understand. . . .'' He looked at Anton again, but did not move.

''I will help you transfer,'' Anton gasped. ''I will recommend you.''

''You are too kind,'' Azal said. ''Too kind! I will go get Najil.'' Unspoken quid pro quo met, Azal vanished at a run.

After a moment to let his eyes adjust to the darkness of the Internal Security office, Anton saw the solemn man behind the desk, who jerked a thumb toward the back of the room. There, behind several cases of memory cubes, some water-pumping equipment, a cord of aromatic wood, and several lightweight bicycles with null-friction magnetic hubs, was a set of double doors, behind which was a secure comm booth. Anton slid into the padded seat with a sigh of relief. The interior was black and, except for a small control console, featureless. The booth checked his thumbprint, his retina pattern, as well as his cytoplasmic protein spectrum and his genogram, via a small sample of skin. Once it had convinced itself that he was who he claimed he was, it shut its door, sealed itself off, and hummed to life.

''Anton!'' Monboddo's voice said. It sounded as if he were sitting right in front of him, and Anton was surprised by how relieved he was to hear that reedy, weak voice. "How good to hear from you again. Are you having a pleasant trip?"

"Quite entertaining," Anton said. Monboddo always insisted on social form, even when it regarded an intelligence mission. "But the Academia Sapientiae's blocked my access to the Hypostasium. I think I've worked out a way to get there, but—"

"Wait, Anton, wait. I do have a question for you, before we go any further. Let me see, let me see." There was a sound of papers being rustled. "Param cannot find what you did with the accounts for August. We received a shipment of crocus and gladiolus bulbs, and he wants to check it against the order. Lanfrank, the gardener, thinks he remembers ordering paper-white narcissus, as well."

Damn. Anton reordered his thoughts and tried to think. He'd left in such a hurry. . . . "Um, they're in the credenza in the second-floor dining room, in the, I think, the third drawer."

"The credenza," Lord Monboddo said dubiously. "That twenty-third-century Hungarian horror with the wolf's heads on it? Do you normally keep accounts there?"

"Well, I was going over them during lunch, and—"

"Never mind, Seneschal. Even Homer nods, I am told. Now, I have an interesting piece of information that may relate to the Academia Sapientiae's obduracy in allowing you into the Hypostasium this evening." It was early morning in Boston, and Anton heard the clink as Monboddo poured more tea into his glass. "It might be easier if I showed you a picture, but you're not some easily bored Technic, so you'll have to use your imagination."

"I like to keep in practice," Anton said.

"The Academia Sapientiae was, in 2239, about thirty years after its founding, granted an exclusionary landing zone in the Pamirs, a pentagon roughly covering the eastern half of Tadzhikistan. No spacecraft not directly associated with the Academia Sapientiae is permitted to land there, or even to overfly it at an altitude of less than thirty kilometers.''

''Who thinks these things up?'' Anton asked.

''Clever and corrupt men. Who else runs civilization?''

''Who else should?''

''Yesterday,'' Monboddo said. ''A ship, which identified itself to everyone's satisfaction as the *Sabena's Luck*, officially registered in Glasgow and used by Pfalz Pharmaceuticals for the shipment of high-purity drugs from the manufactories in Luna, landed in the exclusion zone.''

''All right,'' Anton said. ''So who was it really?''

''Unknown. The actual *Sabena's Luck*, leased by Pfalz Pharmaceuticals to a partially owned subsidiary involved in the Asteroid Belt trade, is laid up in ordinary at an orbital dry dock at L5, having its environmental support system overhauled.''

''So someone transferred its identity code to another ship, which landed here. As a result, the Academia has postponed my visit after granting me permission. The ship's landing was obviously unexpected.''

''This appears to be the case,'' Monboddo said.

''This is completely confusing. What ship was it? What did it want? Does this have anything to do with anything else, or is it just some petty illegality that the Academia is involved with?''

''Good questions all. Your simple search for information is becoming more complex.''

''It's going to get more complex yet.'' Anton planted his words carefully. ''I want to go to the Moon.''

Monboddo chuckled. ''You want to dig around Clavius?''

''Among other things.''

''Very well,'' Monboddo sighed. ''Clavius is a tiresome fool, but I will deal with him. I will pull the *Ocean Gypsy* out of mothballs.''

''And after the Moon . . .''

''Oh, Anton. Oh, dear. Surely you—the Asteroid Belt? That zone of madness?''

''It depends on what I find at the Hypostasium, but yes, it will be necessary.''

'' 'Will be necessary.' Don't use passive constructions, Anton. *You* think it necessary. I assume you have good reasons.''

''I do. As the main entrepot of the Belt, the Dead End—''

''Don't bury me with details. The Dead End, run by its mysterious Syndics, is entirely unavoidable if one travels outside the orbit of Mars. You're right in thinking that if anyone has news of Ozaki in the Asteroid Belt, it's someone in the Dead End. Whether they'll tell you is, of course, a completely different matter.'' Monboddo was silent for a long time, and Anton began to fear that he had finally gone too far and that Monboddo would refuse him. ''All right. The Great Ship *Charlotte Amalie* leaves Earth orbit in mid-November, in a week's time, en route to the Moon, the Belt, more specifically the Dead End, and points outward. This becomes interesting. Miriam Kostal, Justice of Tharsis, and her suite are also going to be aboard. I will arrange for a berth.'' Monboddo took a breath. ''I have spent the night thinking about your evidence, Anton.''

No wonder his voice was so weak. ''You should be careful, my lord. Your health—''

''Is my own affair. After some thought I find that I agree with your conclusions about the survival of Karl Ozaki. Ozaki is indeed still alive, or at least lived long enough beyond his supposed death to finish our Dead Christ. An interesting concept. It means that he must have faked his own death in order to escape from Clavius. And Ozaki still owes me fifty thousand rubles, did you know that, Anton? For Anastasia's unfinished portrait head, which we contracted for. I am not so self-centered that I think he went through the incredible rigmarole of pretending to die in order to avoid finishing it, but, still, I would like to find him and discuss it with him.''

"Good," Anton said in relief. "I'll join you on the *Charlotte Amalie*. I can catch a shuttle from Samarkand."

"A curiously mundane thing to do from such a fabled place."

"Can't be helped. I have to be off. It's getting dark."

"Good luck, Anton," Monboddo said softly. "I will see you aboard the *Charlotte Amalie*."

Anton walked out of the booth in deep thought. Azal was in the station waiting room with a slender bald man whose icy gray eyes were slightly bloodshot. "My brother-in-law's cousin, Najil. Najil, meet Mr. Lindgren. As I explained—"

"One thousand rubles," Najil said.

Azal started to protest, to speak of politeness to guests, of Anton's personal importance, of the possible anger of his superiors in Internal Security.

Anton cut him off. "Round trip?"

"Are you crazy? One way. I can't wait around, and if they catch me, I'm dead meat. One thousand rubles. I'll swallow the cost of the fuel."

"Does this include entry?"

"Entry?"

"Look, you can't just drop me at the base of the Hypostasium and expect me to haul out my pitons and climb up the outside. That's worse than useless to me. You used to work for them, and, I presume, are useful to me for precisely that reason. Can you get me in?"

Najil shrugged, expressionless. "It's not so hard. Make it an extra five hundred, for 'key deposit.' My landlady charges me that, why shouldn't I charge you?"

Anton gauged the amount of daylight on the peaks. He shrugged. "Done."

"My car is around the corner."

"Good luck!" Azal cried. "Remember my transfer!"

"I certainly will."

Azal grinned, bright white teeth against his swarthy face. "You are too kind, sir."

Najil walked ahead and Anton followed with his increasingly heavy luggage, trying to ignore the unsteadiness of Najil's steps. A short distance from the Internal Security station the air was full of the clatter of working repair shops, the growl of compressors, the shouts of employers at their workmen. Najil opened a door of crudely nailed together boards to reveal a gleaming vehicle from another age. Cruelly streamlined, it had only two wheels and had obviously been carefully maintained.

"I haven't seen many of these," Anton said, in an attempt at a pleasantry.

"There aren't many of them left. Most of them crashed and exploded."

Najil strapped the luggage in behind. Anton slid into the seat on the left, which was almost horizontal, like the couch in a spacecraft. He closed the door, and found himself bound by a multiplicity of straps, including one across his forehead. He felt confined for execution. In front of him was a control board with many dials.

The engine roared to life. Anton noticed that Najil had no straps on him at all. He asked him why.

"At the speeds this thing goes," Najil explained, "almost every crash is a fatal one. The straps do no good. If anything, they'll keep you from escaping a burning wreck."

"Then why am I wearing them?"

"They're supposed to make you feel more relaxed."

The mountains, icy and sharp, glowed harshly in the late afternoon light. The road clung to the shoulders of the peaks, sometimes smooth, sometimes cracked and broken. Najil drove like someone who did not enjoy life unless he had a sense of its imminent end. Because of its gyroscopic stabilizers the car was capable of incredible speeds around sharp turns. Still, at some point, determinable by some rather elementary physics calculations that Anton was too terrified to perform, the inertia of the car would overcome the friction of its tires on the road surface and fling it off into empty space. Najil was an expert at testing this point.

Anton became glad of the straps that bound him, because he would otherwise have been black and blue from banging against the sides and the roof. Najil rode the car like a cowboy on a bucking bronco, bouncing around madly, occasionally shrieking in delight at a particularly deadly hairpin turn. Anton suspected that these were the only times he showed any emotion whatsoever.

They came around the edge of a rock and found the road blocked by a large wagon pulled by a yak. Najil screeched to a halt. Several frustrated and tired men in many layers of coat with heavy leggings were trying to push the cart out of the road. Fur hats hung low over their faces. With smiles and waves they indicated that they would be glad of some help.

"They seem to be in trouble," Anton said. "Maybe—"

Najil muttered something under his breath, rammed the car into reverse until it teetered just at the edge of the dropoff, then accelerated, still clinging to the edge of the road. The gap between the wagon and the precipice seemed impossibly narrow to Anton. They would flip over the edge and vanish, erased from existence. He held his breath. The car struck the yak a glancing blow and it screamed in pain. Anton tightened his hands painfully on the straps as the mountains whirled around him.

Two of the men reached into the wagon and pulled out long rifles. They blasted away at the car as it sped off, weaving from side to side to make a difficult target. One of the bullets glanced off the fender with a heavy thunk.

"Son of a bitch," Najil grated. "Bandits. They get worse every year."

"How often do they use guns?" Anton asked, in shock.

"Not often. Still hard to get." He slewed around a turn. "God, I want to kill them! As if things around here weren't hard enough. But the government considers them a local problem. They'd have to hold up one of the Gensek's mistresses and steal her panties before anybody'd do anything."

He pulled a bottle out from under his seat. A pull of his teeth opened the top and the car filled with a pungent sour smell.

"Kumiss?" he said, shoving the bottle of thick white liquid in Anton's face.

"No thank you," Anton replied, gritting his teeth to keep his stomach down.

Najil swallowed half the bottle and belched luxuriously. "The bastards," he muttered, and settled back to his driving.

Anton had no idea how long the road was, finally. While he was on it, it seemed to last forever, while in his memory it would remain as one compressed instant of terror.

The car suddenly slowed. "Almost there," Najil grunted.

The Hypostasium had to compete with the mountains that surrounded it on all sides, but it did so with self-assurance that was almost arrogance. It was immense, an arcology, a self-contained city structure that could hold a population of at least forty thousand. The buttresses curved up out of the valley's darkness into the light like the roots of some vast tree, to support the thrusting parapets and towers of the main structure. It owed little to any historical architectural style. At least an order of magnitude larger than anything else ever built on Earth, the features of other buildings would have looked ridiculous on it. The topmost roofs pitched steeply to shake off snow. Spruces and firs grew among them, giving a green to the complex that contrasted with the bare rock and snow of the mountains.

Najil stopped on a stretch of road not perceptibly different from any other. A tube snaked out of the side of the car and touched a depression in the rock. Suddenly the car was full of jagged lightning bolts of colored light. They flared like fragments of a broken rainbow.

"Simple stuff," Najil grunted. "Poor security. They are too proud." He chuckled to himself. "Sometimes I come up here and break in, just to do it. Twenty-first-century technology. High enough, for most purposes. They are idiots. They prefer to use bandits for their security."

"More dramatic and colorful than crypto codes," Anton said. "And fairly effective, for the most part."

"Almost were for us." As the car's computer worked, the jagged lines joined and rejoined, until they were parallel to each other, as if being laid away somewhere for storage. "I could figure out this access code with an abacus." When the last line lay parallel, a door opened in the rock. Najil turned the car and drove up a narrow tunnel, which eventually opened up into a large open space, dimly lit and noisy. He pulled to a halt in front of an elevator door. Anton was forced to pull his own luggage out of the trunk and carry it over to the elevator door.

Support machinery for the arcology far above them filled the cavern, ventilators that thundered like waterfalls, power switching stations, water pumps, communications processors. Lights flickered on control boards, huge engines turned ponderously. A sodium-cooled breeder reactor, Anton knew, provided power somewhere deeper in the mountain.

Najil popped open another bottle of kumiss, closed the car up, and roared away. Anton watched the liquid gleam of the vehicle out of sight. It had the arrogant beauty of a weapon whose apotheosis would be reached only with its destruction.

* * *

The elevator stopped. All four sides slid smoothly down into the floor. A dozen guards with unsheathed swords instantly pressed closely around and hemmed Anton in with gleaming, razor-sharp blades. They wore gold and dark blue uniforms with light metal breastplates. Rage glittered in their eyes.

"Pardon me," Anton said. "I am an invited guest of Preterite Nahum Torkot. I must insist on more respectful treatment."

The blades pulled back. "How did you get here?" demanded the Sergeant of the guard, a man as wide as a door.

They all stood in the middle of a vast interior space that vanished above in misty obscurity. The humid air buzzed with countless voices.

"Not the correct response," Anton said, shaking his head. Over the Sergeant's shoulder Anton saw a curved desk against the base of an immense slab of granite. He stepped deliberately around the Sergeant toward it. "I think you mean, 'Excuse me, my mistake, sir.'"

"Hold it!" The Sergeant grabbed his arm just above the elbow, and Anton felt searing agony. The blades probed at him, moving like underwater grass.

Anton looked longingly at the phones on the desk. One call to Torkot and his presence would have to be officially acknowledged, making his detention impossible. Until then, he could be defined as an anonymous intruder and dealt with in any way necessary. Torkot could make his apologies later. The sharp points of the swords had already cut several holes in his suit, and one of the cuts had penetrated the skin. He could feel blood trickling down his left shoulder blade.

"You must allow me to—"

"I don't have to do anything. Got that?" The Sergeant thrust his jaw out to emphasize his temporary, localized, and absolute power. He reached up as if to push Anton into the blades behind him, then smiled slightly and lowered his hands.

Anton felt a moment of fear. What was Torkot up to? These men and women looked capable of slicing him to pieces. He tugged at his beard in distress, looking into the cold eyes around him and wondering how Vanessa fit in with them. "Look," Anton said. "This is worse than trying to get into the libraries at Harvard. If Preterite Torkot—"

"You can talk tomorrow. Right now, you are going back out where you came from. I hope your ride is waiting for you, because otherwise you will get very cold."

"Anton!" Vanessa's voice called. She strode toward them, her long crimson dress swirling around her feet. Two thick braids crossed above her forehead, and her face glowed with anger. Anton thought that she had never looked more beautiful. She examined the guards as if she had never seen them before. "What's going on here?" Her eyes flicked across his but did not pause on him.

The Sergeant seemed upset to see his carefully articulated universe of authority violated, in the same way a physicist would hate to see his physical laws disrupted by divine intervention. "You know what the situation is! We have our orders, madame. And those orders are to—"

"Who gave you those orders?" Her voice was high and clear, and slightly nervous.

"Why, Preterite Torkot, of course. We . . ." He trailed off, because she had already turned around and picked up one of the phones at the desk.

"Preterite Torkot please," she said. "It's important. No, it can't wait."

"You are confronted with an age-old problem," Anton said to the Sergeant in a conciliatory tone. "That of derived authority, which can vanish like dew in the morning sun. The entire concept of authority, of course, has no absolute validity, being based on a consensus—"

"Oh, shut up," the Sergeant said without heat.

"Is that an order?" The Sergeant's dead-eyed gaze let Anton understand that there are considerations of authority not derived or based on consensus, and that if the Sergeant ever caught Anton alone, he would rip his head off. Anton decided to be silent.

Vanessa looked over at the Sergeant, who glared back stonily. "The Preterite wishes to talk with you." He took the phone reluctantly, knowing that he was about to be chewed out for having done his duty, a common fate of soldiers. He listened impassively, responding with an occasional "Yes" or "No," and once an "I don't know," then quietly hung up the phone, giving the distinct impression that he would have liked to slam it down violently.

Not looking at either Anton or Vanessa, he barked a quick command at his squad. They sheathed their swords, turned as one, and double-timed off across the floor.

"What's gotten into them?" Anton said. "Haven't you been feeding them?"

"I don't know," she said. "But I apologize. They were extremely rude." She leaned one elbow on the desk and reached the other hand across to hold that wrist. Her dress had a high collar, open in the front, and she wore a cameo around her neck. She looked improbably perfect. She glanced up sideward at him, dark eyes beneath soft lashes.

Anton ruefully examined the holes made in his suit by the guards' sword points. "The main difference between a sword and a gun is that a sword gives you the ability to do degrees of damage." The wound on his back seemed to have stopped bleeding. "That's why we live in such a subtle age."

She laughed. "And why the Sergeant is such a subtle man."

"An artist, in his own sphere." He took a deep breath. "Thank you."

She shook her head. "You looked so . . . I don't know, so serene there, as if they were just buzzing insects."

Anton peered upward into the hazy glow of the upper reaches of the atrium. "How far up does this go?"

"More than five hundred meters," she said. "We're not even at the bottom, you know, just on a larger-than-average balcony."

As they walked, the space opened up. The soaring atrium was broken up by crisscrossing walkways and balconies. Anton could not understand its powerful and contradictory structure, or even truly perceive its scale. They finally stopped at the edge of the balcony. The space extended below as far as it did above and he felt as if he were inside a vast, pulsing human heart. The place implied that all actions within it possessed significance.

Vanessa put her hand on his arm and leaned closer to him. "Be careful," she said. "Nahum's angry. Angrier than I've ever seen him. He has everyone in an uproar. My letting you in won't improve his mood."

He was so distracted by her touch that he almost failed to attend to her words. "What about?"

She shook her head but kept her eyes on his. "He won't tell me. He'll have to eventually." She dropped her hand and shifted her weight. Suddenly, though they were still standing next to each other, they were not together. Anton looked over his shoulder. Torkot's blocky silhouette stood near the reception desk like a symbol of observation. Internal Security used agents with distinctive shapes like his whenever they wanted one of their subjects to be aware at all times that he was being followed.

Torkot seemed to have no intention of moving from his place. Vanessa walked toward him and Anton followed.

Torkot nodded at Anton. "Sorry for the misunderstanding." Anton waited for Torkot to ask if he'd had any trouble getting there, so that he could say, with heavy humor, that he had had a pleasant and relaxing trip, but Torkot was smarter than that. Obviously, Anton had found a way to get around the roadblocks, and thus, just as obviously, it was a subject no longer worth discussing. Torkot would have to reexamine his security procedures later, when Anton wasn't there to sneer.

Torkot was in a high rage. Anger gleamed beneath his long eyelashes and the leathery skin seemed more tightly drawn across the harsh planes of his face, covered with a fine sheen of sweat.

"Let me help you with your luggage," Torkot said, and lifted Anton's heavy suitcase as if it were empty. Having lugged it all over Dushanbe, Anton's arm sockets were in agony, and he was glad of the assistance.

Guest quarters were in one of the bastions, separate from the quarters of Academia Sapientiae personnel. If the mood of the Hypostasium was disquiet, as Torkot had maintained during their dinner conversation aboard the *Bay of Bengal*, then Anton's room exemplified it. The floor area was pentagonal, three meters on a side, but the room stretched upward two stories, with a drastically sloped ceiling. Three of the walls were rough-hewn rock, one light blue plaster, and one a mirror. The bed was a shelf that projected from the wall about four feet off the ground. Harsh lights beat down from far above, as if the room were an experimental chamber. In addition to the bed there was an armoire, a small table, a writing desk, and a metal sink. A single grated window looked out onto the spaces of the Pamirs. It was as cold as a Martian room.

With the air of an experienced personal servant, Torkot opened up Anton's trunk, removed his suits and shirts, shook them out, and hung them in the armoire. The toiletries went on a shelf above the sink. He looked through the books, selected the one with the silk bookmark in it, Boswell's *Life of Johnson*, and put it on the table next to the bed. He unwrapped the small bust of the Gensek Timofey and set it on the writing desk.

"Martian work?" Vanessa asked.

The question somehow embarrassed Anton. That frowning little head was tied up with so much, with the duel in Pyramid Square, with Miriam's bed, with an entire vanished life that he still pulled along with him. "Yes," he muttered. "Twenty-third century."

As he spoke he realized that acting as a servant had given Torkot an excuse to thoroughly search his luggage right in front of his eyes. Vanessa's question had distracted him at a critical moment. Had Torkot found the false bottom that concealed the Ozaki notes?

Acting as a gentleman's gentleman had not relaxed Torkot and he now stood tensely by the door, a man with other, more urgent business who was wondering how to cover his back. "Ms. Karageorge will take care of you," he said. "Good night, Mr. Lindgren." With a sudden turn he loped clumsily off down the hallway.

"Now you're here," Vanessa murmured at his shoulder. "What would you do now?"

Anton yawned. "I think I'll get some sleep. It's been a long trip." He glanced at the bed. Uncomfortable-looking though it was, if he lay down on it he'd be asleep instantly. So, after Vanessa left him, he'd sit at the desk and write some notes. After half an hour or so, it would be safe to get up and see if he could find his way through the collections on his own.

She raised her eyebrows. "Are you serious? You struggled all the way up here tonight so that you could go to sleep? Isn't there anything you particularly wanted to see?"

He was trapped. He could go to sleep, proving himself a lazy fool, try to sneak out later, proving himself untrustworthy, or go with her as escort. "Let's go." Besides, she was starting to look more than a little tired herself. Perhaps he could wear her out.

The Hypostasium could have housed forty thousand people, but its actual population was less than a tenth that number. The research collections filled most of it, set up as a series of environments.

The Academia Sapientiae was interested in the representative, the objects that shaped the mental universe of a given civilization, rather than in the greatest works of art.

They stopped in a small village of mud-brick houses. A hot blue sky stretched overhead. A dusty open area marked the center of the village. Large colored pots and stone tools lay scattered, dating the place to the late Neolithic, around 3000 BCE.

"See that saddle quern?" Vanessa pointed at a large rock with a flat top and a curved surface underneath. A stone roller lay on top of it. "I used a duplicate of that to grind emmer and einkorn wheat, which grow wild in Anatolia." She sat down next to it, back straight, incongruous in her bright red dress, and ran her hand across its worn surface. "I harvested that wheat with a sickle made from a piece of wood set with the sharpened teeth of a wild boar. We sacrificed a pig and danced in the hot sun." For a moment there was a look in her eyes that was not hers, an ancient look, weary yet exalted, the look that, in the midst of unremitting labor, had elaborated the first gods. Anton imagined her, rough-skinned, tanned, her hands callused, digging day after endless day in the fields to raise primitive wheat, then, in a time of wild celebration, decorating herself with bronze ornaments and abandoning herself to her gods and her men. He looked around the room at the rough implements, the structures of dried mud brick, the pathetic withered grains of wheat in their pots, and realized that to her these had the resonance of childhood to them, of things once used and loved even if now put away. That was how the Academia Sapientiae studied the past, and how they hoped to influence the future.

She shook her head, putting the memories back where they belonged, and was once again crisp and serene. "People aren't more fully themselves with a hoe in their hands,'' she said. ''No matter what some claim. But they are something different from us.''

In the next chamber a wool-felt yurt on a wooden wagon stood in the middle of an endless plain of lush grass, a small dung fire burning in front of it. Cumulus clouds towered overhead. A shaggy pony nickered and pressed its wet nose into Anton's hand. It wore a red felt saddle and a bridle with copper cheekpieces shaped like long-maned horses. Inside the yurt Anton found embroidered wool clothing, rugs, and two cups made of human skulls, the insides gilded. He hefted one and felt the hair on the back of his head stir. These were certainly not ancient Scythian artifacts dug out of a tomb in South Russia. These were relatively new. How far did the Academia go in its exploration of mind and environment? Had those domestic troops that had harassed him by the elevator ever ridden swift ponies across the steppe and cut their enemies' skulls to make drinking cups?

Vanessa waited for him outside, an elaborately chased bronze sword in her hand. Her face was thoughtful and distant. A massive round shield rested against the side of the yurt, its central ornament a beautiful recumbent stag of solid gold. Anton felt that the Scythian soldiers had just gone off to forage their horses and would soon be back. He did not want to meet them.

Behind each of the environments was a thorough collection of artifacts. They walked on and on. After hours of wandering through corridors of seventeenth-century Polish cooking utensils and twenty-first-century Argentinean antiradiation equipment, Anton was ready to surrender. Vanessa seemed indefatigable. He forced himself to go on. Suddenly, she stumbled against him, and he realized that she was even more tired than he.

He caught and held her. Her body was taut in his hands, like a strung bow. Her muscles shifted under the soft fabric of her dress. For the first time she was close enough for him to smell the clean scent of her. She relaxed into the support of his arms, just for an instant.

Then her body tightened and she twisted away; stopping to check the buckle on her shoe as a way of explaining the movement. He tried to catch her eye, but she wouldn't look at him.

They walked through rooms of moving images, of recordings of long-dead singing or shouting voices from the eras of reproducible experience, the twentieth century and onward. Scents wafted through narrow rooms, the smells of flowers, of putrefying flesh, of burning incense, of a freshly waxed pine floor. Anton found himself appalled by the immensity of historical experience. He was a citizen of Earth, where too many people had lived before. For a fleeting instant, here in the center of Earth's dedication to remembering, he understood something of the Technic desire to forget. It startled him.

He began to perceive the structure of the exhibits, the logical or whimsical connections between them. They were not related by strict chronology, or even by normal historical succession, but often by emotional sympathy, so that remains of the religious community of Qumran, which had produced the Dead Sea Scrolls, were adjacent to those of Mormon Salt Lake City, some eighteen hundred years later, and the grotesque displays on the late Roman Empire led naturally into those on the Soviet Union, as did Byzantium into the Orthodox Russian Empire of the twenty-second century. So Anton guided their path past Albigensians, Shakers, and Nizari Isma'ilis, called the Assassins, to the chamber dedicated to the Dispossessed Brethren of Christ.

They found themselves in the stone hall of a monastery. A cold wind howled outside. Anton peered through the narrow windows at a landscape of frozen sand dunes, barren of life. A map reference carved into the wall told him that this monastery had stood in the desert of Takla Makan, in the Tarim Basin of Chinese Turkestan. The Brethren's other monasteries had been in the Sinai, on the Moon at Clavius, on Mars at Hecates Tholus, and in the Asteroid Belt at the asteroid Jerusalem the Lost. The windows at the other end of the hall showed the crisp peaks of the Moon against a black sky. Otherwise, the room was strangely and chillingly empty. The walls showed traces of pictures, the floor of display cases, but there was no sign of either. Anton couldn't say whether they had been removed a decade ago, or the previous night.

Vanessa watched him narrowly, as if his response were important. With what he hoped was convincing casualness, Anton shrugged and ambled into the next exhibit, as if the empty room in the howling wilderness held no specific interest to him.

"All this information," he yawned. "I'm starting to lose track of what I'm seeing."

The hall beyond the Brethren's empty chamber was large and vaulting, filled with the detritus of Acherusian digs. The late-night mood gave the spirals and spikes of the artifacts a threatening aspect. The hall was set up like an amphitheater, and the artifacts stood on stands on banks of risers, an audience examining the humans far below them. A hologram of the Moon, Mars, and the asteroids spun above, with glowing symbols keyed to the artifacts to show where each had been found. Anton looked up at it. Clavius and Cap Acherusia, Hecates Tholus. The correspondence with the Brethren's monasteries was close. There was even a symbol on their great temple of Jerusalem the Lost. Something about that didn't quite make sense.

Vanessa's gaze was fixed on something out among the artifacts. Her eyes flicked quickly away, but he noted the empty spot among the artifacts. He would never have noticed it without her momentary lapse.

"Let's go," she said, her voice suddenly peremptory. "It's late." Her face was a hard mask.

"It's been late for a long time." He took several steps into the artifacts. What did he hope to see? It would be hard to examine something that was gone.

She took his arm. Her grip was strong, and not at all sensual. "Let's *go*."

He ranged one more look across the ranks of Acherusian artifacts. A tiny pink spot on the floor caught his eye, only because it was so incongruous. Vanessa looked briefly away from him, to glare off into space, and he knelt and scooped it up. He wondered why a single pink rose petal lay on the otherwise clean floor. What would Rabiah have made of this sign?

It wasn't worth fighting with Vanessa, and he realized that it would be a fight if he tried to stay. He walked ahead of her as they left the room, ignoring her tight lips and angry glare, as if leaving had been his idea.

The savor had gone out of the evening. She marched him back to his room as if he were a prisoner she had escorted to the bathroom. She ignored his remarks, or answered them with taut monosyllables that made him prefer silence.

To take his mind off the sinking feeling her irritation had given him, he thought about the display that hung above the artifacts. He hadn't had enough time to be sure, but it seemed to him that none of the artifacts that still stood in the room were keyed to the symbol that had been on Jerusalem the Lost, now called the Dead End. That symbol might well have marked the site where the missing artifact had been discovered.

But the Dead End had started life as a featureless chunk of nickel-iron and was now a totally artificial creation. There had never, at any time, been even the trace of Acherusian remains there.

An hour and a half after Vanessa, still silent, had put him back in his room, Anton rolled out of bed and tried the door. It was locked as solidly as the entrance of an Egyptian tomb. That decided him. If they wanted him to stay put so badly that they would lock him in, he desperately wanted to get out. He opened out the appropriate section of his suitcase.

It took him only a few seconds to trace the delicate microgauss magnetic field that marked the door's lock. He felt a moment of satisfaction. They could have locked him in with a brass-bound door and a metal bolt, more suited to Academia style. In that case he would have been helpless, but such a massive dungeon portal would have been too obvious, so they had used an invisible magnetic lock, giving them the ability to deny all. "The door got stuck at night? My goodness, your room must have a pressure leak. The Hypostasium is pressurized, so the door was squeezed against the jamb. Happens all the time." Anton was sure that it did.

He was taking a calculated risk. As far as he knew, Torkot and the Academia Sapientiae still considered him to be the nosy curator of an important Judicial Lord. Breaking through a security lock might alert them to the possibility that he was something more.

He countered the field and the door swung open. He slid out and heard it click shut behind him. The hall of Acherusian artifacts would have been a natural first goal, but he suspected that it was too late by now. It would be sealed, or guarded. Instead, he headed in the opposite direction. He had spent most of his evening with Vanessa figuring out the arrangement of the Hypostasium, since maps of the place were carefully unavailable. The Academia Sapientiae liked to keep its secrets. What was the most natural path for someone to carry an Acherusian artifact from the hall to a spacecraft that had come down from orbit? From what he could tell, there were few places the pseudo-*Sabena's Luck* could have landed on the Hypostasium itself, and he doubted they would have tried to lug the artifact over icy cliffs.

The arcology was like an extrusion of magma from the Earth's crust that had, as it thrust its way up into the air, cracked and fractured, forming a variety of columns and odd projections. Often he would pass a window and look out, to see only an arrangement of steep roofs, already covered with early winter snows. A few other windows were glowing in the darkness, indicating other wakeful souls, but there was no way he could reach them. They might as well have been stars, or the campfires of distant armies.

He finally found himself on a high observation deck. It was filled with a profusion of mirrors and ornate columns, which distracted and confused him. He almost ran into his own image several times, and on other occasions avoided perfectly clear passages because he thought they were illusions.

He was almost at the windows when he walked around a pillar and almost stumbled into the plump, ornately dressed woman who was leaning against the other side of it.

She shrieked and jumped back, looking around herself wildly for assistance, but there was no one else around. She recovered herself. "And *who* are *you*?" she demanded.

The woman wore a long, embroidered gown with a high collar. Her eyes were elaborately made up, despite the fact that she was obviously wandering around because she couldn't sleep. She had jewels in her hair.

"Forgive me, madame," Anton said with a deep bow. "I'm afraid I did not see you." He straightened up, and recognized her. "You are Ida Nastra, are you not? Of Chicago?"

"Why—Anton Lindgren! I remember you. I'm sorry I screamed like that. I'm very high strung, very. But of course you remember that."

"I do," said Anton, who didn't. He was pleased enough with himself for having managed to remember her name.

"There are such *strange* things going on here, really. Arnold and I are on a tour of Asia, we were in Samarkand, looking at some old tombs, and of course, you simply *must* stop in at this place for a visit, else everyone will say you have no sense of what is important. You remember Arnold, of course."

"Your husband."

"My son," she corrected with a quizzical look. "He likes museums. He likes to look at the funny ways people used to dress, before they knew any better. He says it helps him understand progress. Arnold dresses very well."

"I remember."

"I don't see how you could, when you met him we were at a costume ball, and he was dressed as a chicken."

Anton realized he was getting himself into trouble. "I simply assumed, knowing your impeccable sense of style . . ."

She giggled, instantly mollified. "Oh, you're too sweet, Mr. Lindgren. Anyway, there isn't much here to interest *me*. I prefer the more active life. And there are so many strange people around here. I ran into one on one of these decks or other, I even think it may have been this one, last night. A soldier."

Anton felt a sudden tension. "A soldier?"

"Or *something*. I don't think he was a waiter, and he wasn't one of those *terrible* security guards they have around here. I'd heard some kind of thunder in the middle of the night. Probably an avalanche, or something, these hills are dangerous, what with all that snow all over them. I put on this wrap, a nice robe embroidered with flowers that I always wear when I wake up in the middle of the night. I mean, my hair's a mess, and I must look a horror, so I might as well have on something nice that covers most of me up. It even has a hood, for particularly trying times."

"You look superb," Anton said. "I am in the same boat as you, unable to sleep, but I look it. How do you do it?"

She dimpled. "Attention to detail, Mr. Lindgren. That's what does it, believe me. And you look fine. Just a little frazzled, that's all, and that's only natural. Anyway, I wandered out and ended up in one of these . . . these *rooms* they have around here, all full of old junk

and mirrors, and of course I got lost, and started to
wonder if I was awake after all. That's when I saw him,
standing and looking out of the window. He wore a black
uniform, with long gloves that went up almost to his
elbow. They made him look like a gardener. It wasn't a
tunic, but more a coverall, tight, like a second skin. It
wasn't really the most flattering thing for him to be wearing, since he was a little plump, and stood with a slouch,
like someone who's a little sick and feels like his arms
and legs are too heavy. I get that way sometimes, and I
have this water retention problem . . . anyway he had a
curved sword and little marks on his chest, like medals,
so he really was a soldier, you see. He had a big wide
cap on too, so that you couldn't see his hair. He looked
like he was breathing hard, but I couldn't hear any noise.
Oh, and his boots had toes. That was odd.''

"Toes? What do you mean?''

"They were split, the big toe separate. Like they were
mittens, except on his feet. Then he saw me, and disappeared. I tried to follow him, since he'd been the most
interesting thing I'd seen in a while and that's when I
knew why I hadn't heard him breathing. I was looking
at a mirror. I wasn't even sure where he'd been standing.
I wonder who he was.''

"Oh, probably someone's bodyguard," Anton said.
"They dress in all sorts of strange ways.''

"I guess," she said, then forgot the matter. Mysteries
disturbed her, and now that she had passed this one on
to someone who was better equipped to handle it, she
saw no reason to continue to think about it. Anton was
impressed by the fact that, while superficially breathless
and silly, her description included every single significant
detail of the intruder's appearance and of the circumstances leading up to it. She had no idea, obviously, that
the soldier's posture indicated that he was used to a low-
gravity environment, and that the bifurcated footwear
indicated that he had spent a lot of time working in
weightlessness, where legs were largely useless except

as two extra grabbing limbs, just as she didn't know that the thunder of what she thought was an avalanche had been the atmospheric entry of a spacecraft.

"Well," she said, "it's been pleasant, but I simply *must* find Arnold now." And so Anton—polite, courtierlike, and grateful for yet another brightly colored puzzle piece—bowed and backed away, though she was the one who had just announced that she was leaving.

It was the final clue he needed. How would a soldier from a spacecraft have appeared on that observation deck?

The deck was actually cantilevered off a shoulder of the mountain itself. Just beyond the windows to the left, Anton could see rock and a snowfield. A few minutes search was enough to find a door that led outside.

He went through the door without giving himself time to have second thoughts. The sharp wind rubbed ice into his bones. He tried to convince himself, as he had ever since childhood, that while he *felt* cold, there was no reason whatsoever that his mind should interpret cold as a negative stimulus. It was just a signal, an indication of external temperature. This never worked, but it gave him something to think about.

The night was clear, which made it even colder, but the moon shone across the snowfield, revealing the depressions of a spacecraft's landing skids. With the feeling that he was collecting entirely meaningless information, Anton paced off the distance between the depressions. Obviously a short-range vessel, with no interplanetary capability.

The cold had turned to literal pain, no longer a debating point. Anton started back for the door and spotted an odd glitter by a rock that thrust out of the snow about where the spacecraft's loading doors would have been. It curved like a walrus tusk. He scooped the thing up and ran for the door.

Once through, he continued to run, as fast as he could, down through the halls, trying to get warm. By the time he made it back to his room he was sweaty and hot, though his hair and beard were still stiff with ice.

He sat down on the bed and pried open the fingers of his right hand. His walrus tusk gleamed there, smooth-textured, like a fossil he had found once as a child and kept until he lost it, an ancient sea snail that had been replaced by shiny, dark gray hematite. Had he found it lying on a path somewhere he would not have given it a further thought. Given the context, it was perfectly clear what it was. The thick end was broken, as if snapped from a larger object, and cracks radiated through it from the impact point. Someone, perhaps unused to the heavy gravity of Earth, had dropped what they were carrying on the rock just below the cargo doors of the spaceship. What they had been carrying was the missing Acherusian artifact.

The sharp peaks glowed above the Hypostasium. A cold wind blew down the valley, carrying snowflakes that had become dissatisfied with their initial resting place. Vanessa felt the wind as a merciless force of purity. She paced a high parapet and her eyes teared whenever she turned into the wind. Rabbit's fur caressed her hands. She'd killed the rabbits that now formed her gloves in the grasslands of Anatolia, in approved Neolithic fashion. A rabbit running straight away from you makes a difficult target, but it always lays its ears back just before it turns. Throw a rock to one side of the rabbit at that instant, and half the time you'll kill it. The fur of the gloves did more than just keep her hands warm, it kept her memory warm as well.

She could just make out a high trail on the slope across the valley. It led into the higher mountains beyond. Dozens of trails ran through the lower valleys, intersecting each other, but as they climbed they became sparser, until just one ran into each high valley. A poor choice made below, if not corrected, could lead to an arduous climb to a dead end at an indifferent glacier.

A favorite art teacher at Northfall, Gail Fortescu, a very old woman, or so it had seemed to Vanessa at the time, had given her a warning. "Be careful of what you do, my dear," Fortescu had said. "When you do something base, you do it in the present moment, and no one sees it. After that, it's in the past, and you always have it in front of your eyes, unable to change it. Guilt's an emotion with good intentions, but it's stupid. It comes only after you've done something bad, not before, when it would actually do some good. This lesson I'm giving you is the same way: you'll only understand it when it's too late."

Remembering Fortescu, Vanessa quirked her lips, despite her pain. The rectors of the Northfall Lyceum were right. The best teachers for the young were cynics who had managed to keep a sense of humor.

Her last night in Boston with Theonave had been painful, for no good reason. He had been as polite and attentive as ever, but actions are seen in context, and the context of his mysterious nocturnal assault on the Monboddo Household changed her view of his character.

Unspoken suspicions are the barriers cooling lovers defend themselves with. Theonave's character made the claim that he was an obvious man, simple and direct. Since Naples, Vanessa had begun to see that this was an illusion. The added complexity in her lover annoyed her rather than interesting her. Subtlety is not an attractive trait in a bull.

So who was he, this man who had served her breakfast in bed, and knotted a red scarf around her neck the one and only time she had managed to convince him to walk outside along the beach? She realized that she had no idea. His motivations seemed now like elaborate contrivances. She suddenly felt that she had taken the wrong trail in the forest, the one leading up to the glacier.

Anton Lindgren was leaving the Hypostasium that morning. If Theonave was a man who hid complexity under a show of directness, Anton was an outwardly complex and intellectual man who was driven by relatively simple passions. When she had met him, she had thought of him as nothing more than an aesthete. A brilliant one, or, as Cezanne said of Monet: "He's nothing but an eye, but what an eye!" but still, a curator of a museum. Now, she was startled by the drive she saw in him, and the other night, before they reached the Acherusian artifacts, she had been ready for almost anything, as, she thought, he had been. The discovery that one of the artifacts was missing, obviously the event that had enraged Torkot, had forced her to defend the Academia's interests and treat Anton as an enemy.

A heavy figure was suddenly pacing the parapet with her, Nahum Torkot, his eyes dim and bloodshot, a light topcoat barely shielding him from the wind. She didn't give him a chance to speak.

"Why didn't you tell me? I never would have let Lindgren go anywhere near the artifacts if I'd known. I had to hustle him out. It made him suspicious." Of her. What did he think of her now?

Torkot turned away from her. "There wasn't time . . . I couldn't decide . . ."

Vanessa felt as if all the supports of her world were being pulled out from under her. First Theonave, now Torkot, obviously pushed beyond his limits. His contacts in the Esopus Palace couldn't help him here.

"They threatened me at gunpoint," he said thickly. "Right here, in the Hypostasium itself. They said the deal was going through, whether we got the figurine of the Dead Christ or not. They suspected me of having stolen it for myself. They said I planned to miss the rendezvous in Naples. Why else—"

"Never mind that!" Vanessa said angrily. "What are we going to do now? Are we going to recover the Acherusian artifact? Its name was Nehushtan, wasn't it?"

"Recover—" He looked at her. "How did you know that the artifact had a name?"

"The man who delivered the Dead Christ told me,

just before he died. What is that supposed to mean?''

"It means that it has more importance than either of us can realize.'' He shivered in the cold wind, looked around as if suddenly realizing that he was outside, and gestured Vanessa to precede him through the door back in.

"Who is it?'' she asked, refusing to budge. "Who are these people?''

He shook his head. "Can you believe it? I don't know. But I do know that they need the artifact. They need it to commit some great act. So I traded it to them.'' He flicked his eyelashes at her. "I wanted to act.''

"A noble ambition. You know more than you're telling me.''

"No, I don't. I suspect more than I've said. You can draw conclusions as well as I can. Better. You tell me.''

"You'll let me do what I want then?''

He looked at her, a slight smile on his lips. Had her desires once again coincided with his plans? "I will,'' he said. "As long as you observe as well as act. You will be recording an act of history.''

She turned and headed quickly down the stairs.

"I'm traveling,'' Vanessa gasped, breathless from her run down from the parapet to the empty, echoing garage. "On the *Charlotte Amalie*. Academia business.''

Anton stroked one of the forks of his beard. "So will I, as you no doubt know. I'll be glad of the company,'' he said, giving notice that she could not expect either indignation or surprise from him.

"I have some research obligations on the Moon—''

He raised a hand. "No explanations, unless they are the true ones. And you know what I mean by truth.'' His eyes had a hint of frost in them, as they had since her sudden anger in the hall of the Acherusian artifacts. Frost could melt on the next warm day, or it could harden into the ice of a long winter. It looked as if the choice, suddenly, was hers.

"I'm sorry." She looked beseechingly at him. "But I can't say, yet."

"Nor can I," he said. "Though you know more of my secrets than I know of yours. Just be careful." He reached out a hand and she took it. His hand was strong and callused, like that of a man who worked the land rather than the library. "If we raise our swords against each other, I don't think either of us will ever put them down."

"I don't want that."

"I know. I'm sure the Caliph doesn't want it either."

Vanessa smiled at what had become their private nickname for Torkot. She heard a low hum. A boxy vehicle crept down a ramp from somewhere inside the mountain and rolled up to where they stood.

"Ah, a formal vehicle," Anton remarked. "Still no brass bands, banners, or speeches from dignitaries. But a substantial improvement over my reception."

She picked up one of his suitcases. It had, she knew, false compartments, but Torkot had been unable to find out what was in them. And had Anton indeed managed to get out of his room that first night? Indications were unclear. Who was this man?

8

From "The Tale of the *Mariamne*," in *Myths of the Commanders*, by Lowen Fronstock, Innsmouth Press, 2347:

The drugged guards lay snoring amid the ruins of the immense meal, their swords loose at their sides. Tarana slipped by them, softly, softly, her earrings still tinkling their song, as they had through her own dinner with the Captain. She held a glow globe and warmed it in her hands as she walked. The Captain awaited her, as she had asked, in the Observation Room at the other end of the Ship. The Observation Room's crystal walls glittering with the ruddy light of receding Mars. The Ship hummed and whispered to him, and he felt, for once, at peace. He ran his hand along the crystal wall, hearing it sing beneath his fingers, and dreamed of love, as all Captains do.

Tarana thought not of the Captain's love, nor of the First Officer's rage, nor of the coming despair of the engineers when they found their engines destroyed and useless, leaving the Ship to drift aimlessly among the planets. She thought of beauty, and of all she had been denied. The hatches behind her were sealed. She reached into her bodice and pulled out the Captain's access tool, with its curves and edges, now hers, finally, after all her painful efforts. It fit smoothly into the hole in the control core though it had never been used, not once in the Ship's one hundred years of life. The machinery inside hummed. The engines suddenly shut off and, somewhere in the distance, alarms wailed. Lights died throughout the Ship and were replaced by their paler emergency brothers. The control core rose up out of the floor, even as Tarana floated up in weightlessness, even as the Ship drifted, dead.

She gathered her dress around her and pulled herself forward. If there was residual radiation, she didn't care. There in the heart of the Ship, the Ship that had never been kind to her, the ngomite gleamed with the beauty of frozen suns, just as her mother's stories had said. She levered a piece out, not caring about the nanocircuitry she destroyed. It glowed in her hand, like the Earth seen from the Observation Room. Her eyes filled with tears, but the tears did not fall. Instead they moved about her as she floated in the darkness, tiny liquid moons. . . .

The *Charlotte Amalie* bulked on the shuttle's viewscreen. Anton gazed at his destination distractedly. It seemed unreasonable that he was here so soon. Not six hours ago he had been at the Hypostasium. The bus had taken him to Samarkand, and he had immediately been hurled out of Earth's atmosphere as a supercargo on a supply shuttle to the Great Ship. He was unused to such rapid transitions, and it was odd to see the globe of the Earth entire beneath him, so that it seemed that he could trace out his long journey from Boston to the Pamirs with a single flick of his eye. He couldn't really trace it out that way, of course, since the journey had consisted not of miles of topographic distance, but of the places and people that linked it together. The approaching spaceship filled the screen.

One of the largest Great Ships, the *Charlotte Amalie*

had first been built a century and a half before, and
expanded substantially since. Its two-kilometer-long
main structure was a long, straight backbone, like the
spine of an immense fish. The front third was the main
body of the ship, built and extended with additions until
it was a vast complicated junk pile. Several hoops spun
around it, providing gravity areas when the ship was not
under acceleration. These, and the three engine pods that
thrust out of the rear of the blocky foresection, were its
only symmetrical features. The long main spine extended
back to the main engines in the rear, far from the inhabited areas. At several points along the spine junk-pile
areas appeared again, one with its own spinning ring.
These areas were called ''niduses'' and had specialized
functions. Nidus 2, for example, contained gambling
dens, dueling pits, and dream parlors. Nidus 3 provided
engineering support.

A number of ships had already linked up to various
sections of the spine between these areas. The *Charlotte
Amalie* carried both individual passengers and a variety
of spacecraft that otherwise did not have the range for
interplanetary travel. The various vessels were linked into
the *Charlotte Amalie*'s own structure, piggyback, provided with atmospheric support, and served, essentially,
as extra cabins, already designed precisely to the passenger's specifications. Somewhere in the complex tangle, Monboddo's ship, the *Ocean Gypsy*, had already
linked on, as had, most likely, Miriam Kostal's vessel,
the *Rapier*. Anton looked for it, but dozens of vessels
floated around the Great Ship, some being maneuvered
in for docking by stubby tugs, and the *Ocean Gypsy* and
the *Rapier* were invisible in the chaos.

The *Charlotte Amalie* never landed on a planet, since
its structure could never permit such a thing, and never
stopped anywhere for long. It was an independent world
that could travel anywhere it pleased. Many of its crew
were born, lived, and died aboard, and never felt the
need to live anywhere else. No more or less honest than

the general run of humanity, the name of their ship caused them to be known as Charlatans.

In any future Solar War, the role of the dozen or so Great Ships, and their lesser brethren among the interplanetary ships that bore allegiance to no planet, was an imponderable that occupied huge bureaus filled with busy diplomatic officers in both the Union of States and Nationalities and the Technic Alliance. They were a potential military resource that could not be allowed to fall to the other side. If the *Charlotte Amalie*, for example, was in Earth orbit when hostilities broke out, Terran vessels would be obliged to compel its submission and put it under dependable command. Given the Great Ships' traditional independence, this would certainly be more easily ordered from an office at the Esopus Palace than carried out by a sweating military officer in a corvette trying to attack a ship two kilometers long, armed with unknown weapons.

The robot shuttle docked with a dull thud. The air acquired a complex odor, dusty and aromatic. The hatch unsealed and Anton floated into the *Charlotte Amalie*.

Anton walked across a sloping floor tessellated with stars, each glowing with the correct spectral intensity, though much larger than the scale of the distances between them. He paused on Betelguese, huge, red, and pulsing, captured in the matrix of the dark transparent floor. Nameless stars surrounded it. Cryptic silver lines flowed between the stars, symbols of the mysterious astrology of the space dwellers, who had an infinity of stars for their prognostications.

The star map on which he walked was centered on Sol. Ahead of him, past the warm, homey lights of Procyon and Tau Ceti, the floor sloped down to the flaring nova of the dueling pit, the bottom of the bowl of stars. It occupied a space ten light-years across, swallowing up Sol and Alpha Centauri. The crowd around the dueling pit cheered as one of the combatants scored on his opponent.

Anton reached into his breast pocket and once again felt the visiting card he had placed there. His left hand reached automatically down along his side, but his sword was not there to reassure him. Personal weapons were not allowed in the *Charlotte Amalie*. He felt naked, since he wore a dark suit of formal cut, incomplete without a sword.

The visiting card was one of his own. He had met Monboddo, Fell, and Osbert at the *Ocean Gypsy* but had not stayed to rest. As soon as the Great Ship had accelerated, leaving Earth orbit for the Moon, he had set out to Miriam's ship, the *Rapier*. The Martian vessel had joined the *Charlotte Amalie*, despite the fact that the ship's course would take it out through the Asteroid Belt and the moons of Jupiter before returning to the orbit of Mars. Miriam, he was beginning to suspect, had her own goals, which did not necessarily coincide with his and Monboddo's.

The attendant on duty at the *Rapier* had returned his card, saying that the Justice of Tharsis was indisposed. That may or may not have been true, but she had left him no note on his card, quite unlike her. The Justice was obviously elsewhere, but wished to be thought at home. Anton had moved quickly down the hallway. The ship had not been under acceleration long. Perhaps he could catch her.

Charlatans labored everywhere, termites in their interplanetary colony. The ship was old and she took constant maintenance, which the Charlatans provided with stoic irritation, like a farmer with a favored but balky mule. Anton interrupted one Charlatan, who was repairing a large pipe that ran under an immense photograph of Captain Golgotha. The photograph showed a tall, dark man with flashing eyes, here dressed in the uniform of a Maintenance Tech. The Captain's pose was oddly hieratic, as if he were an Egyptian Pharaoh or

Byzantine Emperor. His topknot was high and elaborate, with some carved ornament in it. He held a drill in one hand and a voltage probe in the other.

"Have you seen a woman go down this hallway?" Anton said. "She may not have been alone." He described her.

The Charlatan, a balding man with sloping shoulders, did not stand or even look up. He had barely enough hair for a topknot.

"Yeah," he said.

"Which way did she go?"

The man pointed silently and Anton went in the direction indicated. He passed several more photographs of Captain Golgotha, one of him as a Navigation Officer, and another as a Steward, holding a platter full of canapés. In both of the photographs his eyes stared out past the viewer.

He found another Charlatan, this one pensively sorting colored wires. "Woman?" he said. "Another Nidus for that."

"No," Anton said. "A specific woman." He described Miriam.

"Oh." The Charlatan seemed startled by the idea of searching for some woman in particular. He looped wires around his hand as he thought. "Dueling pit." He returned to his sorting, clearly dismissing Anton.

Anton found a Charlatan who condescended to point out the dueling pit. It was apparently against Charlatan mores to impart more than one piece of information at a time.

The circular dueling pit, twenty meters across, had a surface of raked white sand. Most of the spectators gathered around immediately above the pit, though some, like Anton, preferred to keep a discreet distance. Were they interested parties? Bookies? Since they kept a good distance from each other as well, Anton could not tell. High above the pit, a Justice Officer sat in a glass box, insuring that the rules were observed.

Two men, stripped to shorts, fought in the pit with swords. They were frightened men and fought clumsily. Anton could hear their ragged breaths from where he stood. They attacked each other only reluctantly, and it seemed that the duel would end at any moment from simple lack of interest. What deep-seated dispute had brought them here, to this sugar-white field of maiming and death? The dueling pit was the only place that Charlatans could hold a weapon, which accounted for their obvious lack of experience with the implements of death in their hands. Over the months and years something had grown between these two men. Unable to escape each other, and unable to live together, they had come here. Scheduled and structured violence was an ancient Terran habit that had found favor throughout the Solar System as a solution, of sorts, to otherwise insolvable conflicts.

Finally, one of the men, with a grunt, brought the edge of his sword across the other's neck. The blade was dull, but it had enough of an edge to rip the other man's neck open, flinging his head back. The blow tore the jugular vein, but not the carotid artery, so blood poured out onto the white sand but did not spurt. Death would not come quickly. The wounded man shrieked and fell to the ground, where he writhed in agony, trying to hold his shredded throat closed with his hands. His shocked opponent looked down at the victim.

"Jon," he said inanely. "Are you all right?"

At a signal from the Justice Officer, a medical technician emerged from a doorway onto the dueling surface. He knelt over the wounded man solicitously. Anton saw the glint of a hypospray. When the technician stood, the man lay quiet. The spectators applauded politely, and those who had had a personal interest in the dispute started to leave. It was only then that Anton realized that the man was lying quietly because he was dead. Stretcher bearers appeared and carried the body away. The technician gave the sobbing victor an injection also, a calming rather than lethal one this time, and led him away.

New spectators appeared. The previous crowd had been almost entirely Charlatans, but many of these appeared to be Martians. Some were honeymooning couples, some businessmen, others elderly tourists, all sorts and conditions of men, but all had some indefinable quality of discipline. They looked like soldiers. And not like soldiers on leave. If he had seen them individually Anton would have paid them no attention, but en masse they seemed to be at parade rest.

Workers cleaned up the blood-soaked sand and replaced it with fresh. The sand regained its immanent purity.

It was then that he saw her. She sat just near the booth of the Justice Officer. He hadn't recognized her at first. She wore her hair pulled back severely, emphasizing her high forehead. Her outfit was a dark dress with padded shoulders that changed her profile. Nevertheless, it was definitely Miriam Kostal.

Anton slid through the crowd and sat down next to her. She glanced up at him, then looked back at the dueling pit. Her knuckles were white on the railing. The next two duelists had emerged onto the sand. One of them, still as expressionless as a statue, was Torstov Plauger.

It wouldn't do to demand an explanation. Anton tried to sit back, but his back and legs were as tight as metal cables. Plauger was slender and muscular, and held his sword with cold command. Martians learned swordplay as soon as they could stand up. The other man had the topknot of a Charlatan. He was heavy but strong muscles played under the apparent softness of his flesh. Plauger whipped his sword through an intricate salute. The other held his sword negligently in his hand and stood watching Plauger. His look of stoic composure struck Anton. He stood like a man who understood what faced him and did not fear it.

A bell sounded and the two men began to circle each other, trading feints and probes. Each of them used what

was obviously his own sword, not the standard-issue
blades that had decided the previous dismal contest.
Plauger's was a Martian saber with a simple hilt. The
Charlatan's resembled a Japanese *katana*, its blade
gleaming with an elaborate crystal structure, its sword
guard a complex knot of metal. Anton longed to get a
closer look at it. Beautiful as it was, the Charlatan obviously knew how to use it. It whispered along Plauger's
blade and bounced off the hilt up at his face. He parried
and stepped back, sweat springing out on his forehead.

Miriam's body trembled, just slightly. He could hear
her hectic breath. The two men moved with such smooth
grace that they might have been performing a dance, feet
stamping and blades ringing. Light flared from their
swords as off ice on distant sun-lit mountains. Muscles
moved under skin, defined by sweat. Their eyes locked
into each other. No one else existed. The two men danced
with their unseen third partner, Death.

Anton tore his eyes away. Graceful and compelling as
it was, the contest on the sand told him nothing. Like
sex without love, the interest of death without meaning
soon palled. The crowd was tense, watchful, professionals witnessing a brilliant performance. He fixed the
faces and postures in his memory. Most of them were
definitely Martians. Others were Charlatans. A few were
ambiguous, from the Technic Alliance or the Belt.

A gasp and a whisper. "Well played," Miriam
breathed. "Damn him." The Charlatan's blade had
sliced across Plauger's forehead. Blood poured down into
his left eye. The Charlatan pressed his attack. Plauger
fell back, jerking his head to clear the blood from his
eye. A shaky leg slid out from under him and he dropped
on one knee.

The Charlatan's blade swung like a scythe. Plauger
tumbled forward. Suddenly the point of his sword darted
up into his opponent's rib cage. The Charlatan hacked
down desperately, cutting across Plauger's neck and
shoulder, but the Martian forced his blade home. They

stood still for a moment, Plauger on one knee looking up, the Charlatan, arched back, supported by the length of steel embedded in his chest like an empty suit of armor on a pole. His eyes glazed and he flopped backward, loose-limbed, and lay bloody in the sand. His right hand still held tight to his sword.

Plauger struggled to his feet. Blood from the cuts on his head, neck, and shoulder sluiced down over his bare torso, ran down his legs in scarlet ribbons, and dripped down onto the sand, leaving a trail as he walked over to the supine corpse of his opponent and saluted him with his sword. Then, calmly, without a glance up at the crowd of Martians, who had greeted his victory with an indrawn breath of appreciation and a respectful silence, he walked with shuddering legs out of the dueling pit.

Miriam took a deep breath. "Come with me, Anton," she said. "We need to talk."

Anton's breath steamed slightly in the sharp cold air of the *Rapier*'s tearoom. He pulled the quilted robe around himself and watched the water rise in the tube of the teamaker. Coals glowed red under the bowl of water ready to boil. Miriam fed the fire with twigs of sandalwood, filling the air with aromatic smoke. The octagonal chamber, its walls hung with blue damask, was dark, and the fire caught the muscles of the silver panther that leaped across her hair.

A sword in a scabbard of dark lacquer with embedded silver crystals rested across Anton's knees. While it was illegal to carry a sword in the passageways of the *Charlotte Amalie*, it would have been impolite not to carry one within the *Rapier*, so she had lent him one.

"I remember this," he said, running his hand across the scabbard's old nicked and scratched surface.

She looked up, her dark agate eyes unreadable. "You learned on that sword, and fought your first duel with it, in Pyramid Square. I thought it would help you."

He held it tightly, with all of its memories, and felt a

mixture of pride and melancholy. In other words, he felt Martian.

When the tea was ready, Miriam poured them each a glass. Anton took a sip of his tea. It was strong and bitter, and its smell and flavor completed the work of the sword. The years dropped away. He sat in a room alone with a woman he had once loved desperately and once again felt an inconvenient surge of lust. He had been young and she had been wise, perhaps not the best combination, but it had changed him forever.

Miriam lowered her eyelashes at him. She now wore a domestic robe of midnight blue, darker than the damask of the walls, so she seemed a deeper shadow in gathering night. They hadn't talked about the duel, and wouldn't, though Plauger now lay somewhere aboard the *Rapier*, badly wounded. The refusal to discuss what everyone knows to be true is the essence of civilized behavior. He rather suspected that they were not going to discuss Martian troops crawling around a space vessel bound for the Neutral Zone either.

He looked at her and imagined another woman, slender, with dark eyes and braided black hair. Vanessa Karageorge was now somewhere aboard the *Charlotte Amalie*. Where was she? How could he find her?

"Have you ever fallen in love with someone you thought could betray you?" Anton asked. "Not personally betray you—that's almost anyone. We are never safe there. I mean betray what you believe in, your House, your profession, your world."

She did not have to think. "No," she said. "I don't think that's possible. That implies an emotional laxness I just cannot accept." She looked levelly at him, realizing that he was not just asking an abstract question.

He wanted to lean on her Martian certainties. "But we can't help falling in love. . . ." He stopped, realizing that he sounded ridiculous. What could he say? Vanessa's loyalties were obscure, and so, for that matter, were Miriam's.

"We can't help defecating either," Miriam said contemptuously. "But we can choose where and when we are going to do it." She softened slightly. "You are from Earth, Anton, but you come from a good family and you lived with us on Mars. You are more than half a Martian."

She slid around the teamaker to him, and rested her head on his shoulder. He stroked her hair. "I know you," she said. "You'll find out soon enough that you cannot love someone who would betray what you believe in, and then you will have to die." She pulled herself against him and drew a shuddering breath.

Questions tried to push past his lips, but he remained silent.

"You talk about trust and honor, but you don't trust me, do you, dear Anton? What are the Martians up to, you ask yourself. What of my Miriam? Why did Torstov fight in that pit?"

"And can you answer these questions for me?"

She tossed her head back. Her eyes glowed with tears. "Who is it that you love, Anton? Who is this woman who would betray you?"

"Her name is Vanessa Karageorge. I can't really say if I—"

She silenced him with a finger on his lips. "Don't tell me. But if you don't know if you love her, then you don't. And if you don't, you cannot trust her." Her tears wet his neck. "I love Torstov. Stupid, you think, I know. A stiff man, honest, honorable, and dull—shh, don't say otherwise, it's not worth your lying. Not much after the youthful ardor of Anton Lindgren, but men have never understood why women loved them."

"Have women understood themselves why they do?"

She almost laughed. "Perhaps not. Does she love you, this beautiful dark woman? You see, I remember her, from Lady Windseth's *vyecher*. I saw her right away."

"She is, I suppose, my type."

"Not your type, Anton. Your individual. I can see.
Does she?"

He scowled. "I think she loves someone else. A Technic, believe it or not."

"I don't. Women never truly love the one before. Ask
any of us and we'll tell you. She was waiting to love
you, then. And you don't trust her because she belongs
to an organization whose interests are not identical to
yours, and to which she owes her loyalty. You *are* a
fool, Anton."

It was absurd, but her words, as aphoristic as ever,
lightened his heart. Comfort, sensible or not, always had
to come from someone else.

"I am, Miriam. Some things never change."

"Some don't. Some do. You, for example." She ran
her hand lightly across his cheekbones. "You are now
awake. And there are now so many decisions, eh? So
much easier to lie in bed and snore. So much safer."

Voices murmured behind the curtains and Kalmbach,
one of her Lieutenants, thrust his head in. "He wants to
talk to you," he said slowly, examining Anton.

Both of them stood. She stroked his arm, her gaze
distant. "Excuse me, Anton. If he is conscious I must
speak with him."

Monboddo sat up in bed as Anton entered his cabin.
He had been lying on his pillow reading Dante, and his
white hair stuck out in all directions.

"Dante was thirty-five when he started to write *The
Divine Comedy*," he said, closing the book and putting
it on his night table. "Young men's thoughts of death
always have a curious, vigorous charm to them, at least
to us who are old. Young men regard death with the
same hot passion they feel toward their lovers. Old men
live with it the same way they live with their wives, on
intimate, not quite respectful terms."

Anton slouched down on the floor against the wall.
"Plauger had a flirtation with death today, in the dueling

pit of Nidus 2, if you want to put it that way. He may yet succumb to its advances.'' He tugged pensively at his beard.

"Ah, yes. Martians have always been death's greatest teases. Death eventually has its way with them all. What happened?''

The walls of Monboddo's cabin were covered with a lightly patterned blue-green fabric. Under his bed Anton could see the elaborately joined rosewood chest that held the traveling treasures: a copy of the 1595 edition of Montaigne's *Essais*, an Egyptian scarab, and Caroline Apthorpe's Blood Bowl. To Anton, Monboddo sometimes seemed like a tortoise that crept along in a shell encrusted with rare jewels.

Anton described the duel to him. Monboddo looked thoughtful. "How did Plauger and this Charlatan manage to offend each other and make arrangements for a duel in less than an hour? They must have had some earlier association.''

"Miriam didn't say.''

"I'm sure she didn't. So the *Charlotte Amalie* is filled with Martians. That should be interesting. I just discovered that it's filled with Technics as well.''

"What do you mean?'' Anton asked.

Monboddo looked sour. "As a gesture of firmness in response to the *Sulawesi* Incident, the Esopus Palace has, more or less at random, declared several hundred Earth-resident Technic citizens persona non grata and ordered them home by next available transportation, that being, of course, the *Charlotte Amalie*. This is the firmness of a pudding covered in hard sauce, an action that benefits no one, but irritates everyone.''

"Lady Windseth predicted that. So do you suppose we'll get to fight the Second Solar War aboard the *Charlotte Amalie*?''

"I'm afraid, Anton, that that's more than likely.''

* * *

"This is intolerable!" de Borgra said in a rage. "Landing privileges denied! Have you ever heard of such a thing?"

Sellering was placid. Her fingernails were pulled back in so far they looked like a child's. "I don't see why you're so surprised. We have been declared persona non grata. Why should they let us off on the Moon? We're still in Union space."

"Yes, but, but—" De Borgra's face turned red. "I have to get down there. I can't stay up here, cooped up in this ship." They sat in the main cabin of their vessel, the *Hans Lesker*, a Ganymedean cruiser. A screen at the end of the fussy, overdecorated room showed a pattern of swirling metallic water. The rest of the crew were prudently going about their duties, letting their superiors argue.

"It looks like you're going to have to."

"After all that trouble I took to get us swept up in the deportation? It's ridiculous." It had been, he had to admit, a masterstroke on his part. Lindgren and Monboddo were going off-planet, in pursuit of . . . whatever it was they were pursuing. Both he and Sellering had become convinced that it was important, even vital, to keep track of them. So de Borgra had used influence and bribery and managed to get them and a half dozen of their agents declared persona non grata by the Esopus Palace, and forced, much against their will, to be put aboard the *Charlotte Amalie* along with their quarry. It pleased de Borgra to have the Gensekretariat itself assist him in his intelligence activities. It was unlikely that anyone would check on the reason for the Technics' presence. Who, after all, bribes people to get himself deported?

"Are you going to try to tell them that you should get special privileges?"

"Dammit, those two are up to something." He hit the table with his fist. "And I have to sit up here, while they do—"

"What, Theo, what? It's the Moon they're going to, to pay a social call. There's nothing for them to do there. And there are enough things aboard the *Charlotte Amalie* to keep us busy."

"Oh, you still think the ship's full of Martian troops mounting an invasion of the Alliance?" De Borgra had settled on a project and found Sellering's insistence on bringing up peripheral or contradictory issues extremely distracting. The Martian troops, if any, were obviously linked with the Monboddo operation. "They're tourists, Tamara. All Terrans are tourists. That's why they've made their whole planet into an amusement park."

"These aren't Terrans, they're Martians." De Borgra tended to the Technic shorthand of calling all members of the Union of States and Nationalities "Terrans," which annoyed her. "The distinction is important."

"Bah. I have other things to worry about."

De Borgra stalked out of the *Hans Lesker*, leaving Sellering to her concerns about Martians. Martians. The woman really did have a way of being distracted by nonessentials.

The current style had altered his long-lapeled red jacket into something stiffer, more formal. Its pattern of lines, starting at the high collar and spiraling down to the long tails, glowed with the fluorescent colors of the visible spectrum, red at his neck, green at his waist, and violet at his knees. He felt pleased, having gotten the stylistic jump on many of the other Technics, who were still wearing last month's dowdy jackets, their lapels flapping ridiculously.

The *Hans Lesker*'s computer had given him an interesting piece of information about the passenger list. Vanessa Karageorge, as an agent of the Academia Sapientiae, had booked an open passage aboard the *Charlotte Amalie*. This fact both dismayed and interested him. Personally, he would have preferred that she vanish from his life without a trace. To de Borgra, a completed love affair was like a completed meal, nothing but pleasant memories and dirty dishes. He preferred to leave and let someone else take care of the cleaning up.

Professionally, however, he needed to keep an eye on her, for she had some connection with Monboddo and Lindgren's interests. It was now professionally that he stalked her. Did she know that their affair was over? Perhaps not. Women often had trouble figuring that sort of thing out, he was never sure why. They held tighter rather than letting go, and squeezed him out between their hands like a wet bar of soap.

She wasn't an agent of the Division of External Security. That seemed clear enough. But what, then, was she after? He toyed with the idea that she was pursuing him across interplanetary space because she loved him and could not be parted from him. Possible. Definitely possible. But unlikely, he concluded reluctantly. When he found her, would she make a scene? Cry, throw things? Beg? He entertained himself with various scenarios as he made his way to her cabin.

Theonave lay naked on the bed and watched Vanessa get dressed. She moved with sharp energy, precise, as always. Too precise, he thought suddenly. After making love she was usually languid and sleepy, like a cat sunning itself. A button on her dress caught on her hair as she pulled it on over her head and she swore under her breath. He admired her body for one last instant before it vanished under the fabric.

She had not been pleased to see him. That hadn't really bothered him, since it had been easy to turn the slight irritation into guilt. Why, after all, should she be angry with him when he was such a charming, innocent man? No reason at all. It had been, after all, an amazing thing that he had been tossed off Earth and suddenly found her aboard the same ship. Fate was on their side. It didn't matter if a woman was quickly or reluctantly persuaded, so long as she was persuaded. But now Vanessa was acting like a man, eager to leave the bed after sex, while he lay alone in the cooling sheets.

The cabin was tiny, undecorated, silent, a storeroom for people. She had not brought any of her own decorations into the cabin, leaving it blank and anonymous. That also was not like her. Vanessa could not move more than an arm's length away from him, but moved as far as she could. She sat down in front of the mirror and started brushing her long dark hair, tangled from the pillow. Her back was rigid. She pulled the brush viciously through her hair. It caught on a knot, and suddenly she was crying, back still straight. Her shoulders shook slightly, and he could see the tears in the mirror. She cried silently. The brush continued its regular motion.

Theonave felt a sharp irritation. It was bad enough that women cried, even when they had a good reason. It was worse when they cried just for the hell of it, usually to reduce their own guilt by washing it in tears, and induce it in someone else. To Theonave, tears were the most frequently used and least effective weapons in a woman's armory.

"What's wrong?" he demanded, his voice harsher than he had intended.

Her shoulders froze, then relaxed again. "Nothing. Just a mood."

He scratched himself languidly and watched her. You knew a lot more about a woman once you'd gotten her to take her clothes off, but now he wasn't sure if he knew what was important about Vanessa Karageorge. "Where will you be going on the Moon?" he asked.

"Oh, I don't know." Her voice was calm, but she didn't turn to look at him. "Here and there. I haven't decided yet." She wiped her eyes and was calm again.

He couldn't imagine that Vanessa had come all the way to the Moon and had not planned her itinerary out well in advance. He could find out where she was going. She would have to take one of the *Charlotte Amalie*'s own shuttles, and the passenger lists would be available.

What was she after down there? Did she know anything about the Union Division of External Security and its search for ngomite, or was she just a coincidence, or window dressing? His inability to find out was galling.

He started to get dressed. "I can't go with you, of course. I'm restricted to the ship while we're in Union space."

"I know."

"What are your plans after the Moon? There are a number of interesting places I can show you, in the Belt and in the Alliance. Isn't it lucky that we ended up here together? When they threw me off the planet without a day's notice, I thought I had lost you forever. It's like a miracle."

"A miracle," she murmured to herself. "Yes. I suppose you could call it that."

He looked at her back. She was locked tighter than a military database, her thoughts hidden under layers of crypto codes. Why? It seemed that making love to her had chilled her. He had felt it even as he lay thrusting on top of her, energetic, yet skilled and patient, as he always was. It had been like drilling through successively denser and more resistant layers of ice on the surface of Ganymede. He had succeeded, finally. He didn't think she had faked her orgasm, and it had been a good one too. So what had happened?

He tugged his jacket on. It was enormously irritating. There had been a power failure in their love somewhere, and no matter how much he twiddled the knobs, nothing happened.

"Dammit," he said. "You Terrans always pretend innocence. You attack us at Europa, steal some damn artwork, and then blame us for searching the *Sulawesi*." He was as angry as he had been the night at the Brasilienne, before his futile journey to Fresh Pond. Sometimes it seemed that all events conspired against him, that the damn Terrans, fussy and aesthetic, would still defeat him. That would be utterly intolerable. He looked at Vanessa, who had listened calmly to his diatribe, and felt like kicking her.

Instead, he kissed the back of her neck and she flinched. "Let's have lunch. I found a good place, just down the corridor." He hadn't, but he was sure there must be one, somewhere.

"I—all right." There was no decent way for her to refuse, and he knew she wouldn't fight, not right now. Eventually, he was certain, she would have to tell him what she knew.

9

From *A Tourist Guide to the Human and Alien Antiquities of Luna*, by Basil Krummorn, New York, 2353:

. . . Siesta Cliff, as it is generally known, is a fairly stiff climb up the rill. Surprisingly, though humanity has been settled on the Moon for only three hundred years, there is some argument about who carved these bounteous yet sullen-looking nymphs out of the soft rock of the bluff. Some say the first explorers found them here. Who knows? It was more likely some artist in the service of one of the Households, which tend to be extravagant. They are very pretty ladies, however you look at them, though they seem to have no idea of how to play the musical instruments they hold in their hands. Sit on one of their laps and enjoy the view out over the Sinus Iridum. If the sun glares in your helmet, sit beneath the violinist, and her outstretched instrument will shade you. . . .

. . . The site of Apollo XI, in the Mare Tranquillitatis, is, of course, the premier historical site on the Moon. Look down at those spidery little contraptions and think about firing off into the unknown on them. Then go have a beer at one of the restaurants I recommend at the end of the chapter. Ramps have been built everywhere to preserve the scene, and you can still look down on the undisturbed footprints of Armstrong and Aldrin, left there as they lumbered around in their primitive spacesuits with Collins circling forlornly overhead, the only men who were not at that moment standing on their native planet. . . .

. . . As to whether the remains near Cap Acherusia can be called "Antiquities" or not is subject to sometimes violent argument. Much of this area is undisturbed, unlike the remains at Clavius, which have been extensively looted. There are curiously shaped chambers and odd metallic extrusions galore in both directions from Cap Acherusia, on the edge of the Mare Serenitatis. Walk around for long enough and pretty soon every twist of the hills and every irregularity in the surface of the ground look like deliberately planned structures. And who's to say that they aren't?

By the following morning the *Charlotte Amalie* was in orbit around the Moon, where she would remain for a week. Private ships and the *Charlotte Amalie*'s own shuttles scattered down like falling leaves to the various Lunar communities with their ancient names: Copernicus, Ptolemy, Alphonsus, Mare Crisium, Endymion, Sacrobosco, Gagarin, Mare Moscoviense, Oppenheimer.

The *Ocean Gypsy* descended to Clavius.

Fell piloted her down. Osbert, having taken the previous evening off, now sat behind Fell, drawn and miserable, which meant that he had had a good time indeed. Anton knew that he would remain alert until he crashed into unconsciousness when his services were no longer required. They lowered themselves slowly on their landing jets, the walls of the crater rising up all around them. The surface of the Moon was always stark white and gray, overhung with a dead black sky, matter reduced to its essentials, the skeleton of the universe made visible.

In Clavius, humanity had imposed its own order. Human inhabited areas looked like translucent ice, tinged with green. They covered the wall and floor of the crater Rutherford, which was inside Clavius, intersecting at one length of their outer walls. The cities of the Moon depended on solar energy, and absorbed as much as they could through the two-week Lunar day.

The *Ocean Gypsy* came to rest in the direct center of the marked circle in the landing area. The circle sank into the ground. The walls of the pit rose up and the opening to the surface closed off. Air rushed in when the elevator halted. The ship now rested in the middle of a large domed space, surrounded by a field of grass and flowers. A flock of yellow butterflies, disturbed by the draft caused by the *Ocean Gypsy*'s entrance, settled back down on the flowers.

A large man in a blue tailcoat emerged from a doorway with several other people. He waved at the ship and yelled something.

"That's Clavius," Monboddo said. "I think he wants us to come out." He fussed with his shoes, and then with the straps on his luggage, as if reluctant to proceed. "There's nothing for it. I must deal with that buffoon for a week." He took a deep breath. "Come along, come along, we don't have all day."

Clavius was a large, beefy man, with a heavy-jowled face and a disconcertingly high forehead. His nose was long and bulbous. He grinned as they approached. "Monboddo!" he bellowed. "It has been too long." He seized Monboddo and hugged him. The tiny Interrogator vanished in Clavius's grasp like a child being misused by an overenthusiastic uncle. Monboddo did not kick or struggle, as this would have been undignified, not to mention useless.

"Delighted to make your acquaintance," Clavius said, pumping Anton's hand, after he had set the flustered Monboddo down. Anton felt like he had grabbed a bunch of bananas. Though Clavius was only a little taller, he was at least twice as wide as the slender Anton Lindgren. Close up, he smelled of some spice not normally used as a personal scent, cinnamon or nutmeg, which irresistibly led Anton to regard him as some giant gingerbread man. Clavius's dark brown eyes examined him closely, recognizing an antagonist. Anton wondered how much of the buffoonish impression was real, and how much was a deliberate screen.

The air around them was heavy with smells, as if they stood in the middle of the jungle. Squeaks and whistles of countless birds filled the air and far above, just beneath the dome, a snowy owl circled slowly. A blue jay with a crested head tried to land on a shoulder of the *Ocean Gypsy*, but could not find a purchase. It spun off the smooth surface twice, then landed on the platform just beneath one of the landing legs and cocked its head up at the ship, as if wondering if it were small and shiny enough to haul back to its nest. Deciding against it, the bird squawked in annoyance and flew off.

"But you must be taken to your rooms!" Clavius said. He always spoke a little too loudly. The dome overhead threw back distorted echoes. "Pick up their bags and let us go."

Three servants in elaborate livery seized the luggage and trotted off. Clavius managed to walk heavily in the weak Lunar gravity, his shoulders hunched over and his head forward. He was like some great bear, bent with age and craft, that could still easily get its head stuck in a beehive while searching for honey. They all spun upward on a spiral escalator, mysterious rooms flashing past too quickly to be examined.

"Here is your floor, the guest floor," Clavius said, stepping off the escalator. They followed him clumsily. "Once you are settled in your rooms, ask anyone you see, and they will guide you to my breakfast. Good-bye! Good-bye!" He waved his arms at them and lumbered down the corridor, vanishing through a round green door in one wall.

Anton's room was a miracle. It was high in a wall of the crater. The two windows on either side of the bed

were of heavy leaded glass, in a Tree of Life motif,
which broke up the stark landscape outside nicely. Lush
green plants grew up the walls and dangled down from
the ceiling. His feet sank into the dense grass of the floor.
The thick gnarled trunk of an orange tree formed the
bed's headboard, shelves and drawers cut into it. Fruit
hung down low over the bed. A tiny hummingbird, no
larger than Anton's thumb, drank nectar from a heavy
blue flower just over the bureau. A stream of clear water
ran through the center of the room. The contrast between
the dense growth within and the bone-white, dead exterior visible through the window was stunning.

Burbling to itself, a quail wandered into the room from
some passage Anton couldn't see, bent over to drink,
tilted its head back, and, finally spotting Anton, waddled
off to hide under the night table. It sat under there, in
the shadow, and waited for him to leave, meanwhile
making so much noise shifting around that it was impossible to ignore. Anton washed up in the bathroom
and chewed a little of the peppermint that grew around
the deep, low-gravity sink.

He sat down on the bed and opened a panel in his
suitcase. It contained two things: Ozaki's hidden notebook, and a curved metallic tusk from an Acherusian
artifact. He held them in his hands and wished Vanessa
could have helped him with these mysterious signposts
on a midnight road. He leafed through the drawings of
the Brethren's monastery, which lay somewhere in Clavius. If all went well, by the time he and Monboddo left,
they would know all that could be known about that
place. He hid his treasures again.

Dressed in a light silk suit, for the air of Clavius was
warm and humid, he headed down to breakfast.

He emerged on the upper level of a large room roofed
with an elaborate trusswork. It, and the heavy stairs along
which he descended to the floor of the Great Hall, were
living wood. No matter how many feet walked up and

down these stairs, they would not wear away, as long as the wood was kept watered and cared for.

Hunting trophies hung on the walls, not so many that they looked like the result of a slaughter, but enough to show the Justice's inclinations. They included a magnificent twenty-four-point head of a red deer stag just over the main door, an impala with its spiraling horns, and a huge boar's head with enormous tusks. The centerpiece was a bizarrely twisted set of stag antlers, officially forty-two-point, which Clavius had taken on one of his hunting trips to Earth, in the deepest reaches of the Bialowieza Forest, a hunting preserve since the sixteenth century. Hunting enthusiasts often came quite a distance out of their way just to look at them.

A collection of hunting spears and halberds hung beneath the trophies. One wall was almost covered with the short, stiff bows characteristic of the Moon, with its low gravity and enclosed spaces.

Clavius sat in a huge, high-backed chair at the head of the table, looking over some documents. He drank beer out of a large tankard. While birds sang and twittered in the trusswork overhead, dogs, retrievers and setters, disported themselves at their master's feet, gnawed on bones, and sniffed each other. Several fluffy cats watched the scene indifferently from various shelves of an almost-empty bookcase along one wall. Birds at one end of the ceiling shrieked as a squirrel with a long bushy tail tried to climb the trusswork. Several blue jays drove it off.

People milled around the Great Hall. No one paid the Terrans any attention whatsoever, except to see what they wanted for breakfast. Fell was already sitting at one of the tables with some pancakes. He ate them quickly, glancing up occasionally, obviously worried that some bird was going to make an unwelcome addition to his syrup before he could finish.

Monboddo was already there, pensively buttering a muffin. Monboddo hated eating breakfast in public. Two broad-chested men with short-cropped hair sat on either side of Clavius, going over the documents with him. They wore the uniforms of Huntmasters, recognizable anywhere in the Union. Anton often envied the Huntmasters their obvious skill and control. As they grew older and more experienced, they could become Wardens and develop a complete and intimate knowledge of the wildlife of several hundred square miles of forest, guiding hunting parties and making sure only animals slated for cull were hunted. Such men often lived in the forest and grew to look like earth gods, bearded and venerable. Clavius's two Huntmasters, however, were young men and, being Lunar dwellers, could only become Wardens of one of the underground Environments, a much more limited and much less mystical thing.

"That is as far as we can go without the city fathers," Clavius said. "It is their city, after all."

"Very well." The two Huntmasters withdrew, taking some of the dogs with them.

Clavius clapped his hands together and the room grew quieter. "Be aware." He pointed at the four Terrans, for Osbert had since joined them and was preparing to eat a soft-boiled egg. "These are our guests, the Lord Monboddo, his Seneschal, Anton Lindgren, and their two associates, who go, it seems, only by the names of Fell"—Fell waved cheerily—"and Osbert." Osbert ignored the commotion and worked intently on his egg, as if it might explode if handled incorrectly. Introductions over, the room grew noisy again.

Someone set a large platter of steamed pork buns in front of Clavius. He picked one up and engulfed it, grinning at them the whole while. "Now," he said before his mouth was empty. "How can I help you boys?" He picked up another bun. One bun, one mouthful.

Monboddo nibbled a bun. "As you know, I am subject to fancies, to strange nervous disorders. An effect of my childhood, which was entirely taken up with darkened rooms and old romances. A traditional upbringing, with the traditional flaws. I long to go on a spiritual retreat."

Bun eaten, he wiped the ends of his fingers with his napkin and made a temple of his fingers, fingertip against delicate fingertip. "I must meditate."

"Eh?" Clavius was taken aback. "A spiritual retreat? Here?" He took the last bun on the plate and was about to eat it, then thought better of it. "Why here? Why not someplace on Earth? The Antarctic, maybe. Nobody there, is there? Good place. Take some good dogs with you. Huskies or malamutes. Maybe samoyeds. Nothing like a good dog to clear out your spiritual problems." He took the bun and held it out at knee level. "Here, Nikita. Here. This is for you." A lanky borzoi trotted up, grabbed the bun, and ran off to eat it at his leisure in the corner. The rest of the dogs looked at him jealously and growled, but dared not express their displeasure at this favoritism any more vehemently with the master present.

"That would simply not be adequate." Monboddo shook his head. "The lonely howl of the wind is not what I seek. I need the memory of other men to keep me company."

"No problem there, what? Memories of other men are all over Earth. Soaked into the soil. Blood, piss, spit. Everything. Churned over with it, I should think. Right? You could sit in your own yard and count the generations, and pick pieces of their bones from between the roots of your daisies."

"That also is not right," Monboddo continued obstinately. "Too general, a hum of distant voices when I want a clear, clean whisper. I understand that there are the ruins of an old religious brotherhood, long gone and forgotten, in Clavius. Is this correct?"

Clavius blew out his cheeks. A dog licked his hand and he patted it absently on the head. "Yes . . ." he said slowly, reluctantly. "There are some rooms dug in the rock, empty of everything. They lived there once, those whatayacallem, those Brethren of the Forgotten Christ. At least I think they lived there. They certainly died there, their coffins are all over, like shoe boxes in a lady's closet. Ugly place. Just as soon meditate in a storage locker down in the air plant, eh? Nothing but dust and bad memories.''

"That is what I am looking for," Monboddo said. "I wish to meditate on the evanescence of human aspirations, the transience of—''

Clavius stared at him. "What? Why do you fuss with things like that? There's a hunt tomorrow, a big one. Stags, boars, rabbits. A real treat, we don't get to do that much. Afterward we meditate on the evanescence of beer and the transience of roasted boar hams. And you want to sneeze in an empty tomb?"

Monboddo looked pious. "Exactly, my dear Clavius. The better time you have, the more effective my meditations will be. Do I have your permission?"

"I guess there's no harm in it." He peered at Monboddo suspiciously, suspecting a trick.

"You are too kind." Monboddo leaned back in his chair, tiny against its vast back.

"Always happy to be of service." Clavius looked up, and, to distract himself from thinking about the decision he had just been forced into, picked a serving man out of the crowd and yelled at him. "Hey, you! Yes, you. Where's Addison?"

Anton's ears perked up, and he leaned forward.

"I don't know, sir."

"He doesn't know. What does he know, then? You! Do you know how to scrub out the main oven in the kitchen, so that we can use it for the feast tomorrow evening?"

"Well, I—''

"So find the idiot, will you! Or you'll spend the night polishing the inside of that oven until it's cleaner than my sword blade, eh?"

The serving man fled.

"Artists and servants. All incompetent dullards, fools, drunkards, and philosophers. Always talking and mess-ing their minds up with things. No bottom to them. No keel. A breeze of the mind and they tip over.'' He slammed his empty tankard down on the table, and it was instantly replaced by another, so that he could not even bellow about poor service. This frustrated him and he drummed his fingers on the table.

A man slouched into view, a strong man with large, powerful hands. His hair was a stubble, quite contrary to style, his narrow chin poorly shaved. His wide, pale blue eyes were as expressionless as marbles. He had a thin, straight mouth, the mouth of a Puritan divine rather than an artist. His rough blue smock was covered with rock dust, two clean circles around his eyes marking goggles. ''Yes?'' he said with the air of a man who had been interrupted while doing something important.

Clavius smiled, trying to be pleasant, though obviously irritated. He had large teeth, like a horse. ''Mr. John Addison, my artist. Meet Lord Monboddo and his Seneschal, Anton Lindgren.''

They shook hands, Addison reluctantly, obviously having no idea of who he was meeting and with no interest in finding out. He did not stand still, but twisted and shifted, like underwater seaweed. With a gesture, Clavius offered him coffee, a piece of cornbread, anything, but Addison just shook his head with one emphatic motion.

''John has been working on a major work for me,'' Clavius said. ''It is—''

''I'd rather not discuss it now,'' Addison said.

Clavius's face flushed, but he forced a smile. ''Ah, yes, of course. Ha ha. Artists, don't you know. Temperamental.''

This last was obviously not a word that appealed to Addison, and he walked away, stepping over the dogs on the floor, to pick a white fluffy cat off the bookshelf. Anton watched him with interest. Artists were not, by tradition, supposed to be borderline lunatics like mathematicians, or sexual perverts like lawyers, but they were by common understanding supposed to be moody and irritated, and Addison fit that model as if he had been practicing for it.

Successful court artists were typically men and women of some social grace, sometimes outrageous flatterers. Even a brilliant artist would starve if he relied on the good taste of the public, so he depended on patrons and governments whose ready wealth derived from taxing that very public that would not buy the artist's work directly. Patrons and governments needed nonaesthetic reasons for giving up money, and that was where the successful artist turned showman.

Clavius, for all his boorishness, was obviously a man who preferred great art to good behavior. He glanced over at Anton and Monboddo from beneath his brows, wondering what to do next. He had wanted to display his pet artist, as if he were one of his dogs or artworks, and this attempt, predictably, had failed. Addison was now wandering around the room with the cat in his arms, petting it and not looking at anything in particular.

Clavius shrugged, embarrassed. "He's been busy, you know. Things for my chapel. Hard work. He's like a child sometimes, you know?"

"Ah, the ways of artists," Monboddo sighed sympathetically.

Anton walked over to Addison, who was standing by the bookshelf looking at one of the few books in it, a heavy volume of differential equations. Anton couldn't tell whether he was actually following the equations or just looking at the complex curves graphed by their solutions. "Mr. Addison," he said.

"What the hell do you want?" Addison said, not looking at him. His face twitched as if he were thinking of putting on a facial expression but was not sure which one.

"I bought one of your works recently, for Lord Monboddo," Anton said, not to be daunted. "*The Hand of Phidias*. Superb. I'm trying to figure out how to light it properly. Texture is really important in that piece.''

"Ah, *Phidias*." Addison's gaze turned inward. "A tough piece. I did it years ago. Garbage, of course. I'm surprised anyone would pay money for it.''

They started walking along the bookshelf together. Anton likewise captured a cat from the bookshelf, a fat black and white one with white paws and a lopsided white splotch on its muzzle that made it look particularly foolish, and began to pet it. It purred loudly. Addison did not seem to object to his presence. "How would you say your work has changed?''

Addison looked at him, then looked away. "I've pushed the surface of the universe back some more. It squeezes in too much. *Phidias* is a wreck, a chewed cracker. I'm stronger now.''

"Have you modified the universe, or your work?''

Addison stopped and glowered at him, suspecting levity. "The work is stronger. The universe is weaker. I keep working on it.'' They reached an arched doorway. Anton prepared to turn around to walk back the other way, but Addison kept going. He glanced over his shoulder at Clavius and put the white cat back on one of the shelves. The cat arched its back elaborately and yawned. "His hunters are here, so the bastard won't miss me. Ah. Lindgren? Right. If you get a chance, come down and see my studio." And with that, he vanished.

Anton turned around. A group of men and women had come into the Great Hall and were gathered around Clavius. They looked like a corporate body of some sort, a board of aldermen, perhaps, or the chiefs of the local board of medical ethics, for they all dressed similarly, in loose dark jackets with wide lapels and trousers with soft boots to mid-calf, and they moved in reference to each other, not simultaneously like a school of fish, but with the symbiosis of effort shown by beavers or wolves. Sober, punctilious men and women, they were anxious to get about their business, and seemed unamused by the disorder of the Clavius ménage, though they were obviously used to it. One of them shook an overly affectionate, boot-biting dog off his leg without even looking at it.

The dishes had been cleared from the large central table and they all gathered around Clavius's end of it, according to some rules of precedence not readily apparent to Anton. Monboddo had left to get ready for his retreat.

Anton slid in next to them. Several of the others glanced up, but since he was not interfering in their arrangement they accepted his presence.

Clavius did something with his hands and a city appeared on the table. It was not an Earth city, with spires and domes, but a Lunar city, all snaking passages alternating with large open areas. Such models were partially holographic image and partially a stimulation of the orientation centers of the brain, so that the complex arrangement was spatially perceptible. So, for a few moments, Anton had a perfect comprehension of the arrangement of the public areas of the city of Rutherford, which occupied the smaller crater within the bowl of Clavius. "Where do you want the procession to run?" Clavius asked.

"It will start here, in the Placeo Cordeño," a man with a soft goatee said. He pointed, and the largest of the open spaces lit up. Then, in succession, he touched a variety of streets and created a circuit that ran back to the main town square.

"Good, good," Clavius said, nodding. "That should give everybody a chance to show off. Now, here are the latest stats from my Huntmasters." He handed out several sheets and the committee examined them. "It's a big one this time, eh? More beasties than you can handle?"

The man with the goatee smiled slightly. "That I would like to see."

"Heh, heh, maybe you will. We'll let them loose at the usual places." His touch lit up five areas in the city, on its outskirts. "The boars will run Corvina Road. It lets them build up some speed. Then, look out! Then we got pronghorn antelopes, klipspringers, gazelles, dibatags, dik-diks, you name it. Fast ones too, we've been training them."

"They had better be faster than last time," a woman with a strong jaw and high cheekbones said. "I killed two oryxes myself."

Clavius looked unimpressed. "Oryxes are very pretty, right? Good horns, white coloring. Look good in a lady's parlor, conversation piece, match the decor. Not sporting animals, though. Don't tell me about oryxes. You kill two pronghorns yourself, you come and tell me. I'll have my taxidermist mount them for you, free, and dinner in the bargain."

The woman smiled slowly. "It's a deal, Lord Justice." She stared at the city, as if already planning where her victory was going to take place.

Hunting was universally believed to be an infallible way of building moral character. It was, demonstrably, the way that Earth was kept a paradise, with its wide forests and flocks of birds, since the general taste for hunting prevented the farmers, those eternal spoilsports of human civilization, from taking over the land, cutting down the trees, slaughtering all the animals, and reducing everything to endless fields of one single crop, the way they had before the wars. Between fish, birds, and animals, wild game made up a substantial fraction of an average person's diet, which now included more species than it had since the invention of settled agriculture.

Clavius and his Huntmasters spent a great deal of time drilling wiliness and cunning into the animals they bred. The city dwellers spent an equal amount of time practicing tossing spears and firing arrows. The hunt would continue for eight hours. Whatever animals were, by exertion and skill, killed during that time were to the honor of Rutherford. Whatever animals, by their own speed and intelligence, evaded the hunters were to the honor of Clavius, and were rewarded and fed when the hunt was over. Thus, honor accrued to all, and there was a feast at the end to celebrate.

10

From *Travels in Luna* by Borchart Wieseltier, Gnomon Press, Geneva, 2348:

Doors. That's all there really is to any city on the Moon, wiggling canyons lined with doors. Some have huge pediments, crouching lions, and stained-glass panels; others are blandly featureless; others bear lists of tenants with their portraits. These doors have only one thing in common: no one, not even their nearest neighbors, has any idea of what lies behind them. The pedimented door belongs to a minor insurance manager, the featureless one to an incomprehensibly wealthy minerals investor, the list of tenants is false, or fifty years out-of-date. I have stepped through such doors, and found an ocean, filled with fish, the only solid spot being the step where you take off your slippers. I've wandered through endless snaking tunnels, almost falling into hundred-meter-deep shafts with pools of quivering mercury on the bottom. I've forced my way into an apartment so jammed with rugs and furniture that when the cat died it took a week to find it.

Moon dwellers aren't interested in the other side of a door, any door. Questions only confuse and irritate them. "Behind that door?" they ask, as if you want to know the number of planets around Aldebaran. "Never really thought about it. Why do you want to know?"

My whole time there, I never knew what wonders lay in the rock beneath my feet, or behind the blank wall to my left. Maybe that's the secret to living on the Moon.

Anton found Monboddo in his own room. Its jungle decor resembled a painting by Henri Rousseau, with Monboddo, reclining on a striped satin couch, his old, dried body dressed in nothing but a loincloth, as an improbable native beauty. He had concealed his long hair in a white turban, though several long wisps stuck out from under it. A large crane walked around behind a stand of marsh grass, stalking the fish that lived in the stream.

"I think that Rabiah umm-Kulthum would be driven mad here," Monboddo said. "To see that pristine sterility outside, and yet be forced to live amid this burgeoning life."

It was true. Anton thought that if it were possible, umm-Kulthum would have breathed vacuum and sat out in the middle of the crater under the stars.

A bird chattered somewhere above them. "I am not so sure I like it myself," Monboddo mused. "It makes me feel redundant. In the presence of so much unself-conscious life, why should I hold on so tenaciously to my own?"

Anton didn't like it when Monboddo talked this way. It seemed to strike at the verities of his own existence. "Because you act on the life around you. Would you feel less redundant loping across the Mare Nubium, raising moon dust?"

"Ludicrous image. No, I'll feel less redundant if I figure something out."

"Sure," Anton said, not looking at Monboddo. "Will you be all right in those caves?"

Monboddo grimaced. "Don't worry about me, Anton. I have been meditating for years. Though, I admit, not usually in a necropolis."

"It's absurd." Lindgren paced back and forth irritably, pulling sharply on his beard. He cursed the necessity of putting his frail lord in a deep cavern alone, but long discussions between them had not resulted in any other solution. Anton had to play front man. "I found out where the entrance to the old chambers of the Dispossessed Brethren of Christ is. It's out in the open, though the citizens of Clavius don't seem to pay much attention to it."

"Let us enjoy ourselves then, each in our own way," Monboddo said, and bounced up off the couch, drifting down slowly in the low gravity. He carried a small bag that contained flatbread and dates, his sustenance for the next few days, as well as a flask of water and several biological torches.

They left the guest area, and the area that could be defined as Clavius's palace, and hopped on a moving walkway. It was matter confined by a field effect, and swirled beneath their feet like cream being mixed into coffee.

The walkway moved through that part of the crater wall of Clavius that was shared by Clavius and Rutherford, and out the other side. Along most of its length it ran along the bottom of a twisting canyon, with cliff dwellings hanging over on either side. It ended in what looked like a large, swirling pool, where its matter was recirculated. This was an older section of town, and the tunnels leading away seemed to be cut more roughly, with many stairs going up and down. Anton consulted his map and they climbed a stairway up a narrow passage.

Lights became sparse. They activated their biological torches and walked for quite a distance through abandoned tunnels. A large gateway carved in the rock finally loomed above them. Anton pulled the loose sheets of Ozaki's notes out of his rucksack and examined the drawing.

"This is it," he said. "We are at the old foundation of the Dispossessed Brethren of Christ." They passed through the gateway.

The first chamber held the monumental arm with the eye in the palm. The arm was powerful, almost oppressive. The muscles stood out in agony. They passed through several other chambers, all empty, and finally into the necropolis. Sarcophagi loomed all around them, with their burdens of realistically carved decaying bodies. When Anton moved his torch, it seemed that they moved in response.

Monboddo picked a spot on the floor, not perceptibly different from any other, and sat down cross-legged. "This is where I will meditate," he said.

The ceiling vaulted high above them, covered with stars. A flaring line grew upward along the curve of the dome, ever brighter, until it shattered the sky, revealing the Eye of God at the apex of the dome, gazing impassively down on both the quick and the dead. Anton wandered around the sarcophagi, each a spectacular, if gruesome, sculpture of a specific individual. The eye of the sculptor had revealed more character in their faces than was usual for dead bodies.

The light that exposed the Eye of God turned out to spring from the folded hands of one of the figures. The figure held something in its hands. Anton stood on tiptoe and peered at it. It was an orrery, a tiny mechanical solar system, its components moving slowly but noticeably. Except—he looked more closely. It was not Earth's Solar System, but instead represented a triple star system, two dwarves close together, with another circling them. Five tiny planets circled the outermost star. Anton had noticed similar hypothetical systems aboard the *Charlotte Amalie*. It was apparently a favorite artistic theme of those who felt imprisoned by the Solar System.

The body's face was curious and quizzical, the face of a man who would examine death with the same attention he gave all other fascinating things. He wore a dark red robe, in tatters, so that his ribs showed through. He lay on a bed of roses, eternal roses of stone. What had he seen in Ozaki's notebooks? Roses . . . and the name Abakumov. A holy man famous among the Brethren. Was this his tomb? There was no name on it.

"Perhaps," Monboddo said, "by meditating upon the Brethren's remains, I can discover what happened to them. You may go now, Seneschal. If I do not reappear in three days, come and look for me."

Anton bowed precisely. "Yes, my lord."

The room was dark blue-green, like an undersea grotto. Julie Skirous, Clavius's innkeeper, sat on the other side of the copper table from Anton with the serenity of an exotic idol. She had a large, hooked nose, and a wide mouth that turned down at the corners. Her eyes were black with kohl. She wore a colored shawl over her long hair and smoked a large water pipe as she and Anton talked. Her fingers were covered with countless rings.

"Understand," she said. "I've been innkeeper here for years. Things happen. You'd be surprised at what happens. The stories . . . I plan to write my memoirs."

"That sounds like an excellent idea," Anton said.

"It *is* an excellent idea. God, what I could tell you. Lara Singletary trained a nightingale to sing if her lover was approaching. Nice trick. If she'd ever switched lovers it would have been a problem, but I guess she was conservative. Her husband caught on, though. No surprise. One night he strangled the lover and the nightingale while Lara waited out in the gardens. She waited, almost sitting on her lover's corpse, and in the morning was accused of the murder. You see? I don't want everyone to know these things. I want to save them for my memoirs. They make my memoirs more *marketable*." Skirous used the ancient twentieth-century term, reserved for scandalous revelations.

"Have no fears on that score. I want the information to use, not to retail. I want what you know about Karl Ozaki, and what you remember about the night he died."

She pursed her lips and took a long draw on her water pipe. The tobacco in it glowed orange in the blue shadows. "Talk about stories. Karl Ozaki. He was a genius, they tell me. I wouldn't know about that. Innkeepers don't know who's a genius. They know who didn't sleep in his or her own bed, and whose sheets are stained. They know who drinks too much, who has trouble sleeping at night, and who's waiting for something . . . they can even often guess what."

"And Ozaki?" Anton prompted.

"Ozaki knew a lot of people. A popular man, as men go, though it was hard to guess why. He was not what you'd call pleasant. Liked to yell at the help, though there's a lot who like to do that. Then there were those that were visiting him. Justices, Bishops, all those long robes and titles, drinking tea out of little cups and 'chatting.' Ridiculous. They weren't talking to him, they were trying to seduce his fingers, get them to carve for them. Too bad for them, those fingers were connected to Ozaki, and he'd just ignore them.

"Once he stayed up in his room for two days, watching an ibis hatch. Or so he said. I don't believe it. Who'd sit and watch a bird get out of an egg? He said it was a miracle. What sort of miracle is that? It happens all the time. Miracles never happen. That's what makes them miracles, isn't it?"

Anton made some sort of affirmative noise.

"That puts me in mind of something that once happened to one of my guests, a priest of the American Apostolic Church, who claimed to have had a visitation from the Archangel Michael in his room. . . ."

Once she had finished the anecdote, Anton got her back on the subject of Karl Ozaki.

"Were you around when he died?"

"I was *around*," she said, "but I didn't *see* it, if that's what you want. Nobody saw it. We all heard the story, of course. It should have been a dark and stormy night, though it wasn't, of course, since this is the Moon. I don't know what he was doing, down there in his studio, all the time. He carved those big-breasted women holding up the ceiling down near the Grand Ballroom. Have you seen them?"

"Not yet."

"Well, go. Tell me if you think that's art. Big droopy boobs and faces all scrunched from holding up the ceiling. Caterpillars, he called them."

"Caryatids."

"Whatever. That's not art, though. Art is supposed to be special, not a bunch of fat bimbos who look like they're working like hell to keep the roof from falling down."

"So he was in his studio . . ." Anton said, trying to get the conversation back on track.

"That's right. He was working on some ridiculous project. A huge pile of those Elder Race-type artifacts lying around, from that old monastery he used to go to, the one out in the abandoned tunnels."

"The Dispossessed Brethren of Christ?"

"They dug out a lot of that old junk. I don't know what they used it for. God. We make enough of our own junk, don't we? And here we go, digging around, pulling out junk someone threw out a million years ago. Ozaki liked all of it, and was trying to stick some of it into his own work. Well, he connected all of it up that night, and it blew up in his face. Not enough left of him to scrape into an envelope and mail home. The whole place shook."

"They never found out what happened?"

She threw her hands up in the air. "The idiot blew himself up. He was doing some explosive metal fusing, or something. He said he expected to get some real dramatic effects with that technique. He was right. Everybody was running around that night, through the halls, out into the garden. A lot of things come out in emergencies like that. We had a lady from Mombasa staying here with her suite, and you should have seen what came out of that room. . . .''

After several more unrelated anecdotes, Anton bid her good-bye, after promising to buy a copy of her book when it came out.

On his way out to the garden he took a detour through the domed space near the Grand Ballroom, just to check out Skirous's aesthetic judgment. The space was circular, with two colonnaded balconies running around it and a high dome. The first balcony was held up by four brawny women with large breasts. Their faces showed effort. None of them were particularly pretty women, but they were strong and willing to work. He was sure none of them would have given up her place even had someone offered.

Ozaki's version was a clever variation on the serene, unstrained caryatids of ancient Greek temples, who looked as if the weight of the architraves on their heads was no more than that of a basket of cloth being carried to market. Pretty nymphs danced above the second balcony, and close examination showed that each of the laboring caryatids was glowering at one of the nymphs. Anton left the hall and went out to the garden.

The domed area between the Justice's palace and Rutherford, the largest open space in the crater, appeared even larger by its careful plantings of trees and hedges, which distracted the eye from looking off into the distance. An optical field effect blurred edges, making it impossible to tell where the dome ended.

Anton came out of the door of the palace, plunged into the underbrush, and was soon hopelessly lost. The paths twisted through dense growth, detouring around huge roots, crossing streams on little bridges, and then immediately returning to the first side. It was densely wet beneath the leaves. The Moon had a limited amount of water, not like Earth with its seas, but a properly managed closed system, like that of a Lunar city, could keep most of its water in the form of life, instead of underground reservoirs.

The side of Clavius's palace that faced the garden resembled a conventional Terran building, with columns, archways, and windows. Anton's only landmark, it soon vanished in the trees. He'd been told, however, that the gardener would be found among the Euphorbia. Knowing nothing about botany, he found this information of little use. He found himself on some more open trails, amid a parkland forest of beech trees, where there were other people strolling, an activity as much practiced on the Moon as on Earth, though here everyone floated more slowly. As he wandered, he kept his eye out for Vanessa. His business had not given him time to hunt her down, but he had checked the shuttle passenger lists and knew that she was somewhere in Clavius. He suspected, somehow, that that was not accidental.

Suddenly a slender, well-dressed man dropped from the trees above. He wore a small hat on the back of his head, which he tipped to Anton before spreading out a cloth and kneeling down on it. He pulled out what looked like a walking cane, twisted its end, and started prodding with it in the roots of a beech tree.

Anton was so startled that instead of a coherent question, he only managed to say, "Euphorbia?"

The man considered this. "No, do you?" He paused to see what reaction his little joke would get, but Anton just stared at him. "Is that your usual greeting? I haven't been keeping up with the social trends from Earth."

"It's a family of plants," Anton answered. "I'm looking for them."

"Ah, a botanical expedition. How educational. Let me educate you. You won't find any family of plants named Euphorbia."

"Oh?" Anton said. "And why not?"

"Euphorbia is a genus. Euphorbiaceae, for example, is a family, the very family, in fact, of which phorbs are a member." He waved his cane up toward a ridge to the left. "The distinction is not all that important in this case. Most of them, family and genus, are desert plants, and you'll find them over there, in the dry zone. Why do you need these plants, may I ask?"

"I don't need them," Anton said. "I need you."

"Ah, I am found out." He pulled his cane out from the roots. It turned out to have the head of a trowel. "Drainage problems," he explained as he stood up. "We have pipes underneath all of this. Sometimes the roots block the openings." He took off his gloves and shook Anton's hand. "Bob Schneider, at your service."

Schneider gestured at a bench underneath some trees nearby. "Shall we sit? You want to talk to me about Karl Ozaki. I have a few moments."

Anton thought a moment. "Julie Skirous told you."

"Of course. She's the only way anyone knows what's going on." He pulled at his hat. "I know I do not look, or act, like a gardener, Mr. Lindgren. A defect I suffer from constantly. Gardeners are supposed to look burly and act as if they did not speak any known human language. The soil should be rubbed into them so thoroughly that it penetrates their pores, making them at one with the substance of the earth. They move slowly and ponderously, like trolls. Then people trust them."

"Don't people trust you?"

"Regrettably, no." They sat down on the bench. "My habit of climbing in trees distresses them. They find it frivolous. Ozaki, you know, did not think much of things that were alive, so I didn't see him often. He liked the products of living things, wood, oils, organic colors, things like that, but not the things that produced them." Schneider was pale, and had light blond, almost white hair. He wore his hat firmly perched on the back of his head, as if it had been nailed on. He drawled his words lazily. "That night, the night he died, there was a lot

going on. It was full of people here. I live here, understand, in the trees, so I see everything."

Anton looked up, trying to spot, for some reason, a
treehouse, or a hammock hanging between two branches.

"If you could see my arboreal arrangements that easily, I would be most unsubtle. But, rest assured, I do
spend most of my night hours up there. I don't like to
leave my park, save for formal functions at which my
presence is required. And the night of Ozaki's death had
no formal ball scheduled."

"So you were up in your trees."

"Make sport of it if you will. I was sitting in the big
chestnut tree. You can't see it from here. If I was on
Earth I would have been watching the Moon. As it was,
I still watched the Moon, though from inside. Just before
the explosion I saw an odd man in the garden. He was
dressed in a long formal kimono and was strutting around
as if he owned the place."

"Do you know who it was?"

"Some relative of Ozaki's, his uncle, I think. A Lord
Fujiwara. Bad timing, I must say, coming to visit your
nephew just before he blows himself to Kingdom
Come."

Anton felt a thrill. This was the first piece of evidence
that confirmed Ozaki's survival after his supposed death.
"Lord Fujiwara," indeed. "Do you know what happened to him?"

"No. He disappeared. Didn't even claim the remains."

"Hmm."

"There's a little memorial to Ozaki now, near his old
studio," Schneider said. "If you take this trail up toward
the Euphorbia, which you really should look at, even if
you're not looking for me, you'll come upon it soon after
you pass them. Addison made it. You know Addison?
He's Clavius's new little artist, making noises and stinks
off in his studio. He'd like to think of himself as Ozaki's
apprentice, though I'm not sure he ever even met the

man. Ozaki loved apprentices, molding the minds of the young, that sort of thing."

The image of Brother Theophanos, kneeling in the courtyard and sobbing, was vivid in front of Anton. His had been a harsh apprenticeship indeed. Anton understood why the Abbot had sent Theophanos to pick grapes. There was something peculiarly relaxing about life molded by man. Perhaps Theophanos could take up gardening.

"I suppose artists would like to be in charge of other artists," Schneider said, "instead of being in the hands of patrons, but things just don't work that way. Don't you suppose that I would like to have my own garden, instead of putting in those ridiculous azalea bushes Clavius is so fond of?"

As Monboddo's Seneschal, Anton had done his share of tyrannizing over artists. He felt a moment's discomfort.

"Pleasant as this break is, I have work to do." Schneider clipped the cane to his belt, like a sword. "If Clavius has a formal affair in your honor, I will be sure to be there. Otherwise, look up!" With one single bound, he was in the beech tree overhead, swinging off, branch to branch, like a spider monkey. The Moon's gravity was only one-sixth Earth's, but it was still an impressive exhibition, particularly for a man wearing such a neatly cut suit. He eventually vanished into the haze of the optical field effect. His hat never left the back of his head.

Dry air met Anton on the other side of the ridge. The plants were twisted and spiky, and twined around each other like most dangerous lovers. Anton kept carefully to the center of the path. At the end of the desert he could vaguely see the dome through the disruption of the optical field. In obedience to Schneider's instructions, Anton turned and proceeded through a wilderness of piled boulders, following the edge of the dome like an ant trapped under an overturned bowl trying to get out. Then, suddenly, he found it.

Ozaki's memorial was nestled in a hollow. Anton stopped above. A small Doric temple, its columns were more slender than they would have been on Earth, a change in proportion natural to the lower gravity. Like all classical temples on Earth, this one had no roof, implying that the natural destiny of a temple was to lie in ruins. Dark metal beams marked the vanished roof line. The memorial glowed from inside. The classical style was nearly three thousand years old and, in the right hands, had still not lost its freshness. To Anton it sometimes seemed that the Greeks had discovered the style, rather than inventing it, as if it was part of the natural order of the universe, like the gravitational constant, or the ratio between a circle's radius and its circumference.

He climbed the three stairs into the memorial. The Moon shone within, as seen from Earth. It did not float in space. Four cloaked figures with muscular arms and legs carried it on two poles, their heads and faces invisible. Anton came closer. The Moon's surface features were wrong, the arrangement of dark maria and mountains completely different from reality. He looked for the Man in the Moon; and saw Karl Ozaki. Once he saw his somber, bearded face in the carved crystal that had looked like the Moon, he could not imagine how he had not seen it at first. Ozaki's swollen head was being carried by the cloaked figures like the Boddhidharma, a figure of Japanese legend, a Buddhist saint who meditated so long and hard that his body withered away and vanished, leaving nothing but the head.

The four carrying figures were carved from wood, the folds of their cloaks modeled precisely. Two were men, two women, but all had strong arms and backs, for they bowed under the great head's weight. He had seen the cloaks they wore, just that morning. They had been worn by some of the decaying bodies of the Dispossessed Brethren of Christ, in the necropolis where he left Monboddo. He went around to the front, to look more closely at the face.

Ozaki even looked somewhat like the Boddhidharma as he was typically portrayed in Japanese art, with large, staring, irritated eyes. While the wooden figures had most likely been carved by Addison, the head itself was a self-portrait, *The Artist as Celestial Body*, or whatever, a typical bit of Ozaki egotism. Anton examined the surface of the portrait carefully. The surface features of the Moon that was Ozaki's head were different from the actual Moon, but there were some correspondences. It was also upside down from the way it was usually seen from Earth, but Anton finally determined that the crater Clavius corresponded to Ozaki's right eye.

On the marble wall at the back bronze letters said: "Karl Ozaki." And underneath: "2277–2338."

He left the memorial and stood on its front steps. Ozaki's studio had been here, and so, presumably, was Addison's. He listened carefully. Earth was quiet, now that airplanes and automobiles no longer roared triumphantly everywhere, but on the Moon noise was easily conducted by rock. After a while Anton heard the clink of metal against stone. He walked toward it.

The clink became louder. A few more steps and he found himself in Addison's studio.

The cluttered studio resembled, as sculptor's studios always had, less a place of artistic creation than a factory. Michelangelo's studio had had forges with bellows pumped by apprentices, large brass hammers, piles of clay and sand, men in leather aprons. Addison's studio had electric forges, grinding wheels, manipulator arms, high-intensity vibrational cutting tools, and a man in a leather apron. Addison stood hunched over a chunk of marble clamped in a vise with a sophisticated three-axis mounting. With all the equipment around him, he worked on the rock with a hammer and chisel. With each blow a tiny shower of chips drifted to the floor. His eyes were intent behind his goggles.

Anton stood and watched him for a long time. He couldn't see what the sculptor was working on, but he knew that the focus was here, in a man changing the universe with the muscles in his hands. Later, after he had changed this piece of universe, it in turn would change those who truly saw it, but here only the artist and the rock existed.

Addison yanked the chisel away as if he had suddenly heard the rock scream with pain. He took several quick steps back. He breathed deeply and straightened up, gasping slightly at the released tension in his back.

"Hello," Anton said. "I hope I'm not late."

Addison lifted his eyes, but it took him a moment to remember to focus them as well. Once he had focused them, he stared dully, not much of an improvement. "I don't remember. . . ." He ran his huge hand over the stubble on his head.

"No reason why you should. Artists never do." He sat down on a stool. "Have a seat," he offered, as if Addison were visiting him rather than the other way around. After a moment's thought Addison sat down, still holding his hammer and chisel, which he crossed in front of himself.

"I was just admiring your memorial to Ozaki," Anton said. "Particularly those monks carrying the head. The pattern of their gowns was interesting. Did you make it up?"

Addison stared at him blankly for a long moment, then finally realized that a response of some type was called for. "No, I didn't make it up," he said. "It's historical. But that wood, did you look at it? It's Indian laurel. Beautiful wood, but a bitch to work with. It's heavy, and the grain gets twisted. Got two huge chunks up from Burma. You should have heard Clavius squeal when he saw the shipping cost."

"And when did Ozaki carve that self-portrait?" Anton asked, taking advantage of Addison's sudden garrulousness.

"Just before he died, I think. I don't know, I wasn't here. I never knew him. I met him once, but he didn't know who I was, and didn't talk to me. There were a lot of other people around. It was some sort of party."

Anton could picture the scene, the sullen but admiring young artist visiting his idol, and the idol, as idols always do, ignoring him. All around were sycophants and merchants of art, drinking wine out of crystal goblets and chattering. Addison had most likely insulted one of them on the way out. And good for him.

"I found the head in his studio, when I came here. It was packed in excelsior, and crated, like he was going to ship it somewhere. The crate wasn't labeled. I found it when I was clearing out his stuff. I think it's one of his most brilliant works. For all I know, it might have been the last thing he ever did." The worshipful tone in his voice was clear. "Ah, did you really like *The Hand of Phidias*? I worked hard on it. Clavius, of course, didn't really appreciate it. Called it 'good journeyman work.'"

"Oh, no," Anton said, though the judgment was not unreasonable. "It's much more than that."

"Sure." Addison ran his hand over his head again, and Anton realized why the sculptor's hair was so close-cropped. The sharp edges of marble dust cut hair off at the roots, slowly, over a period of months. Most sculptors wore hair coverings. They wore face masks as well, to prevent the dust's getting into the lungs, although the famous longevity of sculptors might well have been due to the healthy effects of breathing marble.

"What are you working on now?"

"That? It's a figure of the Repentant Magdalene, for Clavius's chapel." Addison walked over and threw a cover over the rock, without looking at it.

Anton choked on some rock dust and started coughing. "What does she mean to you?" he finally managed to choke out.

"I'm not sure what you mean." Addison finally laid his tools down on a bench. "Beauty and grief. She was a prostitute, Clavius said. Name of Mary. Someone she loved died, and she was sorry.'' He shrugged at Anton's bemused look. ''How should I know who she was? It doesn't make any difference. Grief and beauty. Look.''

He pulled the cloth off the statue. A woman, her hands roughened by years of worthless toil, knelt, looking up. Under her poorly dressed hair her face was strong and beautiful. A whore, she faked emotions daily, but now genuine pain and loss showed through, though she tried to hide them, even from herself. Her shoulders and back were still rough stone. That was all Anton had time to see before the sculptor threw the cloth back over her. Grief and beauty. Theophanos would have hated that statue, for his faith was in the specific Mary from the city of Magdala who witnessed the Resurrection, and Addison did not even know her.

''I hate them like this,'' Addison said. ''Cripples, extra rock all over them like cancer. Sometimes I can't cure them. Sometimes they die. I break them in half and they vanish.'' He frowned. ''Clavius wants them to mean something. What? They just are, that's all. He's driving me crazy.''

Anton squinted at him, and felt the first stirrings of a plan. He and Monboddo were looking for Ozaki, and his ngomite. What would they do when they found him? He had hidden for twenty years. Addison, a young artist of the sort Ozaki had once liked to have as apprentices, could well serve to open that long-locked door.

11

From *Rudolf Hounslow and the Massacre of Syrtis Major*, by Lisa Prophuët-Merino, Ophir, Mars, 2355 (restrained by Division of Internal Security Censorate, released to limited distribution 2358):

The bones of several hundred people still lie in the cold sands of the basin of Syrtis Major where they fell on 3 May 2333. Covered with an invisible protective coating, charge generators keeping sand from covering them, they will remain thus for centuries, a monument to what we fondly think of as a unique and unrepeatable disaster, all of their rib cages, femurs thrusting up, skulls rolled against each other like soccer balls.

Unrepeatable? Unique? As I write these words, Union troops, bloodied by the unexpectedly strong resistance at Astrolabe Bay, are fighting their way through the central highlands of New Guinea, on their way to another unique event: the forcible reduction of an entire continent. Before it is over, the piles of bodies will make Hounslow's efforts seem the pathetic efforts of a schoolboy.

Rudolf Hounslow and Murad Luo are not anomalies. The Union of States and Nationalities, founded at Jakarta in 2225, is not necessarily eternal. Australia cannot possibly maintain independence from the rest of Earth, nullifying the Treaty of Jakarta as it wishes, but if it becomes necessary for Mars to take a separate path, it can and will do so. The fact that this was precisely Rudolf Hounslow's position should not deter us from holding it.

The buzzing alarm brought Anton awake. The dense tangle of branches just above him was heavy with oranges and aromatic with blossoms. Lunar plants knew no season and had been bred to flower and fruit continuously. He switched the alarm off, but a lighter buzzing, like a distant echo, continued. Several large bumblebees climbed in and out of the orange blossoms in search of nectar. They were covered with pollen, and the bright, slanting sunlight from the window showed tiny showers of gold as they left each blossom. Sharing the tree with them was a single brilliant blue hummingbird.

Anton slid out of bed, the grassy floor warm and soft on his feet. He looked out of the window. While inside it was morning, outside it was the very end of the afternoon of the two-week Lunar day. The sun was just above the edge of the crater. Long shadows stretched along its floor.

When he got there, the Great Hall was a madhouse, hunters and spectators fighting for food. Anton seized some bread and several slices from a large wild boar ham, and wolfed them standing. The coffee was bitter and scalding hot, as was proper for any morning expedition.

One of the Huntmasters, a whippet of a man named Leary, found Anton. "You want to hunt boar?" he asked.

"That would be excellent," Anton said.

"Good, we needed a fifth." He marked something off on the clipboard that he held in his hand. "You can meet your companions at the Grafton corner of the Esplanade, after the procession. All right?"

"Who am I meeting?" Anton asked.

"They're techs from the crater industries. One's from antibiotic chromatography. People like that." He disappeared.

"People like that," Anton muttered. "What does that *mean*?"

The armorer's noisy, crowded chambers were near the kennels. Anton could hear the dogs howling in anger and disappointment at being left out of all the fun. He knew that several of the more boisterous citizens of Rutherford had, on more than one occasion, invited Clavius to allow the dogs to join the hunt, not as hunters, but as prey. Clavius never failed to react with an explosion of wrath, largely the reason the invitation was repeatedly made.

"Here," the armorer said, handing Anton a short Lunar bow with an elegant line. "You're going for boar, right?"

"That's the arrangement I made with Huntmaster Leary," Anton answered, wondering how the armorer knew this, since he had only just learned it himself.

"Here's your boar spear." The spear had a heavy, leaf-shaped blade with a crossbar. "Good luck. I have others to take care of." The armorer vanished back into the clamoring crowd.

As was customary in these urban hunts, all of the participants displayed themselves in a circuit march of the city before the start of the hunt. Crowds filled the garlanded balconies overhead in the squares and wide main streets like the Esplanade, the Mercado, Anna Akhmatova Street, and the Avenue Jorge Luis Borges and cheered the participants. Hunting horns brayed in their insistent tones. The rows of spears glittered as the hunters marched. The march also gave the hunters their first opportunity to inspect the changes made to Rutherford, the mazes and tangles that filled the streets, giving the animals a better chance of escape. Anton found himself shouting and cheering with the rest of the marchers.

With one last shout, they reached their mustering point at the center of the Esplanade, in the Placeo Juan Cordeño, and separated to their groups. Anton made his way through the crowds to the Grafton corner, bumping his spear against everyone else's in a sort of anonymous hunter's greeting. The air was full of the sound of metal against metal. He saw his group, finally, in the shadow of a deep doorway. Each held a beer. Two of them were named John, one was Alphonse, and one was something Anton never did manage to hear over the sounds of the crowd. If all of them had been named John it would have been easier.

"The boars are coming down from the upper levels," Anton said. "The release point is along Heller's Way. Which way do the boars normally run? Corvina Road was mentioned."

The question puzzled them. "I saw one on the East Walkway once," one finally said. "Boy, did it look confused, wondering why it was moving when it was standing still."

They looked at one another and shrugged, but seemed unwilling to do anything else.

"This way," Anton said suddenly. Right or wrong, they had to move, otherwise they would be rooted there for the rest of the day. He grabbed their beer cooler and started off.

"Hey, where are you going with that?"

"I'm going to hunt boar. Coming?" Grumbling and grunting, they took up their spears and followed him.

A group of men and women, bows unslung, trotted past, and Anton almost dropped the cooler. At their head, her slender body in a red coverall, her hair tautly bound under a kerchief, ran Vanessa Karageorge. She moved intently, and did not see him.

The group stopped at an intersection, and she spoke briefly to a taller, red-haired woman. Then she turned to the others. "He's in that covert there. If you three split off and go up Kalmyrnia and around, we can flush him.

We'll back up the Rue Professor Bernardo de la Paz.
Go!'' Her voice was crisply efficient, and despite Anton's
frantic gestures, she never noticed him. The three split
off and ran up the small street to the left. Vanessa and
the others whirled and took off in the direction they had
come from.

Anton and his companions turned a corner and found
the street ahead of them blocked by brambles and overturned park benches. With a graceful bound, a magnificent stag cleared the brambles. In the low gravity of the
Moon, it flew like a god, head held high. His companions
shrieked and dove for cover as the stag's hooves hit the
paving with a clatter and it ran up the street and out the
other end. Anton turned and watched it fly out of sight.

"Are you there, Vanessa?" a voice called from the
other side of the brambles.

"No," Anton said. "She's the next street over."

"Damn," the voice said feelingly. "They really set
this place up like a maze. I can't find my way, and I
grew up here. Thanks."

"Good luck."

"You also, stranger."

Anton's companions were climbing back up to their
feet and picking up their spears, looking a trifle sheepish.
"I don't think we're anywhere near where the boars are,"
one of them said. "That's in the other direction. I remember that now. It's farther up, toward the Three Tunnels district, near City Hall."

Anton tried not to let the frustration be heard in his
voice. "We'll go that way." He heard a stealthy rustle,
and paused. Then he saw the boar.

It had pushed its way through the lower part of the
brambles, through some passage not visible to or usable
by humans. It thrust its muzzle, with its large, wickedly
curved tusks, out of the brambles, then saw the humans
awaiting it. "Quick!" Anton said. "There he is. Back
off a little, so that he will come out. When he's out,
close up, in a semicircle, and get your spears down. Here

he comes, here he comes!'' The boar forced its bulk out of the bramble barrier and trotted forward. It was a large one, nearly four feet high at the shoulders. Since boars liked to be grounded, it moved in a crouching posture to keep from floating up with each step in the lunar gravity. Its little red eyes glowed as it saw the men waiting for him.

Anton's companions backed up as directed, and kept backing up. The boar sensed their uncertainty, picked one of them, and charged. Instead of lowering his spear, the boar's target dropped it. The others yelled and ran around frantically, trying to dodge the fast-moving tusker, which was rather enjoying its sport. Before Anton could act, it had actually trapped one of the techs against a doorway and slashed the man with its razor-sharp tusks. The boar threw him aside with a toss of its head. The man floated down to the ground, blood staining the pavement.

"What do we do, what do we do?" his companions yelled, longing for the security of computer screens and spec sheets.

"Close up, damn you all!" Anton yelled.

They tried, in a ragged, undisciplined way, but the boar saw right through their imposture and scattered them again. It then charged toward the wounded man who crawled down the street, leaving a trail of blood, as if wanting to finish him off. Without really thinking about it, Anton poked the boar with his spear and drew blood.

The tusker squealed with rage and charged him with the suddenness of a sprung trap. Anton backed away, but slammed his back painfully into the wall. He bounced forward and lowered the point of his spear. His chest pounded and he could barely breathe. The boar, moving too quickly, impaled itself on the spear, its butt solid against the wall. The crosspiece on the point prevented the spear from going too deeply into the boar to be pulled out.

Anton yanked the spear, almost twisting it from his

grasp, and dodged back. His legs tangled with his spear, and he felt himself capering ridiculously in the low gravity. The urge to turn and run was strong, but he convinced himself that that was more dangerous than standing. The enraged tusker pushed forward again. Blood spurted from its side, floating down with dreamlike slowness. It swayed dizzily.

His hands sweaty on the haft, Anton dropped and thrust the spear into the boar's chest. It wailed with agony and jerked back. He tried to look it in the eyes, but it was no longer interested in him. It took one step and toppled on its side, twitching. The painful laboring of its breath was loud in Anton's ears. It finally lay still. Anton slumped down next to it, gasping.

After a moment he pulled himself to his feet to go and help the wounded man. A Huntmaster appeared, seemingly from nowhere. "That's old Bart!" she exclaimed, looking at the dead boar. "He's a real vet." Her eyes took in the scene. A dark-haired woman with sharp features and blue eyes, she hopped over to the wounded man and knelt down next to him. The man moaned piteously. She clucked her tongue. "Nasty," she said. "Bart always was a vicious mother." She spoke into her wrist. A few seconds later two men with a stretcher appeared, picked the wounded man up, and bundled him away.

"All right." She walked back over to Anton. "A sole, unassisted kill?"

"Well. . . ." He looked over at his companions. Ashamed and embarrassed, they vanished after their wounded friend, dragging their spears behind them. "Yes. I suppose that's what it was."

"Excellent. Congratulations." She tagged the boar's ear. "It will be a while before we can pick this up, and it doesn't look like your buddies want to help you carry it. That's too bad, there's nothing like a good procession of hunters who have killed a boar. You're with Clavius's suite, right?"

"Yes."

"OK, then they can handle it. Good work, Mr. Lindgren." She strode efficiently down the street.

He patted Bart on the back. "Tough luck, old friend." The boar's hair was stiff and prickly. The eyes were glassy and half closed, and blood had bubbled out of the jaw and pooled on the street. Anton wondered, as he often did after a successful hunt, at the urge to take a beautiful moving beast and turn it into a lump of dead meat. It was a moral responsibility to understand the death it took in order to live every day, of course, but understanding necessity was not the same thing as enjoying it. He bent over the boar. It took some effort, but Anton finally managed to lever the boar up far enough in order to pull his spear out. He wiped the blood from the blade, and saluted his antagonist. "We'll have a lot of good dinners out of you," he said, then set off.

In a few minutes he had reached the wide-open Esplanade and the Placeo Juan Cordeño. He turned aside and started climbing up the sides, where narrow, steep stairways led up to the upper balconies.

He climbed until he was sitting just below the monumental head of Juan Cordeño, that twenty-third-century Argentine revolutionary who, defeated on Earth, had played a large part in the foundation of the city of Rutherford. The area under the dome was huge, and the whole place was crowded with spectators, hunters, and their dead prey. He rested his spear against the statue's nose. He was still wearing his bow, unused, slung across his shoulder.

Someone hissed behind him, and he almost fell off Juan's beard. He turned. Sitting next to him, still dressed in his loincloth, was Lord Monboddo.

"How did you get here?" Anton demanded.

Monboddo clucked his tongue. "Anton. The correct greeting is: 'Lord Monboddo! What an unexpected pleasure! What blessed wind blows thee hence?' Or something similar. You have an excellent imagination for that sort of thing. I should not have to prompt you.''

"That's all very well, but how *did* you get here?'' Anton examined the ledges all around. There was no way Monboddo could possibly have crept up to him without his seeing him. Cordeño's head was right at the edge of the dome, with no balconies behind him, staring nobly down at the square that bore his name.

Monboddo chuckled. "The Dispossessed Brethren of Christ brought me here. Have a date.'' Anton accepted one. He was ravenously hungry.

"Do you mean that mystically, or practically?'' Anton asked. He stopped himself from asking for another date.

"Quite practically. They left this crater riddled with tunnels. They haven't been dug into by later generations because they lie in the old section of the city, where there is no longer any volume for digging new tunnels. No one seems particularly concerned by them. You know how effectively Moon dwellers are able to ignore things. In addition, tunnels ahead of an excavation are detectable sonically, and no one likes to dig into an unexpected tunnel that may well be open to vacuum.''

"I thought you were supposed to be meditating, not exploring ancient tunnels in your underwear.''

"You're the one who thought the meditation story up in the first place, Anton. Do you really find yourself so convincing?''

"Maybe I just found *you* convincing.''

"Don't try to flatter me, Anton. The tunnels are not the most interesting thing that I have found. The monastery of the Dispossessed Brethren of Christ is quite large and opens into a variety of caverns of most ancient and undeterminable origin. I believe them to be Acherusian.''

"Hmm,'' Anton mused. "That seems to be a persistent trend.''

"Apropos of that, I found something most remarkable, which you have to see.'' He handed Anton a piece of paper with a tangle of lines on it. "Here is a map of the tunnels around the necropolis."

Anton peered at the dense diagram. "What do you want me to do with this? Make a fair copy with silver ink on parchment and have it illuminated by one of Clavius's artists? It would look nice framed."

"Try, if you will, to distinguish between form and content. I want you to meet me at this intersection here sometime after midnight."

"Not earlier?"

Monboddo chuckled. "You'll want to indulge yourself at Clavius's party tonight. Your absence would be noted. Try not to drink as much as you usually do, and then stumble down to meet me at this intersection. Is that comprehensible?" He peered at Anton. "What are you grinning at?"

"I was just reflecting that I'm not the only one who likes to create mysteries."

"I'm not creating mysteries. I'm maintaining suspense. You'll have to see what I'm talking about." Monboddo looked over the Placeo Juan Cordeño and shook his head. "How enclosed these Moon dwellers are that they have to live and slaughter in the same place." He squinted his eyes and pointed. "Say, Anton, isn't that your friend, the one from the Academia Sapientiae? Yes, I'm sure it's her. Over there, wearing red."

"What?" Anton stood up and looked out over the open space, packed with people. He turned back to Monboddo. "Where—" But Monboddo had vanished, in the same way that he had appeared.

Anton settled back against Juan's lips with a sigh. In the aftermath of his kill, he felt cranky. He looked out over the square. It had been a cruel ploy of Monboddo's, to pretend to see Vanessa simply so that he could disappear in a dramatic manner. Entirely unfair.

Then he saw her. He recognized her less by any physical features than by the graceful sway of her walk. Before he realized what he was doing, Anton had stood up and was climbing down the stairs to the square. He felt more frightened than when he had faced Bart.

So he crossed the blood-spattered square, heart pounding. A bonfire, a rare event on the Moon, burned in the center of the square. The overhead lights had been dimmed to allow the flames to hold sway. A crowd surrounded it. Its dry heat stroked the side of his face.

Vanessa stood to one side, still in her red coverall. She saw him and gasped. Her face was flushed, the way it had been before she chewed the guards out at the Hypostasium, and her black hair was bound loosely, obviously in a hurry. One long lock uncurled down her forehead as she turned toward him.

"Anton!" she said. "You're all right. I saw that boar you killed. They said someone was hurt by him, and he had bloody tusks."

"Someone else," Anton said.

She looked at him for a moment. "You have blood on your legs," she said in a matter-of-fact tone.

He looked down at himself. Indeed, his pants were spattered with drying boar's blood. He looked back up at her. "Did you get your stag?"

Her eyes glowed. "Yes! Did you see us? He was magnificent."

"I saw you." He felt overwhelmingly tired. He felt as if his blood had drained away with Bart's.

"There!" she said, pointing dramatically. The stag, now stone-dead, lay trussed on a rack against the wall, along with a pile of dead gazelles and antelopes. It bore an eighteen-point rack. The rest of her hunting band sat around it, drinking and bandaging damaged limbs. "But it wasn't a sole kill. Not like yours."

"Yours took planning and skill. Mine was an accident." He leaned against the wall. "I have blood all over me. Do you have anywhere I can get cleaned up?"

She looked at him. The time for discussion was past. "I have a room over the Avenue Perelandra. It's not far. There's a good view from the windows." As they walked, Anton finally began to relax the tension he'd been holding in his gut. He hurt. The boar had pounded him against the stone wall, and he'd fallen hard on his knees to give the final death thrust. He suddenly felt old and stiff.

The Avenue Perelandra was a long, wide street that led to the outer edge of Rutherford. It had two long rows of windows on either side, alternating triangular and arched pediments with pilasters, and the perspective ended in an arch at the end. Her room was up two flights of stairs. He leaned his spear against the wall. The rear wall and the ceiling were all vines and leaves, hanging down heavy bunches of grapes. Vanessa stood on tiptoe and pulled one down for them to eat. She looked at him over her shoulder.

Despite the quickness of his decision, the kiss itself was languorous, as befits the first. His left hand slid up her back, feeling each of her vertebrae through the thin coverall. His other hand tangled itself in her hair, so untypically loose, and tilted her head back. Both of her arms curled around his back, and their lips touched slowly, with the certainty that demands no speed. Her lips were cool and tasted of pomegranate, or so Anton imagined.

After a long while he pulled back. She looked up at him, eyes bright, and a smile tugged at the corners of her lips. "Please," she said, like a small child.

Being the polite man that he was, he kissed her again. His fingers explored through her hair, feeling its silkiness. Her heart beat against him.

He turned and poked her in the ribs with his bow. She laughed and pulled back slightly. They looked at each other again. He tugged at his jerkin, which suddenly felt hot and filthy. "I'm sorry," he said. "I'm all sweaty...."

"And bloodstained. Don't be utterly ridiculous." She turned and, with one grand gesture, unmade the bed.

* * *

She nestled her head in the hollow of his neck and ran her hand across the smooth skin of his chest. Her breath was warm on his neck. Her black, curling hair was everywhere.

He rolled over and licked her just behind her ear, tasting salty sweetness. She murmured sleepily and stretched, arching her back, shivering slightly like a cat. He put his hands on her waist, marveling at her suppleness, at the long muscles in her stomach and the upturn of her breasts. Her eyelids fluttered.

Their eyes met, that slightly embarrassed moment when minds confirm what bodies have done. She smiled. One of her front teeth had a chip in it, which he had never noticed before. She took his head with both hands and kissed him, tugging at his beard.

They were both now sitting up in the tangled sheets of the bed. Anton looked down at his jerkin and trousers where they lay on top of Vanessa's red coverall, as if in a pool of blood, and contemplated getting out of bed and putting them on. They were dirty, and now cold, and he dreaded the thought of the white flash of his buttocks as he pulled the trousers on. Putting pants on was an inherently undignified activity and he preferred, whenever possible, to do it with no one watching.

"We should have sent them out to be cleaned," Vanessa said, yawning. "They might have been ready by now."

"Oh? And was that what was on your mind at the time?"

She giggled. "No. That's why I didn't think to do it." She pulled him back down to the bed, surprisingly strong. She snuggled against him and rested her head on his shoulder. He felt a deep peace and contentment, the illusory feeling that all was well in the universe.

"Eek," she said, looking at the clock. "The hunt is over. You have to be places, don't you?"

"I suppose," Anton grumbled. "I wish you didn't have to remember it."

She slipped out of the bed, naked as a goddess. Her body glowed, even in the crisp illumination of the constant Lunar light. She bent over and pulled one grape off the bunch that she had picked and not been allowed to finish eating. She put it slowly into her mouth. Her hair cascaded over her shoulders, and Anton thought she looked entirely too perfect to be real. She smiled at him then, a secret smile, for they shared between them something that no one else in the universe knew.

"I have one of these dreadful cocoonlike Lunar showers," she said. "Room for one, barely. I feel like I'm wrapping myself up for interplanetary transport." She tilted her head and looked at him. "Sorry."

Anton wished they were in his room at Clavius's, with its wide, deep tub. "After you."

She came over to the bed, kissed him, then launched herself into the bathroom with a smooth leap. Anton was impressed. He had yet to adjust that well to Lunar gravity.

After his shower Anton pulled on his stiff, sweaty, bloodstained clothing, wincing with each article, much to Vanessa's delight. She was once again the perfectly coiffed and set-up woman that Anton had first met, though now she looked completely different to him. She remade the bed, stripping the now damp sheets and replacing them with clean ones from the linen closet. When she was finished, it was as pristine as it had been when they walked into the room several hours before.

With a fine sense of ritual Vanessa put on a pot of tea, and, after a moment's thought, pulled out some shortbread.

"I brought this to comfort me on lonely evenings," she said, as she put it out on a plate.

"Don't let me deprive you."

"Can you deprive someone of loneliness? I suppose you can. I find it a fair trade."

Vanessa made the tea with a fine delicacy, using a golden-yellow porcelain teapot. While she did so, Anton came up behind her and kissed the back of her neck. She smiled and leaned back against him.

Finally, no matter how slowly they drank the tea, or nibbled on the shortbread, everything was finished, the dishes were washed up, and everything was as it had been, although completely transformed. They left the room together, Anton, somewhat self-consciously, with his spear, and parted, there on the street below the windows of her room.

They made no engagements or agreements to meet again. He had night business to take care of. She did not ask him about the whereabouts of the Dead Christ, and he did not impart to her his suspicions that she was a spy. They just kissed, gently, and parted.

"My dear Mr. Lindgren," Clavius said, slapping him on the back. "That was great! Killing old Bart yourself." He mimed thrusting a spear. "Beautiful! I am impressed. Do you want his liver? An ancient hunter would have ripped it from his side, bloody, and eaten it then and there."

"I wasn't hungry. Could you have your cook make it into a pâté?"

Clavius roared with laughter. "You shall have it! Blood and liver, to spread on fine white bread. Civilization has its uses. Go forward, you have a place of honor." He hugged Anton to his chest for an instant, then pushed him ahead.

In clean clothes at last, Anton preceded him into the crowded and clamorous Great Hall. He knew the old scoundrel had purposely assigned him to a group of hunters with no chance of success, so that Monboddo's Seneschal would not bring home any honor.

"You owe me one, my lord," Anton said quietly.

"Oh, do I?" Clavius rumbled, his expression challenging.

Anton took a bite of wild boar and met the Justice's eyes. "You do. You know what you tried with me, the trick with the boar, and those idiotic techs. And you know what I want to see."

"I seem to know a great many things," Clavius said, draining an immense goblet of wine. "Things I was not aware that I knew."

"Some of us can only live by forgetting, else we wouldn't be able to sleep at night." It was risky to prod Clavius. The man could break Anton in half with his bare hands, or ruin his career at a distant remove. Anton found himself enjoying the sport.

Clavius hid his anger beneath a laugh. "You are too clever for me, Mr. Lindgren." He squinted at Anton, a much more dangerous opponent than a mere wild boar. "We don't need your subtle Terran ways here. Save it for the ladies."

"I could try to taunt you and claim that the . . . work is not worth seeing. Otherwise you would show it. Would that be too subtle?"

"I know exactly what the work, as you put it, is," Clavius said. "*I know.* You can connoisseur all you want. It won't change what I feel."

"I want to see it." The two men locked eyes for a long moment, not a battle of wills but a recognition of them.

Clavius drank another goblet of wine, slammed it down, and turned away. "Come along then."

Anton stood next to the silent, bulky figure of Clavius and looked around in the half-light at the sculptural group that filled the freezing-cold room.

Human figures loomed on all sides of them. It was a courtroom scene, with a host of prisoners in the dock, and four prosecuting attorneys in military uniforms. It was Tennerman's *The Nuremberg Trial.* The atmosphere was redolent with threat and punishment. Blood spattered the walls, and rents in the plaster showed that they were built of rifles and machine guns stacked like a macabre log cabin. Clavius walked up and sat in an empty space in the dock. He looked down at Anton.

The defendants around Clavius had ripped facades of beaten lead. The faces peeled to show the skull inside. Their bodies were made of barbed wire, of wedding rings, teeth, family pictures torn in half, and severed hands. They stared forward, teeth showing through the torn remnants of their lips. A noose hung around the neck of each, except for one, the one who sat next to Clavius, an immense fat man with a grin on his face. He was solid, unlike the other statues, and coated with hoarfrost, particularly in his eyebrows. Hermann Göring had committed suicide with cyanide, cheating the executioner. So had Abe Tennerman.

"He was a great artist," Clavius said, brushing the frost off Tennerman's eyes. "But what else was he?" He shook his head. "I tried to help him. I help all my artists. But what did I get? A sculptural group that makes me sick just to look at it." He shivered in the cold. "Why do they do this to me, eh? I try. I do my best. My collections are respected. People come to look at them, tell me how good they are. And what do I get? Tennerman kills himself. Ozaki kills himself. And Addison looks like he'd like to."

Anton looked up at the insolently grinning face of the frozen Tennerman. No chance here of a faked death and a mysterious escape. Tennerman's bloated body looked made to be dead.

"Why did he—"

"Why kill himself?" Clavius roared. "How the hell should I know? These artists come here. Why? They wander the old tunnels. What are they after? Are they looking for something? Guarding something? Are they Technic spies? Reincarnations of Acherusians, or Possessed Brethren?" Anton had no answers, and Tennerman just grinned.

"I've thought about thawing him out, just to see his fat bulk rot." Clavius stood up. "But I can't destroy a work of art. Even one as sick as this one. Tennerman put his heart and soul into it."

The work was seen by almost no one, but it served the purpose of its creation. Every time Clavius came to see it, it punished him. But he could not stay away.

"What did you do to him?" Anton asked, pushing.

"It wasn't me," Clavius said. "Tennerman felt that he was in prison. He wanted to fly to the stars, like the red-gowned, rose-scented magician of the stories. But he couldn't. None of us can." He glared at Anton. "Is that, then, my fault?"

"Not at all. When we feel ourselves in prison, we see those nearest us as jailers."

"Let's get out of here," Clavius said. "Tennerman was a genius. He always makes me feel like throwing up."

Anton followed the twists and turns of Monboddo's map. He made several wrong turns but corrected himself each time before becoming hopelessly lost. How many would-be explorers of ancient tunnels had done exactly that, to wander until they died of thirst, or entered an area with inadequate air circulation and suffocated? Anton typically calmed himself with such thoughts when he was in a tight spot.

"Mr. Lindgren!" Monboddo's voice cried from ahead. "Would that you had come sooner. We could have used your help."

"I couldn't come any earlier. I had social obligations."

"Ah, the iron rules of society. Come help us."

Anton came around a corner to find three figures. Osbert and Fell wore gray coveralls rather than the loincloths of meditating pilgrims. Fell lay on the ground, a large gash in his left breast, which bled only slightly, staining the chest of the coverall. Osbert was administering a painkiller. Needles already glittered in the acupuncture points, and Fell's blue eyes were glassy, anesthetized.

Anton ran forward. "What—"

Monboddo gestured down the tunnel. "We were attacked. We gave fair account of ourselves and killed at least one, but his comrades hauled him away."

"Martians?" Anton said, bringing out the most likely hypothesis.

"Perhaps," Monboddo answered, dubious. "They matched your Ida Nastra's description, black uniforms, heavy gloves, bifurcated boots."

"What were they doing down here?" Anton asked. "How did they get here?"

"No idea," Monboddo said. "They were surprised to run into us. We disrupted some plan, and gave them quite a fight. Fortunately, they were more interested in getting out efficiently than in killing us, else they would have."

Anton thought about secret armies wandering around in the tunnels underneath the Moon. Did this sort of thing happen often? Moon dwellers probably didn't care. "They landed in a spacecraft," Anton said. "When we get back out, we can check if the surface defenses detected anything."

"Clavius is not like the Hypostasium exclusion zone," Monboddo pointed out. "Ships land here and take off constantly. Their ship no doubt had some perfectly legitimate mission."

Fell was sleeping peacefully now, the bleeding stopped.

"A clean puncture," Osbert said. "Between the fibers of the pectoralis major, and cut some of the intercostalis interus, but the blade caught on a rib, so there is no lung damage." He sounded perfectly cool, but he held his unconscious friend's hand in his. "God damn! Who were those bastards?"

"We may be forced to ask the Justice of Tharsis that question." Monboddo turned to Anton. "I still have something to show you. It will not take more than a minute. Then we can carry poor Fell up to Clavius's infirmary for further treatment. Is that medically safe, Osbert?''

Anton had never actually seen Osbert look indecisive before. "It's safe enough, but—" Osbert was obviously torn between staying with Fell and protecting Monboddo, his duty. His eyes flicked rapidly back and forth, as if seeking a solution written somewhere on the rock walls around him. He kept one hand on the pommel of his sword.

"You remain here," Monboddo said. Osbert started to protest. "No, I insist. We won't be but a moment."

"If you take longer than five minutes, I'm after you," he muttered.

"Excellent," Monboddo said. He gestured to Anton, and the two of them walked up the passage to the right. They passed through a carved portal into the tunnels cut by the Dispossessed Brethren of Christ. Rooms in this part of the complex had tables and heavy racks on the walls.

Anton shone his lanterns into the rooms they passed. "This looks like a research area of some sort," he said. "Look. Racks for scientific equipment. Data plugs. And these tables." He pushed down on one. A heavy slab of stone on four cylinders, it sank slightly under the pressure. "Vibration isolated. You could do cellular microsurgery on one of these things. I didn't know the Dispossessed Brethren of Christ did scientific research."

"Anton, I didn't think you knew anything whatsoever about the Dispossessed Brethren of Christ."

"I don't, but this just doesn't fit in with the rest of what I don't know."

Monboddo laughed. The tunnel ahead opened out into a large spherical chamber, its polished interior reflecting the light of their lanterns with a smooth sheen. They stood on a narrow bridge. Anton sniffed. The odor of roses filled the air.

"Damn," Monboddo said feelingly. "Damn! That's what they were after. That's what they wanted."

On one side of the sphere was a niche, far from the bridge on which they stood. It was empty, save for a garland of freshly picked red roses, droplets of water still glittering on their satiny petals.

"What was there?" Anton said. "What's missing?"

"It was . . . dammit!" Monboddo looked like he was going to throw a temper tantrum. Anton had never seen him so upset about anything. "It was an artifact, an Acherusian artifact, an obviously constructed object, twisted up, like some sort of exotic musical instrument. It was smoothly complicated, and it filled that niche completely, and now it's gone. Gone! They took it with them. They stabbed poor Fell and they took the artifact with them. Damn them to hell!"

Red roses, their petals fresh. Anton remembered the floor of the hall of Acherusian artifacts in the Hypostasium. An artifact was missing and one wilted rose petal lay on the floor near where it had been. He was seized by a sudden fear. Vanessa had accepted his absence for this evening quite easily. Had she, then, had secret plans of her own?

"What made you think this thing was important?" Anton asked.

Monboddo took a deep breath and let it out slowly. He relaxed, and when he spoke his voice had the same reedy calmness it always did. "I must admit, Anton, that I do not know. When I saw it I knew it for an answer, rather than another question. But I could not reach it. Now it is gone."

Something teased at Anton's memory. An Acherusian artifact sitting in a niche. . . . "Wait, wait." He reached into his rucksack and pulled out Ozaki's notes. He handed Monboddo a glittering piece of curved metal.

"That's it!" Monboddo exclaimed as soon as Anton turned to the page where Ozaki had drawn an elaborate Acherusian object in a niche. "And this tusk could easily have come from it, or something very similar."

"Boaz," Anton said.

"A copper column in Solomon's Temple. The man who married Ruth."

"And the name of that artifact."

When Anton awoke he plucked an orange from the branch above him and ate it without getting out of bed. He thought about eating a second one, but reluctantly concluded that it was time to emerge.

After a long search through the house, he finally found Addison in the infirmary, talking to Fell. Fell sat up in his bed and spoke politely, though it was obvious that he had absolutely no idea to whom he was talking. They had smuggled him in the previous night as a hunting casualty.

Anton pulled Addison aside and convinced him to go for a walk in the park. Addison said good-bye to Fell, who smiled politely and uncomprehendingly in return.

They walked along a ridge covered with young maple trees. One patch of them was bright red. The garden knew no seasons, though each individual tree still did, through an internal clock monitored by the gardener.

"The Magdalene is finished," Addison was saying. "I worked on her all night, and made her." He seemed lighter of heart this morning, so light, in fact, as to be mildly hysterical.

"What are your plans going to be now?" Anton asked.

"Now?" Addison laughed. "You know, I really have no idea. None!"

There was a rustle in the branches above. They were passing through a stand of cherry and crabapple trees that grew along a small pool. Brightly colored carp flashed in the water between the lilies. A dense growth of rushes and irises lay between the path and the water. An unseen water bird rustled the grass. A head poked out between the leaves overhead, a head of blond hair with a hat perched on the back.

"Good morrow, gents!" Schneider caroled, and climbed down to join them. He held a pruning saw in one hand and had a loop of wire, clippers, and pliers hanging from his belt. His suit was even more elegant than the last one. "Why, hello, John!" he said with forced heartiness.

"Hi, Bob," Addison replied coolly, an artificer of rock and metal addressing one of plants.

Schneider waved his saw. "Cherry branches twine beautifully, but they tend to strangle each other and need a lot of guidance. They're a lot like children that way." He giggled, and bowed to Anton. "Well, Mr. Lindgren, I hear you killed a big pig yesterday, and that congratulations are in order."

"You are too kind," Anton said.

"Such is the general consensus. How goes your search for the mysterious Lord Fujiwara?"

"Not well at all. He vanished, as if he had never existed."

"Ah, the fugitive Lord Fujiwara. Maybe he was a delusion. We are all moonstruck here, you know. Strange things happen here on the Moon, Mr. Lindgren. Never forget that." While they talked, Schneider dug in the mud of the pond, rooting up dead rushes and planting several more irises, which he had sitting in a box. He put on gaiters and a leather apron to protect his suit.

"Last night for example," he said. "Lots of odd noises, like the scurrying of large rats. We do have rats on the Moon, Mr. Lindgren. They travel wherever humans go. Of course, the noises I heard might just have been John beating the hell out of some rock to make it another shape. It seemed to come from the direction of his studio."

Addison flushed. "How is that different from beating plants to make them do what *you* want?"

"Thank you, John." Schneider looked pleased. "That's the first time you've put my work on an equal level with yours."

"It's not," Addison said, annoyed at being tricked. "I'm an artist. I create the universe."

Schneider regarded him bleakly and planted one last iris. "You create the universe. And I merely use what the universe has already given me to create beauty." He looked up at the intertwining branches of the cherry trees. "An inferior sort of skill altogether. Well, at last we've found something that you and Clavius agree on."

Addison gasped in exasperation. "It's not the raw materials! We carve our way out of the universe, creating it as we go. It's not enough to just change its arrangement. That's all I'm saying."

"You are imprisoned in a metaphor, John. Carve your way out of that, if you can." He stood up. "Take care, Mr. Lindgren. I doubt I shall see you again."

He tipped his hat and walked off. Addison and Anton watched him cross the field just above the pool. He passed beneath an arching bough of an oak, then jumped into the branches and vanished.

"He thinks he's some sort of forest sprite," Addison said. "He's always trying to sound mystical. Instead, he's just irritating. Anyway, what's this Lord Fujiwara business?"

"Don't tell me you don't know who Lord Fujiwara is," Anton said. "Now that's a rather famous open secret." It is always easier to believe something if one thinks other people already believe it.

"And what is it?"

"Lord Fujiwara, my dear friend, was none other than Karl Ozaki." Anton said it conversationally, as if it wasn't important.

Addison did a double take. "What?"

Anton had been watching him closely. His surprise seemed genuine. It was neither extravagant: "My God! I can't believe it! This is impossible!" nor self-consciously blasé: "My goodness, that *is* a surprise."

"I'm saying that Karl Ozaki faked his death and is still alive."

"You're lying." Addison's ebullient mood had instantly vanished. "What the hell for? It's bullshit."

Anton sighed. "Just think about it for a moment, John. Just for a moment. Say it's true, all of it. Ozaki faked his death and vanished from Clavius. Would it surprise you?"

Addison did think about it. He opened his mouth, then closed it. He smiled slowly and his blue eyes unfocused. "It doesn't surprise me at all. Hell, that's the sort of stunt *I* would have pulled." He looked thoughtful. "Maybe I should. That would be one way out of here."

"It's been done. Think of another way. I might have some suggestions."

"How do you know that's what he did?"

"I got my first hint when I saw a sculpture of a knight's head, in the Musée de Cluny, in Paris. . . ." By making the subtle hints of the style and material of the head from the Russian story of Ruslan and Ludmila the basis of his suspicion, rather than the blatant glory of the Dead Christ, Anton succeeded in making himself sound like a person of extraordinary perception and intelligence. Aesthetics was to him what woodcraft was to Leatherstocking, or detection to Sherlock Holmes. He detailed his suspicions about trade practices in the Asteroid Belt and their indications about Ozaki's possible whereabouts. "So we've decided to find him," he concluded. "Our trip here to Clavius has been extremely helpful, and I would like to thank—"

"I want to go with you!" Addison burst out. "This is perfect!" His good mood was back, as suddenly as it had left. "Fate. Destiny. The singing revolution of the spheres. You must take me with you when you go. I can escape! Escape from all of it. All!"

Anton raised his eyebrows. He'd always wanted to be able to raise only one, but had been unable to learn how. "Why should we? It would put us in a delicate situation, you realize."

"You can't do this yourself. Impossible. You'll never

find him. You need me to help you. I've studied him for years, I know things about him that his own mother doesn't know!'' He jumped high into the air and floated down in the low gravity, kicking his heels and humming to himself. He settled down on the wet grass. He didn't notice.

Slowly and reluctantly Anton allowed himself to be convinced that Addison should go along with them.

They left the Moon three days later, the atmosphere at their departure noticeably less cordial than it had been when they arrived. They carried their own luggage. He was waiting for them, Monboddo, Anton, Fell, Osbert, and Addison, when they emerged into the central grassy area where the *Ocean Gypsy* stood. He stood, arms loose at his sides, as woebegone as a child who has lost a favorite toy.

"Mr. Lindgren," Clavius said. "I've had Bart's head mounted for you. That's all right? Pity to waste those tusks, that head. He was mean. Cleaned him up, polished his teeth. Meat's in your freezer, eh? Didn't have a chance to smoke any of it.''

"Thank you very much, Justice," Anton said. "It was an honor to participate in your hunt.''

Clavius glowered at him. "I knew what quarry you were after. Plugged him sitting, no chance for me at all. No chance.''

"My dear Clavius," Monboddo interrupted gently. He was dressed properly again, in traveling clothes, trimmed with lace. "You must understand, it was—''

"Stop it, stop it all of you!'' Clavius said savagely. His face was red, and his voice quavered. "To hurt politely is a damn courtier's trick. I hunt and keep a comfortable house and for that you think I'm a fool, eh? Old Clavius, with blood on his boots, doesn't know what to do with an artist. Loses them all the time, you see. His great collection? His art? Must be a mistake. Him with his dogs. What could he know about art? Ah." He shook his head.

Addison looked stricken. The past few days had been agony for him, and this final scene was something he had hoped that he could avoid.

"Ah, Johnny. You know better than that, don't you? I appreciated you."

"You did." Addison couldn't meet his old patron's eyes. "I'm sorry."

Clavius seemed close to tears. He shook his heavy head from side to side. "I'll clean up your studio. I'm old now, and tired. Three of you artists is enough for me. I'll leave it for the dust and the ghosts. Let it look like those tunnels of the Brothers, with their corpse statues."

"Don't forget the Repentant Magdalene," Addison said, as if worried that Clavius was accusing him of not having done a proper job.

"You finished it, then? Good boy. I've never gone to see it, you know. Always respect an artist's privacy. Always. No matter what kind of schemes he might be hatching." He slapped Addison on the shoulder and walked past him. "Go then, all of you. And be damned to you." He didn't stop to see them get into their ship, but went out through one of the doors and vanished.

Anton felt like joining Clavius in his tears.

"Don't look so surprised, Anton," Monboddo said. "Victory is never purchased but by the common coin of pain. Someone else's or your own."

12

From *Eddies in the Matter Flow: A Guide to the Neutral Zone*, by Nguyen and Castlereagh:

. . . Of course Boscobel is the Belt's main source of null-g and crystallized high-pressure wood, but that is not why it is worth going there. Wood, no matter how fine, is, when all is said and done, wood, but an asteroid filled with immense free-fall trees, their branches spreading in all directions, inhabited by all manners of birds and a particular species of nocturnal hunting cat with orange fur, is something else again. It is said that if the trees were not harvested and trimmed regularly, they would rip the asteroid apart with the force of their growth. Be careful on a visit, the cats bounce like rubber balls with teeth. . . .

. . . All of them have adapted so that they never have to come to the surface at all, both humans and dolphins with artificial gills. Their lungs have atrophied, giving the humans, particularly, a sunken-chested appearance. So be warned, there is very little air to breathe on Dewdrop, just a few hollows here and there for maintenance equipment and activities like spraying corrosion-resistant coatings. The rest of the planetoid is simply a honeycomb of water-filled tunnels, swirling with plants and the strange civilization of those dolphins and humans who are willing to live like this, not the sanest portion of either species. . . .

. . . On Thule, the skaters' legs are as big around as a normal man's waist, while their arms tend to be smaller than average, giving them the appearance of *Tyrannosaurus rex*. Some of them have been clocked at two hundred kilometers per hour on the immense loop of Grevy's Leap. The ice in the tunnels is carefully groomed by a race of helots, virtual slaves, whose only task is to make sure that their masters can indulge in endless skating races. Thule takes the sporting goals of a rural aristocracy to a ludicrous extreme. Picture it: an asteroid with a hundred-mile diameter, entirely filled with great looping tunnels, lined with ice. The Thuleans skate fast enough to cling to the ice's surface by centrifugal force, for there is no gravity. Those areas of the asteroid where food is grown and essential manufactures are performed are by far its lesser part. If you wish to skate, we advise choosing a small pond on Earth. Skating on Thule, with its yard-long, razor-sharp skates, its high speeds, and its dozens of deaths a year, is not recommended unless you have been bred to it from birth, and probably not even then. . . .

Anton was working on an article for *Eclipse* magazine on the so-called Northern Lakes school of landscape painters, a group that had included the incomparable Tarant Hornsby. Actually, "working" was a word he used as charity to himself, since he spent most of the time lying in his cabin idly leafing through volumes of reproductions of paintings, now pausing at one of ice floating in Lake Superior, or sunken coal barges in the shallows of Lake Erie, or the tree-covered sand dunes of the Michigan shore. The Northern Lakes painters had done their work about a century and a half before, around the turn of the twenty-third century, and their work had an underlying melancholy that pleased Anton. Melancholy was a way of feeling sad without being self-pitying, and Anton wanted to manage the emotion a little better. As an initial project, he tried to get over the fact that he was worried about the thinning of his hair. His inability to do so depressed him.

Not that there was any shortage of things to feel melancholy about. Torstov Plauger was dead, of wounds suffered in his duel. Anton and Monboddo had received a terse announcement from the *Rapier* that morning, no details, just the bare fact. Plauger's wounds, though serious, had been easily treatable. Had the Martians refused him treatment? Or had he refused it on his own behalf? Or was the cause of death something completely different? Anton had some guesses but wanted confirmation. He hoped the funeral would provide them.

The funeral was that afternoon. Anton had pulled out the appropriate mourning garments, and had brushed and smoothed them. They lay on his bed like pools of spilled ink.

Objects brought together by chance wove their net around him. Gensek Timofey frowned down from his cabinet, a disapproving older brother. Ozaki's secret notebook lay open to the drawing of Boaz, with its doodled roses and reference to Abakumov, and on top of Boaz lay the curved tusk broken from the artifact in the Hypostasium. The Dead Christ itself was still serenely uncommunicative, but seemed to have conjured these other Acherusian symbols to speak for it.

Finally, Caroline Apthorpe's Blood Bowl stood on the other side of the room. Anton had pulled it out of Monboddo's rosewood chest to keep himself company, for the elegant wide bowl on its pedestal seemed like an old friend. He occasionally touched it, wondering.

Fell interrupted him by coming in with a complaint.

It was, of course, Addison. Fell and Osbert kept an eye on him alternately, and it was wearing on them.

"He's difficult," Fell said. "He gambles in Nidus 2, and gets drunk and expects me to carry him back. He

gets into arguments with strangers. Then he gets all
weepy and wants to be my friend. He apologizes for
things he's done to me, though I don't know what he's
talking about. He keeps asking me if he's made the right
decision. He talks to me about Karl Ozaki. Then he tries
to get away from me and hide in one of the equipment
closets. It's not hard to find him. He collects a lot of
garbage, old ventilator grilles and door latches and stuff
like that and squirrels it away. He's an idiot.''

"He's an artist." Anton shrugged.

Fell stared at him uncomprehendingly. "So? I'm a
bodyguard, you're a Seneschal. Do we act like that?''

"No."

"So why should he?" Fell sighed. "Is he joining the
Household?''

"No, Fell, he is not," Anton said.

"All right," Fell said. "Because Osbert's ready to
kill him.''

"Tell him not to.''

"Yeah. But Addison's an odd duck, that's for sure.
Like yesterday. He pulled all that junk he's been saving
and made a sculpture out of it, right in the middle of a
hallway in Nidus 2. He called it *The Duelist*. It was
something, I have to admit. It was just bent-up pieces
of water conduit, things like that, but it looked like real
muscles, arms, legs, back. Everything. The face was
mean, and had big shiny teeth, and the whole thing was
covered with razor edges. You couldn't get past it without
slicing yourself up, and they had a hell of a time moving
it. Now it's got dried blood all over it, which he says is
part of the conception. I don't know about that. I don't
even know how he managed to put it together without
killing himself. He did cut himself up a little.''

"Did they destroy it?" Anton said. A work of art he
had never seen, destroyed by justifiably irritated people:
that would be a tragedy.

"Oh, no. They liked it, but then these Charlatans are

as odd as he is. They finally managed to haul it off and set it up in a public place.''

''Where?''

''Near the dueling pits, where else? It's right next to the judge's box. There was talk about putting it right in the pit, so that whoever was dueling would have to dodge around it and get sliced up, but they decided that it would interfere with the sight lines for the audience.''

''A wise decision,'' Anton said, resolving to see the statue at the first opportunity. It would have to be after the funeral.

''Like I said, they're as crazy as he is. After he was done with it, he got really drunk. He puked all over—''

''I get the picture.''

''He'd eaten something with lots of peppers and to-matoes in it, so it was real colorful. He's an artist, like you said.''

''I said all right, Fell.''

Fell stretched back, then winced. The wound in his chest had not quite yet healed. ''Sure thing. Well, I have to get back to watching him. Osbert's time is almost up.''

''Thank you, Fell.''

The walls of the octagonal tearoom aboard the *Rapier* had been hung with heavy black cloth. Its shiny surface reflected the lights of the candles around the coffin. Tor-stov Plauger's body, in uniform with sword, lay in the open coffin, frowning slightly, as if in concentration. His wounds were bound with red. Anton Lindgren looked down at him. Plauger had always been a difficult man to deal with, opaque and unreadable, and he was not any more comprehensible in death.

Miriam Kostal wore her widow's weeds, a darkly el-egant outfit with long sleeves and a hood. She looked up and met Anton's eyes. Her skin was tight over the prominent bones of her face, and her brown-green agate eyes looked full, not of grief, but of rage. She turned her head away. She would have a chance to use that rage later, Anton thought.

There were six other people in the room, Lord Monboddo, Osbert, and four members of the Martian suite: Trifon, who had been Plauger's aide-de-camp, Song, Kalmbach, and Father Luvaas, an ordained priest of the Apostolic Church of Mars. Fell was absent, still recovering from his wounds. All wore the obsolete clothing, completely black with long sleeves and many buttons, popular during the reign of the Genseka Agapia a century before, which now served as mourning garb.

The text was ancient and traditional, from Job:

"Man that is born of a woman has but a short time to live and is full of misery. He comes forth like a flower, and withers. He flees like a shadow and never continues in one stay."

Miriam laid her hand on Plauger's forehead. Her eyes were bright with tears. The body was then taken to the *Rapier*'s airlock and launched on a trajectory perpendicular to the *Charlotte Amalie*'s.

The coffin was dismantled and returned to storage. The participants sat down in the dark-hung room for a meal of leeks in a sauce of bitter herbs and salt, washed down with cold water. No one recalled amusing incidents involving Plauger, or clever things that he had said, traditional at such dinners. Instead, the participants made observations about devotion to duty and sober virtue. Anton felt as if they had just fired off a plaster statue rather than a once-living man.

He took another bite of the dark leek stew, which he was beginning to fancy tasted like bile. His heart was pounding in anticipation of the coming hinge point. He knew that he might not leave the room alive.

A Martian messenger slid in, as dark and silent as a deep-sea fish. He murmured something in Trifon's ear, who, with a muttered oath, excused himself and left the chamber, accompanied by Song. The bustle of their departure disturbed the mood, already on the verge of dissipating.

As Kostal put the candles out they heard a thump in the hallway outside the *Rapier*. She ignored it, snuffing the wicks between thumb and forefinger with a savage gesture. She had tossed her hood back. The room grew darker. Monboddo raised his eyebrows at Anton, who slid over to sit next to Father Luvaas. The priest was moodily fiddling with his pectoral cross and staring off into space. Anton caught the fabric covering of the tea table under his boot, and fell over onto Luvaas.

"I'm sorry," he hissed in embarrassment. In struggling to stand up, his left knee somehow pinned Luvaas's sword hand. "These long robes . . . I'm so clumsy." Meanwhile, Osbert slid over next to Kalmbach. Monboddo blew the last two candles out, and the room went dark. There was a moment of silence, long enough for an intake of breath preparatory to violent action.

"That should be it," Monboddo said softly. The light of a glow globe in his hand suddenly illuminated the scene: Anton, sword out, leaning on Luvaas, Osbert behind Kalmbach, ready to strike, and Monboddo standing casually near Kostal. "That's enough, Fell," he said in a louder voice. "Please let Trifon and Song back in here. It is time to talk."

Trifon and Song stumbled in, their hands taped behind them, adhesive patches over their mouths. Fell came after, his sword in his hand. He stripped the tape from Trifon's mouth.

"This is an outrage!" Trifon said. His hair was wild, his cheek bruised. "I went through the airlock and this man jumped us—"

"Both of us," Song amplified glumly. "And bound and gagged us."

"It was an ambush," Trifon said. He glared at Monboddo from beneath his heavy brows. "I demand—"

"Demand nothing, Mr. Trifon. Please sit down, I have information to impart to you. Mr. Lindgren. Let Father

Luvaas up. He looks most uncomfortable." Luvaas twisted out from underneath Anton.

Kalmbach, silent the whole time, rolled his eyes at Osbert as if thinking of jumping him. Though the Martian was a huge man, larger than the Terran, Osbert winked and gave him a little push. Kalmbach stumbled forward and almost fell to his knees. "You've been a good boy so far," Osbert said. "Let's not ruin a beautiful relationship. Sit."

"Lord Monboddo." Miriam Kostal's voice was silky and dangerous. "What is the meaning of this farce?" She had not moved from where she stood.

Monboddo glared at her. "A farce, Justice? Not at all. An earnest of our seriousness."

"An earnest?" Her face started to flush. Her voice quivered with rage. "You come here, to my friend's funeral, to make political demonstrations?"

"Political demonstrations!" Monboddo snorted. "War is a political demonstration. So is murder." He stood motionless, his hands at his sides, as if in court. His blue eyes pierced each person he stared at in turn. "A demonstration? I and my men can now annihilate the entire command structure of the Martian Omega Squads illegally aboard the *Charlotte Amalie*, leaving your troops headless. Is that enough of a demonstration for you?" His eyes glittered dangerously. This was no longer the delightful, eccentric, slightly laughable figure of Lord Monboddo, art collector and bon vivant. This was the Interrogator.

Father Luvaas tugged at his pectoral cross for comfort. Anton noticed that it had sharp pointed ends and could be used as a weapon, not too surprising for a Martian priest. He rested the edge of his sword against Luvaas's throat and ripped the cross from his neck.

"It wouldn't make a difference," Kostal said proudly. "They will continue."

"Will they?" Monboddo chuckled. "I'm actually quite certain, Justice, that they don't even know what their mission is." Her face was carefully expressionless, but he shook his head at her. "Technic troops will wipe them up like spilled beer. Particularly if the government of the Union of States and Nationalities gives official warning to the Technic Alliance of an approaching bandit attack."

"Shit!" said the Justice. "I'm just backing you up, Colonel Westerkamp, you know that." Her tone was bitter, but she had conceded, at least momentarily. "We're assisting your mission."

"Stop it, Miriam," Anton murmured. She looked at him. "You have your own goals, whatever they are. You've been lying to me. Tell us now. Tell us why you want to dishonor yourself, and start the Second Solar War."

She took a step toward him. Monboddo's sword hissed out and touched her on the back of the neck. "Please, Justice. He can hear you perfectly well from where you stand."

"Last time we talked you brought up the questions I should ask you, Miriam," Anton said. "But then you refused to answer them. You were false." He felt bitter. They had known each other for fifteen years, had slept together, hunted together, spent long afternoons sipping tea and discussing the necessities of existence, but he realized that he still did not know her.

She smiled, just the points of her canines showing. "You wanted to talk about love. Men are always talking about something else when they're talking about love. You *are* clever, Anton." Her eyes showed honest admiration. "How did you know you could get us all in one place?"

"I knew Torstov Plauger would die," Anton whispered. "I knew that you had to order him to kill himself. He exposed you."

Her eyes widened, and she nodded to herself. "Everything comes from that. He was a damned fool, that one. Honorable, brave. And he's destroyed us."

"We'll listen," Anton said. "Tell us."

"Wait a minute," Trifon exclaimed. "What's going on here?" He looked at Kostal. "These men—"

"These men are our allies and friends," Kostal said firmly. She looked at Monboddo and Anton. "Our mistake was in forgetting that. Our operations will continue only on their sufferance. Is that adequate, Lord Monboddo?"

Monboddo inclined his head. "You are most gracious, Justice." He sheathed his sword, the cloak of the Interrogator fell away, and he was himself again.

In a practical sense, the game could continue, if the Justice of Tharsis wished. In a moral sense, it was over. She had conceded. Monboddo and Anton knew they could trust her word.

"But . . . but. . . ." Trifon's face began to turn red. "This is outrageous!"

"A consequence of dealing with Lord Monboddo," Kostal said wearily. "You are so slow sometimes, Albert. Do be silent." She turned back. "Three months ago an invading force hit our facilities at Hecates Tholus, in the Elysium Planitia. They came down through our defensive screen. A complete surprise. There was a fire-fight."

"What facilities?" Anton asked.

She shrugged. "Nothing important. That's what's confusing. A refueling site. A water mine. Some mineral extraction plants. Nothing, really. It's a small city. The only interesting thing about Hecates Tholus is the old archaeological museum, for Christ's sake. If we hadn't had a brigade of troops on exercise, they would have been in and out clean. As it was, they lost ten men. They took the bodies with them." She paused. "We lost eighteen."

Monboddo sucked in a breath. For Martians to come up on the losing end of such an engagement was something. No wonder the Martians had reacted: in addition to being enraged, they were feeling embarrassed. Martians in that state were not pleasant to tangle with.

Anton felt the back of his neck prickle. He remembered the maps he had seen at the Hypostasium. "Hecates Tholus was the site of a monastery of the Dispossessed Brethren of Christ, wasn't it?"

Kostal frowned. "Yes. The place was full of their junk, and their excavations of the Acherusian remains in all of the Elysium Planitia. It was a big museum."

"Anything missing after the attack?" Anton said.

"That's hard to say. Several things, including one large work, were missing, but it is unknown whether they were taken or destroyed. One thing that is true is that the object that went missing contained a large amount of ngomite. It had always been particularly well guarded for that reason."

"It had a name," Song said somberly. "Aaron's Rod."

Anton held his breath. An Acherusian artifact in the Moon named Boaz, one named Aaron's Rod on Mars, and one in the Hypostasium on Earth, all associated with the Dispossessed Brethren of Christ, and all collected, by someone, during the past few months. He felt that he was looking at the solution, though he couldn't see it yet, like noticing that what he'd thought was a tree branch was actually the antler of the deer he was hunting, concealed by brush. He had to raise his bow slowly.

It was interesting, though. Mars had been hit by a military assault, but had not informed the Union government, a sign of dangerously growing independence.

"Did you hit the Hypostasium two weeks ago?" Anton asked.

"What are you talking about?" Kostal asked, outraged. "That's on Earth."

"And did you penetrate the tunnels under Clavius two nights ago?"

She laughed. "Oh, God, Anton, you've fooled me. I thought you knew everything, and here I found out that you don't know anything at all. *They* hit those places, not us. You two think you can pull eighteen kilograms of ngomite on your own. You can't. You need our help. Otherwise, the Technics will squash you."

"The Technics?" Monboddo interrupted with gentle irony. "My dear Miriam, whatever makes you think that those troops who hit Hecates Tholus were Technics?"

"Torstov was at Hecates Tholus," Miriam said. "He recognized one of the men he fought, here, aboard the *Charlotte Amalie*. He challenged him to a duel."

"And killed him." Anton was disgusted. He remembered the oddly confident man facing Plauger with a *katana* in his hand. Who had he been? He could have been captured, questioned. Instead he was dead.

"Torstov let his personal hatred endanger our mission." Miriam's voice was musing. "He was always like that. Direct and clean. Complex things didn't interest him. He figured that if they were important, they would be simple."

The tearoom was stripped and empty. Everyone else had gone. The two of them lay huddled on a couch, their mourning clothes at their feet. She held on to him tightly. Her hip pushed against his groin. She breathed shallowly and quickly.

"He lay down on a plastic sheet. I kissed him goodbye, and he killed himself with his own sword. He begged my forgiveness as he died." Her body was wracked with sobs. "You know me, Anton. You predicted it. I had to do it. Just as you had to threaten to kill us."

"More than just threaten." Her fingernails pressed lightly on the back of his neck, the palms of her hands on his jawline. She kept her face down as she cried.

"You would have killed us, I know. Our men would have killed you, but that would have been the end of it. The end of everything. You are insane. How could you do that?" She slid the inside of her thigh along his legs. Her body was warm under his hands, just as it always had been.

"What else could we do?"

His heart pounded in his ears. It had been years since he'd made love to her, since he'd felt her nails on his back. He wanted to. Plauger was gone, she was in his arms, and he wanted to. He hadn't stayed with her to get more information. He had stayed because he wanted her.

Her tears wet the front of his shirt. "Anton. Where have we gone in these years?"

She turned her face up to him and he kissed her, tasting the salt of her tears on her lips. He looked into her eyes. "Miriam. What am I to you?"

She looked at him for a moment, then twisted her hips away from him. "Damn you, Anton. Once again, you've let yourself think too much."

He sat up, dizzy, and put his arm around her waist. Had she really wanted him, or had it been just a ploy, an attempt to forge an alliance on a more ancient level? She leaned back against him. It would have been nice to comfort her in bed, then lie and talk, as they had in older times. He breathed a long sigh.

"You're a bastard, Anton. You come here, interrupt the funeral of my lover, threaten me, extort my secrets, and now you'll make love to me, thinking the whole while that I'm trying to manipulate you. Damn you!"

"And is that suspicion entirely unreasonable?" He took her hand. "Is it?"

"Reason, Anton? Still?" She jerked her hand away. "You should think more about your manners. My lover's dead. You should have given me comfort, and worried about your damn suspicions later. Or do you lose everything at the touch of a woman's thighs? Your honor, your faith?"

He laughed lightly, relieved at being freed from his lust at the last moment, and yet somehow pleased with himself for almost having destroyed something valuable through a momentary passion. For a few breathless moments Vanessa had been far from his thoughts. Not that they had made any oaths of fidelity. . . .

"I—it's too late now, isn't it?" He slid forward, until they sat side by side on the couch. He put his arm around her.

She nodded. "For both of us, I think." Her eyes still shone with tears. "It would have been good, though."

"Of that I have no doubt." He thought about Vanessa and of the unspoken agreements between them. He liked to think of himself as a virtuous man. Suddenly he felt a chilling self-contempt.

They sat together, side by side, silent in the darkness.

Vanessa stretched languorously against him and Anton marveled at the feeling of each individual muscle as it moved under her satiny skin. All of her was essential.

They lay beneath a glowing spiral galaxy, the stars' colors exaggerated, older globular clusters yellow and blue, the stars in the center blue-white, and spots of red throughout the arms. The galaxy's light made the crumpled and wrinkled sheets around Vanessa's legs look like carved marble. Her dark eyes drifted open and she blinked at the stars floating above her.

"Making love in intergalactic space," she said. "You do think of the nicest things." She pulled the sheets up around both of them in the darkness of the rented room and looked thoughtfully up at the spiral. "I think these Charlatans want to reach the stars. Look at all their stars and galaxies. They're trapped by lightspeed, like all of us, but they want to get out. What do you think?"

He moved his nose along her neck and nibbled her ear.

She giggled. "You always think that. Is this the most reasonable man I've ever met?"

"Yes," he said. "It most certainly is." He ran his hand up her back, feeling her spine and curving muscles. She shivered. He had poured his lust into her, forgetting

Miriam and the rest of the world in a frantic union of flesh.

Vanessa pushed herself up on one elbow and looked solemnly down at him. "Anton, who are we?"

Her echo of his own question to Miriam of "What am I to you?" reawakened guilt in him. Who, indeed, were they? If they were to become more than lustful bodies in a bed together, that question would have to be answered.

They had edged away from each other, to avoid, for the moment, the distractions of the flesh. Anton felt that they were at the center of a turning vortex. As long as they held on closely to each other, they were safe. As soon as they separated, even a little, and moved away from the center, centrifugal forces would pull them apart and fling them in opposite directions.

"I am a Fellow of the Academia Sapientiae," she said, regarding him solemnly. "You knew that. For a long time, I have been after your figurine of the Dead Christ. I suppose you knew that too."

"Yes. The figurine carved by Karl Ozaki. I don't know why it's so important to you."

She rolled over and put her head on his shoulder. "And I don't understand why it's so important to you."

"My lord is an art collector, Vanessa. You've even made fun of him for it."

"Anton! Don't!" Her voice was sharp. "You haven't put it on display. You're chasing all over the Solar System when you already have it. It's so obvious. There's something else."

It was a moment balanced on a knife edge, and they both knew it. Opposing forces of duty and love had put them there, and any breath of falseness now would drop them off. But he could not, *could not* tell her everything, not without betraying Lord Monboddo and the Division of External Security. So what could he say?

"I took a trip, once, to Amboise, a chateau in the Loire Valley once belonging to Francis I, King of France.

I walked into the chapel that perched on the fortified wall, examined some indifferent stained-glass windows or other, and then looked down. I stood in the middle of a rectangle laid in some darker rock on the granite floor. The rectangle was marked 'Leonardo da Vinci.' And that was all. Leonardo had come to France to serve the King, and died there. No monument marked the spot of his burial, no enormous reliquary contained his bones, no one came to drop flowers on his grave. There was just a bare rectangle on the floor, and I had not known where I was and so had stood right in the middle of it and ignored it. I thought of that, when I found the tomb of Karl Ozaki in Clavius, a tiny Greek temple in a corner of the garden.''

She looked at him, but did not speak.

"I've discovered that Karl Ozaki is alive, somewhere in the Belt. I want to find him." Truth, as far as it went.

She inhaled a sharp breath of genuine surprise. "Of course! How could I not have seen it? That damn head in Paris. Hah!" Her eyes glowed with joy. "Oh, Anton, that's incredible." She hugged him, as one hugs an appealingly clever child. "But where is he? The Belt! It must be. But that's not a location, that's a concept. . . ."

"Vanessa," Anton mused. "Did that artifact in the Hypostasium have a name?"

"Nehushtan," she said instantly. "The Brethren took it." She looked at him. "I'm sorry I was so rude to you that night."

"What? Don't be ridiculous. You were doing your job." He pulled at his beard. "Are these Brethren the direct descendants of the Dispossessed Brethren of Christ, or another group that's just taken the name?"

"I don't know." She smiled impishly. "Maybe we can figure it out."

"Why did they take it?"

"They wanted it. I don't have a better explanation than that, either. They've wanted it all along. They got in contact with us through some intermediary, and Preterite Torkot offered them a trade: the artifact for the Dead Christ. I went to authenticate and collect the Dead Christ in Naples and . . . I botched it.''

Something in her tone told him that why she had botched it was not now at issue. Someday, perhaps, he would understand. Three men had died of that botch. He could see her in the dark garden in Naples, keen and efficient, just as she had been in the Lunar hunt. "So the Brethren figured they had fulfilled their end of the bargain and went to get the artifact out of the Hypostasium."

"Yes. They threatened Torkot, and stole it."

As they had stolen the artifacts at Hecates Tholus and Clavius. "Do the names Boaz and Aaron's Rod mean anything to you?"

She frowned. "Yes. I got all the information about the Dispossessed Brethren of Christ that I could, little enough. I think they purged all information when they disappeared, and I'm sure that some of what I have is false. But as far as I know, Boaz, Aaron's Rod, and Nehushtan, along with . . . Jachin, of course, were elements of the Brethren's Mass."

"The Mass being called the Dispersal of the Instruments. And the Instruments may have been created by a man named Abakumov. Whose tomb I have seen."

She hit him lightly in the shoulder. "You do know more than you let on, don't you?"

"Until this moment I didn't think that I knew anything." But the focus had suddenly become clear to him. All lines seemed to lead to the Dead End, formerly Jerusalem the Lost, the great temple of the Dispossessed Brethren of Christ. Nehushtan, the artifact stolen from the Hypostasium, had come from the Dead End. Ozaki was closely associated with them. Anton suspected that his quarry was lurking somewhere within that great hollow asteroid.

"And you're looking for Karl Ozaki." She looked

thoughtful. "One thing's clear. He's not where the Brethren are. He's somewhere else."

"What?" he yelped, distressed at having his unspoken conclusions contradicted. "He used their iconography, and his piece was the price of the artifact. It looks like a clear association."

She looked superior. "An association, sure, but that doesn't mean anything. If the Brethren wanted to make a trade, the Dead Christ for Nehushtan, why didn't they just bring the thing with them and do it right at the Hypostasium? Torkot would have agreed. Why go through all the rigmarole of going to Naples, making a night drop. . . ."

"Unless they didn't have the thing in the first place," Anton said, immediately realizing that she was right. "Ozaki delivered directly."

"From wherever he is. It came to Earth separately, not through the Brethren at all. It must be part of a triple arrangement."

"Ozaki gives us something. We give the Brethren something. And the Brethren have something for Ozaki."

"Yes," she said. "I wonder what."

Anton rather suspected that it might be eighteen kilograms of ngomite.

Vanessa regarded him somberly. "Anton. We haven't told each other everything."

"Of course not," he replied, holding her in his arms. "How could we? We might still end up enemies."

"We—" She jerked away and stared at him. "Do you mean that?"

He forced a smile. "Let's find Karl Ozaki. Then we'll see."

She was silent for a long moment. "Just one more thing then, something for you to think about. I think the Brethren already have Jachin."

"Why?"

"It was on Europa, in a tunnel. They hit it, just as

they did the Hypostasium . . . don't ask me how I know, please.''

He felt her body tense against him. ''I won't,'' he said. Several weeks ago Rabiah umm-Kulthum had mentioned the Technic assertion that the *Sulawesi* Incident had been a response to a raid on Europa. He had no doubt that it had been Vanessa's Technic lover who had told her, and felt a chill. Miriam, and Vanessa's Technic businessman. Was it impossible for them to be in bed alone together?

He rolled over and pressed his chest to her back. He cupped her breast with his hand. She sighed, and he nuzzled her neck. There were so many things to do. . . . ''Just a little longer,'' he said.

''The bitch,'' de Borgra growled. ''I knew it. I knew it had to be something like that.''

Sellering looked surprised. ''I thought you'd decided it was over with her a long time ago.''

''Yes, but this . . . they're all in it together. All of them. Martians, Terrans, the Academia Sapientiae.'' He stalked around the main cabin of the *Hans Lesker*. ''God, I've been a fool.'' He whirled on Sellering. ''Well?''

''Do you want me to argue with you? I told you there were Martian troops aboard the *Charlotte Amalie*. You thought it irrelevant.''

''Bah. It was, then.'' He sat down and twisted through several positions, unable to find one that was comfortable. ''Sleeping with Lindgren! How can she do that? And for political reasons!''

''How do you know it's for political reasons?''

''Be reasonable, Tamara. Why else? He's a stick, an aesthete, about as interesting as an evening at the opera . . . don't interrupt me.'' He jumped to his feet. ''And they all had that summit meeting aboard the *Rapier*, under the guise of a funeral. Terrans and Martians all.''

''Was Vanessa present at this summit conference?''

Sellering asked with deceptive laziness. Her fingernails extended slowly as she stretched.

"No! Will you stop interrupting?" He thought fiercely. The room filled with soft pastel light and lachrymose music suitable for the funeral of a stuffed bunny rabbit. It relaxed him and helped him feel sorry for himself. He collapsed back into a seat, which started to massage his back.

Before he knew it her nails were at his throat. He could feel each sharp edge as it pricked his skin. Her pupils were fully dilated. He didn't dare move.

"Theo." Her voice was calm. That just frightened him more. "You've been sleeping with a Terran agent. You thought you were playing her, but all the while she was playing *you*. The great interplanetary stud—"

"Now, Tamara, there's no need to get personal."

"Listen to me! Ngomite, Theo. You've heard the word. You may not be able to pronounce it, but you know it. That's what they're after. Internal Security has been buzzing all over the Earth and Mars muttering it under its collective breath. Monboddo is a man with a reputation for subtlety. He has now allowed Martian Omega Squads to penetrate the Neutral Zone. There's nothing less subtle than a Martian Omega Squad. He's risking war. Why? What are they after?"

"Ngomite! Don't you think I know it? Lindgren has the evidence. He's on the track of it." Images of Anton Lindgren, strapped to an interrogation table, flashed through his mind. The sly bastard. Lindgren was laughing at him. That was obvious. But Lindgren didn't even know he existed. That was de Borgra's great strength. When he finally caught Lindgren they would see who was laughing.

"And your plan is to just follow him around to see where he goes." Sellering was contemptuous.

"What else can we do?"

"We try to get there ahead of him. We're smart enough, aren't we, dear Theo?" Her nails had retracted and she stroked his cheek with her fingertips. He shivered under their touch. He almost preferred the poison nails. "They've hit our base on Callisto. They had a good reason for that. Lindgren is the key."

"Haven't I been telling you that?"

"You've been telling me how pissed you are that he's sleeping with a woman you wanted to get rid of a long time ago. You've gone soft, Theo. In more ways than one."

Her voice challenged him to become angry. He wasn't interested in brawling. His sex life was something Sellering had never understood. He wondered if she was jealous.

"We'll be at the Dead End soon." Sellering was businesslike. "It's time to stop being passive. You must push Lindgren as far as possible. Interrogate him if you can. Kill him if necessary. He and Monboddo are dangerous."

"I know all that."

"Then act as if you did!" She pushed him and slid back. In an instant it seemed that she had spent the entire conversation on the other side of the room. He stopped himself from massaging his neck.

"I've checked out the Martian ship," Sellering said. "We can lock its linkages to the *Charlotte Amalie*, given a few minutes warning."

"Eh?" he asked, startled. Sellering was always trying to distract him with irrelevancies. "What do you mean?"

"We can fuse the connections of the *Rapier*'s air, water, and power lines," she explained patiently, "making it impossible for it to disengage. We may need the time that gives us. When we go after the ngomite."

"We may," he echoed, thinking about something else. Damn it, he knew what to do. He'd push that skinny bastard Lindgren over the edge. That shouldn't be too hard. Then they'd see who was being passive.

13

From *Rattling the Bars*, by Ram Krishnapuram, New York, 2340:

Why did they go through all this trouble? Frustration, obviously. Frustration with the barrier of lightspeed. The final displacement activity for this frustration is the massive manipulation of matter.

The conception was simple, invented hundreds of years before, even before serious space travel. In 2162 the Dispossessed Brethren of Christ went to the Asteroid Belt and found an elongated chunk of nickel-iron thirty miles long. They drilled it out and filled it with water from Ganymede and the rings of Saturn. They spun it on its long axis, and heated it with a rank of parabolic mirrors, each a dozen miles in diameter. It must have been quite a sight, glaring mirrors, glowing molten rock, solemn monks chanting prayers. The water exploded and swelled the molten asteroid like popcorn. The Brethren's prayers and engineering both worked, and the water didn't spurt out through any holes. So they had a spinning hollow cylinder. They moved in. A lot of work for about a thousand square miles of living space, but people built the Pyramids for less reason.

Maybe the Dispossessed Brethren of Christ had some higher plan for their inside-out asteroid. If they did, nothing came of it.

"How did you get them to let the *Ocean Gypsy* dock directly at the Dead End's hub?" Anton wanted to know as they floated through the airlock.

"The Dead End is part of the great human community," Monboddo answered serenely. "And as such it is subject to . . . pressure."

The Reception Chamber was a huge, echoing, weightless space, brightly lit and packed with what looked like half the population of the Belt, most of whom were yelling at each other.

"This way, this way," voices shouted above the hubbub as the passengers from the *Charlotte Amalie* came in through the airlock. Most of them had arrived by way of the shuttle. They were instantly seized and clipped onto a long ladderlike affair. As each ladder was filled with passengers and gear, it shot the two hundred meters across the spherical chamber to the appropriate reception desk, where they would be processed and entered. Enders obviously had no confidence in Terran abilities in free-fall. Anton saw several ladders crowded with Martian Omega Squads disguised as tourists, who studiously ignored the Monboddo party.

"And how about this ridiculous palanquin of yours? In null-g? I didn't even know you'd stowed it."

"Anton, I have no taste for being fired across space like a bundle of rags. As a Terran Judicial Lord, I am entitled."

Fell and Osbert, wearing scarlet capes and satin trousers, acted as footmen. With calm insouciance, they launched themselves from the airlock and shot straight across the Reception Chamber, ignoring the complex rules for movement through the space and serenely assuming that they had the right of way. The blond Fell was in front, and the dark Osbert behind, the ornate bulk of the palanquin between. They banked off a huge bale of cloth, each with a kick of a beribboned foot, and arrowed through the open portal that was their destination. Agape at this sight, the bearded rockhead who had been shepherding his wares carefully toward the correct Goods Receiving portal didn't even have a chance to curse.

Addison was quiet, and held his left arm stiffly against his side. He had slashed it seriously during his construction of *The Duelist* and it was not yet fully healed. Coaxing him out of his cabin on the *Ocean Gypsy* had taken Anton a good half an hour.

The inner portal closed, isolating the six of them from the chaos of the Reception Chamber. Gravity slowly seized them. The dark room opened up, revealing a sunlit desert landscape, piled with great gilded logs, brass caldrons, bales of purple cloth.

"Lord Monboddo!" cried a voice in rolling organ tones.

The speaker appeared, a large, fleshy man dressed in loose clothes of red satin, his elaborate folded headgear resembling a Montgolfier balloon that had crashed over the battlements of a castle.

"Seneschal Lindgren?" he said, with a bow and an elaborate gesture. "Pawel Luria, Expediter to the Lord Monboddo's party, at your service." His gaze was caught by the ornate box of the palanquin, inlaid wood perspective on its side showing a honeycomb being carved out by bees wielding hammers and chisels. "Is the Lord Monboddo in need of special life-support systems? I was not informed. . . ."

"Mr. Luria," Monboddo cut him off. "I am in need of the most essential of life supports: solitude and silence. As, I believe, we have contracted."

Luria pulled back a sleeve and extended his gloved left hand. A glowing column of gold appeared on it, and Anton could see numbers race through it. He closed his hand, and the gold vanished. "The completion of fund transfer from the Bank of Tycho to the Credit Dispensary of Ceres means that the Hadramaut is yours, according to your agreement with the Syndics of Jerusalem the Lost. Let us then proceed.''

Luria seemed to Anton a typical native of the Dead End: suspicious, subtle, avaricious, and polished, he guided their tasks with detachment but a keen attention to detail.

"In deciding on the Hadramaut as the site of your vacation, you have made an excellent choice,'' Luria said as he directed the rest of them in the stowage of the large tent of purple cloth and gilded beams on a wagon with brightly decorated wheels. "It's more peaceful than the rest of the End. Less commercialized. The rules can be difficult.''

He prepared a concoction of lamb and fava beans. He warned them about avaricious merchants. "Most of the relics are false. But God is clever. He can speak through false relics as well as true, if they are made with enough art.'' Luria spoke as if God had imparted him this knowledge over coffee.

Everything was done with finesse, a performance. Anton was full of admiration. As a Lord's Seneschal, Expediter Luria would have been unsurpassed. Was he also, Anton wondered, a member of the Dispossessed Brethren of Christ? Did he know that Anton and Monboddo were in pursuit of Karl Ozaki and eighteen kilograms of ngomite?

"Excellent,'' Monboddo said. "Let us be on our way.''

This part of the Dead End was cut by a maze of deep canyons, deliberate cracks in the asteroid's shell as it cooled. The dazzlingly bright band of the sun arced across the sky. Simply from the appearance of things, Anton would have been unable to tell that they were actually inside of a fifteen-kilometer-diameter cylinder spinning in space. Puffy clouds formed and re-formed in a variety of patterns, now complex geometric structures, now fantastic cities with towers and battlements. Anton got a sense that the stuff of reality, normally so obdurate, was here as malleable as soft wax.

Since Osbert and Fell had to carry the palanquin, Addison and Anton pulled the wagon with the tent and equipment, Addison wincing at the pain in his arm. The ground was rough and sandy, and the wheels sank deeply into it. The sound of their labored breath echoed weirdly from the colored canyon walls as they tugged at the wagon, Addison darkly accepting, Anton swearing under his breath. Luria offered no help. The fusion sunlight was merciless, the air dry and transparent, revealing every detail in the tortured rock around them as if it were under a magnifying glass.

An open area at the intersection of several canyons was to be their dwelling place. Clouds towered atop the surrounding cliffs, obscuring where rock ended and illusion began. Gods could have hidden up there. The wind moaned in an almost human voice, teasingly just short of uttering recognizable words. Osbert, Fell, Addison, and Anton unloaded the gilded cedar posts and purple fabric.

The tent went up surprisingly easily, given its size, being cleverly guyed and supported. Luria's advice never failed to be useful and to the point, but he stood, legs apart, and watched them like a foreman. When up, the tent resembled nothing so much as the Tabernacle of the Israelites. Its flapping added consonants to the wind's voice. Luria struck a rock with his staff and water gushed out, flashing in the light.

"Now, Expediter," Monboddo said. "What is our schedule? I am anxious to be started."

As Luria detailed the wonders that awaited them, Osbert and Fell muttered behind Anton.

"We're going to have to sit and listen when he discusses epistemology with a philosopher?" Osbert said. "What the hell is that?"

"We'll know by the end of it," Fell said gloomily. "We'll have to look at more tombs too."

"Jesus. Are there women here?"

"Must be. Doubt we'll get to see them. We'll just have to learn about piss-whatever."

"That's the way of it, all right."

Grumbling, they escorted Monboddo inside, while Addison and Anton finished unloading the cart.

Enders were proverbial for the restricted compass of their knowledge. They made their small world seem larger by refusing to learn anything whatsoever about areas outside their immediate concern. So it didn't surprise Anton that Luria, an expert on the desert of the Hadramaut, who could dicker over rugs and who knew every relic within its narrow canyons, knew nothing about how many gamelans there were in Bali, or even where Bali was from where they stood.

"It lies upspin of here a bit," he said vaguely, "and toward the trailing hub . . . I think. Is a gamelan something you hunt? Here in the Hadramaut you can hunt desert cats. They are fast and vicious. Good sport. Terrans enjoy that sort of thing."

"No," Anton said. "A musical ensemble of a variety of bells and percussion instruments. Tuned in Aeolian mode, transposed to D." He thought that was right, not that it mattered. "You have Lord Monboddo well in hand. And I . . ."

Luria pursed his lips. "Wish to indulge your love of archaic music?" He rubbed his hands together, gazing off into the middle distance. "Perhaps something can be arranged." Enders kept their itchy palms discreetly gloved. Anton and Luria made the appropriate credit arrangements. Enders did not insist on being bribed with anything immediately physical.

They entered the tent. The interior was scented with myrrh. "And what is our first order of action, Expediter?" Monboddo said.

"First," Luria said, plopping down on a pillow. "We

rest." He lay down on his back on the embroidered
pillows, put his hands behind the back of his head, and
stared up at the complex folds of the tent, no doubt
contemplating the large additions recently made to his
personal account.

Tired as he was from loading, pulling, and unloading
the cart, Anton would have liked to have joined the
Expediter, but he had more pressing business. He gestured to Addison, who had just settled down to what he
regarded as a well-deserved rest. Addison's look of dismay made Anton's own tiredness bearable, knowing that
someone else was equally burdened.

The palanquin rested outside, canted across a rock like
the shell of some creature cast up by the surf. While
Addison grumblingly got to his feet, Anton pressed three
spots on the door and removed two small boxes from the
hollow panel inside of it. One was a portable terminal
for contact with the main computer aboard the *Ocean
Gypsy*. The other contained a half-dozen organic piezoelectric microphones, each the size of a pinhead. The
terminal could pick up their signals. He slid both boxes
into his toiletries just as Addison came out of the tent.

They loaded up two small packs with survival gear,
weapons, and emergency spacesuits, which no one in
the Belt was ever without, and set off like children running away from home, through the canyons of the Hadramaut, following Luria's instructions.

The Cascade Bar & Grill hung halfway up the wall of
the cylinder end. Torrents of water rushed past on either
side, leaping out and crashing down toward the hills
sloping up from below. The tables were arranged on a
large, scalloped balcony, sloped so that the view was
good from every table, underneath a canopy that caught
any random precipitation from above. Anton and Addison were shown to a small table very near the edge.

The view was dramatic. From where they sat they
could see the cylindrical structure of the Dead End, the

land curving up, becoming vertical, then more than vertical, finally vanishing in the glaring haze of the fusion light. A wall loomed at the opposite end, forty-five kilometers away. Anton looked down and wondered how much of what he was seeing was real. Colors melted and shifted, and what had appeared at one look to be a dark forest seemed, when more closely examined, to be a towered city. Or was it an ocean covered with sailing ships? A field of sharp crystals? It always seemed that it would come into focus momentarily, but it never did. Clouds took the shape of mountains, and windblown mountains scudded across empty deserts. Anton felt that he was examining a landscape made of rumors. Sometimes even the cylinder itself seemed to bend, as if squeezed by a massive hand.

Addison stared out at it. "I didn't know you were going to bring me here," he whispered.

"I told you where we were going," Anton said. "If you didn't want to listen . . ."

"But you weren't saying the right thing!" He turned his eyes to Anton. "I can't believe this place. I didn't create it. It has no reality."

"Someone created it," Anton pointed out. "Or don't you think their version of reality is valid?"

"It's not supposed to be valid. Look at it!" He guzzled a drink, his third. "Could you carve truth out of that?"

"I'm only interested in carving Karl Ozaki out of it. Any ideas?"

"Here? He's not here. How could an artist work here? Your chisel has to hit *something*, for God's sake. You can't carve mush."

"Let me put it another way," Anton said. "If Ozaki was anywhere on the Dead End, where would he be?" Addison's reason for concluding that Ozaki was elsewhere differed completely from Vanessa's, but confirmed it. He felt, for a moment, a deep despair. He rested his head in his hands. Everywhere he chased just gave him more signs and symbols, more representations, more hints. He wished Vanessa were there to rub his back and kiss him on the back of his neck. Her touch was the only reality he had encountered between the house at Fresh Pond Verge and the Asteroid Belt.

"Somewhere with a hard center," Addison said. He tore the soft inside of a roll into little pieces and rolled them into cylinders, like a small child. He then formed them into clever little statuettes resembling Easter Island heads and popped them, one by one, into his mouth. "What could they have here that he can't create for himself? He's a genius." He laughed to himself. "What could they give Lord Fujiwara?"

Anton smiled slowly. "The best idea I've heard so far." He leafed through his stack of documents.

He found it in his copy of Nguyen and Castlereagh, and read it aloud to Addison: "'One oddly fixed point is Nippon, installed fifteen years ago, in 2342. The amount of labor that went into this replica of an inn on the Tokaido Road in seventeenth-century Tokugawa Japan is incredible, and incomprehensible. Why build this accurate replica here, in the Belt, where no one is interested in it? Tourists do not come to the Belt in search of six-hundred-year-dead cultures. Earth itself provides enough of that. The rulers of the Dead End, the mysterious Syndics of Jerusalem the Lost, to give them their full and formal title, seem to have some plan, beyond anything a mere tourist can discern.'"

"My God," Addison breathed after a minute's thought. "They built it for him. That's incredible. Two years after he disappeared they built him his own amusement park." He shrugged. "But I bet you he's still not there, and we'll never find him." He relaxed into torpor.

"Ozaki never intended to vanish totally and forever," Anton said. "His ego's too big for that. He has to want someone to figure out how clever he's been. That may be why we've made it this far. But I'll bet that somewhere in Nippon we'll find a clue, some sign of his continued existence."

Anton used the console in the middle of the table to make reservations in Nippon.

Addison looked dreamily out over the shifting landscape. "Do you suppose we'll ever get there?" he asked.

The Dead End made travel deliberately difficult, so that psychological space was increased. Anton plotted a route from where they sat, halfway up the cylinder end. It was complicated, involving a boat ride, a climb up some stairs, a chair lift, and a complex piece of underground transport. The route zigzagged all over a good portion of the Dead End.

It took a good number of wearying hours before they made it to the last segment of their journey. It involved climbing into a rather spidery-looking contraption and being launched into dark space by another serenely superior Ender, this one a woman in a cloak, like a magician.

Anton held onto the handles of his car, trying to see what was ahead. All was darkness. The air rushed past him, and he thought he could hear distant waves, and the clatter of rocks on a shore. Suddenly that sound was obliterated by the roar of an internal combustion engine and the thunder of explosions. He broke through into light and found himself flying over a layer of clouds lit by a full moon above. The control board of a primitive aircraft, a bewildering field of glowing dials, had materialized in front of him, and he was holding the controls.

"Good evening, Lieutenant Palgrave," a voice said in his ear. "It is the night of 21 October 1940. You are flying a Hawker Hurricane Mk1 of the No. 257 Squadron. A German bombing mission, consisting of some fifty Dornier 17 bombers and sixty Heinkel 111's, with a fighter screen of Messerschmitt 109's and 110's, is moving toward London. You have just been scrambled from Northolt airfield to defend. Good luck and good hunting." He could see them, moving slowly in the moonlight. Several Messerschmitts spotted him and peeled off to defend, while the bombers, gravid with bombs, lumbered toward their targets. Anton fired a test round with his machine guns. Everything seemed to be in order.

This was ridiculous. He was just trying to get to seventeenth-century Japan and he would get there even if he did not fire a shot. But . . . he pulled back and climbed for altitude. The aircraft reacted exhilaratingly, pushing him into his seat. It vibrated in his hands, a makeshift of wood and wire. The air was cold and blew viciously through the cockpit.

The ME 110's were twin-engined craft, slow, while the 109's were much quicker than a Hawker Hurricane. Anton dropped the left wing and dove down toward the bombers, the important targets. He fired a burst and stitched across the wing of one of the defending 110's. He must have hit a fuel tank, because it exploded gratifyingly. But now the others were on him. A 109 was on his tail, and another was off his left wing. He swung to the right, away from the bombers now, but both of them stayed right on him. Panic choked him. He heard a long burst of machine-gun fire, his aircraft bucked, and suddenly the cockpit was full of smoke. His left wing was on fire, and partially sheared off. He pulled on the steering gear but it flopped in his hands, disconnected. He could feel himself spiraling down toward the ground, down through the cloud layer, in darkness fitfully lit by the flames of the burning city below, toward the inevitable impact . . .

He pulled into the station and stepped off onto the platform. He was wet with sweat, and shaking. He thought he should smell of smoke from the burning plane, but of course he didn't. Addison, when he got off his contraption a minute later, looked just as shaken.

"Hell of a ride," Anton commented, for lack of anything better to say.

"I'll say!" Addison responded, truly excited for the first time since Anton had met him. "I got three of them before they got me. The bomber went off like a firecracker. Maybe we should go around again."

"We don't have the time." Three? Anton felt irritated. Addison had gotten three? Anton consoled himself with the thought that a facility at games indicated a basic shallowness of spirit.

They walked out into the light. The hills around them had cunning profiles, like the ones in old paintings. Some of them had picturesque temples on them, though whether these temples were real or merely silhouettes was not apparent from where they stood. Ahead of them, nestled in a small valley near a series of lily ponds, was a Japanese inn, a low building with a dark curving eaved roof that spread among the pine and maple trees with no apparent order.

Since it was an imitation of an inn along the Tokaido Road in the seventeenth century, built inside of an asteroid hundreds of millions of miles from Earth, it was not real. But beauty is always real, and the place was beautiful.

Anton paused and looked down at it. He was getting closer to his goal. He could feel it. "I can almost reach out and take hold of your hand, Karl Ozaki," he whispered.

Theonave de Borgra's bulky figure sat jauntily on the ladder as it was fired across the Reception Chamber. Vanessa Karageorge watched him narrowly, her breath tight in her throat. He looked just as he always had, stocky, serene, self-satisfied, hands folded across his belly as he awaited events, but now every posture, every gesture, was charged with threat. How could she not have seen it? How could she have ever let those heavy hands caress her?

He vanished through a portal before her own ladder made it across. It had been an odd whim of hers, to time her arrival just after that of the crew members of the Technic ship, the *Hans Lesker*. Somewhere ahead of her waited the Dispossessed Brethren of Christ. That somehow no longer seemed important. They could wait their turn.

She remembered her old lover vanishing into the dark gardens of the house at Fresh Pond Verge, long before Anton had been anything to her but an oddly interesting man she had talked to in the East Ambulatory. She should have told Anton about it, she knew she should have. But bed with someone for the second time was not the place to discuss former lovers. "I followed my old lover one night, dear, and he tried to break into your house. You know how old lovers can be. . . ." She looked around the Reception Chamber, trying, for some reason, to spot Miriam Kostal, the Justice of Tharsis. What had that woman been to Anton? Vanessa felt a surge of jealousy. If Anton hadn't brought Miriam up, why should Vanessa have brought up Theonave? Oh, God, she realized, she wasn't making any sense at all.

Her thoughts crystallized, much too late. She forgot all about the rendezvous with the Brethren. Theonave was after something. She could see it in his posture, in the smirk on his face. It involved Anton. She was sure of it. Theonave had been, for reasons she still didn't understand, after Anton since the beginning. Anton had to be warned. It was late to be telling him about Theonave, he could ask her why she hadn't told him earlier, he could be angry with her, hurt. It didn't matter.

Once she had made her decision, her mind worked smoothly. If Anton was searching for clues to Ozaki, there were some natural places for him to go. She could find him. Whatever he did, it would take Theonave much longer. He didn't know Anton and he didn't know Ozaki. By the time he managed to get anywhere, Anton would be warned and safe.

Even in the midst of her fear and impatience, she managed a smile. Maybe they could even manage a quick embrace, a kiss. No reason why a practical action couldn't be romantic as well.

* * *

At the inn Anton allowed himself to be taken in hand. Refusing a bath would have been impolite, and conspicuous, so he and Addison were stripped naked and plunged into a hot mineral bath, where they were massaged by three women each. The tension in Anton's body, which had been holding him as rigid as a board, slowly vanished. He did wonder what odd minerals the water contained. Antimony? Plutonium? Enders were capable of anything.

Anton climbed out of the bath as soon as he politely could. His first order of business, after preparing himself in his room, was a close inspection of the entire inn and its grounds, under the guise of a pleasant stroll. Rockheads from all parts of the Belt wandered the paths of the garden, admiring the cunningly twisted bonsai trees, some brought all the way from Earth. One group, kneeling uncomfortably in front of an expanse of carefully raked sand with about a dozen boulders sticking out of it, were listening intently to a lecture on rock gardens given by a shaven-headed monk. He tried to explain how the perspectives from different angles represented mountains and valleys, with only indifferent success, since most of his audience had never seen mountains and valleys.

With the paranoia that he had picked up from Fell and Osbert, he checked for possible escape routes. There was a cut in the ridge, angled upward, probably a relic of the amusement area that had been here before Nippon had been built. It was the easiest way out of the bowl in which the inn was nestled. He had put himself in the middle of a little dimple inside of a spinning tin can in outer space, and he was starting to feel claustrophobic.

The inn itself was a complex of pavilions and outbuildings, none of them more than two stories high. Between them were courtyards, one with a vivid green garden of moss. The dark and narrow hallways, their floors of polished black wood, never proceeded level for more than five paces, always going up or down one or two steps.

In his search, Anton used a simple principle: he moved into resistance. When doors led him to feel the natural path was to the left, he went to the right. When a room was closed, he tried to get into it. When a hallway was impassable because the floor was being polished or led to a dead end, he tried to go that way. The sliding rice-paper shoji screens that served as divisions between rooms were not made to be locked, and the entertainment personnel were unused to practicing concealment and misdirection.

In a room just off the moss garden, a room with a jammed shoji screen, Anton found it. The room was small, and had a wall hanging at one end, which showed clouds and a dragon. Japanese rooms of that period had typically had an alcove at one end, called a *tokonoma*, for displaying works of art normally kept stored away in a cabinet and shown only rarely. The ancient Japanese fear of wearing out their sense of beauty was similar to Monboddo's. This hanging was flush to the wall, where one would expect an alcove.

He pulled it aside. In the alcove, suspended by some field effect, was a flying horse in bronze, its long mane streaming behind it. It stretched its hooves out in tense exuberance, a spiritual relative of the panther in Miriam's hair. Anton had no problem in attributing it to Ozaki. He let the wall hanging fall back in its place, concealing the horse, which seemed to be a permanent fixture there. Ozaki himself did not worry that his work might wear out anyone's sense of beauty. Since it was difficult to remove, someone had attempted a makeshift means of concealment. That made Anton nervous. Who knew they were here looking for Ozaki? He hadn't had time to ask anyone the question. He left one of his piezoelectric microphones there, stuck at the intersection of two slats on one of the shoji screens, and continued his search.

In a back garden stood a small outbuilding where tourists learned to make lopsided sake bottles with matching cups. A kiln, potter's wheels, and a variety of implements filled it. Several people worked on their projects. Anton mixed in unobtrusively.

The pottery studio was provided with the hard wax, slip, and metal ingots useful for lost-wax casting. The rough wood floor was stained with the solvents used to clean off a freshly cast bronze statue, to aid in the start of its patina.

Anton walked tensely around the room. He felt like a hunter who hears the snapping of a twig in the brush ahead, the whisper of leaves in the still air. He picked things up and put them down, not really looking at them. Ozaki worked here, sometimes. When he needed gravity, perhaps? Was he here now? The equipment had not been used for some months, Anton finally decided. Someone had dripped wet clay on the metal ingots and the tools had a layer of dust on them from the drying clay.

He stared at the kimono-clad woman giving instruction. Did she know where Ozaki was? He turned away before she glanced up. He wasn't going to be able to trick Ozaki's coordinates out of anyone under the guise of idle chatter, and he couldn't interrogate anyone. Frustrated, he left a microphone.

He headed back, getting lost only twice on the way. He found Addison, dressed in a kimono, kneeling and sipping sake served him by a beautiful woman. In another room, concealed by screens, a flute played. Anton paused silently at the door. Addison was looking confused.

"But you must know something about him, Sei!" he said. "You must."

"I have never even heard of him," Sei replied, her eyes demurely downcast. The sake flask rattled on the edge of the cup as she poured.

Addison's eyes narrowed suspiciously. "Karl Ozaki is only the most famous artist of our century, Sei. This even seems like the sort of place that he would go, if he could."

"We are far away, here."

"I want you to understand!" Addison pleaded, seizing her by the hand. "I need to find him. The only way to see life is through what we have made ourselves. He can teach me! I don't care about the Dispossessed Brethren of Christ; I don't care what Anton Lindgren is after, I don't care about what I guarded at Clavius; none of that matters. I want Ozaki!"

She pulled her hand free, flustered and frightened. "You are most unfortunate. You have come to the wrong place."

Anton entered the room noisily. Sei jumped in fright and stared at him with wide eyes. Anton smiled at her. By denying any knowledge of Ozaki whatsoever, she had revealed that she knew something about where he was. He took a step, and tripped over the long sash of his own kimono, stumbling against Sei. While apologizing fervently, he left a microphone on her. He and Addison went out into the bonsai garden, leaving Sei behind them, twisting a lock of hair around her finger and staring off into space.

The bonsai garden consisted of rock and bare soil with ancient, gnarled trees clinging to stony outcroppings. Five twisted maples leaned against each other like old men walking in a park, their branches intertwined. Three yews stood on the crest of the small hill. Bonsai trees seemed a perfect phenomenon for asteroids. An entire forest could be encompassed by a few square yards, just as each asteroid was a civilization in miniature. Anton knelt in front of a red azalea in full flower, which clung to a rock gleaming with quartz crystals.

He remembered the garden of Lady Perrine, Inspector of Cincinnati, on a series of terraces above the Ohio River. There, in a porcelain pot, was a thick-trunked, sturdy-looking tree a meter high that Lady Perrine called her family's "project": a bonsai sequoia, already seventy years old. Eventually, several hundred years on, it would reach full growth, nearly ten feet high, and be a centerpiece of that part of the garden. It was this tree, even more than the instructions for a proper English lawn ("seed and roll for six hundred years"), or a twenty-five-hundred-year-old Roman aqueduct that still carried water to villages in Provence, that for Anton symbolized the enduring aspects of the civilization he had pledged himself to defend. He would defend it against the rumblings and shrieks represented by the Massacre of Syrtis Major and the Australian Expedition, against its own internal corruptions, against its external enemies.

"What the hell was that all about?" Anton whispered. It wasn't until he spoke that he realized how angry Addison had made him.

Addison looked startled. "What? I was just trying to find some things out for you. I don't know. I think Ozaki's been here. You were right. It wouldn't make sense for Sei never to have heard of him."

"John Addison, boy detective. You have all the subtlety of a rhinoceros trying to hide under someone's bed."

"God, do you want to find Ozaki, or don't you?" Addison asked aggrievedly.

"You can't flush him like a partridge by making a lot of noise!"

"You don't understand. You don't." Addison's voice trembled. "All this time I thought he was dead. And he's alive! And no one ever told me."

"Who would have told you?" Lindgren was interested despite himself. Addison seemed as aggrieved as if personally lied to.

"No one could have told me anything, of course." Addison spoke quickly. "Who could know he was still alive?" He laughed, a patently false sound.

"Someone does," Lindgren said. "You, in some ways, were closer to him than anyone. I wonder why you never knew."

"Maybe I didn't deserve to know." Addison was sud-

denly maudlin. ''Perhaps I never could have done what
I had to do at Clavius if I had known.''

Anton desperately wanted to attend to Addison's dis-
jointed confessions, but events were overtaking him. He
scratched his ear with his little finger, setting the ear-
phone in properly. The computer display flashed on his
thumbnail. His terminal was in contact with the computer
aboard the *Ocean Gypsy* through the repeater in the palanquin. He closed his eyes in deep meditation, and listened.

The room with the flying horse was silent. A clatter-
ingly noisy crafts class of some sort was using the work-
room. He restrained a wince and turned to the
microphone in the obi of Sei's kimono. She was breathing
hard, her heart beating strongly.

''Hello?'' she said tentatively. ''Hello?''

There was the hiss of white noise as *Ocean Gypsy*'s
computer began to track the communications around the
Dead End for a backscattered maser signal. It would be
coded, but he was interested only in its direction.

''Yes? What is it?'' The voice, on a narrow-band signal, had most of its character squeezed out of it, but its
irritation was obvious.

''Karl?'' Sei asked tentatively, as if wondering if she'd
gotten a wrong number.

''Who else would it be? What do you want?'' There
was a pause between each side of the conversation, several seconds in duration. Ozaki must be about a million
kilometers away.

''Someone's looking for you.''

After a moment of silence, longer than simply transit
time, Ozaki asked, ''Who is looking for me?'' Anton
listened in fascination. So there he was, somewhere in
the Asteroid Belt. Karl Ozaki himself. Alive! Anton
barely kept himself kneeling. He felt like jumping up
and dancing around the courtyard. He'd done it. He'd
finally done it.

''Two men. Terrans. One is a connoisseur. The other

says he is an artist. Lindgren and Addison.''

"Addison . . .'' Ozaki mused. "John Addison, late in the service of the Justice of Clavius.''

"They keep asking questions about you. At least Addison does. Lindgren keeps silent.''

"Ah,'' Ozaki said. "Those are the dangerous ones. Poking around the things I left at Clavius let Addison know I am still alive. I wonder how he tracked me there. Luck probably. Ah, well. I would like to see him.''

"What?'' Sei was confused. "But how am I going to be able to get him to you? You are not—''

"I was expressing a wish, not a desire I expect you to satisfy.'' Ozaki cut across her words, contrary to the etiquette of a long-distance conversation. "I am well aware that it would not be permitted. But they need never find me. You know that. You didn't even have to call me to know that. You could have simply kept them distracted, sent them away unsatisfied, and never bothered me at all.''

",I know,'' she said miserably. "I hadn't heard your voice in so long.''

"I have been busy with the task, Sei. I am still busy with it. Is that all?''

"Yes.'' Her voice was all but inaudible.

"Excellent. Good day.'' He switched off.

Anton looked down at the flashing display on his thumbnail. Location confirmed. He smiled to himself. That was the way it ended. His life had been spent riding in broughams pulled by horses, crossing continents in pullmans, digging turnips in the garden, admiring elegant china coffee cups, but when it came down to business he found himself wired up to a computer, dependent on it, just like the most cyborg-minded of Technics. It was the way of war, when one found oneself increasingly resembling the enemy.

Before he ordered their destruction, Anton listened to each of the microphones one more time.

"You know, Anton, things are more complicated than you think they are."

"No doubt." The workshop was still noisy with students. He gave the order and the microphone sublimed into the air.

"I'm only telling you this because . . . well, it's hard to say. I feel like I'm no longer able to trust anyone. I believed what they told me, and here Ozaki's been alive the entire time. It makes me wonder how much of everything else is true."

"What *who* told you?" Lindgren spoke and then held his breath, listening to Addison and the room with the flying horse simultaneously. . . .

"Oh, God," a woman's voice moaned. "Oh, my God."

Anton recognized the voice. It was Vanessa's.

The frame of the inn shifted and creaked, as if it were a ship at sea. Vanessa nervously edged along the dark corridor, listening. She felt like an intruder, not rustling with silk, untouched by a hot mineral bath. A ridiculous habit, she thought, this following her lovers around. She should cut it out.

She had seen Anton head into this part of the inn, tall and dignified in his blue kimono, his carefully double-pointed beard making him look like some scholarly Japanese spirit. He'd been seeking something, every nerve end alert. She'd lost him somewhere, but he couldn't have gone far.

A board creaked and she whirled, then felt disgusted at her weak nerves. Something about the inn and its noises got to her. Where had Anton gone? She had to find him quickly. She edged along a wall, past a half-open shoji screen.

With a crack, an arm smashed its way through the rice paper and wrapped itself around her neck like a steel spring. She kicked back instantly, but slammed her heel against the wood framework of the doorway. The rigid

forearm crushed her larynx, exposing no fingers for her
to grab. She fought desperately, flopping against the wall
like a gaffed fish, unable to breathe. The pressure let up
for an instant, but before she could move, a hand seized
her wrist, twisted her arm up between her shoulders, and
dragged her into the room. The rough tatami mats
slammed into her face. She slapped down and tried to
roll. A heavy knee crushed the small of her back, knocking the wind out of her. Her assailant grabbed her shoulder and rolled her over. She found herself staring at a
knife blade inches from her eyes. Holding it was Theonave de Borgra.

He smiled. "You never fought me that well in bed,
Vanessa. It's a revelation."

She gasped, still unable to breathe.

Theonave stroked her face with his fingertips, for all
the world as if they were indeed still in bed. "I don't
think I would have found this place without you. But
you're pretty easy to follow. Your boyfriend Lindgren
must be here somewhere."

"Anton?" She frowned. "I don't think so. He and
Monboddo were going to—" She stopped as the knife
pressed against her throat.

"I don't have time for this," he hissed. "No lies, not
even by implication. You'll have to tell me. I've examined you, Vanessa, believe me. You don't have any
autonomic nerve blocks that will kill you before you can
talk. You don't even have any pain receptor suppression.
You're kind of exposed, aren't you?" He curled a lock
of her hair around his finger and tugged it, first lightly,
then painfully.

"I don't know what you're talking about," she said.
It was interesting, she thought in a dissociated way. He
still wore his glittering suit with the spiraling iridescent
lines. He looked and acted pretty much the same as he
always had. He was a single-minded man. It was just
that this time his single-mindedness was going to kill
her.

"I don't have time for this! Where is it?"

"Where is what?"

He slapped her, backhanded. That was good. Angry men make terrible interrogators, and she could stand being slapped around for hours. Someone would find them eventually.

He obviously had the same thought. His eyes narrowed. "I'll offer you a choice, Vanessa. Tell me where the ngomite is, or what you know about it, and I won't kill you. A simple arrangement."

She relaxed her muscles and looked up at him. She shifted her hips slightly. "You always were a negotiator, Theo. Too bad I don't believe you. You're going to kill me, whether I tell you anything or not." She tossed her head. His assault had ripped some of the pins out of her hair, and more now shook out onto the mats. Her black hair spilled out.

"I don't have much in stock, Vanessa. It's the only deal I have. You'd better take it."

They looked at each other for a long moment. If she cried, it would be all over. He would be merciless. Instead, she parted her lips. He wasn't crazy enough to think she wanted to have sex, not now, but then, he was a man, and men saw such things differently. But all she really needed was a moment of weakness.

"What do Lindgren and you know about the ngomite?" he asked softly, leaning forward. "Tell me. I know it's not here. I've checked that already."

"The ngomite?" Her breath came in short gasps. Thank God, she thought crazily, that fear and sexual arousal are so hard to distinguish. "You're right, Theo. It's not here." She arched her back, pushing out her breasts. She was careful not to move her body in a way that he could interpret as a physical threat, an attempt to escape. Rather, it should seem a desire to surrender.

"Then where is it?" He was excited despite himself, she could feel it. He had an erection and his lips were tight across his teeth. He had always been easy to arouse.

She remembered a time when she had liked that. He shifted his weight to one side, just slightly, and she slowly moved her thigh against him. He moved forward a little more.

"It's—" She slammed sideways with every ounce of her strength. His position, weight on one knee, was precarious. He tottered, off balance. She kicked him in the kidney, and he fell. She slammed her heel down on his wrist, knocking the knife from it. He twisted quickly and dropped for the knife. She smashed her heel against the side of his face, rolled across the roughness of the tatami, and felt the hilt of the knife smooth in her hand.

She turned. Theonave bulked above her, already dropping like an attacking grizzly. His face had the thoughtful, slightly quizzical expression she'd seen so many times, when he was trying to understand something he thought ridiculous, like why Terrans stayed outside so much, or built houses with useless ornaments. For an instant she remembered why she had loved him.

He roared when the blade cut him and he jerked back. She pushed again. He stumbled back and toppled against the opposite wall, slamming his head against the corner. He lay face upward. Vanessa stood over him for a long time. He wasn't dead. She could see the pulsing of a blood vessel in his throat. She should cut it, slaughtering him like a hog. She should. Human life was delicate. She was getting repeated lessons in that.

She stumbled away, barely able to breathe, and made it to the next room, where she collapsed on the floor.

"Oh, God," she moaned. "Oh, my God."

She lay there for several minutes, feeling the air that entered her lungs as a blessing. Then she pushed herself to her feet. A wall hanging covered part of the opposite wall, a picture of a dragon flying among clouds. She frowned. That was odd. She pulled it aside and found Ozaki's horse, running through the air, its head thrown back. It looked much more alive than she felt.

"Vanessa," Anton's voice said.

She turned and buried her face in his chest, suddenly crying. She pulled her head back and looked up at him. "He's in there, Anton. His name is Theonave de Borgra. I think he's a Technic agent."

Anton turned away from her and strode quickly into the other room. "How long ago?" he asked.

"What?" She followed him. "Just a couple of minutes."

The other room was empty. Blood stained the tatami mats, much less of it than she had expected.

"Oh, damn! I . . . I couldn't just kill him, Anton. I'm sorry. He was . . . he and I . . ."

"Never mind!" Anton said, holding her. "Technic agents are tougher than you think. Physiological augmentation, blood shunts. You couldn't know. What was he after? I'm sorry I have to interrogate you—"

"He was after ngomite. He said that you—" She stared at him, seeing him, once again, anew. "You must be ExSec then. It makes sense."

He frowned at her, thinking, and reached a decision. "How much do you need to know in order to trust me, Vanessa?"

"Nothing, now. Let's find him! He can't have gotten far."

They stepped out into the hallway.

"He's still dangerous," Anton said. "Understand that."

The hall echoed with the slam of a heavy body hitting a wall. They froze. A figure ran down the hall toward them, and tripped over one of the uneven stairs, almost falling.

"Anton!" Addison cried. "They're after me!" He ran up and grabbed Anton's arm, ignoring Vanessa's presence. "The Brethren! They're going to take us. Oh, God, why did I let you bring me here? We've got to get out. Hurry, for God's sake."

There are times for considered reflection and relaxed, informed decisions. This was not one of them.

"I've put the packs together," Anton said crisply. "Let's get them. Calm down! Pretend you're relaxed. Worry about dinner."

Addison's face was pasty, covered with sweat. His stubbly head and chin were shiny. He gulped and took a deep breath. "I led you here, to find Ozaki. That's what they're angry about. But I didn't know the connection. I didn't know the Brethren were here, for God's sake! I don't think I can explain it to them. Oh, Anton, I'm afraid."

"You're not alone. Let's move!"

Vanessa followed. They got their packs, stepped out onto the porch, and started down toward the transport tunnel. Two men slouched with elaborate casualness at its entrance. They wore kimonos, but looked like a stake-out. Anton backpedaled. He looked out toward the hills, scanning quickly.

The hills turned blue as the band in the sky mimicked sunset. A troop of tourists was returning from a tea ceremony. Several other figures wandered over the hills from the direction of the hub, where the other exit was. Vanessa squinted into the growing darkness. There were not many of them, perhaps half a dozen, but their arrangement was not random. They coalesced and moved in tight formation, like soldiers.

Anton jumped off the porch and ran around to the other side of the inn to look at the hill opposite. He was back in an instant. "More of them on the other side," he said laconically. "Let's head for the cut up there." He pointed.

"Can we escape?" Vanessa asked.

He smiled tightly. "I doubt it. We're trapped like bugs in a jar. But let's go." They ran.

"No, no." Addison had trouble breathing as he trotted after them. "That's not the way. We could go out—but no, we'd need spacesuits, wouldn't we? That's the way I remember it . . ."

"Where is it?" Anton grabbed Addison. "Tell me!"

The sculptor shook his head dizzily. "Let go of me. You keep trying to rip things out of me. It's too complicated."

Anton was close to losing his temper. "Dammit, if there's a way out of here—"

"Please." Vanessa looked seriously at Addison. "It's our only chance."

"This way."

"Let's go!" Anton led the way.

Behind them they heard the sound of a dozen booted feet running down the wooden hallways. They ran out of the inn, down a twisting path among lily ponds, where the frogs had started to croak.

Three intruders loomed from the shadows. Without slowing down, Anton slammed into the middle one, knocked him flat, and kicked him in the head. Vanessa slung her opponent over her hip and dropped on his stomach with both knees. Addison grappled with the third. Anton pulled him off and dropped him into a lily pond with a splash. The frogs stopped croaking for an instant, then resumed.

A cliff loomed ahead, the cut of the old ride black against gray. They stumbled along the rough ground, tearing their ungainly kimonos as they ran. Vanessa, wearing pants, had the advantage.

They stopped in the cut. Addison frowned. "It's hard. It was all a dream when I learned it, a marvelous dream. I didn't think it was real." His voice was dreamy. He turned back toward the pursuing troops. "I didn't know it actually existed."

Vanessa remembered her own researches into the Dead End. There had been access hatches during construction, now used mostly for the disposal of dangerous waste. "This way!" She felt around and found the concealed doorway.

"Yes." Addison seemed less than pleased that the hatch had been discovered. "That's it."

A narrow, twisting maintenance tunnel led down from

the doorway. The three of them ended up in a tiny room, far down in the shell of the Dead End. In the floor was the hatch of an airlock, a mechanical one worked by air pressure with no associated electronics whatsoever. It looked unbelievably primitive.

Anton started to remove his clothing, and froze. He stared at Vanessa. "We have two skintites," he said, his voice dull. "Calculated to our body sizes."

"Go!" she said sharply. "We can argue it out while you put them on."

Anton gestured, and Addison found the compartment in his pack, revealing a small stack of plastic sheeting. He pulled the spacesuit out and rolled it on.

Anton put his on slowly, like a child getting dressed reluctantly for school. "Vanessa, I—"

"I led the bastard here," she said viciously. "It's my fault. There's nothing you can do."

"De Borgra has nothing to do with these people. It's not your fault."

"Get dressed, goddammit! We can settle this later."

Anton took a deep breath and finished putting on the lightweight spacesuit. He reached into his pack and handed her a curved metal tusk. "This is part of Nehushtan, broken off when they stole it from the Hypostasium. Use it as a negotiating point with the Brethren, if you have to. It's all I have."

Vanessa put her arms around him. She could feel his strong body through the resilient fabric. She kissed him quickly. "Get in the airlock. I'll give you as much time as I can."

Voices shouted in the tunnel. Anton and Addison dived into the airlock, flipping up their helmets, and Vanessa slammed the hatch shut. The airlock cycled. She turned and waited.

Her face—drawn, intense, with dark, burning eyes—vanished as the hatch closed. Anton stared up for an instant at the unfeeling metal, then swung to the exit hatch. If what she had done was to have any meaning, they had to move. The hatch to space was at right angles to the interior one. The reason for this became clear as soon as they had emerged into space. Addison whimpered, and even Anton, who had been expecting it, felt a moment of panic.

They stood on a tiny platform that hung from a rocky ceiling, nothing below but the uncaring stars. They were on the outside of the spinning cylinder that was the Dead End. If he stepped off he would fly off at a tangent trajectory. This little bit of physics did not calm him. He would fall down to the stars, and be dead long before he hit bottom.

Other than the ship radio messages crackling in his headphones it seemed that the two of them were alone in the universe.

The stars passed by in procession, like a huge school of luminescent fish. Anton looked along the rock surface around him, which his mind persisted in seeing as above him, and saw a series of handholds left over from the early construction, along with a slot where a safety line would be attached. They had no such safety line, but he felt the clunk of the airlock through his fingertips, as their pursuers figured out where they had gone. What had they done with Vanessa?

"Come on," he gritted to Addison over their comm channel, gesturing toward the handholds. Addison groaned in fear. Anton swung out hand over hand. Ahead of him another platform stuck out, where he could rest.

Meanwhile, his terminal was broadcasting a private distress call. Anyone else would interpret it as a monitoring signal, but to Monboddo and the *Ocean Gypsy* it was a cry of panic. If they could hear it. He'd set off the alarm the instant he saw that the Brethren were closing in, but had no idea if that had given Monboddo, Fell, and Osbert a chance to escape.

Anton made it to the platform. He turned and looked. Addison had, after what had obviously been an extremely long pause, decided to follow and was about halfway toward him.

A familiar voice crackled in his headphones. "Mr. Lindgren. Are you there?"

"Thank God!" Anton said. "Where are you?"

"Ah, thank goodness." Monboddo tried to keep his voice calm, but Anton could hear the relief in it. "It would be more useful if you would tell me where *you* are."

"Addison and I are on the surface of the Dead End, directly exterior to Nippon."

"Clever of you to have gotten there. I see your location signal. When I give you the word, Mr. Lindgren, you will let yourself fall. Is that clear?"

"Just let go." He could barely breathe. "I'm terrified."

"Of course, Anton," Monboddo said gently. "But you're safe. We'll catch you, like catching the first snow-flake of winter on your tongue."

"Disgusting image," Anton said. "Later." He switched circuits and conveyed the direction to Addison.

Addison froze halfway along the length of the hand-holds. "No," he said. "I can't. I *can't*. Just leave me. This is ridiculous. They are my friends. I can just explain what happened. How was I supposed to know that Ozaki had anything to do with them? I'm sorry, Anton. . . . I should have explained, but I just didn't know." With that, he turned and started to work his way, slowly, back to the airlock.

Anton growled with frustration and, without a further thought, leaped out and started swinging himself hand over hand toward Addison, like a gibbon in a jungle canopy, with no further thought of the risks of slipping and letting go. He keyed the other circuit. "How much longer?" he gasped.

"I will count down," Monboddo said. "Fifteen sec-onds, now."

Ahead, past Addison, Anton could see the heads of

three of their pursuers. They wore their own skintites. Asteroid dwellers were always ready for space. They climbed out of the airlock and started along the handholds in the direction of Addison.

"Ten seconds," Monboddo said. "Nine. Eight."

Anton swung desperately toward Addison. Space was silent, and Addison had no idea that he was back there.

"Three. Two. One. *Now*." Anton launched himself forward at an angle to Addison, calculating the trajectory and trusting to luck. He fell away from the asteroid and to the left, and grabbed Addison's legs. With a shriek, Addison was pulled loose from his handhold and the both of them fell outward from the Dead End. Their pursuers might have been able to do something about it, if their suits had rocket packs, but they did not react quickly enough. In a couple of seconds they had swung out of sight, as Anton and Addison proceeded on the tangent.

Addison sobbed desperately and struggled with Anton, as if escaping from his grip would somehow save him. Anton held on.

"Stop it, John," he gasped. "If we break loose from each other, our center of mass will continue on the same trajectory, but we—"

"What? What?" Addison was in a panic. "What are you talking about?"

"Physics, dammit!" He elbowed Addison in the solar plexus and the other stopped struggling. They spun slightly as they floated. The Dead End drifted past Anton's field of view, smaller each time, like a dirigible that had lost its mooring lines and been caught by the wind.

"We're going to die!" Addison wailed.

"Don't be such a baby." Addison's panic had absorbed his own, so Anton felt he had the right to act tough.

Between one turn and the next, the *Ocean Gypsy* appeared. Anton had a chance to appreciate her smooth lines and realized that he hadn't seen her from the outside since he'd left Earth. Her hatch was open. Fell and Osbert appeared on either side of it, outfielders. The thin blue of a fusion flame corrected *Ocean Gypsy*'s position. Osbert and Fell reached out and caught them.

The impact was hard, and for an instant it seemed that all four would be pulled free of the *Ocean Gypsy* to fall into outer space. Osbert and Fell hustled them into the hatch, and the *Ocean Gypsy* accelerated.

14

"The unfortunate Expediter Luria tried to jump us," Monboddo explained. "He has a number of skills, but hand-to-hand combat is not one of them. We took measures."

They sat in the main stateroom of the *Ocean Gypsy*, catching up on each other's affairs after the events of the past forty-eight hours. A stunned and suddenly resentful Addison had been almost forcibly put to bed. He had gone meekly enough, not yet decided on a mood. Anton was going to let him stew for a while before appearing for an interview. A calm Addison was as quiet as a forest pool, and as uncommunicative. A hysterical Addison might actually part with some information.

"He jumped you by himself?" Anton asked.

"Oh, no indeed," Monboddo said. "That would have been absurd. He had the assistance of a round half dozen of his brethren. Osbert and Fell dispatched them with their usual efficiency."

"Hah!" Osbert said. "All three of us. The Lord Monboddo took out the guy who was trying to kill me. Smooth."

"Entirely fortuitous," Monboddo explained. "I tripped and slid under his legs, taking him down. Osbert then dribbled his head a bit, and he was at peace."

"Nothing difficult, really. They thought we'd go down like a cheap bimbo at the whiff of a hundred-ruble bill. Hah! Pushovers we aren't."

Monboddo winced. "Please, Osbert. Don't try so hard to be colorful."

The *Ocean Gypsy* followed the direction of Sei's maser communication toward one statistically anomalous group of rocks. Fell set a high-acceleration course toward them.

When Anton had explained what had happened to Vanessa, Monboddo had silently hugged him. Anton had been startled by how light and frail his lord was, like a bundle of reeds. Monboddo could offer him comfort, but he could not change their mission, not for anyone.

In the small galley just off the main drive, Anton made eggs. As he watched them fry, he wished he'd decided to make something more complicated, something that took more of his attention. Vanessa kept walking through his mind, hunting a deer, striding across the reception area of the Hypostasium toward him, strolling through the East Ambulatory among the carved mourners. Each time, her image vanished behind a slamming airlock hatch. The Academia Sapientiae had made arrangements, he told himself. She was contacting the Brethren. She was all right. They'd stabbed Fell at Clavius and killed eighteen Martians at Hecates Tholus, but they wouldn't harm her.

An alarm whistled as the eggs burned. The smoke made his eyes sting with tears. He flipped the charred circles into the recycling slot and started anew. He had to be careful. They didn't have many eggs. He dropped some gravlax in the pan with them. He realized that he had no idea how Vanessa liked her eggs. Probably fried a little harder than he himself preferred. He should ask her. De Borgra hadn't managed to kill her. She would live. She had to. This time he caught the eggs before they burned completely. He flipped them onto a plate.

Addison sat up on the bare pad of his stripped bed. Sitting opposite him was a grotesque puppet made out of the bed's sleeping fabrics, knotted together. It slouched ominously, huge fat arms drooping down, a troll awaiting schoolchildren. He looked up and stared at Anton, then reached with his foot and kicked the puppet. It collapsed back into a shapeless mound of sheets.

"Hello," Anton said. "I brought you some breakfast."

The way Addison looked at the food made it obvious that he was starving, but he did not want to concede anything. "Breakfast?" he said. "Is it morning?"

"You have it backward," Anton said. "Breakfast defines morning, not vice versa. This is always true, but even more true in outer space." He folded a chair out of the wall opposite Addison and sat down. The ship was silent, but they felt heavier than usual, because it was moving at high acceleration.

Addison ate hungrily. Anton watched him for a moment, and tried to lean back in the seat. The wall was vertical at his back, the seat was perpendicular to the wall, and leaning back was impossible. "John," he said severely. "This is all very well, but you really should have told us that you were a member of the Dispossessed Brethren of Christ."

Addison looked up at him. He had yolk on his upper lip. Anton handed him a napkin, and he wiped it off. "I'm not," he said.

"Now come on—" Anton began with some heat, his irritation at Addison's meddling in Nippon flooding back. He'd been played neatly, and resented it.

"Dammit!" Addison said, also angry. "I said I'm not, and I'm not. Let me explain. I tried to tell you the story, but you cut me off." He ran his hand over his nearly bald head. In sympathy, Anton tugged at the waxed ends of his own forked beard. It could stand a trimming, he thought. Vanessa had said that it was getting a little long.

"It's so easy to get trapped," Addison said. "The world is always waiting for it—hell, that's what the world *is*, after all. A gigantic trap. And all of us stuck inside it. Flies in amber."

" 'We are all conceived in close Prison,' " Anton quoted. " 'In our Mothers' wombs, we are close Prisoners all; when we are borne, we are borne but to the liberty of the house; Prisoners still, though within larger walls; and then all our life is but a going out to the place of Execution, to death.' "

"Who—?"

"John Donne. A poet."

"Don't know him. Sounds like a member of the Brethren."

"He wasn't," Anton said. "I doubt if he would have been if he could."

"And I'm not either! Can't you listen to what I'm trying to say? They took me young, and never let me go, making me a—what?—close prisoner. I was an art student at the Kokand School of Design in East Turkestan, in the middle of the desert. It gave peace and quiet to work, they said. Peace and quiet, with the wind shouting obscenities at you."

"The Takla Makan," Anton said, remembering the exhibit in the Hypostasium. "Near the old Brethren monastery?"

"Actually within what was left of it. That's where I met them. You know how it is, at school. Secret brotherhoods, special handshakes, mysterious meeting places. It's all part of the fun. You don't know what it all means, or how serious it can get. And there wasn't anything else around. The school had started at the monastery, and kept on after the Brethren vanished. But they hadn't vanished after all, of course. And I . . . I don't know how I lost my freedom to them. God is trapped in the universe . . . we are all trapped. My freedom of action just went away. They helped me, and I found myself helping them."

"Is that what brought you to the Moon?" Anton asked.

"I wasn't doing very well." Addison grabbed the

sheets and wrapped them around himself. He folded and draped them to give himself exaggeratedly wide shoulders, concealing his own form. "I wanted to be on my own but the times aren't for it. Everyone belongs to an association, a family, a group. They give up their freedom for security. I wouldn't do that. I lived like a dog, trying to sell my art, day by day. Sometimes I just couldn't produce. Then I would starve. But I was on my own. They knew when to come to me. One day I got a message that I could find a position with Clavius, where Ozaki had worked. And all I would have to do was watch some relic in a cave. I was a fool. I went."

"It sat in a spherical chamber of polished rock."

"Yes. A big tangle of tubes. It looked like a bassoon."

"A bassoon," Anton said. "An Acherusian artifact."

"No. It looked like an Acherusian artifact, all right, but it was made by human hands. I know that. I can tell the difference. It was left there by the Brethren sometime in the past. I have absolutely no idea what it was for. It was called Boaz, and I even had a title, Warden of Boaz. But I didn't go there for that. I went because of Karl Ozaki."

"Who had been Warden of Boaz before you," Anton said with dawning understanding. "And Tennerman before him. All of you sitting and watching an underground artwork. Not something any of you were particularly qualified to do."

Addison stared off into space for a long moment, and took a breath. "Yes. I didn't know that he was associated with the Brethren. I didn't believe it. How could he have been? Ozaki was his own man, always. He didn't need joining. He didn't have to belong to some corporate group, a Household, an Academia."

"A valid approach. But, as you said, the times aren't for it. We live in a century of transcendent corporate spiritual efforts." Irritated at not being able to slouch down in his seat, Anton finally folded it back up into the wall and collapsed to the floor. He twisted and turned there for a moment, like a dog trying to get comfortable in an unfamiliar spot. "So that's why all of you ended up at Clavius. But why did Tennerman end the way he did?"

"Clavius is smarter than you think, than any of you think. He's had years to check out the crater and its tunnels. He knew that he had something on each of us, and used it. The Brethren pulled me there, and then he squeezed me because he knew I had no choice. He forced the work out of all of us."

"Brilliant work too," Anton said.

"He made me feel like a tool in his hands!" Addison exclaimed. "I hated it. Tennerman couldn't stand it. I think it finally drove him mad, watching a cave in the rock and having Clavius always pushing, pushing, shoving Tennerman's head into the work until it was finished. Ozaki faked his death to escape."

"Clavius has as much right to create the universe as you do," Anton said, just to be difficult. "He didn't have the skill, so he used yours."

Addison glared at him, but Anton met his eyes. The sculptor looked away. "The Brethren finally came to collect Boaz. They came through a passage Tennerman had built at the back of the sculpture studio. Fell got hurt. I thought it was my fault. There wasn't anything I could do. But afterward, I was empty. What was there left? I had belonged, but then didn't anymore. When you offered me the chance to go after Ozaki, it was a godsend."

"And it took you back to Jerusalem the Lost."

"I didn't know! I swear to you, I had no idea." Addison was bitter. "I'd learned all about the home temple, the great Cathedral, the Ark, as they sometimes called it. It's part of the faith. I knew its passages and its uses, but I didn't know where it was, or what it was. It was just a grand hypothesis, the place that shifts and changes, concealing the reality of God beneath the flickering, whirling lie of the universe. I didn't know that the Dead

End was Jerusalem the Lost until I was there, seeing its eternal change, and by then it was too late.''

Anton remembered Addison's sculpture *The Duelist*, which had startled him with its simple power. It portrayed a muscular man, a gladiator, with his head thrown back, teeth bared in pain or triumph. A work of genius, and the man who had created it was incapable of the simplest sort of reasoning. Fate scattered its gifts like jewels, and it was a fortunate man who collected more than one or two.

"So it didn't occur to you that the Brethren's ship was using the *Charlotte Amalie* to move?" Anton said. "Europa, Mars, Earth, the Moon. And now back to Jerusalem the Lost. The Grand Tour."

"I don't know what you're talking about. I watched Boaz."

Monboddo's head popped around the edge of the doorway. "Gentlemen, if you would be so kind, we are approaching that cluster of asteroids that Mr. Lindgren has chosen for us. I would be gratified if you would join us on the bridge for the approach."

They proceeded up the spiral stairs to the control room. Halfway up, the gravity vanished, since the ship had arrived at its destination, and they pulled themselves along the curving banisters.

"Now," Monboddo said. "How shall we find our mysterious artist? We know his location only approximately, and the volume remaining is quite large."

"Let's take a look," Anton said. "I suspect we'll see the answer."

Fell flicked on the screen. For an instant there was nothing on it but stars. He tracked the view in on the nearest rock.

Queen Victoria tumbled slowly toward them. She wore an elaborate full-length dress and had, in her outstretched hands, a globe of the Earth, at which she stared disdainfully. Her face was pinched and resembled that of a herring.

"My God!" Anton said. "That thing must be two hundred meters long! I think that's a clue."

Queen Victoria tumbled on. They passed the hem of her dress.

"Look!" Fell said. "Bloomers."

"Two hundred meters long," Monboddo said in awe. "He carved a statue two hundred meters long, and he uses it to make fun of ancient undergarments. What sort of man is this?"

Anton knew that this group of asteroids was probably an orbiting sculpture garden, full of brilliant works, and he would have liked to spend hours searching through it. There was no time.

"Here's another one!" Fell sang out.

A gargantuan head with malevolent yellow eyes appeared. The face was that of an elderly Asian man, a wispy beard clinging to the chin, skin pulled tightly over the substructure of bone. Every feature was revealed with the clarity of genius, a masterpiece of the stone carver's art.

The eyes stared into the cabin with the petulant anger of a god disturbed in the middle of creating a universe. "He certainly looks angry," Monboddo said.

"Yes," Addison said. "Worse than his other self-portraits. More powerful too."

"A growing sense of cosmic self," Anton said. After the initial shock of the head's appearance, more details became apparent. Around the lower part of the beard floated a "broomstick," which amounted to a reaction drive with a seat on it, and an arsenal of large-scale sculpting devices that, on Earth, would have rated as banned weapons that could have changed the balance of power in any twenty-first-century war. It took a lot of power to turn a two-hundred-meter-long chunk of rock into Queen Victoria. Gutzon Borglum's heads of the Presidents at Mount Rushmore were one-tenth that size.

Floating on the side of the head opposite the sun, somewhat incongruously, was a brightly decorated Jap-

anese kite, blowing in the solar wind. Its body was a
concave circle, highly reflective, while around it were a
series of small reflecting planes. The planes changed their
angles periodically, through some control mechanism,
and made the kite flutter and drift from side to side as
if it were in an actual wind.

"That head doesn't look any friendlier," Anton said.
"I think what it means is 'no peddlers or solicitors.' "
He wondered how they could they get Ozaki's cooperation. His cooperation? Anton suddenly realized that they
were here to steal his ngomite. They could quite possibly
have to proceed against his active resistance.

"Why hasn't anyone mentioned seeing any of these
things?" Addison wondered. "They seem so obvious."

"They're obvious only when you've finally found
them," Anton said. "And not before. The Asteroid Belt
is a damn big place, almost entirely empty space. Normal
statistical fluctuations give you rock concentrations like
this. Besides, this simply confirms what we all feel about
Ozaki's personality. He is ambiguous about his anonymity. I'm hoping that he is ambiguous enough to let us in
to talk to him."

The communicator sounded, indicating an incoming
call. "Just in time," Monboddo said. He gestured. "Osbert. Could you please retire to your cabin? I shall need
you in reserve."

"This area is private. Please leave immediately," a
synthetic voice said. A stylized skull and crossbones had
appeared on the screen. "This area is defended with laser
mines. Leave the area immediately."

"Karl Ozaki," Monboddo said calmly. "Could you
appear? You will not fire lasers off where you could risk
damaging your work. You cannot expect anonymity if
you present a portrait bust a hundred meters high."

The skull and crossbones was replaced by Ozaki's
scowling face.

"What do you want?" he demanded.

Monboddo smiled. "Is that the prodigal's response?

He that was lost, and now is found? Ah, Karl, I had not thought that you would be thus inhospitable.''

''What?'' Ozaki scowled at Monboddo. ''Who—oh, I remember. Lord Monboddo. Ah . . . yes.''

''We have some unfinished business, do we not?'' Monboddo said, the smile fading from his face. ''A matter of work contracted, but not delivered, through the good offices of our mutual friend, the Justice of Clavius? Is my recollection in error?''

Ozaki was distinctly taken aback. ''Well, I . . . I . . .'' Expecting to have his resurrection from the dead greeted with glad cries, he was instead being chastised for his personal failings.

''You died, is that what you are trying to tell me? Hah! Utter nonsense, I see now. How taken in I was! I am ashamed to admit it now. I even shed a tear or two, in memory of a great man and a great artist. I did! And now, what do I see? The artist himself, owing some fifty thousand rubles, and the project still uncompleted twenty years later. My beloved wife's portrait! I had my heart set on it. Beware the rage of the unsatisfied patron, Karl Ozaki,'' Monboddo thundered, as well as he could with his weak, reedy voice. ''It is an earthly token of the worm that dyeth not and will consume you in the end. Oh, what ingratitude! Swindled. Swindled, like a babe on his first time at the art auction. It is unbearable!''

''Look, Monboddo, I'm sorry,'' Ozaki said, hastening to mollify him. ''We'll take care of it. Uh, did you really hunt me down like this over that contract? I've wondered what to do about it, but it seemed inappropriate for me to do anything whatsoever, even through a third party.''

''Lest anyone see through your imposture. Of course. But no, Mr. Ozaki, I did not hunt you through the barren spaces of the Asteroid Belt over the matter of an unsatisfied contract. If that had been the matter, I would simply have sent my solicitors in an armed gunboat, with one battery of writs and another of laser cannon.''

"Ah!" Ozaki said, startled. "That violates the Treaty of Juno. You can't do that."

"The Treaty of Juno does not prohibit private citizens from seeking justice. I merely thought I would mention it, seeing as I had you available. No. Several weeks ago I was visiting my old friend Clavius—"

"Friend. Hah. That's a good one, Monboddo. You and him—"

"Mr. Ozaki, the personal relations of Judicial Lords are of interest to no one but themselves, and I would thank you to control your references to them."

Anton watched, marveling. In a few short sentences Monboddo had put Ozaki into an inferior position from which he was forced to complain. This position did not please Ozaki, who was used to getting his own way, and had for most of his adult life, but he found himself in it anyway, fight and struggle against it as he might.

"As I was saying," Monboddo continued with an air of great forbearance. "I was visiting Clavius. In his employ at that time he had an artist, who may be accounted your successor."

"John Addison!" Ozaki said. "Yes, I know him. He's good."

"You are to be commended on your attention to the current art market on Earth," Monboddo said with heavy sarcasm, obviously irritated at having been interrupted once again. "That is quite true. Mr. Addison had become less than satisfied in the service of the Justice of Clavius. I offered him a position and he accepted. Less dramatic, I suppose, than creating an explosion that breaches the atmospheric integrity of the dome over Clavius and faking one's own death, but that is the way of it, sometimes. Life treads an even and regular pace, and some of us, at least, are glad at the quiet of it."

"What are you saying?" Ozaki said, growing impatient.

"Has the clink of chisels made you deaf? Mr. Addison took service with me. Upon hearing that we were bound for the Asteroid Belt, he indicated an interest in meeting you. Your traces are all over that crater, and you could not have expected that your role as the beneficent Lord Fujiwara would go forever unrecognized.''

''Actually, I had hoped that everyone had forgotten all about it.''

''Mr. Ozaki, you hoped no such thing. You may delude yourself, but you cannot delude me. At any rate, if you will permit me to reach my point, after some detour and digression, I will say that I acceded to Mr. Addison's request, and have brought him here to meet you and pay his humble respects.'' He stepped aside and dexterously slid Addison into the field of view.

Ozaki regarded him, carefully showing neither approval nor disapproval. ''John Addison? You carved that piece called *The Sarsen Stone*, did you not?''

''Yes,'' Addison said, eyes wide. ''I don't know what happened to it. It was bought anonymously at the TWA Terminal Show, at the old Kennedy Airport.''

Ozaki suddenly smiled. ''*I* bought it, my boy. I still have agents on Earth willing to perform favors for an old man. Ah.'' He looked at them thoughtfully. ''But who is your third?''

''Anton Lindgren,'' he identified himself. ''The Lord Monboddo's Seneschal.''

''Of course. And the author of *The Works of Carlos MacReady*, are you not?''

''I am.''

''Interesting. There are several points I might argue with you, particularly as regards your opinions on his attempts to revive the antirealist traditions of the twentieth and twenty-first centuries.''

Anton inclined his head. ''I am always willing to discuss my opinions.''

Ozaki stared at them for a moment longer. ''Very well,'' he said finally. ''I cannot deny a clamorous public. There are . . . only three of you aboard?''

''No,'' Monboddo said. ''We are accompanied by a

bodyguard as well." Fell stared at Ozaki, who seemed nettled by his opaque appraisal. "That makes four. And we are all getting rather tired of one another, if I may say so."

Ozaki looked annoyed with himself. He had made the mistake of asking a direct question. Question asked, and answer being given, he had no choice but to accept it. Gentlemen do not demand to search each other's ships, at least not on ostensibly purely social occasions, and if it was one thing that Ozaki had always wanted to be, it was a gentleman. Artists from Velásquez to Benvenuto Cellini had managed it. Why not him?

"If you would like to enjoy our hospitality," Monboddo added after letting Ozaki twist in the wind for a moment, "we would be happy to have you over for some tea. I could show you the *Ocean Gypsy*. I have worked hard on her, and there are some aspects of her design that I think might very well interest you." He did not say, "Come over here and search my ship, if you're nervous." That would have been crass.

"No, no, that's all right. I would like to have you come over here instead." His eyes examined those parts of the cabin visible behind Monboddo, Anton, and Addison, as if still wishing to search the ship but unwilling to accept Monboddo's hospitality in order to do so.

Monboddo frowned for a moment, considering the offer. Did they have time for it? Didn't they have a dinner engagement elsewhere, for which they were already late? Was this the right Ozaki, or had they made a terrible mistake? Finally, he smiled. "Certainly. We would be delighted. Fell will remain with the ship, of course." He managed to sound as if he was doing Ozaki a signal favor.

"Ah, certainly. I'll take you on a tour." His face vanished, to be replaced by its stone image against a sea of stars. Having finally seen the all-too-human, vacillating, and easily bullied Ozaki, Anton could see that this unsmiling, eternal image was Ozaki's desire for himself. He was further from achieving it than he ever had been, since stern dignity and dominion over others are acquired not in isolation, but by interacting with other human beings.

"Into your suits, gentlemen," Monboddo said.

Vanessa wiped the blood from the corner of her mouth. "Is this the way you treat the official Academia Sapientiae observer?" Gingerly she pushed herself up from the floor where she'd been thrown, and stood. No bones seemed to be broken.

"Official observer?" the woman facing her asked. "I don't recognize that office." She was old. No, Vanessa corrected herself when she had looked more closely. The woman was ancient.

"No, I suppose you don't. There seem to be many agreements that the Dispossessed Brethren of Christ do not recognize."

"Don't talk to me about agreements," the woman snapped. Beneath the black felt hat that hid her hair, her eyebrows were white and bushy, her eyes piercing. "You have just aided the escape of several of our enemies."

"How am I supposed to know how to define your enemies when you refuse to give me any information whatsoever? You forced me into ridiculous extremities just to get into contact with you." Vanessa craned her neck around. "Is this a council chamber of some sort? Where the Syndics of Jerusalem the Lost meet?"

The chamber was a half dome, a dais in the front faced by ranks of seats in semicircles, about sixty in all, each equipped with a data hook and a writing desk. Around the base of the dome ran a frieze of portraits in severe style, about twenty-five in all. Each was of a stern-faced man or woman wearing a dark red robe, a gold chain of office, and a black felt hat. The woman who now stood facing Vanessa wore the same uniform. One portrait, about halfway down the line, was blacked out, as was the name under it. The blacking had a perceptual effect, pulling in on the portraits on either side, like a blind spot in the visual field. It took some effort to see that it was there.

"Ms. Karageorge, I am not obliged to give you any information. The Academia Sapientiae feels that it has the right to know everything. This is not true."

"We do have an obligation to history, Grand Master." Vanessa counted portraits. "The twenty-fourth Grand Master of the Dispossessed Brethren of Christ. Or do you count that as twenty-three?"

The Grand Master's eyes were as sharp as needles. The old often become washed-out all over, with white hair and pale eyes, but all of her character had been concentrated into two intense points. "You need an education in our ways," she said, her voice flat and ominous. "If you survive, we can talk further." She turned away slightly, as if to issue a command.

"Wait!" Vanessa said, dismayed to hear her voice crack. "Do you still need the missing part of Nehushtan?"

The Grand Master's eyes bored into her. "Where is it?"

"A safe place. I want to make a deal."

"Why should we negotiate with you? Since we now know you brought it with you, we simply need find it."

Vanessa managed a laugh. "Good luck. It's about five centimeters long, and this asteroid isn't short of hiding places. How long do you think it would take to find it?" Her hope was that the Grand Master would believe that Vanessa had possessed the fragment since the Hypostasium, and thus could have hidden it anywhere on the Dead End, rather than hurriedly in the airlock chamber.

"What do you want?" the Grand Master asked, finally.

"I already told you. It's simple. I want information. History. That's my job. A fairly low price, I think. History isn't a commodity. You can start with your name."

"Very well. I agree. Where is it?" The Grand Master

scowled when Vanessa told her where the fragment was. "Clever, and foolish. But I will not renege. You see, we keep our agreements, when the other party does not violate them." She stepped behind the dais. "My name is Deborah Durogin. Do you know how Nehushtan came to be in your collections at the Hypostasium?"

"No. I don't think anyone does."

"Very well." Durogin vanished. She was replaced by a scene of a rocky desert, sharp ridges rising like the backs of fossilized dinosaurs. "The Brethren arose in the waste areas of the Earth. God is everywhere concealed, everywhere imprisoned in His creation, giving the greatest gift of all, Himself."

A solitary spacecraft rose up from behind a ridge and vanished into the sky.

"The Brethren decided to give a gift in return. They would purge themselves of the dross of existence, carve away the flabby material world that hangs on God, and free Him, so that He once again stood alone, contemplating."

Blocks of stone appeared and were carved into statues of ecstatic saints and wild beasts by spacesuited figures. The statues stood in bare vacuum, unblinking stars above them. Vanessa did not recognize any of them. Great works of art, they had long since been concealed or destroyed.

"That was our glory, to reveal with each motion the God that lay beneath. Those who had eyes could see. Finally, the greatest carving of all was attempted." A red-cloaked figure appeared, hunched over a complex shape: one of the Instruments. "Abakumov gave form to chaos and gave us the chance to carve the universe!" Abakumov turned and, face still invisible, disappeared from the scene.

"Then arose a Grand Master who wished to turn his back on the great task and return us to the Earth we had so long ago fled." The council chamber reappeared, but now its seats were filled by long-dead Syndics. Vanessa noticed that the wall behind them now held only a dozen portraits, none of them blacked out. The Syndics gestured angrily down at the dais, where a man stood, dressed in the dark red of a Grand Master, chain of office gleaming. He had no face. It wasn't as if the face had simply been blotted out. The concept of face just did not apply to this man. Armed soldiers burst into the chamber, dragged two of the Syndics out of their seats, and killed them at the foot of the dais. The faceless man stood motionless.

"He betrayed our dreams," Durogin's voice said. "He tried to change our work when it was almost finished, to turn us back from the direction we had chosen, back to Earth, back to prison. He wished God to remain trapped."

"Who was he?" Vanessa asked.

"He had no name." Durogin's tone was matter-of-fact. "He did not really exist."

"That's not history."

"No matter how deeply a name is carved in stone, it can be removed, until there is nothing but the virgin flatness of new marble. That may not be history, but it is fact." The faceless, nameless Grand Master marched out of the council chamber. He was replaced by four complex, twisting artifacts.

"Jachin, Boaz, Nehushtan, Aaron's Rod," Vanessa said.

"The Instruments. Our greatest work. Abakumov's creation. The goal that was to be betrayed. But some had seen the coming conflict, and prepared for it." Figures seized the Instruments, hauled them down dark tunnels, and placed them aboard spaceships. One was thrust into deep ice tunnels on Europa. One was hidden at Hecates Tholus, on Mars. One vanished into the tunnels under the crater Clavius on the Moon. One was hauled to a monastery in the desert of Sinai, on Earth.

"We disappeared," Durogin said. "The Dispossessed Brethren of Christ vanished from the visible universe. The monasteries on Earth, the Moon, and Mars were eventually destroyed. Nehushtan was hidden in a collection of Acherusian artifacts, though it was made by the hands of men, and in this disguise went to the Academia Sapientiae. The Dispossessed Brethren of Christ had ceased to exist." Her voice lowered. "But we survived. The world had forgotten us, but we continued to live. The time has come for us to complete our task. The Dispersal is over, the Instruments are in our hands again. We can carve the universe." The four Instruments gleamed enigmatically.

The council chamber filled with light. Vanessa found herself surrounded by Brethren, hands on their swords. Grand Master Durogin glared down at her from the dais. "You want to understand. I will give you the opportunity to perceive the essential nature of our task. If you survive your necessary education, you can observe its culmination."

"Dammit!" Vanessa shouted as they seized her and pulled her out of the chamber. "We made a deal."

"We did," Durogin said, watching calmly after her. "The piece of Nehushtan for information. You are getting your information. We did not agree that you would survive to impart it to anyone else."

"My ancestors, overcrowded and away from nature, invented the rock garden to represent nature in microcosm. An ocean filled with islands, a range of mountains, a vast river: all could be represented by an arrangement of rocks in a tiny area. One could look at them, meditating, and *see* in their pattern and texture the larger world from which they came."

Anton, Monboddo, and Addison floated in the midst of Ozaki's orbital rock garden. The broomstick had passed many of the asteroids Ozaki had collected for his work. A crater marked each where the thrust vector passed through the center of mass. Anton was impressed. Moving these massive rocks had been an incredible labor, totally uneconomic. Only an artist would have done it.

"Although I do not lack for space here," Ozaki said
with a self-deprecating chuckle, "man is still trapped in
his solar system. Therefore, I have represented the universe here, in these rocks."

It took a while to see. A large collection of variously
sized rocks floated in a protected position between several
large shepherd asteroids, one of which was covered with
the spidery cranes that must have moved the rocks to
their current orbits. For a moment those rocks were nothing, a bunch of debris in an unusual concentration.
Slowly, something began to appear. Order? Structure?
That family of rocks there: a solar system? What was
that peculiar glint in the distance? Was that one rock
ringed? As with any rock garden, it took patience, and
willingness to accept, but the result was worth it.

"The Solar System," Anton murmured. It wasn't a
simple model like an orrery, but something else—a symbolic representation. An orrery. He thought about the
effigy on a man's tomb in the tunnels on the Moon, a
model solar system in its hands. How did that representation relate to this one?

The collection blended together in the distance, becoming planetary nebulae, clusters of stars, galaxies. The
boundaries of the garden were uncertain. It seemed to
go on forever.

To Anton's critical eye something was missing, some
intention unfulfilled, some plan gone awry. What? He
looked more closely. Each of the rocks had a small crater
in it. Why? Surely they had not been moved to their
current locations by heavy thrusters, as the huge asteroids
around them had. These were deliberate dimples, with
no function, either aesthetic or practical. Anton thought
about asking Ozaki, but decided against it. One should
always be concerned about the information given away
by one's own questions. A searchlight reveals the search-
er's own location first of all.

He looked back over the rock garden and thought of
ngomite. He realized then what he was seeing, what those

small craters were intended for. It was a heady experience. He was a collector of finished works, and did not truly understand the nature of the artist's task, the will that brought forth a work of art where none had been before. For the first time, his mind leaped ahead from the materials to the finished work, and he had at least an inkling of creation. He saw each of those dimples occupied by the appropriate chunk of ngomite. Each piece of the vital mineral glinted as it caught the attenuated sunlight, catching the knot of light. The rock garden was suffused with a glow, the clear light of morning. For an instant, Anton could see what it would be like.

The image faded, and he once again saw nothing but tumbling rocks. But the memory of that vision would stay with him.

Anton Lindgren, however, was trapped by the world of events. He was concerned with the consequences of things, with their meaning in the larger scheme. In addition to his awe at the glowing vision of Karl Ozaki, here in the wastes of the Asteroid Belt, he calculated costs and consequences.

The amount of ngomite needed to realize the vision Anton had been vouchsafed would make this rock garden the single most costly work ever created. Where could Ozaki possibly find that much ngomite?

It could only have come from the chunk whose existence Anton had so long ago concluded. He made a rough estimate of its necessary volume, given the holes it must fill, and looked for it. And found it.

A rough stone cylinder spun amid the rocks. He stared at it. Somewhere beneath its dull surface, he was certain, lay the ngomite they had been searching for. It had to be there. The cylinder was a model of the Dead End. This gave him pause. When it was broken up for the ngomite to be put into the proper places, the Dead End would vanish. He was getting used to thinking in the symbols and signs so beloved of the Dispossessed Brethren of Christ, and knew that this was not an accidental feature.

The ngomite was about one hundred meters from him, in the middle of Ozaki's rock garden, surrounded by other rocks in orbit with it. He could not get to it from where he floated. It was only possible to look at it, spinning just out of reach.

Anton fought down disappointment. Was this what he had been seeking? The puzzle had been important. Karl Ozaki had been important. The ngomite, now, was left over as some sort of unpleasant aftereffect. One that could turn deadly.

He looked across the rocks, to find Addison staring straight at him. Anton thought back over his own actions. Had he done anything unusual that would have revealed the specific point of his interest?

"Anton," Monboddo's voice whispered on a private channel. "Fell just got a message from the Martian ship the *Rapier*. The Technics have broken loose from the *Charlotte Amalie*, at full emergency acceleration."

"They're on their way here," Anton said decisively. He tried to picture Theonave de Borgra, wounded and enraged, piloting the *Hans Lesker* toward them. He'd never seen de Borgra. He wondered what Vanessa's former lover was like. "They can track our fusion emissions, if they wish."

"They ripped loose without detaching umbilicals and damaged the *Charlotte Amalie*'s systems. In addition, the *Rapier* is stuck."

"What do you mean?" Anton felt a chill.

"I don't know!" The tension in Monboddo's voice was clear. "The Technics have gimmicked their linkages. Rather a clever trick, actually. It will be some time before they pull clear."

Anton looked off into the stars as if he could spot the flare of the Technics' fusion drive. It wouldn't take more than hours.

15

"You're an idiot, John," Anton said wearily. "An absolute idiot."

"Shut up," Addison said. "Just don't move." He'd wrapped his feet around a column for stability and held the meter-long carving laser tightly in his hands, the innocuous-looking glass of its business end pointed at Anton.

"I can't help moving," Anton said as he floated. "I'm not attached to anything. Neither is Lord Monboddo. You should have thought of that before."

"Shut up!"

They all floated in the brightly lit interior of Ozaki's asteroid, divided into vast, curving spaces that seemed made from bone, as if this were indeed the inside of Ozaki's skull. The air was full of dust, of floating particles, of tiny liquid globules. A large snake writhed past them, snagged a sphere of water, and swam up toward the next chamber. An amazingly graceful tortoise followed, its shell inlaid with the face of a Japanese demon.

Ozaki hung in the air behind Addison, thin beard and hair floating around his head like a nimbus. Anton realized, at that moment, how old the artist was, how unprepared for the chaos that he had allowed into his space. He was perturbed, not used to controversy, and things were happening too quickly for him. Three men had followed him through the airlock, and then one of his uninvited guests had turned a weapon on the other two. "This is most odd. I don't understand—"

"I don't know who they really are," Addison said, his eyes as expressionless as the blue sky seen from the bottom of a well. "But they're after something. They're enemies. They've hidden an extra man aboard their ship, Osbert."

"Nonsense. If you don't know who we are, how do you know we're enemies?" Anton asked reasonably. He and Monboddo drifted slowly apart, widening Addison's target. He'd expected suspicion, but not this suddenly violent reaction. He cursed himself. To come this far and be killed by a lunatic artist would have the absurdity of all true tragedy. He watched Addison closely. The sculptor was not used to carving human flesh. How long would it take him to learn?

"By the way you're acting!" Addison said. "You're opposing the Brethren—"

"Oh, so now we're suddenly all worried about the Brethren, are we?" Anton asked with heavy sarcasm. "Those people who manipulated and forced you into courses of action you didn't want? I'd think you'd be more worried about the Technics."

Ozaki blinked. "The Technics?"

"Don't listen to them," Addison muttered. "You don't know these two."

Monboddo floated wide-eyed near one of the curving walls. "The Technic vessel *Hans Lesker* is approaching this asteroid. It should be here in less than an hour. While the *Ocean Gypsy* is unarmed, this is certainly not true of the *Hans Lesker*." He turned his gaze on Ozaki. "What could there be here that would interest the Technics, Mr. Ozaki? They don't usually travel such distances for purely aesthetic purposes."

Ozaki's face betrayed astonishment and fear. He had spent the last twenty years alone or with the sycophantic and respectful inhabitants of Nippon, so his ability to conceal his feelings was almost lost. Before his self-imposed exile, Ozaki had been a tyrant. Tyrants and children are seldom obliged to hide their feelings.

"I . . . I can't imagine—"

"He's making it up!" Addison cut across his words. "There aren't any Technics. It's a lie."

Anton shook his head wearily, like a theologian at a petty doctrinal error. "You can check it all out, of course. And you'll find that it's true. The Technics exist, even if you did not personally carve them out of marble. They'll be here in an hour, and I suspect they'll get what they want. Whatever it is."

"But why are *you* here?" Ozaki wailed. "What do you want?"

"Just let us get out of here," Anton bluffed. "The current political situation being what it is, I'd rather not have to deal with them, if you don't mind. If our presence bothers you, you can deal with the Technic warship on your own. The sooner the better, though. We're far from the regular space lanes, and they might just destroy the *Ocean Gypsy* on general principles. It would be a slaughter. We're completely unarmed." He sensed solid wall behind him. He felt behind him for a handhold, almost pushing himself back off. At the last instant, he found a raised edge on the rock and was able to hold on. "Please! Don't hold us here."

Addison leveled the laser at his now-stationary target. "Damn you!" he said. "You're twisting everything. This is all your doing. I know it!" He stared at them, knowing the truth, but unable to articulate it. Anton did not envy him the role of Cassandra, telling the truth and not being believed, but didn't have any energy left over to feel sorry for him.

"Why are you doing this? After what the Brethren did to you?"

"The Brethren have nothing to do with this. They're just an excuse to you. It's Karl Ozaki I'm worried about.'' He did not look at the old man, who stared at all of them in horror. "It's him that you're after. And you used me to get to him.''

Anton looked at Monboddo, rejecting Addison's arguments, though they were all completely true. "On the other hand, my lord, we could just talk to the Technics and claim neutrality. They'd probably let us go. They couldn't risk bullying a Judicial Lord.''

"Perhaps not.'' Monboddo shrugged, as if the matter were of little interest. "However, it would be a pity if they did a lot of damage here.''

"It depends on what they're looking for. And how rowdy they get. They might just take their frustration out on the sculptures. Napoleon's soldiers used the nose of the Sphinx for target practice. It's an old tradition.''

"Yes.'' Monboddo frowned. "But why would they want to come here in the first place?''

"Who knows?'' Anton said. "Who can figure out why those maniacs do anything?'' He looked at the old artist.

"The ngomite,'' Ozaki whispered. "I don't know how they found it, but they must be after the ngomite. Twenty kilograms of it.''

The silence stretched. Addison stared at them, his hands now loose on his weapon. Anton thought about jumping for it. He wouldn't have to. He desperately hoped he wouldn't have to.

"Do you want the Technics to have your ngomite?'' Anton asked. "Or do you want us to save it for you?''

Monboddo held the Blood Bowl gently in his hands. The brilliant simplicity of the red-flecked bowl with its slender pedestal asserted itself, as if it were the Platonically ideal bowl made flesh, the bowl from which all other bowls took their nature. Monboddo ran his fingers along the edge.

"Sometimes this bowl makes me feel unreal,'' he said, "as if I were the created object, and it the creator. And truly I would not be who I am if I had not held this in my hands.''

"Caroline Apthorpe carved it in 2198," Anton said harshly, as if the factual information would somehow reduce the enormity of their coming action. "Its substance is lazarite. Aya Ngomo named it after Lazarus, because she was almost dead when she found it and it gave her the strength to go on."

"You are right, Anton," Monboddo murmured. "This bowl is specific, not Platonic. Still . . . it seems that it exists outside our petty world. Perhaps it is better that it leave a world much too harsh for it."

"We can't excuse ourselves that way either, my lord."

They floated with Addison in Ozaki's null-g studio. The curving walls around them held all of the apparatus necessary for what they were to do. Ozaki himself was in another chamber, awaiting the approach of the Technics. Almost catatonic with terror, he was unable to make a decision.

Monboddo handed the bowl to Anton, who looked down into its liquid depths and stroked its smooth surface. He felt miserable. Reason had taken him here, and the conjunction of the Technics and Ozaki's ngomite did not seem to allow any other conclusion. But did even the needs of the entire Union, or even the entire human race, take precedence over beauty's right to exist? He remembered the way Vanessa's fingers had stroked it, so long ago, that first night they had met.

Addison took the bowl and, with a shudder, clamped it into a vise. "Is this all we can do?" he asked plaintively.

"Do you have a better idea?" Anton snapped. "Do you want the Technics to get everything, and our lives into the bargain?"

Monboddo patted his shoulder. "Quiet, Anton. Are you ready, Mr. Addison?"

Addison stared down at the object he was being compelled to destroy and shook his head slowly. "This is insane." He looked up at Anton, expressionless, his face purged of suffering. "Insane. But you planned this all, didn't you? It's not an accident, something that just happened. It's happening because you want it to."

"Do it," Anton said harshly. "You're the only one with the skill. You have to do it."

"You hold me in your hands," Addison said. "I am your instrument. Are you sure this is the reality you want to create?"

"Do it!"

Addison cut into the edge of the bowl with the saw. "It's like carving through living bone," he whispered.

Anton felt an almost sacred terror, a sense of necessary sacrilege. Addison worked with a calm fury, shivering the beautiful bowl into fragments, which he then shaped and joined together, until, when he was finished, he had a replica of the spinning model of the Dead End in Ozaki's rock garden. He filled the model with rock, so that it massed around the same amount as the ngomite. Twenty kilograms. Anton had calculated not less than eighteen.

Lazarite was quite a different substance from ngomite, but if things worked properly, the difference would only become apparent too late. Technics tended to depend on their technology, and their instruments would detect the Island of Stability elements that ngomite and lazarite had in common. If all went as planned, it was that similarity that would prove decisive. If the plans went awry, then they had made a cruel and vile sacrifice.

Addison pushed himself away from what he had just done and huddled against a wall. "We carve and we carve, and all we have when we are finished is a tomb." He looked tearfully over his shoulder at Anton. "Have you made yourself real by this?"

"Damn you, I'm not acting to define myself," Anton said.

"Why else do we act?" Addison wrung his hands, an

oddly melodramatic gesture. "I don't see the blood. But I can feel it."

Having waited discreetly out of sight until he was necessary, Osbert floated in and took possession of the model. Without a word, he floated back out. The Blood Bowl no longer existed save as an image burned into Anton's soul.

They waited until they knew that Osbert had put on the walkabout, the single-man spaceship carried by the *Ocean Gypsy*, and vanished into space. He would float there, virtually indetectable, until needed. If things did not go well, he might float there forever.

This is what it came down to. After months of careful planning and concept, of delicately laid operations, the denouement of their plot depended on a desperate last-minute contrivance, which might shatter into a thousand pieces should de Borgra and Sellering launch a blow in an unexpected direction. Gone were any concerns of cultural superiority, of the forces of history. This pivot turned on a pin of mere cleverness.

They all regarded each other, the officers of the Terran Division of External Security, the agents of the Technic Alliance, and the two artists, trapped between them. All around them the walls were carved with a bas-relief of endless staring faces. They peered in, goggle-eyed, all the races of the Solar System, all of them equally moronic. They reduced whatever they were looking at to the status of ludicrous shenanigans. Ozaki had named this work *The Great Public*.

"Anton Lindgren," de Borgra enunciated with satisfaction. He floated stiffly, newly bandaged, his face puffy, but was dressed in shining new clothes that swirled iridescently around him. Behind him were Sellering, and two of his men, Thurman and Vangwill. "I had wondered what you were like." He examined Anton not contemptuously, but with an objective intentness. "Interesting."

Anton was too tense and drained to want to trade words with Vanessa's ex-lover, particularly when de Borgra might kill him at any moment.

De Borgra leaned toward him. His silver eyes bored into Anton's. Anton examined the face before him, dimpled chin, soft features, an insolent strength underlying all.

De Borgra smiled, his lips full. Had Vanessa found those lips sensuous? Had she enjoyed their kisses? "She's quite something, our dear Vanessa, isn't she? You know what she really likes? She's probably been too embarrassed to ask you yet. She's that way. If you spread her legs wide . . ."

Anton remained carefully expressionless, as if de Borgra were giving him a recipe for chocolate-chip cookies. He couldn't even find it in himself to be particularly angry. The situation was too deadly ludicrous.

"You do go on, Theo." Sellering pushed up next to de Borgra and whispered to him. He glowered around the room, irritated at being interrupted in his speech. "The ngomite isn't on this asteroid. Where is it, Ozaki?"

Addison tried to relax. They'd had a long and tense discussion. Several times Ozaki had refused to speak any longer, had pulled away and stared blankly at a wall as if contemplating it for further carving. But finally Anton and Monboddo had convinced him that there was only one course of action. At least, the old man had seemed convinced. What he would do now was another matter.

Ozaki turned slowly toward de Borgra. His pale eyes took the measure of the Technic and he nodded. Despite the lack of gravity, he sagged all over, a defeated man. "I came here to escape you human beings. Rock is hard to carve but it is never cruel."

"Never mind the philosophical statements!" De Borgra was contemptuous. "You Terrans are full of them. It makes me sick." He drifted toward Ozaki and loomed over him. "We've checked this place. The ngomite isn't here. So don't try to be smart. Just tell us where it is."

"I will show you. It is in another orbit. As long as there is no violence."

"That is up to you. And"—de Borgra looked at Lindgren and Monboddo—"your overly clever friends."

Ozaki didn't look at anyone. Addison just hung, looking at his hands as if he had never seen them before.

The four Technics, unwilling to split their forces for guard duty, hustled all the Terrans out of the airlock. There they were joined by Fell. Lindgren made eye contact with him, but there was no expression in the other's face. They were all helpless prisoners dependent on one ridiculous gamble.

"This way." Ozaki's voice was barely audible in the headphones. They all drifted toward Ozaki's rock garden. Before them was the massive shape of the *Hans Lesker*.

Anton looked at Monboddo's tiny figure as it floated in front of him. What was he thinking now? Having calculated all the probabilities and made all the possible decisions, Monboddo was probably thinking about something completely unrelated: creating obscene limericks about de Borgra, imagining new constellations, or remembering the rooms at Fresh Pond.

Again the rock garden appeared. Once a brilliant artwork, to Anton it was now nothing more than a collection of matter spinning through space. It was an instrument that might save him or might kill him. Art, he reflected gloomily, had no soul. But what, then, of the Blood Bowl? What destruction could a man encompass in order to survive?

De Borgra glanced over the rock garden. "Ah, how clever. Where to hide a rock? With a bunch of other rocks. Stupid, but it works."

They all gathered in a knot near a shoulder of the shepherd asteroid. The cranes embedded in it hung like silent whips above them. Addison kept as near Ozaki as he could, just below his arm, but looked at no one.

"The Brethren gave it to me," Ozaki said. "For a great work."

"And in exchange," Lindgren said, attempting to solve a few final mysteries, "you gave them your statue of the Dead Christ."

"Yes. That was mine to dispense with. This ngomite is not."

"Do you need a signed contract?" de Borgra grated. "We can write it with what's left of your bodies."

"A simple business deal." Ozaki was no longer interested. "And now the ngomite goes to you. Much luck may you have with it."

He activated one of the cranes. "I saw it, and the great monument came to my mind. A monument . . . to my own stupidity." The crane extended itself as if reaching out to the ends of the universe, stretching and stretching. It finally dropped a filament down through the countless delicately orbiting stones and pulled the model of the Dead End, still spinning, out through some passage not visible to the eye. "The ngomite inspired the work. As soon as I found it, I knew what it was for, how I could use it. Did the Elder Race put it here for that purpose? It was to be a final memorial to the Solar System, once they have left it."

The crane moved slowly and smoothly. The cylinder drifted along. Anton clenched his jaw fiercely, until he felt his teeth were going to crack. It was such an insane risk!

"Stop it!" de Borgra shouted. "Stop it this instant!"

"What?" Ozaki turned back to de Borgra, puzzled at the other's rage. The ngomite accelerated. Ozaki's face was sharply carved, each plane cleanly defined. He stared at de Borgra with distant contempt.

Ozaki had moved the crane so that it would whip the cylinder away from them at high velocity, like an angler casting a fly. Once it had been flung from the crane no one would be able to find it again. It would drift slowly out of the Asteroid Belt and vanish forever.

Without a further word, de Borgra fired twice, catching Ozaki in the chest. The old artist had done exactly what

Anton had asked. And for that he died. His body spun slowly away from the controls.

The heavy cylinder moved past, just out of de Borgra's reach. If it disappeared into the darkness, the Technics would never be able to radar-track it out from among the other rocks in time. The Martian ship had managed to free itself from the *Charlotte Amalie* and was almost on them.

"Son of a bitch!" de Borgra screamed, and launched himself after it. "Home on my transponder. I'll be right on that damn rock."

Anton could just see his figure, arms outstretched, chasing the ngomite. He passed to the other side of the big head of Ozaki, toward the Japanese kite that floated out behind, blowing in the solar wind.

"Got it!" de Borgra exclaimed in satisfaction. "A stupid goddam trick. Terrans think they're so clever. Hah! I—aaah!" His scream choked off. His figure flared brightly against the stars for an instant, and vanished again.

"Okono!" Sellering called sharply. "Do you have it?"

After a long, tense pause a voice answered from the *Hans Lesker*. "I think so. I'm still getting his transponder signal. We can recover. The Martian ship is approaching. ETA three minutes."

"Damn and damn. Hurry up and get that rock!" Two suits flared out of the *Hans Lesker*. She turned back, gesturing with her gun. "What happened?" she demanded. "Quickly! What did you do?" Her skintite had modified fingertips. They could see her fingernails fully extended in primitive rage.

Anton tensed again. She should just kill them, all of them, and leave their bodies tumbling through space, silent and unrecoverable. But she had to find out what happened, so that such a trick could never be played on her again.

"We didn't do a thing, my dear," Monboddo said.

"You and Mr. de Borgra were simply unobservant. That kite floating behind Mr. Ozaki's asteroid is one of the dozen or so mirrors that was used to melt Jerusalem the Lost during its construction. It concentrates quite a bit of heat. It is a parabolic reflector, but I doubt he had to pass very close to the focus to be, ah, burned to a crisp."

The two Technics returned, the cylinder between them. Anton tried not to look at it. Had Osbert managed the delicate legerdemain that substituted the lazarite, with its Island of Stability elements, for the ngomite, setting it on the same trajectory? De Borgra's transponder had been an extra bonus. Anton hoped that he would live to find out if they had been successful.

"Thank you very much," Sellering said. "Good-bye." She raised her gun.

Before she could fire, Fell launched himself at her. One shot tore through his arm, and then he wrapped himself around her. They struggled, blood spurting and crystallizing on the outside of his spacesuit. As he did so, Monboddo and Anton sprang in opposite directions, so that Fell's sacrifice would not be in vain. Trying to help him would have been worthless. Sellering finally fought free of his desperate embrace, shoving his body off into space. A shot grazed past Anton. Addison remained where he was, holding the withered dead body of Karl Ozaki in his arms.

"The Martians, dammit!" the Technic aboard ship yelled. "We don't have time. Come on!" Sellering and the other four Technics dove for the airlock with their cylinder of ngomite. The *Hans Lesker* blasted out of the area at full acceleration.

A few moments later the bright flare of the *Rapier*'s fusion drive cast sharp shadows across the rocks.

Vanessa slammed to the floor of the cell. She jumped to her feet, but the hatch above her had already closed with a hiss, merging seamlessly into the curve of the ceiling. The only sound remaining was her own breathing.

The cell was a cylinder perhaps ten meters long and three meters in diameter. She wondered if all the Brethren's detention cells were this geometric shape, or whether others were spheres, icosahedra, parallelepipeds, rhomboids. Anton might be in one of those other cells. She pictured him, pacing back and forth, tugging on his forked beard, checking out the physical limits of his world, curiously examining the vertices and regular polygons that defined his space. He might be dead, pinwheeling through space forever. No, that was absurd. He was much too alive to be dead.

One of the cylinder's ends was rough rock veined with glowing light, like a cheese filled with phosphorescent fungus. The rest of the cylinder was a dull gray metal. Light came from a strip along the top. A hammer and chisel lay in the center, gleaming silver. She picked them up.

The chisel wouldn't even mark the metal walls. The point of the chisel would slide aside as soon as she hit the end with the hammer. The dull tock it made when she hit it was derisory. The rock at the end, however, turned out to be much softer. It powdered under blows from the chisel, and she carved several grooves across its light-veined surface before losing interest. It was pointless occupational therapy for a prisoner. She let the hammer and chisel clatter to the floor and walked back to the opposite end, where she slumped down. This was the Grand Master's education for her. The universe is a series of prisons, some more obvious than others.

The metal walls around her were so smooth to her touch that they felt as if they weren't even there, as if she were trying to reach into a painted still life to feel the fur on a dead rabbit. How was she to get food and water? How was she going to relieve herself? The way to behave when imprisoned was an important part of cultural indoctrination. A child on the Dead End probably knew where the floor of the cell would absorb feces, and where to wait to be fed. He would also know the purpose of the hammer and chisel, and the odd glowing stone wall. He might even know if he should expect to survive. Vanessa looked up at the veined stone cylinder end. Some detail struck her as wrong. She walked back over to it.

She had let the hammer and chisel fall, but now the chisel lay snug against the stone. She hadn't dropped it there. Not exactly. She pulled one end of the chisel slightly away from the wall and stared at it. Nothing. She walked back to the opposite wall, where she spent several minutes jumping up and touching the ceiling, trying to feel out the location of the hatch, without success.

When she went back to the stone wall, the chisel once again lay flush against it. She stared at the wall. The conclusion was clear. Slowly and steadily, like a plunger, that wall was pushing in along the cylinder. If it didn't stop she would be crushed, a banal and mechanical death.

She picked up the hammer and chisel and looked at the cylinder end that was moving slowly toward her. She realized what she had to do. "What the hell's this supposed to prove?" she shouted at the walls. "Goddam symbolic object lesson." She felt like throwing the instruments to the floor, but she had no choice. She could refuse to move, and die. Or she could carve.

Her first frenzied pounding brought little progress, just a shower of tiny stone chips and a pain in her shoulders. Then she adjusted to the character of the rock and the strength of her entire body and began to chip off larger and larger flakes. She dug in slowly. The work was slow and painful.

When the agony in her arms and shoulders became too great, she would turn away from her task and rest her forehead against the opposite wall, trying to ignore the constant pressure behind her. The walk from one wall to the other became progressively shorter. She was desperately thirsty, her throat parched dry. Eventually, as the pain receded, she would turn back to her task. When she picked them up, the hammer and chisel seemed to have gained in mass, and the rock grew ever harder.

Eventually she succeeded in carving a rough lozenge out of the rock. By this time the distance between the two cylinder ends was less than half a meter. She kept testing the shape of her carving, to make sure that there wasn't an edge that would press just one centimeter too far, cracking her collarbone, or squeezing her chest so that she would be unable to breathe. She suspected that she was carving a tomb out of that rock, a narrow and uncomfortable place in which to die.

She began to hit her elbow on the back wall as she carved. Then it pushed on the back of her head, forcing her, millimeter by millimeter, into her tiny, rock-cut tomb. The two cylinder walls finally ground together with a drawn-out, dismal groan. The rock above her cut off the light from the ceiling strip. In darkness and silence, unable to move more than a few centimeters, her arms held down at her sides, she waited. She wept as time ground to a silent halt.

"You are not a military commander, Anton," Miriam Kostal's voice snapped. "You are a Lieutenant in the Division of External Security. You can't give me such an order."

Anton sat in the padded couch in the control room of the *Ocean Gypsy*, staring off at nothing. Fell's and Oza-ki's bodies had been stowed in a cool hold, where food was normally kept. Addison remained down with them, shivering in the cold. Osbert kept watch outside. He had not spoken a word since he had returned triumphantly with the ngomite to find his friend dead. Monboddo sat in his cabin, cleaning the rock covering off the ngomite cylinder.

"I know that you will suffer heavy casualties," Anton said. "That's inevitable."

"Numbers of casualties aren't the issue." Kostal's

image did not appear on the screen, but the anger in her voice was clear. "You know that. But we need a better reason to die than your say-so."

"You know me, Miriam. Would I ask you to assault the Dead End with your Omega Squads unless I had a good reason?" And would he ask it knowing that Vanessa was somewhere on the asteroid and would probably be executed when the assault began? His hands shook, and he clasped them together. "Unless I had no other choice?" Please live, Vanessa, he thought. Please.

"What is it, Anton? We are distributed throughout the Dead End. My troops will seize it if I give the word. It does not matter how many of us die. We will succeed, if we make the attempt. I don't need authority from you. I have that myself. But I have to know why!"

Ozaki had given him the final confirmation. It was interesting. The last thing the great artist had done in his life was confirm the hypothesis of the man responsible for his death. "I suspect that if you do not make your assault soon, the Dead End will vanish from our Solar System completely."

With just the slightest whisper, the wall behind her slid aside. Vanessa stumbled backward, but managed, somehow, to regain her footing. The hammer and chisel fell from her hands. She found herself out in the open, bathed in the Dead End's artificial sunlight. She squinted through her tears. Facing her was Miriam Kostal, Justice of Tharsis. Behind her she heard the wall close again. They stood together on a height above what looked like a ruined medieval European castle. Part of it was in flames. It didn't look like part of the entertainment.

"Ah, there you are," Kostal said, her voice calmly modulated. She examined Vanessa closely. "Are you all right?" She wore a formal gown, off one shoulder. The panther fluidly made its way across her wavy brown hair. "You need water. Drink." She pressed a bottle into Vanessa's hands.

Vanessa pushed her tangled, sweat-soaked hair out of her face. Her lips were cracked, and her hands were scratched and bloody. Her eyes were red with frustrated tears. She gulped the water. "I'm all right," she croaked, and stepped forward. Her legs buckled beneath her.

Kostal swung and caught her, supporting her under one arm. "I've got you, dear, don't worry."

The two women regarded each other for a long moment, Kostal's agate green-brown eyes against Vanessa's black-olive dark ones. Kostal's slightly parted lips revealed the tips of her canines. Vanessa tried to imagine this fluid but sharp-edged woman with Anton. She was a vigorous and powerful woman. Could Vanessa hope to match her? At that moment Vanessa felt like ancient moldy leftovers discovered in the back of a refrigerator.

"Why are you here?" Vanessa asked.

"I'm here as a favor to a friend. Now that you're safe, I can proceed with my other tasks."

There were shouts from below. A man ran clumsily along a crumbling wall, pursued by two others. Their balancings and contortions would have been comic if it hadn't been obvious that they were in deadly earnest. The first man jumped off the wall. His leg twisted under him and he rolled. The other two descended more cautiously. They slid down the slope and confronted him with drawn blades. He lay staring up at them.

"What is going on?" Vanessa was frightened, afraid that the man would be killed outright before her eyes. She could see other soldiers running crouched past the keep, swords at ready. They covered each other past doorways and dove to the assault when a defender was discovered. There was the distant sound of sword on sword, like the cracking of a miniature crystal. A body lay near a futilely spinning waterwheel.

"War." Kostal was curt. "I have lost many dear friends in the past few hours. I was told it was necessary. You see but the aftermath."

Vanessa turned back to her. "Anton." She took Kostal's arm in a strong grip. "Where is he? Is he all right?"

Kostal examined her levelly. "I doubt that you and I shall ever be close friends," she said, quirking her lips. "But at least Anton has chosen well. That much I can see. I can also see the pain of the sacrifices he was willing to make."

"What do you mean?"

Miriam shook her head. "It is not for me to say. He will tell you. I have my own tasks to take care of now, my own dead to bury." A hint of the pain she concealed leaked through her eyes. "I have already made *my* sacrifices. Let's go. Can you stand for a moment?"

Vanessa nodded. Kostal knelt and picked up the hammer and chisel. "Keep these. If you ever need a reminder of how much work it is to survive, you can hold them in your hands and remember."

A woman's body lay facedown in the lily pond, her hair spreading over the flowers. Her sword lay half in the water, its blade resting on a moss-covered rock. A Martian soldier who had entered disguised as a tourist, she had lost her life in the vicious fighting that had won the Dead End for her comrades. Her opponent, an Ender wearing a dark blue kimono, had fallen through a rice-paper wall and lay on his back on the tatami mats of the room beyond, his sandaled feet protruding. Anton thought about pulling her out of the water, of covering him with a blanket. To what purpose?

The *Ocean Gypsy* and the *Rapier* had arrived back at the Dead End in the aftermath of the Martian conquest. The battle had been fought almost entirely with swords, bows, and lasers. Explosive and projectile weapons had the same effect on an asteroid as thermonuclear weapons did on Earth: they were instruments of destruction, not conquest. Neither the Martian Omega Squads nor the Dispossessed Brethren of Christ had wanted, even in the last extremity, to destroy the Dead End.

The Martian's blood had stained the lily pond's water

a delicate pink. Carp darted around her outstretched fingers. A nightingale sang its liquid syllables in a stand of bamboo. The inn's dark eaves were silent around Anton, its attendants and guests gone.

Suddenly, like a breath of air in a close room, Vanessa was holding him, the sound of joy deep within her throat. "You're alive," she said.

She shivered in his embrace. Her lips were rough and when he pulled back from their first kiss he saw that her face was drawn, streaked with rock dust. "So are you," he said. "So are you." He looked at her as if not believing in her existence.

She smiled up at him. "It's my hair, isn't it?" She pulled at her tangled locks. "It's always my hair."

He felt the weakness in her normally taut body as she leaned against him. Her heart fluttered. "What happened to you?" he asked.

"Oh, just a little exercise the Brethren dreamed up. An illustration of how to carve a niche in the universe. But you." She pulled at his beard, a habit he realized he would have to learn to like. She was as solemn as a small child. "Your eyes. What have you seen, Anton? What horrors have you looked upon?"

"I killed him, Vanessa. I found Karl Ozaki, and not an hour later he was dead. We have his body aboard the *Ocean Gypsy*. If I hadn't found him he'd still be alive."

She didn't ask any questions. "You couldn't have known that when you went looking for him, Anton."

"Fell is dead too. Our mission is accomplished. I think we can call it 'minimal casualties.'"

"Anton! Stop it. You did what you had to. Did you think that everything would come for free?"

He thought of Theophanos kneeling and begging him to destroy Ozaki's notes. He thought of Clavius's face as they swindled him out of his artist. He thought of the Blood Bowl, destroyed forever as a piece of elegant misdirection in a magic trick. He thought of the dead faces of Fell and Ozaki, one a friend, the other a man he had longed to meet for most of his life. "No," he said. "I didn't think it would be free." He held her and ran his hands down her back. "What did happen to you?" He smiled through his tears. "You look like hell."

She laughed. "You were always such a charming man, Anton. That's why I fell for you."

"You need a bath," he said, tugging at her sweat-stained clothes.

He had half feared that they would find a scene of carnage in the bathhouse, bloody corpses lying on the smooth wood floor, but the tubs steamed as if nothing had happened.

Anton and Vanessa stripped. Before she did anything else, she washed and rinsed her hair in the small preliminary bath. Then they both slid into the hot aromatic water.

"I didn't know I hurt in so many places," she gasped.

He thought for a long moment before he spoke. "I almost killed you too. I didn't have a choice about that either."

"How?"

"I contacted Miriam Kostal when the *Rapier* rescued us. I told her to seize control of the Dead End with Martian troops. I knew that if you weren't dead, you were a prisoner of the Brethren. I gave the order anyway. The Brethren could have killed you during the assault. Dozens died as it was."

She raised her eyebrows. "Well, Anton. Are you going to tell me why you ordered the attack? As one of the potential sacrifices, I think I have a right to know."

Anton winced. "I was afraid that the Dispossessed Brethren of Christ had succeeded in reassembling the Instruments. If they had, and activated them, I think they could have taken the Dead End out of our Solar System." He looked at her. "There is every indication that the four Instruments together are a working star drive."

* * *

"It sounds more like you guessed it than that you figured it out," Vanessa said as they floated up the passage.

"I suppose so. Everyone from Brother Theophanos to Ozaki himself knew some part of the puzzle. A model of an unknown solar system in the hands of the man who designed Boaz: Abakumov. Three suns, two closer together, a third circling them."

"The Centauri system."

"Now who's guessing? But the orrery Abakumov held in his hands had the planets of that system as well, and they have never been observed. Then there is the Lunar legend, which Clavius mentioned to me, of the red-cloaked magician who could fly to the stars. The Charlatans are associated, somehow, with the Brethren, since they let the Brethren attach their attack vessel to the *Charlotte Amalie*, and they have an obsession with space and interstellar travel, which you yourself pointed out to me."

Vanessa smiled. "That's right, I did. Do you really pay that much attention to what I say? I'll have to be more careful."

"Ozaki gave me the final clue. His work was intended to serve as a memorial to the Dispossessed Brethren of Christ once they had left the Solar System. When they left, the ngomite cylinder representing the Dead End would have been broken up, and the pieces put in the proper places. The Brethren's iconography is always precise. There is nothing accidental about it. And, just before he . . . died, Ozaki said it out loud, that the Brethren were about to leave. Yes, it was a guess. But a good one."

They emerged into a vast space shaped like the inside of an egg, larger than the Reception Chamber at the opposite hub though just as brightly lit. The egg's axis was occupied by a featureless cylinder of polished metal. Attached at its base in the wider part were four complex shapes, the Instruments: Jachin, Boaz, Nehushtan, and Aaron's Rod.

"In digging through the Acherusian deposits at Clavius, the Brethren discovered a remnant of an Acherusian spacecraft. They were fortunate in that they had a genius, Abakumov, who was able to figure out how it must have worked. He built the Instruments. He tested them by flying to Alpha Centauri. Look at them! In his notebook Ozaki said that if Abakumov had been an artist rather than a physicist, he would have been considered a genius."

On each of the Instruments hung a garland of roses, an ancient attribute of Abakumov. Anton remembered the meticulously carved roses on which Abakumov's effigy had rested, and the one single rose petal on the floor of the Hypostasium that had been his first clue.

"He was a genius," Vanessa said. "But who were the Acherusians?"

Anton shrugged elaborately. "Still no one knows. They vanished a million years ago. Did they come in the spacecraft that Abakumov found, run around the Solar System leaving us clever substances for our art and our spacecraft, and then vanish? Did they come from somewhere in our Solar System, perhaps the mythical planet between Mars and Jupiter that has become the Asteroid Belt, and leave on spaceships like the one in Clavius? Who knows? I don't even know why the Brethren never succeeded in their designs, even though there is evidence that Abakumov made at least one successful interstellar voyage. Why it stopped there I have no idea."

"They built Jerusalem the Lost as an interstellar spacecraft," Vanessa said. "But a civil war destroyed them before they could leave." She told him the story Durogin had allowed her.

Anton stared at the Instruments. He had been looking for ngomite, and had found it, finally, but the true mystery had been there right next to what he was seeking.

He held Vanessa, seized by a sudden insane urge to make love to her, there above the massive engines of the Brethren's star drive.

She divined his intention and fended him off, laughing. "Stop it, you maniac. We have plenty enough time for that."

He stopped and just held her within the circle of his arms. "Do we? How much time is that?"

They looked at each other. They had sworn no oaths, made no agreements. The time for them had only just come.

"As much time as there is."

The council chamber of the Syndics was a place for drama, and Anton had taken full advantage of it. The Syndics sat in darkness. A bright beam of light illuminated the cylinder of ngomite resting on the dais. Monboddo had removed the covering of rough rock under which it had been concealed.

The ngomite gleamed like a dragon's egg.

Grand Master Durogin stared at it in silence. She walked slowly to it, then reached up and touched it. Her hand caressed the side of the rich stone. She could touch it, so it was real.

Lord Monboddo, Miriam Kostal, Vanessa Karageorge, and Anton Lindgren stood together and watched her.

"The Technics stole a copy," Anton said. "A cylinder of lazarite stuffed with chondritic asteroidal rock. Ozaki threw it through the focus of the solar mirror, where Osbert was waiting, and was then killed. Osbert seized the ngomite and swung the decoy out in a matching trajectory. The lazarite's high atomic weight elements fooled the Technics just enough. They didn't have time for a closer inspection. They must know by now, but there's nothing they can do."

Durogin shook her head. "You were all so clever.

Truth is concealed by the universe, and you seek to hide it under more and more lies.''

"We did what we had to," Anton said. "Didn't it ever occur to you that Truth might be concealed for its own protection? Of course it did. You have been concealing yourselves for centuries. I don't blame you. Hiding the truth in your circumstances was no more a crime than is burying a seed so that it may germinate. Do us the courtesy of accepting the validity of our concealment as well.''

"What do you want?"

The Martian troops had been removed from the chamber itself, but they still remained in occupation of the Dead End. Anton looked up at the ranks of Syndics. Many of the seats were empty. Those who remained alive glared down at them, hate in their eyes. Among them Anton spotted Pawel Luria, their erstwhile Expediter. Luria glowered down at him.

Miriam spoke. "We have discussed the matter and are agreed. In front of you is the ngomite that you gave to Ozaki, in exchange for his figurine of the Dead Christ in his winding sheet. It is now in our possession. If you agree, it will be returned to you, and our troops will leave this asteroid, if you grant us access to your technology of interstellar travel. This is generous on our part. You have little choice.''

"We can fight!" Durogin said, her eyes savage. "We can destroy you.''

"You can. You can destroy Jerusalem the Lost, and all that it stands for. You can bring the temple down just as Samson did, allowing no one the victory, and give up forever your hope of reaching the stars. You can fulfill the work of your nameless, faceless predecessor. Do you want to do this?''

Anton waited tensely. Vanessa slipped her hand into his, and he tried not to squeeze it too tightly. If Durogin decided so, they could all be dead.

"You've killed Karl Ozaki," Durogin said bitterly.

"And like good people of business, you have brought us John Addison to replace him. Everything is a matter of process." She took a breath. "We will agree."

"Don't thank me, Anton," Miriam said. "Thanking me for doing the right thing implies that I did it as a favor, rather than because it was right."

"Stop it." Anton glared at her. "You saved Vanessa's life. That deserves my gratitude."

Miriam sat, gracious and dignified, on the other side of the teamaker. She had not offered him any tea, and he had not asked for it. "I'm not at all sure that's what you're thanking me for."

"For what then? For finally agreeing to deal with the Brethren? It only took us several hours to convince you to go along." The argument between the Martians and the Terrans had been long and intense.

"And I'm still not sure that it was in our best interest. If we'd played the game correctly, we could now have the star drive *and* the ngomite." She glanced at him. "And you would have a stronger sense of guilt, the guilt that you get from victory. That, I fear, was the decisive factor." She stood up and clenched her hands together, irritated with herself. "I held all the strong cards. My troops occupied the Dead End. But you and Monboddo ... you and the eternally gabby, agreeable, and unswervable Monboddo, you bent me to your will. Just so that you could sleep comfortably at night, knowing that the sacrifices you made had not been in vain, and that Ozaki's great work can be completed."

"We convinced you to be reasonable," Anton said. "That's far from a sin. I don't think it's possible to bend you, Miriam."

"Reasonable. I'm catching your disease, then. I'd hoped never to become reasonable. Was saving your lover reasonable?"

"No," Anton said. "It wasn't. That's why I'm grateful."

"And wise enough not to bring her here. She thanked me when I pulled her from her tomb. She was soaked with sweat, bloody, like a newborn infant. She thanked me, and asked about you. I hated her at that moment." She looked at Anton and smiled. "Do you think you deserve her?"

"We don't deserve love any more than we deserve God's Grace," he said.

At that she laughed. "You stole that line from me, Anton. I'm sure of it." She reached her hand out to him and he took it. "We, however, do deserve to be friends, Anton. I think we've both earned it." He kissed her then, and held her. The panther in her hair, made by the man he had killed, seemed to wink.

It would have been simpler to simply let him go, allowing him to vanish, but Anton could not let it happen that way. So he waited near the airlock and when he saw John Addison floating through the chamber, he approached him.

"What do you want?" Addison grated. His eyes wandered, not focusing on Anton.

"I wanted to see you," Anton said soberly. "To apologize."

Addison's eyes swiveled toward him. "You bastard," he said. His voice cracked, as if he had not said anything for a long time, and was now compelled to speak only by overwhelming passion. "Your apology isn't for me. It's for you. The same way . . . you told me once, didn't you? You apologized to that wild boar as you wiped its blood off your hands. So apologize and go to bed easy. Everything will be easy."

Anton's saliva had turned to acid and burned his throat as he swallowed. Is this what victory felt like? If it did, he was getting used to victory.

Anton thought about all the things he could say, about the necessities of state, the threat of the Technics, the need to preserve the human race, but none of these things would mean anything to this artist whom the great world had barreled over in its career toward the future. The arrangements had been made. Addison would complete Ozaki's last great work, the rock garden that was to be the memorial for the vanished Brethren. The ngomite was being returned, having been exchanged, in its turn, for something even more valuable. Anton had not stolen it with that intention in mind at all, and he had to struggle with himself to keep from imagining that he had. He was terrified that in future years, wishing to think of himself as a good and virtuous man, he would convince himself that everything had come out just as he had planned.

"Mr. Lindgren," Osbert said behind him. "It's time to go." Fell's funeral had been only several hours before. Fell and Osbert had met in Monboddo's service only a few years before, but now it was difficult to imagine only one of them, making his way through life alone.

"Thank you, Osbert." He turned back to Addison. "I don't expect forgiveness from you, but I want some understanding. We did what we had to. Lord Monboddo and I lost Fell, an associate and a friend. Justice Tharsis lost over fifty of her men, as well as her friend Plauger. We could have stayed home, sipped coffee, and none of this would have happened. But now everything is different. Human beings will move out to the stars. Our world will be transformed. Is this good? I can't say. I may well have contributed to the destruction of the culture I love best. At least our survival as a species is made more likely by it. And I can't regard that as a bad thing. But we acted. That's what counts."

"And that's all that matters?" Addison demanded, having waited wearily for Anton to finish his speech.

"Are you asking me whether Caroline Apthorpe's Blood Bowl, a brilliant work of art that Lord Monboddo and I have always loved, mattered less than that? Don't you understand?" The bowl floated before Anton's eyes. "Don't you understand? Though I live to be a century old not a day will pass in my life when I will not think

about that, and regret what I did? If I you don't understand that, you are incapable of understanding anything.''

Osbert took Anton's arm and clumsily patted him on
the shoulder. Anton slapped his biceps in return. ''Let's
be on our way.''

BIO OF A SPACE TYRANT
Piers Anthony

"Brilliant...a thoroughly original thinker and storyteller with a unique ability to posit really *alien* alien life, humanize it, and make it come out alive on the page." *The Los Angeles Times*

A COLOSSAL NEW FIVE VOLUME SPACE THRILLER—
BIO OF A SPACE TYRANT
The Epic Adventures and Galactic Conquests of Hope Hubris

VOLUME I: REFUGEE   84194-0/$4.50 US/$5.50 Can
Hubris and his family embark upon an ill-fated voyage through space, searching for sanctuary, after pirates blast them from their home on Callisto.

VOLUME II: MERCENARY   87221-8/$4.50 US/$5.50 Can
Hubris joins the Navy of Jupiter and commands a squadron loyal to the death and sworn to war against the pirate warlords of the Jupiter Ecliptic.

VOLUME III: POLITICIAN   89685-0/$4.50 US/$5.50 Can
Fueled by his own fury, Hubris rose to triumph obliterating his enemies and blazing a path of glory across the face of Jupiter. Military legend...people's champion...promising political candidate...he now awoke to find himself the prisoner of a nightmare that knew no past.

VOLUME IV: EXECUTIVE   89834-9/$4.50 US/$5.50 Can
Destined to become the most hated and feared man of an era, Hope would assume an alternate identify to fulfill his dreams.

VOLUME V: STATESMAN   89835-7/$4.50 US/$5.50 Can
The climactic conclusion of Hubris' epic adventures.

ARTHUR C. CLARKE'S VENUS PRIME™

by Paul Preuss

VOLUME 6: THE SHINING ONES 75350-2/$3.95 US/$4.95 CAN
The ever capable Sparta proves the downfall of the mysterious and sinister organization that has been trying to manipulate human history.

VOLUME 5: THE DIAMOND MOON
75349-9/$3.95 US/$4.95 CAN
Sparta's mission is to monitor the exploration of Jupiter's moon, Amalthea, by the renowned Professor J.Q.R. Forester.

VOLUME 4: THE MEDUSA ENCOUNTER
75348-0/$3.95 US/$4.95 CAN
Sparta's recovery from her last mission is interrupted as she sets out on an interplanetary investigation of her host, the Space Board.

VOLUME 3: HIDE AND SEEK 75346-4/$3.95 US/$4.95 CAN

VOLUME 2: MAELSTROM 75345-6/$3.95 US/$4.95 CAN

VOLUME 1: BREAKING STRAIN 75344-8/$3.95 US/$4.95 CAN

Each volume features a special technical infopak,
including blueprints of the structures of *Venus Prime*